THE SHOPKEEPER'S WIFE

Also by Noëlle Sickels

Walking West

THE SHOPKEEPER'S WIFE

NOËLLE SICKELS

ST. MARTIN'S PRESS ❧ NEW YORK

Library of Congress Cataloging-in-Publication Data

Sickels, Noëlle.
   The shopkeeper's wife / Noëlle Sickels.—1st ed.
     p.   cm.
   ISBN 0-312-19333-5
   I. Title.
   PS3569.I269S55 1998
   813'.54—dc21   98-21118
                                     CIP

First Edition: November 1998

10 9 8 7 6 5 4 3 2 1

FOR VICTOR,
PIERRE DE MON COEUR

THE SHOPKEEPER'S WIFE

ONE

🙦 THE TRAIN from the country had been late, and the progress of the crowded streetcar was maddeningly slow, traffic being busy and the horses decrepit. The Society for the Prevention of Cruelty to Animals kept special watch on the street railway lines, but the sad pair pulling our car had escaped their vigilance. As we rattled through the press of trolleys, delivery wagons, omnibuses, and dashing pedestrians, I was repeatedly jostled against my neighbor on the overhead strap; he had had garlic for supper.

When, at last, I got off the streetcar, I still had a short distance to walk to reach the Delaware River piers. It was an area of wholesalers—teas, candles and lard oil, spices, wool—but I passed a few shopfronts, too, all closed for the night, their window displays only dimly visible in the light from the streetlamps. A dry goods window caught my eye nevertheless and was cunningly enough done to make me stop and study it a moment, late as I was.

A rolling landscape had been made all of fabrics, with folds of green and brown tarlatans for woodlands, hills of tulle, a blue satin river, and pale linens and muslins shirred into fields of spring growth. Mr. Edwin would have appreciated it. When Isabelle and I cleared out his desk, we found a leatherette box of sketches for merchandise displays, though none as fanciful as the fabric landscape.

There was nothing particularly private about those sketches, nor about anything else in Mr. Edwin's desk, but I didn't like emptying the drawers. I'd never had anything to do with the desk before, except to dust its surface, and there I was throwing away worn-down gum erasers and pen nibs, and his calendar diary and reading spectacles. It didn't help that it was all under Isabelle's supervision. I felt the same when she had me clear away other things that couldn't be sent to charity, like his shaving brush with its splayed bristles and the half-used bowl of shaving soap, and a dressing gown he so favored that the oft-darned cuffs and shawl collar were fraying again. It's things like that—ordinary things that show the wear of common use—that bring home to you that someone is really gone.

I sensed the presence of the river before I reached it. Of course, I knew it was there; I had lived quite near it for a year. But it was more than plain familiarity with the river's existence that informed me. There was a difference to the atmosphere, a coolness apart from the winter evening's chill, like a bassoon behind violins. There was, too, an opening up of space, a feeling that some large edge was close at hand. Lights were fewer ahead; sounds broke up, spread out, and died thin.

Perhaps, however, it was only my state of mind that made the approach to the river so suggestive. Isabelle Martin awaited me there, and the course our meeting might take was anything but clear. I could have said the "notorious" Isabelle Martin, for she had been called that and more—evil, conniving, immoral. (To be fair, there were those as well that called her better things, like tender and diligent.) It was her house near the river in which I'd lived that year, hers and her husband's. And more passed there for all three of us than some folks meet in the full of their lives. For though everyone encounters death somewhere along their way, few are acquainted with murder, and fewer still accused of it.

———

꧁ THEY TALK about the pursuit of happiness in the Declaration of Independence, but when was it people really started expecting that they ought to be happy? When was it they started thinking it was all right to do whatever it took to get personal happiness? It must have begun sometime while I was a child, for I know my parents never had such a notion, nor my grandparents, and yet, when I was grown, there it was, showing its face with greater and greater boldness in more and more places.

Isabelle Martin certainly considered she had a right to be happy. And she was clever enough and sure enough to use whatever came her way, including me. I remember her clearly on that last night in 1887, waiting on the pier at Philadelphia's waterfront, ready to set sail for a new life. She was going to France to revisit the places of her childhood, and then someplace else, where, I did not want to know. I had asked her not to tell me, and she had agreed to my request without question.

Isabelle's slight figure seemed even smaller in the shadow of the great ship, yet she stood straight and still, looking calmly out across the harbor as if she were viewing a rose garden on a fine summer's day. While I shivered despite my thick wool shawl, Isabelle, in her trim silk traveling suit, seemed not to feel the dampness in the fog curling around us carrying with it smells of wet rope, decaying fish, and sewage. Other passengers bustled past us, porters behind them dragging trunks on wheeled carts or hoisting cases on their shoulders. Rough seamen in threes and fours strode noisily by on their way south to the alehouses and oyster bars on Water Street; they eyed us openly, made curious by two lone women standing wordlessly and without apparent purpose. But Isabelle ignored the staring sailors and the busy travelers and porters forced to detour around us.

I'd wondered, at first, why she wanted me to see her off. But when I saw her so serene in the misted darkness, I knew. She wanted to show me she believed she had been right, that her conscience was clear. I also knew, as cold water seeped through the soles of my thin shoes, that I had come because I wished to see just that which she desired to show.

I wanted to witness Isabelle Martin on the verge of what she expected to be a happy life at last, if only to observe closely again her fierce impulse toward happiness, for though I was only a servant girl of twenty-four, it seemed to me that this was an impulse that would mark the movements of women and men in society more and more, and that it deserved careful watching.

TWO

I CAME to Isabelle Martin when she needed me most. She had had maids before, but they had always been older women who did their work in crisp silence, Irish or English women who, despite their lower station, looked a bit askance at Isabelle Martin because she was French and had too high an opinion of herself. Honestly, that was one fault I never could find in her. Her long vowels and the soft way her French accent caressed words could make her sound aloof and conceited, but really, she was in many ways a burdened woman, only slightly vain, and very lonely.

Because she was expecting their first child, her husband, Edwin Martin, was feeling indulgent toward her, so he put in at the domestic agency for a servant girl closer to his wife's age, and one with experience of babies, to ease her confinement. I was twenty-three then; Isabelle was twenty-seven. I came from a family of six living children, of which I was the oldest girl, and I knew not only about babies, but about birthing, as my grandmother had been a midwife and had taken me along as assistant from the age of eleven.

I thought at first I had the wrong address, for number 15 Chestnut Street was a grocer's shop in the commercial district, just west of the trolley turnaround at Market and the dock where the ferries crossing the Delaware to New Jersey put in, but a clerk inside directed me to a red door beside the plate glass front of the shop and told me to ring the bell, as Mr. and Mrs. Martin lived overhead.

The house was red brick, like most of the buildings in the area, with three stories above the shop and a dormer window standing out from the sloped slate roof. There were four tall windows on each story, and lace curtains at all of them except one window on the third floor that had a shade instead and those on the second floor, which I later learned were the offices of Mr. Edwin and his partner, Mr. Cox. The neighboring building on one side housed a dry goods store and on the other side was a ship chandler's; both appeared to have residences on the floors above.

Mr. Edwin answered the door himself, huffing from the long staircase, though he was a spare man, with no extra weight on him. I learned later it was his manner to breathe excessively whenever he had to deal with household matters, as if it were a great indignity or confusion to have to order a meal or ask about the arrival of the laundry or inquire when his wife was expected home. I had immediate reason to regret this quirk of his, for Mr. Edwin had a most disagreeable mouth odor, and in the narrow, enclosed staircase, his foul breath wafted back to me as he led the way up to the apartment.

Isabelle was sitting on a circular stool at a piano when we entered the parlor. She looked up from an open folio of sheet music on her lap as if we had surprised her, though surely she'd been awaiting us. It was a trick of hers to seem to be discovered absorbed in some task. It afforded, initially, a view of her shining dark hair, which she wore twisted in a thick knot on top of her head, and then of the pale smoothness of her comely face lifting to encounter her visitor, an engaging smile dancing over her large, wide-set eyes like sunlight on wind-ruffled water. She had the kind of looks and coloring that at certain angles conveyed a startling and exotic beauty, while at other angles, her features appeared heavy and excessive.

Men liked to come upon Isabelle Martin in a room empty of other people, so they might see that trick of the slowly lifted or turned head, that retrieval of herself from some occupation or private thought. It appealed, perhaps, to the explorer in them. But that first day, I knew none of this. I only knew that the young woman who might soon employ me had, by a simple tilt of her head and a sigh close to relief, made me feel that I was the one person in the world she had been waiting for.

"Well, my dear, here she is," Mr. Edwin puffed. "I'll leave you to it."

Fixing her empty gaze a foot above my head, Isabelle held her cheek toward her husband, who bent and kissed it. Then she turned her attention to packeting the sheet music, and he left the room, backing out as if he were in the presence of royalty.

During the few moments of this scene, I scanned the neat parlor. Besides the upright piano of dark wood, there were a number of chairs, a tall bookcase, a settee piled with fat cushions worked in needlepoint, and an étagère arranged with scores of decorative trifles. Near the windows, which looked out onto the street, stood a row of small tables holding potted ivy, violets, ferns, and other houseplants. Two walls were papered in a floral print and two in a paisley embossed with bronze flecks. On the walls hung pictures of landscapes, and over the fireplace, in a large gilded gesso frame, the portrait of a robust old man I later learned was Mr. Edwin's father, Sylvester Martin. A dark, polished parquet floor gleamed around the edges of wool rugs patterned in crimson and indigo.

"My husband's time is much taken up with business," Isabelle said, putting aside the music folio. "Your name?"

"Hanna Willer, ma'am."

"I understand you've not held a position before."

"No, ma'am."

"But you know housework and cooking, I gather. And about . . ." She laid her hand on her big belly and looked down at it as if it were not a part of her, but a puzzling package someone had mistakenly left on her lap.

"I've had a lot to do with babies, ma'am, from their first squalling moments and on," I said, hoping it was not improper to be so frank.

I had had little direct experience with people like the Martins, who had pianos and owned shops and hired girls like me to keep their homes and their children clean and provisioned. Though my family and my upbringing were respectable, they weren't refined. My father was a carter; he hauled beer, mostly, from the German breweries between Girard and Columbia Avenues along the Schuylkill River to saloons and stores all over Philadelphia. It was honest work, but coarse.

"Well, I've had nothing to do with babies," Isabelle said, smiling at me and putting me more at ease, "and I have embarked on motherhood like a schoolgirl leaving home on a cloudy day without an umbrella."

She got up and walked to the plants at the window. Seeing her figure erect, I guessed that her time was no more than two months away. As she passed before me I smelled her scent, roses, and the fanciful thought came to me that a rose might sound as she did if it could speak. She stood a few moments plucking dead leaves from a begonia. I wondered if the interview were over.

"Shall you be my umbrella, then, Willer?" she said so softly I was not sure I had heard her correctly.

"Ma'am?" I ventured. She turned to face me.

"I wish to engage you," she said, in a more practical voice. "I believe the agency described my needs accurately. I'll take you through the details day after tomorrow, if you are willing and able to start by then."

"Yes, ma'am," I said. "I've only to gather a few things from my father's house, out in Montgomery County."

"Then it's settled," she said and came forward to shake my

hand, which I hadn't expected. Her grip was light and fleeting, but the gesture afforded me another whiff of roses, and that, coupled with my youth, stilled the vague questions scratching like cupboard mice at the back of my mind.

THREE

I NEVER had direct cause to dislike Mr. Edwin (which is what both he and his wife said I should call him). He had little to do with me; I was under Isabelle's charge. But he was always an object of curiosity for me.

Mr. Edwin was different from the kind of man I was used to, cool and meticulous, cautious with his words and even more with his smile, though I think that was partly to hide the blackened teeth that occasioned his bad breath and which he knew Isabelle lamented. During my time with the Martins, I was in every one of Mr. Edwin's five shops, and the clerks all said he was a firm master, strict on appearances and punctuality and, of course, the accounts. But Mr. Edwin's firmness was not like the firmness I had seen in the men of my childhood, and so I thought him superior to them.

Most of our neighbors were farmers or laborers of one sort or another, but some had underlings, young boys to fetch and carry or simpletons to do the dirtiest work like mucking out stables or swilling latrines, and their idea of firmness was most often a threatening curse and a stray blow or two for emphasis. Even my father, whose tempers were more often shown by sulks and mutterings than by outbursts, could be inordinately sharp over small annoyances, and we all skirted him watchfully, like minnows round a snapping turtle or hounds round a skunk. My brother, who worked with him three years in the carting business before going west to the Dakota plains, said he had a reputation in the city for ferocious speech when other drivers blocked his way.

Now I am old enough to understand that someone can wither beneath someone else's power and authority even when it is administered without harshness, and though I still think of Mr. Edwin in manners and some points of character superior to my father's rougher friends, I find him, in the unthinking comfort and self-satisfaction of his position, to be their equal.

Mr. Edwin made the rounds of every one of his shops every day, which often kept him away from home from dawn till dusk, like a farmer. My grandfather had been a farmer, and my grandmother told me she never saw him in daylight for years on end. During Mr. Edwin's long absences, Isabelle occupied her time with needlepoint, at which she excelled, and piano practice, and reading, though it was common wisdom that too much reading could make a woman nervous and even ill, as if she were cream that would curdle in an overheated room.

These activities and the few duties involved in running her small household still left Isabelle with idle hours that seemed to chafe at her like tight shoes on bare ankles. She appeared to regret the lack of her husband's company, yet when Mr. Edwin was at home, Isabelle often remained fretted, for he tended to fall asleep during her piano playing and to ignore her needlepoint, never noticing the completion of a new one. There was no hope of discussing books, either, because he read only the newspapers, and Isabelle had no more than passing interest in them.

I, on the other hand, became quite attached to newspaper reading. I always had the news a day late, as I could not chance taking Mr. Edwin's papers away to my room before he was quite through with them, but that did not dilute my interest in all I read. Actually, I was regularly several days behind, as I tended to read so much of each edition; not just the headline stories, but editorials and advertisements, the obituaries and the shipping news.

As Isabelle's lying-in approached, her discontent with her husband eased. Mr. Edwin more frequently took midday dinner at home, and he even put his head in sometimes just to pass a few minutes or to bring her a little cake. Isabelle declared she had not eaten a decent piece of pastry since her girlhood in France, but she took the little cakes graciously and seemed genuinely pleased at Mr. Edwin's attentions.

My father had never shown such courtesies to my mother, at least not that I had seen or heard of. My grandmother said that my father did make one change in his routine whenever my mother presented him with a child: he went out and got so drunk he had to be carried home and washed and put to bed like a baby himself. He did that even the last time, when the baby girl came much too early and lived only one night, pulling my ill mother along so soon after her that we wrapped them both in one shroud and buried them together in the same coffin.

Isabelle followed an unusual regimen for her pregnancy. She put wet compresses over her loins and belly and took cold sitz baths; she swore off meat, alcohol, and hot drinks and drank great quantities of water. In all this she was following a book called *Esoteric Anthropology (The Mysteries of Man)* by Dr. Thomas Low Nichols. Dr. Nichols and his wife, Mary Gove Nichols, were water-cure enthusiasts, as was Isabelle, even though the water-cure was not as fashionable as it had once been.

Isabelle consulted and obeyed that book the way other people do the Bible. She believed an enthusiastic adherence to its principles would guarantee a quick birthing, an easy child, and what she called a "pure" marriage. I had never witnessed these three things together at one time in any woman's life, and none of them seemed to me subject to influence. The first two were up to chance, and the third required an aged or infirm husband. But it was not my place to voice opinions, however much Isabelle solicited them.

"Willer," she said to me one day after I had been at the Martins' a month, "what do you make of the free-love thinkers?"

"I have seen their pamphlets, ma'am."

"I want you to go this afternoon to a lecture by Mrs. Digby, a disciple of Mary Gove Nichols. I got my ticket long ago, when I heard she was to be in town from the Nichols' clinic in England, but Edwin doesn't like me to be in public now, in my condition."

"I was going to beat the rugs this afternoon."

"Leave them till tomorrow."

"Yes, ma'am."

Isabelle shifted her gaze from me to the window.

"I only wish someone had given me an opportunity to know the Nichols' ideas sooner," she said. "Then, perhaps, mine would be a finer marriage."

I nodded, though Isabelle was not looking at me, and moved to pick up the tray I had come into the parlor to collect. It was one of Mr. Edwin's long days out; Isabelle didn't like to eat at the dining room table alone, but preferred a tray in front of the street windows. I was glad to see she'd taken the sardine rolls; I believed a pregnant woman needed more than rice porridge and apples and roots, no matter what Dr. Nichols and Dr. Graham and the other food reformers said. When I was near the door with the tray, Isabelle spoke again.

"I really have no room for complaint against my husband, Willer. But I never chose him, you know."

"No, ma'am?"

"My guardian arranged it. I knew Edwin only slightly. His cousin and his cousin's wife were our neighbors. And his younger brother, Frederick."

Isabelle was still staring out the window; her voice was trembling a little, as if she might start to cry. I knew women near their time were quick to cry or feel melancholy. I rested the tray against my hip so I might stand and listen. I thought it more important just then to keep Isabelle company than to clear away dirty dishes.

"My guardian chose Edwin because he was an established businessman and could give me a comfortable future. And because, as a grocer's wife, I would be inconspicuous."

"Inconspicuous?"

Isabelle turned. Her large, dark eyes studied me, and I wondered if I had been too familiar. In hindsight, I think she was judging herself more than me, to see how much of her heart she was willing to open.

"My guardian was acting for my father, who is a wealthy gentleman. It would be a great embarrassment to him if my existence were known. He's provided for me all my life, but he cannot acknowledge me. Do you understand, Willer?"

"Yes, ma'am, I think so. Was it your mother, then, who was French?"

"That's right. She died when I was two. My grandparents kept me awhile in France, then I went to a convent school, and finally here, where I expected to study further."

"Your plans weren't realized?"

Isabelle smiled, but there was no mirth or warmth in it. She shook her head no.

"Not exactly. Immediately after my marriage, I did go away to school for two years—it was part of the agreement with Edwin. But I have never felt complete in my learning. I try to read philosophy and mathematics and even novels, and I often feel I don't understand all that's there to be got."

"I'm sure you must be too hard on yourself, Mrs. Martin. You have so many books—I could never get through them if I were to read every day until my last."

"Would you like to read my books, Willer?" Isabelle asked, her face brightening for the first time since our conversation began.

"Why, I don't know, ma'am," I said, feeling shy, though I was eager to do just that.

"Please, I would like you to."

"Well, then, ma'am, thank you, though I suspect a lot will be beyond me."

"We could discuss what you've read, if you like. I wouldn't be a remarkable teacher, but I'd be an earnest one."

I smiled at her in answer. I was truly pleased at this turn of events, too pleased to put into words. The Bible had been the only book in my parents' home. I had read it regularly to myself and to my brothers and sisters, but despite its many stories, it was still, in the end, only one book. Before my mother died and I wasn't needed at home so much, I used to stay late at school reading the books there, though they were sometimes dull or confusing and almost always practical.

"You know, Willer," Isabelle continued, her voice again sounding mournful, "Mr. Edwin received a large settlement upon our marriage, enough to add four new grocery shops to the prospering one he already owned. It was the making of the busy, contented life he finds himself in now; I gained only a name and obscure, friendless days."

"Surely not friendless, ma'am."

"We've moved four times in the past seven years. I see no one except Edwin and occasionally Mrs. Cox, his partner's wife. Or Edwin's father, who does not like me."

"That will change with the baby," I said cheerily, anxious not to hear any more family business and wishing to end on a hopeful note.

"Perhaps," she said, and turned again to the window.

I took this as a cue to leave, but she followed me into the hall and rested her hand on my arm to stay me longer.

"Will you be my friend, Willer?" she said, as plaintive as a little girl.

It was an odd request for a mistress to her maid, even, some would say, an improper one, but there was such innocent longing in her expression, my sympathy was aroused. Besides, I, too, at that time, was friendless.

"I'd be happy to try, ma'am, if you think Mr. Edwin wouldn't object."

She grinned, this time with full measure.

"You must call me Isabelle. And I shall call you Hanna— no, Nanette, from the language of my childhood."

"Nanette," I said dubiously. "I'm not sure I could get used to that, ma'am."

"Nan, then," she said. "Nan and Isabelle."

And so it was.

FOUR

THE LECTURE by Mrs. Digby was held at Forepaugh's Theatre. It was an off afternoon for the theater, which on other days was featuring the temperance play *Ten Nights in a Bar-room*. Large posters outside proclaimed the next month's show, a varied entertainment that included pantomime, clowns, lady velocipedists, a family of acrobats, and Egyptian jugglers. The renown of each attraction was indicated by the size and elaborateness of the type naming it and whether or not there was an accompanying illustration. A smaller printed bill beside one of the posters announced Mrs. Digby's talk, "The Case for True-Love Marriage."

I had arrived for the lecture a half hour early, so I took advantage and visited the theater's Hall of Justice museum, where a series of wax figures depicted the history of crime. For twenty-five cents, I was admitted to the uncomfortably realistic company of murderers and thieves, all immortalized in the very moment of their worst deeds. I entered the theater in a bit of an agitated state; still vivid in my mind were the sights of panicked gunshot victims, huge-handed stranglers, and demon-eyed poisoners.

Mrs. Digby's listeners were mainly women, which I attributed to her topic and to the fact that, unlike at evening performances, ladies could attend matinees without escorts. There was a lot of chatter on all sides as the audience found their places. Most of the ladies seemed to have come with two or three friends. My seat was in the fifth row from the stage, on the center aisle. I was pleased to be so close. I had never been in a theater before, though we'd acted a play, *The Two Orphans,* once in the school basement, and I'd seen Christmas tableaux at church.

The woman in the next seat glanced questioningly at me when I sat down, but I was too busy looking around to care. I took in the plush chairs, the sloping floor, the ceiling molded with plaster angels and garlands, the side walls draped in an arabesque brocade of pink and gold. I would have liked a peek at the set for *Ten Nights in a Bar-room,* which I imagined gave a satisfying contrast to the sumptuousness of the theater, but it was hidden behind a thick velvet curtain that hung the full length of the stage.

Presently, several ladies and one gentleman filed on to the stage. There was a line of gilded chairs, and the ladies settled into them, while the man went to a wooden lectern at the center of the stage. The audience quieted.

The gentleman was a Mr. Gass, and he was meant to introduce Mrs. Digby. He began to do this, but as soon as he had mentioned her training under Mary Gove Nichols, he digressed into a long tale of his own experience, years ago, at the Dansville Water Cure, which was run by Harriet Austin, another of Mrs. Nichols's disciples.

"I suffered for years from dyspepsia, irritability, and lack of concentration," he explained. "And I suffered almost as much from the remedies: mercury tonics, silver nitrate, asafoetida, quinine, opium, ipecac syrup, cathartic pills, and muriatic acid baths. Then, at Dansville, I met God's own medicine—pure, fresh water. I underwent the Crisis; my body was cleansed of waste and age and morbid matter, and I was cured and renewed."

Light applause skittered across the audience. More water-cure veterans, I supposed. Isabelle told me a friend had convinced Mr. Edwin to send her to New Lebanon Springs for three weeks during the third year of their marriage, when she had sunk into an inexplicable weakness of both body and spirit. There she'd worn loose, unrestricting clothing, eaten small vegetarian meals, and drunk twenty-four glasses of water a day. She'd had various temperatures and pressures of water applied into and on every part of her body, including plunge baths, wet bandages, enemas, sitz baths, showers, vaginal injections, and steam sweating. Her Crisis, as they called it, had brought uneasiness and insomnia, then high fevers and visions, breaking through at the end into a new sense of well-being in body and outlook.

Though New Lebanon Springs did not sound like a peaceful place to me, Isabelle insisted her stay there had been one of the most restful times of her life. A refuge, she said. But Mr. Edwin had not wanted her to go back, as many women did at regular intervals. He'd missed her too keenly. He had relented, Isabelle said, two years ago, and let her take a week away, but she was sure he would never countenance another stay.

"I am proud to say I met my wife through our subscriptions to *The Water-Cure Journal*," Mr. Gass was finishing. "In my ad, I specified a woman of good size, with a natural waist, a solid education, and undoubted piety; I was well answered in Mrs. Gass. In turn, in her ad, she described herself as possessing a cheerful, healthy glow and as a young lady able to be ruled only by love. She pined, she said, for a tall, dark vegetarian. I think she was not disappointed."

Mr. Gass smiled and bowed to one of the ladies on the stage, a full-figured, uncorseted woman, who, indeed, did look cheerful and healthy. She smiled back at him. Mr. Gass then abruptly left the lectern and went to sit next to this lady, in the remaining empty seat on the stage. Mrs. Digby took his place in the center of the stage, moving slowly and buoyantly, apparently undistressed at having been so scantily introduced. She was a stately woman, plump but not overly fleshy, dressed plainly in an unfitted gray gown.

"Ah, yes, water," she began, and paused to look carefully

out over us like a shepherdess counting sheep. "Water. The universal solvent. The life saver."

Again she paused and scanned the audience, as if searching for naysayers. But there were none. Her voice was as resonant as a man's, and her pauses were artfully held. Just as I would begin to yearn for her to resume speaking, she did. Others must have felt the same, for I noticed quiet shuffles near the end of each pause, as people leaned slightly forward in their seats or held themselves ready, like children hunting fireflies, waiting for the next flash to guide them where to reach, when to grasp.

"Able to be ruled only by love," she intoned. *"Pining* to be ruled by love."

She spoke with fierce reverence, hushed yet seemingly loud.

"True love, ladies and gentlemen. Another universal solvent? Yes, I say to you, that and more. As necessary as water. As pure. Worth waiting for. Worth fighting for. Even if that fight sets daughters against parents, wives against husbands, women against society. Because, in the end, just as the Water-Cure Crisis saves the individual body, so true love—and marriage based on true love—is the only thing will save society and renew our boasted civilization."

Again, applause skittered through the theater, more vigorous in some quarters than in others. There were mutterings, too, as people made comments to their companions or aloud to themselves. Mrs. Digby, encouraged, warmed to her theme, declaring that every woman has an absolute right to a true-love marriage, or, failing that, the right to exercise control over her life within marriage, particularly in the bedroom. The ideas from the water-cure spas were novel enough to me, who had been raised where the consumption of meat was copious and the hygienic use of water scant. But to consider that a woman, especially a married woman, might be in any sense free was like considering the possibility that cats might fly.

"Sexual union without love—even inside marriage—is prostitution," Mrs. Digby said emphatically. "A woman's body is hers to give or withhold, independent of the wishes of her husband, who must wait upon his wife's desires, trusting in her love for him and her natural instinct to become a mother."

I wondered exactly how this would work. Being unmarried, I had no direct experience of how husbands and wives consorted, but as my grandmother's assistant, I had entered many households and heard many stories. Sometimes just the way the furniture was laid out hinted much about a family's private life.

A midwife is in a unique position for receiving confidences. My grandmother not only attended births, she also visited the mother weekly in her last month and then two or three times afterward. In all those moments, a woman can be as unguarded and revealing as a child who has not yet learned how to tell falsehoods. Even the fathers were subject to the thawing society of a midwife. Once in a while, a man might pass a remark or question to my grandmother that, all unawares, showed tenderness or callousness. I never did figure which leaning was shown by my father's drinking while my mother bore his babies.

It's easier, I suppose, to puzzle out the way other people are made and how they fit with one another than it is to understand the workings of your own family. Although I ought to know my parents' marriage and my own doings with them and with my brothers and sisters better than I know anything else in the world, I am too much a piece of them to do it.

But going on what I saw and heard in the bedrooms and kitchens of the homes where my grandmother took me, bobbing like a dinghy behind a sloop, I knew that women sometimes did withhold themselves from their husbands, though it often seemed a troublesome and short-lived practice. I knew, too, that there were women who tried and failed at this, or who wished to try but didn't dare, judging their husbands' embraces more tolerable than their tempers. Then there were those women for whom Mrs. Digby's ideas would be so foreign as to be akin to nonsense or even blasphemy, for they believed that a wife could not shirk that duty any more than she could stop the sun setting or the rain falling.

But there were two or three or four women over the years in whom I beheld an affection for their husbands that longed to be expressed by touches and caresses. I recall sharply one young mother who cried piteously when my grandmother advised that her husband sleep apart from her for two months because her birthing had been such a hard one and she needed healing time and sound rest. Then her husband held her in his arms and licked the tears on her cheeks and kissed her throat and her shoulders, and she took his hand and guided it to her breast, where he curved his fingers around her and laughed and promised he would lie with her every night until she fell asleep.

When the husband began stroking his wife's nipple with his thumb, my grandmother stood up and shoved at me and said it was time to leave, we would be back tomorrow to check the baby and the mother, and maybe she would only need a month and not two for healing.

"A woman in a loveless marriage is no better than a slave," Mrs. Digby declared. "A slave with no chance of escape—either because she has no means to earn an honest living for herself or because she is unwilling to give up her children to their owner. The only hope of dignity for such a woman is to stand up to her husband's sexual tyranny and insist on total abstinence except for the purpose of childbearing. I will go even further, ladies and gentlemen, and say that for a woman trapped in a loveless marriage, entering a love union which the world labels adulterous is no sin."

This bold pronouncement met with much comment within the audience, but with less shock than I would have expected. I heard a few gasps, but I also saw many bonneted heads nodding affirmatively. This was an idea I would have to think about. I resolved to read more of the Nichols's writings on free love.

Mrs. Digby went on to say that all women, even those in true-love marriages, should remain chaste throughout pregnancy and nursing because amative excesses then could lead to ovarian tumors in the mother or masturbation in the children. But pregnancy and lactation could easily cover two or three years. I could not imagine many of the women my grandmother had attended accomplishing abstinence this long, and I marveled at the self-control of Dr. Nichols, Mrs. Nichols's husband, who had written the same advice in his book that Isabelle was so fond of quoting. There were two beds in the Martins' bedroom, a double and a single, and each one had to be made up each morning, so I knew both were being used. How long would Mr. Edwin indulge Isabelle in this separation?

"I urge you all," Mrs. Digby closed, "to choose your mates based on mutual love, and to esteem each other. Happiness will follow as a natural result. Though pleasure should not be an end in itself, pleasure will inevitably be part of sensual union when true love forms the beautiful basis of a marriage."

I felt as if I had encountered a whirlwind. Mrs. Digby's words, and the sureness with which she spoke them, set something stirring in me, just as a whirlwind lifts up unsettled dust and unnoticed, forgotten bits of rummage, mixes them together, and then drops them, rearranged, into a new neighborhood.

Later, I dated Mrs. Digby's lecture as the start of certain changes in me, but, in truth, that was simply a convenience. Wherever I might lay my finger on the calendar of 1886—on the day I moved to the city, or the day of the lecture, or of any other distinct event—there was no single, clean turning point. Indeed, I could not have been turned by anything that happened in that year if my life had not been already seeking and set to change. I was like an untended garden plot—a hungry, waiting garden—and the seeds most likely to take root and flourish were those that could best feed on the minerals and humus that had been laid deep in the soil during my childhood.

I grew up in a cottage in Montgomery County, at the edge of Philadelphia. It and the five acres it sat upon were all our family used of the forty acres that had been my grandfather's small farm. The rest of the land was leased out to a neighbor who planted it in seed corn. In my childhood, the area was still very rural, but by the time I moved to the Martins', its eventual fate as a streetcar suburb was on the horizon for those who could look ahead with modern enough eyes. The north end of Broad Street, which led out of the city into the Montgomery County farmlands, was yet unpaved and was widely used for horse racing, and places like the Lamb Tavern, the Punch Bowl, and Markley's Tavern crawled with jockeys, pugilists, politicians, and horse-trading gypsies, but the city was beginning to inch out from its center at Penn's Square. Already, many Philadelphia businessmen had built new homes around Poplar and Broad Streets, and within a few years of my transplantation to town, some of Philadelphia's richest families had claimed generous lots even farther north for their brownstone palaces, and large row houses were starting to fill the spaces between.

My parents had moved in with my grandmother when my brothers were babies because my mother did not like the soot and noise of city lodgings. She had put up with them when it had been just herself and my father, but she believed the countryside to be the only place for children.

It was the one thing I knew my mother to have insisted upon in the whole of her married life, and my father never let her forget it. Every time he had to get up especially early to go into the city for cargo, every time the dray or the wagon got stuck in a muddy country lane, every time he heard of a "lesser" man getting a hauling job that he felt would have been his if only he'd been on the spot to claim it, he railed and growled like a great bear caught in a leg-iron trap. At these times, his complaints and invectives against my mother and her "milkmaid daydreams" flowed as steadily as our backyard stream when it was swollen with rainwater and rushing mud. Sometimes his voice, rising and falling as he dredged up new ways to say the same things, was the last sound I heard before falling asleep at night and the first one upon waking in the morning, preceding even the cock's crow.

I think my father would have made a good orator if he had been born into a different place. His is a deep baritone, and he has a natural talent for lowering and raising it at the points most likely to move his audience in the direction he wishes. He's weak as a conversationalist, but he shines at monologues.

My mother, as audience of one, was often made meek under his upbraidings (though she never surrendered the cottage), but I remember once creeping down the ladder from my bedroom to spy on them beside the hearth and finding her listening to him with a rapt smile on her firelit face. I supposed he was telling her a story, as he occasionally did to us children. His stories were never complex—no dragons or princesses or magic spells; he kept us enthralled with simple tales of his daily encounters or his boyhood adventures because of where he put the details and how he used his voice. My father was the center of the group when he and his cronies were standing about on a street corner or lolling on the grass on a warm Sunday afternoon. As on the night I spied on my parents from the ladder, I never came close enough to these groups of men to hear my father's words, but I recognized the cadences of storytelling.

I have always been glad I witnessed that quiet fireside scene between my parents. It has allowed me to believe my mother's life with my father was not empty of mutual affection, as it often appeared to be on the surface. As I said, my parents did not expect to be happy. My father expected work and respect and attention to his physical needs, and he got them. My mother expected children, a country home, and protection from want. But I had desired happiness for them, particularly for my mother. Somehow, even at an early age, I knew that if happiness were beyond the reach of my mother, then it might be beyond me, too.

FIVE

THE DAY after Mrs. Digby's lecture, Isabelle decided to rearrange her sewing room. She directed, and I moved furniture. She wanted to make space for a second Turkish chair so that I might sit and sew there with her from time to time.

"And converse as friends do," she said.

The sewing room was on the floor above the main living quarters. There were two other rooms—a guest bedroom and adjoining it, a small sitting room that had been newly decorated as a nursery. At one end of the hall, carpeted stairs connected this floor to the downstairs entry hall outside the parlor, and at the other end, narrower staircases spiraled down to the kitchen and up to my attic bedroom.

The sewing room was a place for practical work, and as such, it was simply furnished with a chest where Isabelle kept her yarns and scrims for needlepoint, her embroidery hoops and threads, and her collection of velvet, satin, and silk scraps for crazy quilts; a table for laying out patterns and cutting; a sewing machine cabinet with a straight-backed chair in front of it; and an upholstered chair set next to the window. The wood floor had been left bare except for a woven rush mat near the door. But there were touches of beauty amid the simplicity. The muslin curtains at the window had insets of cotton lace, and the sewing tools arrayed on the chest were very fine and included two velvet pincushions, one cased in ivory and one in silver, and steel sewing clamps and scissors cast in the shapes of birds.

The sewing room boasted a full-length mirror framed in dark wood carved with curling vines and leaves. Isabelle had a full-length mirror in a corner of her bedroom as well. I had never before encountered such large looking glasses; no one of my acquaintance had one, and it was not because of the expense. In the country, we were taught that young women should not see themselves naked. After a certain age, girls put talcum powder into their bathwater to cloud it and obscure their reflections. As far as I knew, Isabelle only used her mirrors to judge the fit and effect of her clothing, but I could not help but imagine temptation crouching within the mirrors' silvery surfaces. Sometimes, when I dusted the mirrors, my attention would be caught by my own image, and I'd pause to regard myself almost as if I were another person, once even turning my body slowly to view my profile and the unknown aspect of my back.

After things in the sewing room had been shoved around a few times, Isabelle sat down in one upholstered chair and asked me to take the other so that she could evaluate the amount of light falling from the window and the ceiling lamp onto the chairs. Once we were seated, however, she seemed to forget her purpose. She stared dreamily out the window and never even glanced down at her lap, where her sewing work would be held. The February sun gleamed on the tips of long icicles hanging from the roof edge above the top of the window.

"What did you make of Mrs. Digby?" Isabelle asked, turning to me after a few minutes.

"I thought she was right in much of what she said," I replied.

"You are not a dissembling girl, Nan," Isabelle said. "I can see you thought more than that."

Isabelle was right. I had found Mrs. Digby especially admirable in condemning laws and customs that put women's property, children, and very manner of living in the complete control of their husbands, but in other ways she seemed too strict and unsympathetic. Her advice that women in loveless marriages insist on abstinence as a way to soften their desperate plight seemed, to me, of little use and even less comfort. But I was still too shy of the new footing between me and Isabelle to show her so bold an opinion.

"I did wonder," I dared to say, "if it is really possible that a husband would willingly limit relations with his wife."

"I'm afraid I'm hardly more an expert on husbands than I am on babies, Nan, but the point is, I think, that it is the woman, not the man, who has the right to choose when she will bear children."

"I think there must be times, though," I ventured, "or unavoidable circumstances, when a woman is not free to claim that right."

"But it is a right, all the same," Isabelle declared, "and nothing out of reach is ever gained if one is not willing to risk claiming it."

At that moment, Isabelle looked like a person prepared to risk or claim anything if she wanted it enough. Her dark eyes were almost feverish with resolve, and her chin was lifted as if ready to take a blow, as if inviting one in order to show the immovability of her will. But what was it she willed or wanted that she had been thwarted in? She was in the seventh year of her marriage, and this was her first pregnancy. Assuming normal health and normal relations, that gave some evidence that she had been permitted choices. She had said she'd not chosen Mr. Edwin on her own, but she'd also said she had no complaints against him.

"I know what the first book should be that you borrow from my library, Nan," Isabelle said, suddenly jumping up and leaving the room. "Wait here."

I stood and looked out the window. The view was of the flat roof of the neighboring house, which was shorter than ours. A maid was gathering cold-stiffened sheets from a clothesline. The wind slapped the sheets away from her so she had to stand on tiptoes to reach the clothespins; it caught, too, at her skirts and her apron, tangling them with the sheets as she tried to fold them.

Before lifting the laundry basket to carry it back inside, the young woman paused to rub her hands together and blow on her fingers. The sight brought a strange melancholy seeping into my heart. Here was someone engaged daily in the same tasks as mine, living and working right next door, and yet we were strangers to each other. I gazed across the patchwork of rooftops and building faces and rears visible for blocks in three directions, and I imagined all the other girls throughout the city doing the same things, perhaps thinking, sometimes, similar thoughts and sighing sighs whose sources would be familiar and understandable if ever we met and talked about them. Yet we were all separated and alone, so that our work and our thoughts and our sighs stayed unique and seemed small and inconsequential.

Late summers at home, I used to help farm wives cook for the harvest hands, who expected food and found along with their wages—board and room, they call it in the city. There were teamsters, sack jigs, sack sewers, roustabouts, and barn men. On the bigger farms, that meant eighteen to thirty-five hungry men needing five meals a day for ten days or longer. Neighbor women took turns helping one another, but they weren't enough, so there were always several young girls hired on, too.

We worked from 3:00 A.M. to 10:30 P.M., cooking in sheds or shanties to keep the heat of the woodstoves away from the main house, and we never put away just-washed dishes, but set them right on the table again for the next meal. It was hot, continuous work, but there was pleasure in it, too, because of the company. We found time to talk while we baked bread or made lemonade or carried the midmorning and midafternoon sandwiches out to the fields.

I put the palm of my hand against the frigid windowglass

of Isabelle's sewing room and held it there; I could not feel the wind, nor the chilled sheets, and I could not call the maid next door by name, but I would share this one fragment of her life, the cold touch of a Pennsylvania February.

"Here it is," Isabelle said behind me.

I turned, and she handed me a book, *Mary Lyndon,* by Mary Gove Nichols.

"It's a novel," she said. "About the despair of her loveless marriage, before she found the water cure and before she met Dr. Nichols. He was her second husband, her true love."

I smoothed the cover of the book with my hand. It was not the first selection I would have made, but I didn't feel I could object.

"Thank you," I said, smiling, deciding it was far better to be loaned a book I didn't want than to be folding cold sheets in the wind, without the comfort of knowing that sympathetic eyes were watching.

AFTER *MARY LYNDON,* Isabelle let me pick books at will. She didn't even prescribe a pattern for me, so I skipped around without design; sometimes a book had a link to the one that had preceded it, but more often not. In the first weeks of jumping from shelf to shelf, I read some stories by Sarah Orne Jewett, Lucy Larcom's autobiography about her girlhood in a textile mill, parts of *The Homeopathic Domestic Physician,* and some slight essays on cats and tea and such things by Agnes Reppelier, whom Isabelle said was a homely but witty spinster, having met her once at a literary evening at the Contemporary Club.

Though I found it gradually more comfortable to talk with Isabelle in a conversational way, about books or other things, I was never easy in it unless I was engaged in a chore at the same time. Nor did I ever initiate our exchanges, but left that always to her. Sometimes, she'd let a day or two pass without encouraging any familiarity between us, as if she'd lost interest or forgotten that it was possible; then, unexpectedly, she'd come into the kitchen and read poetry aloud while I cooked or call me up to the sewing room to sit and do mending while she embroidered baby clothes. Once I saw that such ons and offs were simply part of her nature, I didn't worry about it. Besides, I knew that a woman nearing birth often folds more into herself, like a bird building a nest.

I saved my reading for nights in my room or when supper was simmering and Isabelle was napping and Mr. Edwin hadn't come in yet. Somehow, it seemed a very private thing. I did not want to be observed doing it. When I was reading, my awareness of my surroundings fell away from me; interruptions startled or confused me by bringing me too suddenly back.

I had a small, secret plan to have, someday, a tidy set of rooms of my own. I would furnish them just as I liked, and I would be free to read in them without any chance of disturbance. Because I had no steady expenses, I was able to save a good part of my wages, though I did send something to my sister Elsinore each week so that she'd have a little to spend on herself; she was the last one at home with our grandmother and father.

My room at the Martins' was not much more than a large closet under the eaves, with a shaded dormer window at one end and a small skylight that let in the morning sun and made a dance floor for rain, but it was the first room I had ever had to myself, and the simple, sure privacy of it had given me a taste for seclusion. As I lay in my narrow iron bed and stared through the skylight at the stars, I wished for one year in two or three rooms of my own before I should meet some man and marry and keep his house.

SIX

"AIDEZ-MOI, NAN," Isabelle said, desperately gripping my hand. "Help me, please."

Her face was terribly pale, her large eyes dark with fear, like the eyes of a horse too near a fire. I had just finished wiping her brow and wrists with rosewater, but it could not overpower the salty smells of tired sweat and body fluids. Mrs. Nostas, the midwife, was napping on the single bed near the open window. Isabelle had been in labor all night, and it had been a hard labor, more so than most I'd seen, and I think the pain was made worse by Isabelle's disappointment. She had so counted on a quick job. Only two days ago, she had repeated to me Dr. Nichols's description of births to water-cure patients.

"It says in his book," she'd reminded me, "that sometimes there is no pain, and that often it is all over in an hour or less. I have been so careful in my preparations, I'm sure my baby will drop from me like a ripe apple from a tree."

"Sometimes apples need shaking and knocking to get them down," I'd replied.

She smiled at me as if she were sorry for my ignorance, and I said no more to contradict her. She seemed to have forgotten that two pages past the description of one-hour labors in Dr. Nichols's text, he mentioned waiting through twenty-four, thirty-six, and forty-eight-hour labors. Still, it was possible that things would go as Isabelle hoped. I had seen births like that. But not many.

"*Aidez-moi,*" she said again now, but more softly, and her fingers lessened their grip on my hand. She closed her eyes and fell into a doze. In two minutes, her face began to contort, and she threw her head back and forth on the pillow and moaned. Then she suddenly arched her back and shrieked.

"Isabelle," I said loudly. "You must keep yourself light and loose, like a leaf in a stream."

She moaned again and rolled to her side, but I could see her trying to obey. She erased her frown and let her arms and legs fall limply away from her body. I pitied her. If will alone were required, she'd have had her baby hours ago.

Mrs. Nostas arose and came over to the double bed and looked down at her patient. Isabelle was dozing again. Mrs. Nostas put her hand on Isabelle's shoulder, and Isabelle raised her eyebrows to show she was awake though she remained motionless, with eyes shut.

"I want to examine you, dear," Mrs. Nostas said.

"Dr. Nichols says . . . avoid examinations." If I didn't know better, I'd have said Isabelle was drunk, her words sounded so slurred. I guessed it was the exhaustion and discouragement.

"Even Dr. Nichols does examinations when there's need, dear. Now, onto your back. Quickly, before the next pain."

Isabelle complied, and I got up so Mrs. Nostas could have my chair beside the bed. I handed her oil for her fingers, and she slipped her hand under the sheet and along Isabelle's thigh. When the next pain began, Mrs. Nostas leaned forward and moved her hand up.

"Oh!" said Isabelle. "Nan!"

I put my hand on her head, which seemed to calm her, and she rode that pain tolerably well, even with Mrs. Nostas's judging fingers inside her.

"Willer," Mrs. Nostas said to me. "Go tell Mr. Martin we need a doctor's advice here. I don't like how this dear is suffering to so little purpose."

I paused in the hall for a few minutes before going to find Mr. Edwin. Except for a half hour in the kitchen to eat a cold supper around midnight, I'd not been away from Isabelle's bedroom since late yesterday afternoon. It was a relief to be out of the grip of that grinding drama, though I did feel a twinge of self-reproach knowing that she had no such escape available to her.

Mr. Edwin was breakfasting. A neighbor woman had come in to fix his meal, a big piece of haddock, brown rolls, fried eggs, and coffee. He looked up expectantly from his newspaper when I entered the dining room, and pushed his chair a bit away from the table, as if preparing to get up and go to his wife.

"Bearer of good tidings, Willer?" he said.

"No tidings yet, sir."

"Oh." Looking puzzled, he pulled his chair back in and took a sip of coffee.

"Mr. Edwin, Mrs. Nostas asks that you call a doctor."

"A doctor? Is there an emergency?"

"No, sir, not that I can see, and Mrs. Nostas hasn't said so. It's just for advice, sir. Because things are slow and Mrs. Martin is wearing down."

"My wife is young and fit, and I won't have a doctor putting hands on her. This is a business for women. Mrs. Nostas came highly recommended."

When I relayed this to Mrs. Nostas, she looked cross but she did not say anything. Two hours later, she examined Isabelle again and was satisfied that she could start pushing. But the pains had faded, and Isabelle had no inclination to push. Mrs. Nostas said we might wait a little while, that Isabelle could use a short rest. She smoothed the bedclothes around Isabelle and beckoned me to the door.

"I'm going to insist Mr. Martin bring in a doctor," she said to me in a low voice so Isabelle could not hear. "There's something not right here. Don't you feel it?"

I nodded. Throughout the night, despite our concentrated

work, I had felt a kind of emptiness in that room. Isabelle was in thrall to the pains; Mrs. Nostas and I kept busy doing what we could to make her comfortable. Yet all of us had seemed as futile as wooden animals on a carousel going round and round in pursuit of nothing.

"I fear for that child's life," Mrs. Nostas said, and though she could have meant Isabelle, I knew at once she meant the baby, for I recognized suddenly what it was that was absent. The baby was not trying to be born. It was not giving anything to our work. The missing piece was the baby's vitality.

Mrs. Nostas finally convinced Mr. Edwin to send for a doctor. He assured Mr. Edwin the outcome would have been no different if he'd been summoned earlier. Before the new night had fully entered, Isabelle's little girl was delivered, still and blue, with the cord wrapped three times tightly around her neck. She'd been gone before we'd half begun.

SEVEN

⁓ THERE WAS a small funeral for the Martins' baby two days later. They had named her Agatha Yvonne, after both their mothers. The chief clerk in each of Mr. Edwin's five shops came, and Mr. Edwin's partner, Mr. Cox, with his wife, and two elderly ladies who, Isabelle later told me, went to all the funerals in the congregation.

Mrs. Nostas, the midwife, was there too. She and I kept close behind Isabelle at the funeral parlor and during the graveside service in case she looked faint, but though her complexion was sallow and she had to receive condolences seated in a chair, she never wavered and only cried when it was time to leave the cemetery. The ground was frozen from several days of very cold weather, so interment had to be delayed. I wept a little myself to think of the baby waiting out there in her white christening gown of stiff pineapple cloth that Isabelle had so carefully embroidered, and then to imagine her, later, being put into the ground in her icy metal box with only the gravedigger as witness.

Mr. Edwin's father, Mr. Sylvester Martin, came late to the viewing at the funeral parlor. He was a large man, much more robust than his son, with a red face and a full head of pure white hair, and a white beard that made his lips look as pale and fleshy as raw veal. I would have noticed him in any case and was interested to compare him with his portrait in the Martins' parlor, but his lateness and his loud apologies to Mr. Edwin drew everyone's attention. Isabelle shook his hand and gave him her cheek to kiss, but her eyes were angry, and it looked like an old anger. I shook the impression from my mind. She might be running a low fever, which would show in her eyes. Plus, she'd been agitated when Mr. Edwin, because of his father's lateness, postponed closing the coffin past the time she was ready for that to happen.

Isabelle stood beside the old man while he viewed his tiny granddaughter, and she would not let me or Mrs. Nostas or Mr. Edwin support her. As soon as Mr. Sylvester Martin turned away from the little box, she motioned to the funeral director to close the coffin lid. Or rather, the casket top.

"It's a casket, not a coffin, Nan," Isabelle had corrected me only the day before when she showed me the engraved illustration of the one she'd chosen from the catalog Mr. Edwin had brought home.

Her selection was one of the more elaborate models, draped in fringed black serge, with tufted white satin inside and, on the outside of the top, a silver-plated ornament of a woman's hand holding a lily and a scroll underneath saying Our Darling. It was guaranteed against leakage. A delicately lettered sentence at the bottom of the catalog page stated that a price list would be furnished on application.

I thought about my mother's death nine years ago. Her untreated body and that of her newborn infant had been wrapped in a shroud and put into a simple, human-sized, human-shaped wooden coffin. My father knew it was becoming customary in the city to embalm bodies and to hold funerals in funeral parlors rather than at home, but he could not afford these services. It was just as well, for my grandmother, who was my mother's mother, frowned on such practices; she said decay was a natural part of the cycle of creation and that people should leave for their final rest from the place they had lived, not from some house of the dead.

It would not have eased my sorrow over my mother if she had been buried in a better container, or if it had been called a casket, like the boxes ladies use to keep jewels. And if she'd been laid out looking as if she were asleep, as they did with Isabelle's baby, I would only have felt taunted. But the special care and trappings seemed to help Isabelle, at least on the day of the funeral.

For days after, however, she sat long hours listlessly on the couch in the parlor, propped with pillows and coverlets, and on several nights, just after the Martins had retired, Mr. Edwin had to call me into their room to help Isabelle to bed because she was weeping too piteously to do it herself. In this period, in order to divert Isabelle from her grief, I put myself forward for the first time, using any small thing to kindle conversation. Each day it was a little easier to lead her, and when the week's anniversary of Agatha Yvonne's birth, and then of her funeral, had circled by, Isabelle was nearly herself again, a bit more active in the household routine, talkative on her own—in her characteristic rhythm of ebb and flow—and needing no help at bedtime.

I deemed her recovery complete when she came into the kitchen on a Tuesday, ironing day, set up her board opposite mine, and took up a flatiron and a stack of damask napkins. We sent Mr. Edwin's shirts to Chinatown for laundering, but that still left a lot of garments and tidies to be ironed, especially as Mr. Edwin liked his sheets and pillowcases and his undergarments pressed. I welcomed Isabelle's help.

It was nearly mid-March, and the weather was beginning to soften, so I had pushed the windows up a little; the occasional breath of damp breeze that came into the stove-warmed kitchen carried a refreshing chill and hints of the river, which blended pleasantly with the clean aroma of the heated cotton and linen under our irons. We worked silently for some time, but it was a comfortable silence. I didn't see the need any longer of drawing Isabelle out; I had fallen out of that short-lived habit.

"I'd like, Nan, to pack up the baby's things tomorrow."

Isabelle had avoided the nursery so far, not even going to her sewing room, which was next door to it.

"We could lay tissue paper and red cedar chips in the drawers to keep the clothes," I said.

"I don't want to keep them," Isabelle said.

Holding her gaze down, she turned over the blouse on her board, exchanged a cooled flatiron for a hot one from the top of the stove, and continued ironing. I wondered if she feared that using Agatha Yvonne's clothing for another baby would be bad luck.

"She didn't even wear them," I protested gently. "And you made such lovely things. Your next baby will get good use—"

Isabelle looked up sharply. "There's not going to be any next baby," she said.

I knew from Mrs. Nostas that the doctor had pronounced Isabelle sound and perfectly capable of bearing more babies, with no reason to expect another loss. But I saw it would not be prudent to remind her of that just then.

"I intend to give the clothes to the Interchurch Child Care Society," she continued, as coolly as if she were discussing some old vests of Mr. Edwin's.

"You don't want to wait a little longer?" I suggested.

"Wait?"

"In case you come to feel differently later on. Right now, the disappointment is still so fresh."

Isabelle left her ironing board and sat down in the easy chair next to my mending basket. She leaned her head back and closed her eyes.

"You're right, Nan," she said, her head still back and her eyes still shut. "I am disappointed. But not in the way you think."

"No?"

"I had counted on the baby bringing me some relief."

"Well, Isabelle," I said, puzzled, "babies bring relief from pregnancy, but otherwise, they bring a lot of new work." She straightened up and stared at me. There was a hardness in her face I had never noticed before, though the longer I looked at her, the more I began to think it was something I *had* seen without being aware of it, something that had always been there, only veiled over, like dust covers on furniture in an unused room.

"I had been counting on some relief from my husband," she said.

When I did not reply, her expression turned to annoyance, clearly directed at me. She stood up and made to leave the room. As she passed my board, she stopped and spoke in an exaggerated whisper.

"You understand, Nan. You heard Mrs. Digby."

What Isabelle did not understand was that my silence had not come from missing her meaning; it sprang, instead, from an absolute grasp of her meaning and from the wish that we both might be allowed, in the future, to forget what she had said, or, at least, to pretend to forget it.

I HAD A half day off a week, usually Thursday, though Isabelle sometimes changed it if she needed me on a Thursday. When the weather was especially grim, I stoked the small stove in my room and spent most of the hours there reading books and newspapers or writing letters to my family. But I bundled up and went out for at least a little while even on bad days, just to feel that the time was truly my own. I slogged through slush and rain to take cocoa in a small confectioner's shop near the amusement museums on Arch Street or pushed against the cold wind to go sit with a book in Franklin's Library Company.

By the end of March, spring was flirting seriously with winter, and I began taking all my half day out, walking all around the city, avoiding, of course, the rougher areas, stopping sometimes to rest on a bench or low wall. I was sitting in Rittenhouse Square one mild afternoon when a rubber ball bounced into and then out of my lap, leaving a round smudge of dirt in the middle of page 52 in *Jo's Boys*. I immediately brushed at the mark with my glove, but the surface of the ball must have been damp, for the dirt smeared across the page and onto the adjoining one, making the stain worse. Isabelle liked Louisa May Alcott far less than I did, but I was nevertheless distressed to have a brand-new book marred. Isabelle hadn't even read it yet.

"Wesley! Come here!"

I looked up to see a young woman chasing after a little boy, who, in turn, was running after the rolling ball that had fouled Isabelle's book. The boy caught up with the ball and scooped it from the ground, tucking it under one arm just as his pursuer reached him. She took hold of his free hand and led him toward my bench.

I watched them approach. The young woman was about my age; she wore a shabby coat of spring wool and an unseasonable straw hat brightened with a new sash of tartan plaid ribbon. The boy's Norfolk suit was of more expensive cloth and looked to have been cut by a professional tailor. I assumed the woman was a nanny, though her dress was more individualistic than was typical; Rittenhouse Square was a favorite place for nannies to bring their charges.

They stopped in front of me, and the young woman pushed the boy forward so that his knees were nearly touching mine. He hung his head and stood very still. He was close enough that I caught that smell little boys can have, even rich little boys, of sweaty puppies and raw corn.

"Go on, Wesley," the young woman said, and the boy raised his head, showing me an expression of childish misery.

"I'm sorry, miss, if my ball hurt you," he said softly.

"I wasn't hurt, just startled," I said, "but my book—"

"It isn't a bad ball, miss, only it's a new ball—for my birthday—and it's not very good yet at coming back when I throw it up high."

Thinking of Jo March and Professor Baer and their tolerant love of boys and boyish ways, I closed the book to hide the dirty pages. Would Jo and her professor have cared that a wayward, disobedient ball had bounced across their story?

"A new ball needs a lot of looking after," I told Wesley. "I'm sure you'll be in charge of it soon."

Wesley bared his teeth and pointed to a gap in the top row.

"The ball did that," he said importantly. "But the tooth was already loose, and Papa said now that I am six, I'm not to cry anymore over such little things."

"All right, Wesley, that'll do," the young woman said.

The boy skipped off, stopping several yards away from us to bounce the ball up and down on the stone walkway. The ball went awry once and landed in a freshly turned flower bed of black mud. Wesley retrieved it and resumed his studious bouncing.

"He'd have been telling you next about the blood down his shirtfront," the young woman said. "He does like an audience. There's not many at home with the patience to listen to him."

"He's not yours?"

"Oh, no. I'm a maid-of-all-work in his father's house. The nanny's been sick in bed for three days, and the boy's been cooped up alone in his playroom, so I asked his mother if I could take him out for a bit, and she said I might if the cook didn't need me, and the cook didn't, though she said I'd been too forward in asking his mother that."

The young woman started to laugh.

"Well, it seems I've spared you Wesley's ramblings only to tire you out with my own!" she said.

Her round, dimpled face was vastly freckled, and she had bright blue eyes and gleaming coppery hair. With her easy laughter laid over these lively features, she was the picture of friendliness.

"I'm Hanna Willer," I said, holding out my hand.

She took it without hesitation, a good sign in a woman, and her handclasp was firm but relaxed, another good sign. My favorite brother, Leonard, said the way a person shook hands was a reflection of character, and that that held for women as well as men. He thought women who would not shake hands untrustworthy and secretive, and women who shook weakly to be capable of foolishness and deception. He did not understand that women often find themselves in situations where secrecy or deception or even foolishness are the only wise courses. I did not try to enlighten him. I loved him and wanted him always to think well of me, so I cultivated a forthright handclasp and used it liberally, and somewhere along the way, I came to adopt my brother's prejudice and belief that character *could* be read in a grip and that women ought to pay more heed to theirs.

"Matrona Morrison," returned my new acquaintance, smiling. "Mattie."

She turned to check on Wesley, and I looked over at the boy, too. He was trying a new trick, raising first one leg and then the other, bouncing the ball back and forth under his uplifted knees. This feat required not only the coordination of arms and feet, but also the switching of hands. Wesley often missed a beat or inadvertently kicked the ball, but he pounced on it before it could roll far and resumed his practice. We watched him silently for a few minutes, me sitting with the book closed on my lap, Mattie standing in front of my bench.

"Have you children?" she said at last. "You were very kind with him."

"No, I'm in service, too. There's no children there, but I did help raise my little sister."

Mattie nodded and sat down at the end of the bench, as if enough personal information had now passed between us that she could. Before sitting, however, she did lift her eyebrows and tilt her head, ever so subtly asking my permission, and I made a slight, smiling nod in answer.

"So, you don't come to the square regularly?" I said.

"No. I'm about as penned in as poor Wesley. But that's to change soon."

"Oh?"

"I'm going to a paper-box factory. And I'm to be married." Mattie grinned at me. "That sounded odd, didn't it?"

We laughed a little together, and I found myself thinking how likeable she was.

"I only meant," she continued, "that I won't be living in some dreary boardinghouse, carrying a midday meal of cold fried eels wrapped in newspaper. You know, I had a friend whose landlady gave her pickles and cake most days to take with her to the factory, and didn't even put sheets on the beds. But I'll be with my husband and his brother, and we'll eat decently and live in clean rooms, and then, someday, we'll get a little house all our own. Paolo's already got shares in a savings and loan association."

I admired her certainty. Perhaps I envied it a bit, too. I always see too many sides to every question, always anticipate how plans might become blocked or snagged, always fear that some greater machinery than my small hopes will determine the final outcome of a course of action. I do not trust contentment. I do not believe in safety. There is only more or less safety. More or less freedom. And bargains to be struck between them.

When I evince confidence it is often because I have deliberately taken on its guise in order to force myself forward on something. But it is amazing how effective appearances can be. I am my mask as much as I am the person behind the mask, because it is the person behind the mask who fashions it and decides when and why to put it on.

Wesley came over to us and carefully propped his ball against the side of the bench. Squatting down, he cradled his head in Mattie's lap. It was touching how sure he was of her welcome.

"Tired, are you?" she said, pulling off his cap and stroking his tangled hair. "And the ball, too?"

"Yes," came the muffled reply. "We're tired."

"Let's go, then. There's just time for a bath before your mother comes upstairs to see you."

The boy straightened up, and Mattie stood, smoothing out her skirt.

"I enjoyed our chat," she said to me.

"So did I."

She took Wesley's hand and turned to go, then turned back.

"Will you be in the square again?" she asked.

"Sometime, I suppose. I usually have Thursday afternoons off, and I like to go walking when the weather allows."

"My half day rotates. It'll be Thursday week after next. Shall we meet here? I can bring some oranges."

"Yes," I said impetuously. "Yes, I'd like that. I'll bring something, too."

She smiled at me and left, walking at a good pace, Wesley marching staunchly alongside, with an occasional hop to keep up. The boy's face was turned up toward Mattie the whole way, and her head was canted toward him. I saw her nod once or twice; I imagined he was telling her a momentous story and she was listening with just the right mix of gravity and merriment.

I stood and watched them until they reached the corner at Eighteenth Street and exited the square. Then I headed for the other end of the square to begin my long walk home, deciding to go east along Spruce Street awhile before turning north. Spruce was a quieter street than Market or Chestnut, and I felt a desire for quietness in order to savor the pleasant frame of mind meeting Mattie had put me into.

Only ten weeks out of my father's house, and I had two new friends. Of course, Isabelle was a queer friend; my position as her maid would prevent us ever being close, and I expected I'd never be wholly easy with her. Mattie, on the other hand, promised to be a jolly and full companion, one with whom I could exchange private thoughts.

But it's Isabelle who has marked my life most. We are no longer friends, if we ever truly were, but, like the ghost of a twin lost at birth, I will never be free of Isabelle Martin.

EIGHT

☙ "COME, COME, Nan, you can get them tighter than
that. Here, I'll hold my breath."

Isabelle drew a deep breath and held it while I pulled on
the laces of her whalebone corset, shrinking her waist another
half inch. She was a small, delicately formed woman and did
not, in my opinion, need stays, even now, with the lingering
roundness of pregnancy still softening her shape.

In the book Isabelle had set such store by, Dr. Nichols
swore that tight lacing was injurious to a woman's health, pre-
cipitating backaches, interfering with the functioning of organs, and causing the womb to fall. But since the stillbirth a
month ago, Isabelle had been less enthusiastic about Dr.
Nichols and about Mary Gove Nichols and her disciple Mrs.
Digby. Mr. Edwin, who had been tolerant of Isabelle managing her pregnancy as she wished, encouraged her defection
from the Nicholses now. Despite Isabelle's arguments, he had
never succumbed to vegetarianism, being too fond of sausages
and spicy gravies; his one concession to the philosophy of the
water cure was his daily cold bath. Isabelle had convinced him
this practice warded off illness, which Mr. Edwin thought lay
perpetually in wait for him like a hungry tiger craftily hidden
among dappled jungle foliage.

"Let's see the fit now," Isabelle said, lifting a dress of forest
green faille over her head. She closed the tiny cloth-covered

buttons down the front of the dress, but the ones at her waist were visibly straining the fabric. Annoyed, Isabelle took the dress off.

"Tighter," she said, turning her back to me so that I could work at the laces again.

Isabelle had eaten no breakfast in order to aid in this reshaping of her figure, and after I had tightened the laces yet again and she had put on the dress and declared herself satisfied, I doubted she'd manage lunch either, as how could her stomach expand to receive any food? I reminded her that she was still recovering her health and should not be fasting, but she just waved her hands at me as if I were a fussy old nursemaid.

"I'm too nervous to eat, anyway, Nan," she said. "Too excited, that is. Just think, we haven't seen Mr. Edwin's brother Frederick in two whole years. There's never been a livelier guest in our home than he used to be. And he's sure to have wonderful stories about Australia."

I wondered how any of Mr. Frederick Martin's stories could be unknown to Isabelle, she received such fat letters from Australia so regularly; additionally, whenever Mr. Edwin had a letter from his brother, which happened less often, he read it out to her. Mr. Frederick closed his letters to his brother by asking to have his regards conveyed to Isabelle, which always caused her to bow her head and smile shyly, as if she'd been paid a compliment during a church service.

Mr. Edwin was a keen stamp collector, but Isabelle gave the canceled stamps off her letters from Australia to me, telling me not to let Mr. Edwin know, and I kept them in a box on the little table beside my bed. I thought I'd mount them on a board and hang them in my own place, when I got it, they were so remarkable: fine-lined pastel-colored drawings of kangaroos and koala, of seashells and trains and the queen. When I think, now, of Isabelle, I sometimes imagine her in that faraway land, living a pastel existence, her small, dark self moving dreamily through a vague, muted landscape of pinks, mint green, and eggshell blue. It's just a fancy, of course, yet it seems the right kind of setting for her, which is odd, when I apply my intellect to it, for Isabelle certainly proved herself capable of being as unambiguous as a gravel pit or the baked summer mud of a vernal pool.

Isabelle's father-in-law, Mr. Sylvester Martin, was also invited to luncheon that day. He was cordial when I opened the door to him; he greeted me by name, and asked how I was getting along in the Martins' employ, and said his son had spoken well of me and how composed I'd been in the tragedy of the little dead baby. But next came a glimpse of the underbelly of his dislike for Isabelle, and I saw that she had not exaggerated it.

"My son coddles his wife, as I'm sure you've noticed," he said. "It did him good to see these things must be taken in stride."

"It was easier for me, sir," I replied, "since I was not the bereaved mother."

He paused before entering the parlor and frowned at me, trying to decide whether to put my remark down to intentional impertinence or mere callowness. Or perhaps he was just realizing the harsh tenor of his own comments.

"Life does go on, though, doesn't it?" he said. "And a husband has rights . . . certain needs . . . which he should not be expected to defer indefinitely, baby or no baby."

I was surprised that Mr. Sylvester Martin would be so bald with me about such a private matter, and I was equally surprised that Mr. Edwin had confided it to his father. The single bed had not yet been removed from the Martins' bedroom, and I knew from Isabelle herself that since the birth, she had not been able to bear even sleeping beside her husband. She said he respected her wish that their relations have nothing sensual about them for the time being. I took Mr. Sylvester Martin's remarks as a sign that the "time being" which Isabelle expected to stretch lazily and effortlessly into the indefinite future, had a very different meaning to Mr. Edwin, who, apparently, was anxious to attach a distinct finale.

When I let Mr. Sylvester Martin into the parlor, Mr. Edwin stood up from the settee and welcomed him with a warm handshake and a clasp of his arm. Isabelle looked up from a book she'd been reading and put out her hand to be taken next, but I noticed that she kept the fingers of her other hand between the pages to hold her place, as if she intended the old man to be no more a distraction than a delivery boy.

The bell took me to the door again, this time to admit Mr. Frederick. He was a finely built man a bit over six feet tall, with a graceful carriage. In his well-favored face were reconciled his father's vigor and his brother's quietness, and something more, a touch of playful devilment that rendered him not only handsome, but immediately appealing. Perhaps it was only my foreknowledge of his having adventured in Australia that made it so, but it seemed to me Mr. Frederick was a man of daring and magnetism. He smiled at me and asked my name and remarked on the day's warmth in so friendly and leisurely a manner, it could have been thought he'd come to visit me and not his family, who eagerly awaited him only steps away. At last, briskly rubbing his hands together, he plunged toward the parlor like a man anticipating a bracing dip into a cold river. It was all I could do to reach the doorknob before him and let him in properly.

The father and elder son were standing together near the bookcase, and Isabelle was at the window with her back to the room. The two men burst out into guffaws and shouts when Mr. Frederick entered, and there was much hugging and back-slapping among the three of them. Then a kind of hush descended, and they all looked toward Isabelle, who turned slowly to face them, as if their gaze had been a tap on her shoulder. She did not step away from the window, but stood there like a beautiful picture coming to life, her dark green dress and cinched waist silhouetted against the paler greens of

the plants behind her, her piled hair haloed by sunlight slant-
ing through the glass, half her strong face in slight shadow, the
other half brightly lit, her eyes seeming to glow with their
own light.

After a moment's hesitation, Mr. Frederick strode across
the room with both hands outstretched. Just as he reached
her, she lifted her hands, too, and they exchanged a sympathetic but temperate embrace.

"You never change, Isabelle," said Frederick.

"No," she said, with peculiar concentration.

She walked quickly across the small room then and stood
beside Mr. Edwin, laying one hand on his coatsleeve as if she
meant to pull him aside for a private conference. Instead, she
spoke to me.

"Nan, we'll visit here a half hour; then you can lay the luncheon in the dining room."

"A round of sherry is called for, I think," said Mr. Edwin,
patting Isabelle's hand, which still rested on his arm. "Willer,
four glasses, please."

"Three glasses," Isabelle said.

"Surely you can relax your rules this once, my dear," Mr.
Edwin chided. "Fred will think you don't wish him welcome."

"Will you think that, Fred?" Isabelle said.

"Certainly not. Three glasses, Willer," Mr. Frederick
replied, continuing to regard Isabelle even as he was addressing me. "Mrs. Martin shall drink to me only with her eyes."

Mr. Edwin laughed, pleased at the pretty sentiment directed to his wife.

"Ah, Fred," he said, "we've missed your quick ways."

When I returned with the glasses, the men were crowded
together on the settee sorting through a score of African
stamps Mr. Frederick had picked up for his brother when his
ship stopped over at Capetown. Isabelle stood behind the men.
She was holding the cut-glass decanter of sherry in her hands,
and I had the amusing impression she was about to bring it
down on one of their heads momentarily.

They came into the dining room forty-five minutes later, and it was clear that more than one glass of sherry apiece had been taken. The old father, especially, appeared a bit unsteady; Mr. Edwin guided him to his seat as if he were an invalid. Isabelle looked exercised, but I thought it might have been the strain of wanting everything to go well. She had spent all day yesterday planning the menu, ordering the food, arranging flowers; she had even helped me polish the silver.

While Mr. Edwin settled his father, Mr. Frederick pulled out Isabelle's chair for her. He seemed lost in thought a moment after she had sat down, for he stared at the top of her head as if it were a map. Then, with a quick jerk, he moved to his own place, rubbing his hands again as he had before entering the parlor earlier.

"What a treat," he said, turning his head to survey the sideboard, which held a quiche Lorraine, brioche, a platter of lamb chops, mashed turnips, spinach soufflé, and cold beets. "We don't eat well in Australia. It seems steak and eggs and fried potatoes are all Australians care to cook."

"It's bachelors everywhere who don't eat well," Mr. Edwin replied, taking two chops from the platter I offered. "What you need, Fred, is a good wife like Isabelle, and you'd have no more complaints about your meals."

"Might have other complaints, though," Mr. Sylvester Martin mumbled, seemingly to himself. Everyone heard him clearly, however, as could be told by the awkward silence that followed this comment, and I'm sure it's what he intended.

"Do they eat kangaroo in Australia?" Mr. Edwin said loudly, as if his brother were not right there at his elbow.

"No," Mr. Frederick said. "Hunted for their hides only."

"Have you hunted them?" Isabelle asked.

"Got better things to do with his time," Mr. Sylvester Martin said. "Out to make his fortune, you know. Hard work anywhere, but in a foreign land, thousands of miles from his own people, no family . . ."

I would have thought the father was getting sentimental,

which would be understandable, since it must be hard to have a son so obviously beloved as Mr. Frederick out of reach, except that the old man's voice was flinty and challenging rather than melancholy.

"Yes, I know how difficult it can be to make your way in a place that is not your own. . . ." Isabelle began, and her voice did sound wistful.

"And it's your doing he's there," the old man said to her.

Isabelle suspended in midair the serving spoon she was using to dish out soufflé. She turned very pale and then very flushed, put down the spoon and took it up again, as if confused.

"Father, please," Mr. Edwin said.

Mr. Sylvester Martin turned his fiery stare from Isabelle to Mr. Edwin.

"It's unendurable!" he declared. "To have one woman blemish the lives of two sons, and then to be restrained from making any objections to her. Unendurable!"

"Blemish?" Isabelle exclaimed. "How dare you say such a thing? You know nothing of my life. It's you who are unendurable."

"Know nothing? I know you spent an unlawful week with your husband's brother, disgracing them both. I know—"

"That's not true!" Isabelle shouted, slamming her fist on the table.

"Father," Mr. Frederick said. "I told you it was coincidence we were away at the same time. Let's not stir this up again. Think of Edwin's feelings."

The old man ignored his son and kept his fury aimed at Isabelle. They faced each other like mortal enemies, which, in a way, I suppose they were.

"Your own father—whoever he is—didn't believe you. Why should I?" he snarled at her. "Do you deny his agents paid my son to leave the country?"

"My father only wanted to quiet the scandal you were set on inventing," she answered icily.

54

"Conceived in sin, continued in sin," the old man said.

"Really, Father, I think that's quite enough," Mr. Edwin said.

"Enough, is it? Is it enough I have to go to restaurants to see my own son because his wife finds my company too rough for her parlor? Is it enough that you sleep in a cold bed and are forced into solitary vice?"

"Edwin!"

Isabelle stood up so forcefully, her chair fell backward. I had to jump in order to miss being hit by it. Throughout this awful scene, I had been unsure whether to go or stay. I knew I should not be witnessing it, but I feared, with the embarrassed unreason of youth, that my exit would draw attention away from the heated interchange, and that that would be somehow disrespectful on my part.

"My dear, Father's had too much sherry. And the overexcitement of seeing Fred again has perhaps induced—"

Mr. Edwin did not finish because Isabelle interrupted him with a wordless sob and fled the room. He stood up, then hesitated, as unsure as I had been, it seemed, whether to go or stay.

"Come, Father, let me take you home," Mr. Frederick said. "You've made a spruce mess here today."

I walked ahead of them, opening doors. The old man leaned against his son and looked much diminished by what had transpired.

"It's those books he lets her read," he was saying. "Have you looked at that Nichols's tract, *Mysteries of Man*? Unnatural reading for a woman."

"You must let Edwin manage his own life, Father."

"If truth be told, she's been unnatural from the first. Delaying married life two years while she went off playing at being a schoolgirl! I don't care what arrangement Edwin made with her father, nor how much he was paid. It's unnatural, all of it. She ought to be the daughter I never had, and instead she's taken both my sons from me."

Here we reached the entry hall, and the two men exited the apartment with not even a glance at me. I could hear the old man's voice, though not his words, continuing his aggrieved tirade as they slowly descended the stairs to the street.

NINE

$\mathcal{QR}$ THE FORSYTHIA along the country lane were in full bloom, and even though the way was a bit muddy, Mattie and I descended from the Philadelphia-Horsham coach early in order to be able to walk a while beside the generous bushes of bright yellow flowers.

How those simple blossoms used to cheer me as a girl, with their splash of optimistic color in a world still gray and cramped with winter. Everything is going to be all right, the forsythia seems to say, a new time is on its way. I used to set buckets of them in all the corners of our house, or up on shelves if there was a crawling baby about who might try to eat them. I felt like eating them myself sometimes, they looked that fresh and tender. Only last week, rounding a corner in Philadelphia, my mind taken up with the errand I was on, I'd been surprised by a lone forsythia bush shouting its yellow promises in a tiny front garden, and the encounter had touched my heart.

The April afternoon when Mattie first went with me to my father's house, the forsythia along the lane helped lift my spirits, which had been considerably strained during the three days after Mr. Frederick Martin's visit to my employers' home. The family quarrel was of no direct consequence to me, but the house had been a cheerless, broody place since, and whenever I entered a room where Isabelle and Mr. Edwin were sitting, I felt gloom brush against me like sticky strands of spider silk. They both spoke as little as possible, to me and to each other, as if that would mend or erase what had happened. But their silence was becoming part of what had happened, as a fungus becomes part of the tree on which it grows.

"How old did you say your sister is?" asked Mattie, pulling my thoughts away from the Martins.

"Elsinore is fifteen," I said, glad to steer my mind on a pleasanter course. "She's the youngest, and my pet, I'm afraid," I added. "She was only six when our mother died, and I was fourteen. We were naturally drawn together. She was such a pretty, easy child, taking care of her was no chore, and doing it gave me great comfort."

"What of your brothers and your other sisters?"

"The boys were older, off with their friends when they weren't working, and in a couple of years, out of the house altogether. And the twins had always kept to themselves. Even now that they're married, it's as likely on any day that you'll find one in the other's house as in her own—they are neighbors, and their husbands are cousins. It was Elsinore kept joy in my life after Mother died."

"You must miss her. If only you were married, perhaps you could have her with you."

I nodded, but I felt pinched by guilt. It was true that I missed Elsinore, and I knew that her days were often laborious and dull; yet when I spun my daydream of the little suite of rooms, I did not envision her there with me. I was ashamed to be so selfish that I didn't want to consider my sister sharing my refuge, even in imagination. But my tiny, fragile hope for space of my own could not bear the weight of wishing on behalf of two people. If it could, it would not be the same hope, nor the same wish, and so it would not be mine.

"My father needs her here," I said, making an excuse though Mattie had not looked for one. "My grandmother is too old to do much housework, though she still bakes the week's bread and won't let anyone else brew the morning coffee and cocoa."

"When I am a grandmother, I shall certainly let someone else make my breakfast drink and whatever more they will." Mattie laughed. "And I shall sit in the sun like an old cat."

I shook my head at the improbable picture of Mattie curled lazily on a sunny windowsill. I couldn't imagine her sprightly, engaged energy being diminished by anything, even old age.

Mattie and I had spent only a few afternoons together so far, but I felt I had already come to know her well. At our third meeting, as we were wending our way through a crowd outside Fox's New American Theatre, Mattie had linked her arm with mine; once clear of the congestion, she'd kept a light hold, and our steps fell at once into a coordinated cadence. The whole of our feelings seemed like that walk, an easy, natural pairing.

Perhaps Mattie and I had knit close so quickly because we did the same work and understood the small tyrannies of it, and because, as two country girls in the city, our eyes picked out similar sights and our hearts held similar memories. Yet there was more to it than commonality. We were becoming the kind of friends whom even differences connect. Not a reader herself, Mattie nevertheless liked to hear me talk of books; she had the satisfying trait of asking about characters as if they were real people. In turn, her infectious merriment loosened my reserve. There is nothing like sharing laughter with someone to make that person dear.

"This way," I said when we had reached the cinder path that led up the small hill on which my father's house stood. As we climbed the path, I tried to look at the house candidly, as if, like Mattie, I were seeing it for the first time. It was a commonplace whitewashed stone cottage, with a low-ceilinged ground-level porch along the front width of it and a broad wood door centered between two mullioned windows set deep in the thick walls like eyes in a fat man's face. A small casement window above the front door indicated a usable second story, in reality a long, narrow attic.

A pair of huge sugar maples flanked the house, tiny green buds adorning their dark branches, and a gnarled wisteria vine clung to a post at the south corner of the porch. The hilltop had been flattened into a dirt yard tufted here and there with clumps of hardy grass. A half dozen Rhode Island reds were scratching in the yard, circling an old rocker with a torn cane seat and a split back; their rooster surveyed them from atop this abandoned chair like a king on his throne.

Elsinore opened the door to us and flung her arms round me as if it had been years since she'd last seen me. My grandmother stayed in her place by the fire, which was well stoked despite the spring weather. The house was always chilly, a blessing in summer, but a discomfort otherwise, and my grandmother's age made her feel it more. She was wearing a black shawl; a crocheted afghan lay over her lap.

"Hello, Sippy," I said, going to her and kissing her smooth cheeks. She smelled of talc and old wool. She wrapped her cool, bony hands around my wrists and squeezed affectionately. Her grip was strong and steady; if her eyesight were not failing, she'd probably still be catching babies.

"Sippy, Elsinore, this is my friend, Mattie Morrison," I said. "Mattie, this is my grandmother, Beatrice Hood, and my sister, Elsinore."

"How do you do?" said Mattie, putting her hand out first to my grandmother and then to my sister.

"Welcome," said my grandmother. "Elsie, put the tea water on. I just baked this morning, Miss Morrison; I hope oat cakes and currant loaf are not too countrified for you girls."

"Sounds perfect for what we brought," Mattie declared, pulling jars of pineapple marmalade and guava jelly from her string bag. "You see, Mrs. Hood, city living does have its compensations."

"Well, I'm glad our Hanna's got someone to keep her from lonesomeness in the city."

"We do that for each other," Mattie said. "Though bringing me here is the best thing Hanna's done for me. My folks are ever so far away, in the north of England; it's a great pleasure for me to come into a homey place like yours."

I smiled, feeling proud to have a companion of such goodwill, and looking around, I saw that the simple cottage, though sparsely and plainly furnished, did have a definite homeyness to it. A canning jar filled with lily of the valley stood in the center of the rough-hewn table, which was set for tea with mismatched blue-and-white china and napkins of undyed homespun linen. The few ladder-back wood chairs had goosedown-filled pads on their seats, and the one upholstered piece, a wing chair my father had gleaned from the ruins of a fire, was draped with a faded quilt to hide its smoke-stained arms. The mantle held a parade of cream pitchers, a collection slowly assembled over many years by my mother and grandmother. While my grandmother was still midwiving, additions were made to it regularly by grateful local women who knew of it. Staring out from among the creamers, like dogs among sheep, were a few daguerreotypes of the family, startlingly lifelike despite the stiff poses and serious, staring eyes.

Framed needlework samplers done by me and my sisters hung on the walls. There were none by Elsinore, as my mother had not been there to teach her, and I had not been inclined to do it. But Elsinore had found her own wherewithal. Hung beside the samplers were boxes of mounted butterflies and shiny-backed beetles, striped bees and wasps, and hairy flies. It was to keep her stocked in nets, choloroform, pins and boxes, and insect books that I sent Elsinore money each month.

My father thought Elsinore's preoccupation unfeminine, but he could find no true moral objection to it; so as long as she did not neglect her chores for her bugs, he let it continue. I suspect he thought it was a fascination that would fade with the passing of childhood. My grandmother voiced no opinion on it, but she often sat across the table from Elsinore when she was working on an insect, asking where she'd caught it, what its "book name" was, how it lived. My grandmother contributed facts of her own about Elsinore's specimens, stories from her girlhood: about the baby who'd been bitten in his cradle by a brown recluse spider and died; about the man who'd been chased a half mile to the river by a swarm of hornets he'd disturbed while chopping up windfall branches; about the infestation one summer of bombadier beetles so numerous that they were always underfoot, shooting out their puffs of noxious gas everywhere and sounding like little pop guns.

Tea was soon ready, the breads and jellies set out, and Sippy settled beside the teapot to pour, just like a lady of society. Indeed, there was more warmth and ease in the simple scene than had ever been in Isabelle's elegant luncheon setting, even before the outburst by her father-in-law. I was sorry for Isabelle and did not think she deserved humiliation, whatever her past, but I wondered how she could have been blind to the possibility lurking in her guest list, or, if she had seen the risk, what had led her to so recklessly ignore it.

Before Sippy served anyone, she put two oat cakes, a piece of currant loaf, and three slices of cold roast beef Elsinore had fetched from the kitchen on a plate, tucked a napkin over it, and set it aside.

"Your father may be by," my grandmother explained. "He had a job carrying some pigs this morning."

"You must give good time to your collections, Elsinore," said Mattie, pointing to the cases on the walls. "Do you hunt every day?"

"Oh, no, miss. Summer mainly."

"I suppose that's when insects are most abundant."

"There's always some kind of insects about, but the summer days still have light after the house is done."

"There's school, too, in winter," I put in.

"She don't make that so often," my grandmother said. "She's not as steady as you were, Hanna."

I knew that to be true, for I used to have to sit with Elsinore every evening while she was at her books. She was a solid enough reader to handle the work alone, but without me across the table from her, her mind frequently strayed into woolgathering, and if, by chance, I was not at home, she managed to find any number of reasonable excuses to be busy with something other than studies.

I had wanted my sister to finish school so that she'd possess a sense of the wider world and have the satisfaction of interests beyond the chores and events of everyday existence. Since living in the city, following my own reading and observing the multitude of lives around me, I'd broadened that simple ambition. I'd begun to think that Elsinore might be able to continue her education, as some wealthier young women were doing, though I had not worked out how, precisely, that could be managed. Nevertheless, I'd written to Elsinore to champion the idea and elicited a promise from her that she'd work hard at her studies despite the absence of my company. Now, after Sippy's revelation, Elsinore would not look at me, though she knew I was looking at her.

"I found a pupa yesterday," Elsinore said, pointedly addressing Mattie. "Would you like to see it?"

Mattie had just taken a bite of bread. With a quick glance at me—she'd noticed my displeased expression—she nodded yes to Elsinore, and the girl bounded away from the table and up the ladder to the attic bedroom.

"Don't be hard on her, now, Hanna," my grandmother said. "She tried to keep up, but sometimes she'd fall asleep over her books and then feel unready for the next day, and once she stayed home to make sausages when your father was butchering, and another day to scrub the floors when the corner of the roof came in from a heavy rain and we was all muddied, and then another day to doctor me when I was feverish and coughing. It came to be a habit, I guess."

"Oh, Sippy, you should make her go," I said.

"She's not steady like you, Hanna. And she's a plainer girl, meant for plainer things."

"I'm a housemaid, Sippy. That's plain enough, I expect. Elsinore has the mind of a scientist."

"A scientist?" My grandmother laughed. "I only hope she has a whole raft of sons, so she has someone to tell about her bugs that'll take an interest."

"She has *your* mind," I said softly.

"I'm sure I don't know what you mean," Sippy said, but beneath her sun-browned skin, I detected a blush. "Anyway, my girl, you won't stay a housemaid. Though I won't live to see what you might do."

Elsinore clattered down the ladder, making more noise than was necessary, suspecting, I'm sure, that she was our topic of conversation. In her cupped hand, she carried a small white rag. She carefully unfolded it, exposing to view a fat, reddish brown pupa wrapped as tightly as an expensive cigar. Mattie gave an appropriate gasp of amazement, and Elsinore grinned at the success of her display.

"What will it be?" asked Mattie.

"I'm not sure," said Elsinore, "but I think a Mourning Cloak." She began to fold the pupa up in its cloth again. "That's a butterfly," she added.

"It must be a wonderful thing to see, the birth of a butterfly," Mattie said.

"Yes, wonderful," said Elsinore energetically. "It takes great effort. You wouldn't think a soft, trembling thing like a butterfly could have such strength."

The door opened, and my father stepped inside, then stopped uncertainly, brought up by the sight of a stranger at the table. It was only a moment before he moved forward again, but in that brief pause, I glimpsed the kind of shyness I had seen sometimes when I worked with my grandmother, the kind a young husband shows when he suddenly realizes he is the only man in a room full of women busy at tasks mysterious to him.

"Hanna," he said, nodding at me in greeting. He came over and smoothed his hand once over the top of my head.

Mattie stood up to be introduced.

"My friend, Mattie Morrison," I said.

"Miss Morrison." He gave her a nod, too.

"There's a plate for you, Robert," Sippy said.

"I'll make some new hot water," said Elsinore, slipping the pupa into her apron pocket and taking up the teapot.

My father carried the distinct odor of pig with him. Since he had been with the animals all day, he was probably beyond noticing the smell, but in the close, heated room, it had as pointed a presence as another guest at the table. I was embarrassed lest Mattie think him low or rude, but she showed no sign of distaste and in no way altered the sweet, friendly demeanor she'd had since arriving. Of course, neither my grandmother, my sister, nor I would presume to suggest my father change his jacket or his boots, though it was something my mother might have managed with graceful indirection.

Elsinore brought the fresh pot of tea and a bowl of apples. She brought, too, a small jar of horseradish for my father's beef. He ate heartily, telling us about his day, which included a stubborn boar who fought being crated and a man who'd hitched a ride for a few miles and played a fiddle the whole way.

"Ned threw a shoe," he told my grandmother, referring to his favorite horse. "Got to walk him down to the smith in Davis Grove."

"Did it slow your work?" Sippy asked.

"No. Happened later, on the way back here."

"Can I come to the smith, Father?" said Elsinore.

"Sippy needs you to fix supper."

"Hanna can start it, Robert, before she goes; it'll only delay it a little," my grandmother said. "Take some more oat cakes to fill in."

She pushed the platter toward him, and he looked at it thoughtfully. Then he stood up, took three oat cakes, and slipped them into his jacket pocket. He also picked an apple, turned it around in his hand as if it were an unfamiliar object, and finally bit deeply into it.

"Bring my pipe, then, Elsie, and your jersey," he said around his mouthful of apple. "I'll get Ned and wait at the lane. Good day, Miss Morrison. Hanna, give a kiss now, won't you?"

I walked my father to the back door and watched him head for the small stable behind the house. He had a laborer's stride, heavy-footed and dogged. I thought of Mr. Edwin's father and of how his opinionated directness was much like my father's rustic belief in his own judgments and in his right to express them when and where he wished. But I did not think my father would have behaved as Mr. Sylvester Martin had, at least not with someone outside the family present. There is not much privacy in rural living, which is why, perhaps, my father guarded the privacy of personal knowledge. He spent what he knew very judiciously, and he taught his children to do the same.

When I turned back inside, Elsinore was rushing about, first to the hearth, where my father's pipe lay on a small table, then to a row of hooks in the kitchen where her jacket hung. She was untying her apron strings as she went, and in her hurry, the apron slipped out of her hands to the floor and she stepped on it.

"Oh!" she said, hearing the tiny crunching sound her footfall had made.

She stooped and retrieved the wrapped pupa from her pocket. When she unwrapped it, it was found to be crushed.

"Oh," she said again, this time sorrowfully.

"Maybe you'll find another one," Mattie offered.

"No, I won't," she said, near tears. "They're terribly rare to find."

I went to her and hugged her.

"I'm sorry you lost this one," I said, "but there will be another one someday."

I felt her straighten her back and take a deep breath. She brushed a wisp of blond hair off her forehead with the back of her hand. Her face was smooth and open, childish, but her eyes bespoke a quality of resignation quite unchildlike.

"It's part of nature, too," she said. "Not every pupa gets to be a butterfly."

A loud whistle came from outside; Elsinore gave me a quick but resounding farewell kiss and flew to the door, turning before she exited to smile at Sippy and call good-bye to Mattie. She was, after all, still a child in many ways, excited by small outings, forgetful of small tragedies.

TEN

⁂ "THERE, NAN, what do you think of that?"

Isabelle laid a typewritten paper on the kitchen table where I sat peeling potatoes for stew. She was still wearing her hat and gloves; she had gone out with Mr. Edwin that morning, an unusual thing, and now, upon her return, she had come directly through the apartment to me, without even pausing to put away her outdoor things. I wiped my damp hands on my apron and picked up the document, which was on the fine white stationery of a firm of lawyers.

"Read it aloud," said Isabelle, unpinning her hat and sitting down opposite me.

" 'Having made statements reflecting on the character of Mrs. Isabelle Martin, the wife of my son, Edwin Martin,' " I read, " 'which statements I have learned to be altogether untrue, I hereby withdraw all such statements. I apologize to the said Mrs. Isabelle Martin and Mr. Edwin Martin, and I authorize Mr. Edwin Martin to make what uses he pleases of this apology.' "

Below this paragraph were the morning's date, the signature of Mr. Sylvester Martin, and the signature of a lawyer as witness.

"I shall write out a copy of this and send it to Fred in Australia," Isabelle said, reaching for the paper. "And the original will stay locked in my desk as a defense against further insult."

"Did Mr. Martin senior take much convincing?" I said, impressed at what Isabelle had accomplished.

"*I* didn't speak to him," Isabelle said, as if such a thing would have been beneath her. "Edwin spoke for me. He wanted to know what would soothe me, and when I told him nothing less than a public apology would do, he arranged it."

I resumed my potato peeling. The disastrous luncheon party had occurred nearly two weeks ago, and Mr. Sylvester Martin had not been by since. I had not even heard Mr. Edwin mention his name, whereas before, he spoke of his father often; apparently they met regularly during Mr. Edwin's daily rounds to his shops. Though Mr. Sylvester Martin had been indisputably fractious that day at lunch, I felt some pity for him when I pictured the scene at the lawyer's—his son reserved and formal; Isabelle swelled, even gloating; the lawyer officially neutral yet betraying, perhaps, some distaste for such base family quarrels; and the old man himself, feeling, I'm sure, humbled and browbeaten, however politely the others behaved.

"In France," Isabelle said, standing up and going to the stove to look in the stock pot, "a woman can be imprisoned for adultery, and the sole evidence may be her possession of love letters. A man, on the other hand, can be legally accused only if he installs his mistress in his wife's home, and even then, he will only be fined."

"But surely adultery is not a crime in the way theft or murder is," I said.

"You think not?" Isabelle said. "In most people's minds, I believe it casts as horrible a shadow—perhaps, in the case of a woman, a more horrible one."

"That shouldn't be."

"No, Nan, it shouldn't. But it is." Isabelle smiled at me, a crooked smile such as someone might give who has heard a stupid or offensive joke told by a person who cannot be challenged.

After Isabelle had left the kitchen, I chopped carrots and

celery, and browned some cubes of beef to add to Mr. Edwin's portion of the stew, and started the dough for slippery dumplings. Throughout, my mind was not on cooking, but on the state of a society that would place a love letter on the same plane of sin as a knife coated with the gore of a murder victim, and that could render the specter of wagging tongues as fearsome as that of the gallows.

I recalled Mrs. Digby's lecture and her bold assertion that, in some cases, adultery was permissable and forgivable. I had found it a surprising notion, and I still thought it unworkable in the real world of conventions and jealousies and law, but just contemplating the idea had jarred me loose from certain set ways of conceiving society, had made me realize that there might be more legitimate ways than one to conceive of it, and, consequently, more ways than one to act within it. Like a wobbly kitten venturing from its mother's bed into the scented wilds of backyard and alley, my curiosity and sympathy had begun to reach beyond the maps of what was and what should be that had been given to me as a girl.

To me, there seemed to exist imbalances in society that could not be righted by water cures and loose clothing and physical education for girls, nor even by free love, fair property laws, and reforms in factories and madhouses. There were ways of seeing that needed to change. In the newspapers I consumed, which spanned *The Philadelphia Inquirer* and the *Woman's Journal,* I was encountering women who had begun a new seeing. They had looked at themselves and at the mirrors around them—the mirrors on walls and the mirrors in men's eyes—and they had found inconsistencies and mistakes, false faces and falser standards. I was not sure, then, what was to be done about this, but I felt that, once glimpsed, it could not be turned from. I wondered where to assign Isabelle's action that day. Was she washing a mirror or draping it with scarves? Was she opposing a judgment or certifying its power? And I wondered what part I might ever be called on to play in the shifting world around me.

ELEVEN

THE MORNING after Isabelle achieved her written apology, the single bed was removed. Two stock boys came up from the shop below and carried the bed to a storeroom across the small yard behind the building. Mr. Edwin supervised with disproportionate energies, moving furniture that was not in the way, giving directions that were superfluous, and generally confusing a simple job. From the window, I watched the boys wrestle the bed and mattress through the storeroom's narrow door, and when they reemerged, I saw Mr. Edwin give a few coins to each. I thought this odd, since as his employees, the boys probably had not expected special payment. I put it down to Mr. Edwin's high spirits, which had been in evidence since early morning when I heard him singing in his cold bath.

During all this, Isabelle was nowhere in sight. I assumed she was busy in the sewing room. I was sitting braiding strips of clean rag to make a new doormat for the backstairs entryway when she came into the kitchen. She had a large skein of scarlet wool in her hands.

"Nan, this has to be wound," she said.

"Do you need it right away?" I asked, splaying my fingers to hold tight the three strands of thick braid.

She looked distractedly around the kitchen, as if searching for something. Finally, she sat down on a chair near mine and laid the red wool over her knees, petting it dreamily. Then she got up again, untwisted the skein, and looped the ends of it over the uprights of the ladder-back chair. Locating a loose end, she began winding the yarn into a ball.

"As you're already on a monotonous task, I'll start this one myself," she said.

"Monotony with a rhythm and an attainable end is very soothing, I find," I said. "It helps one think."

"And if one doesn't wish to think?"

"It can aid that, too."

We worked in silence some minutes. The small kitchen window was open, and from below came the morning noise of commerce—men and women huckstering oysters, vegetables, flowers; the scrape and thud of wooden crates as carts were unloaded into the rear of the grocery shop; the clop of horses's hooves and occasional neighs; the reedy, nasal chant of a newsboy. This trellis of sounds was punctuated regularly by the screech of gulls who had swooped in from the Delaware River to glean overfull garbage bins and fallen produce trodden into slippery pulp by traffic and pedestrians.

When the wind was right, as it was today, we could smell the river from our house. Musty and dank, the smell could inspire discouragement or pleasant daydreams of grand escape, depending on one's mood and the day's weather. Only a week ago, in the rain, a woman had thrown herself into the river from a ferry. Perhaps for her, the river had forged a compelling partnership between discouragement and escape. The papers said she was pregnant. They also said she wore no wedding ring. Though the description of her was quite detailed, no one had yet come forward to claim or identify her body.

"Did you sleep well?" Isabelle asked. It was an unusual query.

"Reasonably well," I replied.

"I only ask because I thought I heard you up."

"Yes, I did get up to make myself some cocoa. But I took it to my room to drink. I'm sorry if I disturbed you."

"No, no. It was nothing."

Indeed, it had been my intention the previous night, when easy sleep eluded me, to sit at the kitchen table with my cocoa and my current reading, *A Lady's Life in the Rocky Mountains,* about a solitary English woman's 1873 tour of the Rockies on horseback. But politeness drove me back upstairs to my little bedchamber. In the quiet of midnight, I had heard sighs and labored breathings coming from within the house that could mean only one thing, and though I was unobserved and probably unconsidered by the Martins at that moment, I felt I should nevertheless withdraw out of earshot. Now it seemed Isabelle was concerned to know what I had noticed. She could not think I was unaware that she and Mr. Edwin had resumed relations—the ceremonious departure of the bed was alert enough—but I guessed she would be embarrassed to find that I had actually heard the groans in the night.

"After my cocoa, I slept quite soundly," I added. "The dawn surprised me, it seemed to come so quickly."

"Did it? It seemed, to me, slow to arrive."

The skein of yarn was no more than half wound, but Isabelle set the ball on the seat of the chair. She went to the stove and lit the fire under the kettle.

"Tea?" she said.

"Yes, thank you."

She busied herself scooping tea from the caddy into the teapot, setting out saucers and cups, lump sugar and milk, but in all these actions, she moved with unnatural slowness, like a figure in a dream, so that it seemed the chore would never see its end. I reflected that although Isabelle's languid tea preparations were of the opposite cast to her husband's spry bustle over the bed's exit, both had the same effect of rendering ordinary jobs extraordinary and momentous.

"A wife must be many women in one," Isabelle said, her back to me. "It would be better, I think, for a man to have more than one wife, for all the separate duties marriage entails."

I could not help but laugh, though Isabelle's tone had not been light.

"No, really, Nan," she said, turning. "I myself should prefer to be a companion—I am better suited for it—than to be a housekeeper or a nursemaid or a . . . a . . . paramour."

"Well, Isabelle," I said, still unable to take her seriously, "I daresay there are many men who would be glad to follow your plan—many, in fact, who already do, in their own fashion."

"You're speaking of men with mistresses or men who go to prostitutes. But those same men still expect access to their wives and will not be put off by notions of pure friendship. Nor do they feel it necessary with wives, as perhaps they may with mistresses, to engage in romantic tenderness or courtship."

The kettle had begun to whistle as Isabelle was speaking, its insistent shrill rising steadily. She turned away to answer it. I studied her delicate shape, the trim waist set off by a soft ruffle of lawn, the rounded forearms bared by three-quarter-length sleeves, the smooth swell of hips and buttocks beneath her thin white dress. Her hair was pinned back from her face, but it fell loosely down her back; she often wore it thus at home. It gave her the look of a girl, fresh and untried. I could not imagine a husband who would want such a woman for friendship only, and I wondered how she, after seven years of marriage, could still entertain the idea as at all feasible.

While the tea brewed, Isabelle again took up the ball of yarn and continued to unwind the skein.

"The baby," she said quietly, as if to herself, "the baby was the only time. . . ."

"The only time?" I prompted.

She looked at me then, and her dark eyes were fierce, but with what, I could not say. Fierce with wishing? With recall? With despair?

"Edwin and I refrained . . . until I hoped for a child . . . we didn't . . ."

"You conceived through only one act?" I said doubtfully.

"We had relations only once. In all our years. Only once."

The invasive sounds of last night came to mind. Isabelle stared at me defiantly. To avert my eyes from hers, I put down my braiding and poured the tea. Even so, my face must have betrayed my disbelief.

"Only that once . . . without protection," she said.

She leaned over the table to add sugar and milk to her cup, then sat down and stirred it, again moving slowly, like an imagined being.

"How much nobler, Nan," she went on, "since I do not want to attempt another pregnancy, for Edwin and me to live as chaste companions. But he says he cannot control his sensual desires, that that is why men marry in the first place. He even asserts it is proof of his love for me. To me, it is proof only that he is unwilling and that my will is unimportant."

It did not appear to me that Isabelle's will or wishes were unimportant to Mr. Edwin, though he certainly did not heed them all, but I did not say so. She reminded me too much, that day, of a bird with a broken wing, hopping on a high window ledge, yearning for the sky that beckoned above her, gathering her courage for the gamble of a plunge off the ledge, or for a resigned settling in to a circumscribed, earthbound life.

TWELVE

MATTIE'S WEDDING was to be held at my father's house on a Wednesday in early June. She and Elsinore and I had been sewing for weeks to make her a small trousseau. Isabelle let me use her sewing machine nights, which allowed the trousseau to be fuller than it would have been if we'd had to rely only on handwork.

One night three weeks before the date, Isabelle came into the sewing room, where I was set up working. Mr. Edwin was away on a buying trip to Baltimore, so I supposed she was finding it hard to fall asleep all on her own. I glanced up from the machine and smiled at her when she entered the room, but I did not stop the treadle. She returned my smile and went with no formal word of greeting to one of the Turkish easy chairs by the window.

It had become like that with us—an almost sisterly slackness when we were alone together. For each of us, the other's presence was familiar and comfortable enough to need no remark on it. In rooms where she was, I could move around or be still with the confident ease of a lordly housecat, though like any cat worth its salt, I paid heed to my "whiskers" and stayed, beneath the ease, alert to any signal from her that I was to behave in a more upright and orthodox fashion. And, of course, in front of others, I always showed deference, and Isabelle always sat in charge.

"This is agreeably done," she said, coming to the table after a time to finger a length of crocheted lace I was attaching to the hem of a muslin nightgown.

"My grandmother made it," I said. "I took it off an old slip of my mother's."

"You're fortunate to have such things, Nan—ties to the past, a sense of your place."

"My grandmother is a keeper of things. She has a lock of hair from each of her children, and her grandchildren's baby teeth, and even some mud-stiff old shoes of my grandfather, who died twenty years ago."

"Did they have a happy marriage? A marriage of true love?"

I shrugged. It seemed an odd thing to consider concerning my grandparents. In my memory, my grandmother had always been solitary. She did not appear to regret her widowed state, yet she only spoke well of her husband when she did mention him. I'd heard her say at various times that he was hardworking; that he showed an almost unmanly affection for young animals; that he did not interfere in her midwifery, even when it took her from his bed and his kitchen at all hours and kept her away from home overnight. Were these the marks of a happy marriage? Or only of two people who had learned to live together harmoniously? Would my grandparents have said there was a difference? I suspected Isabelle would.

For years, there was an old pipe of my grandfather's on the kitchen windowsill, left, probably, by his own hand on the day he died. I used to put it in my mouth sometimes when no one was around. It had a bitter taste when I sucked on it, and the bowl still smelled of burnt tobacco. I could feel with my tongue the indentations his teeth had made on the stem. I thought, with a child's logic, that the flavor and feel of that pipe would give me some sense not only of my unremembered grandfather, but also of what, in general, it might be like to be a man, to think a man's thoughts and make a man's motions. It felt a very daring thing, putting that pipe in my mouth and strutting around the house with it. It took me to the edge of what I wanted to know, to the edge, I guess, of myself.

"And your friend," Isabelle continued, not put off by my silence, "is hers a true love, do you think?"

"She's thoroughly convinced of her man, if that's what you mean," I said.

"I mean is theirs an ennobling passion, a tenderness of the heart and soul, not a mere surprise of the senses?"

"Really, I don't know," I said between my teeth as I bit off an end of thread.

"No, I suppose not," Isabelle said, sighing. "It's a private matter. But still, they're not marrying for practical reasons, are they?"

"My, no." I laughed. "Mattie will work now in a paper-box factory so she can go home nights, but if she gets with child, she'll have to stop, and then they must rely on Paolo's wages alone. If anything, their marrying is quite impractical."

"Ah, well, that's something, then."

Isabelle stood up to leave, then turned back at the doorway.

"Your friend knows about certain devices, I assume, Nan? The Goodyear Rubber Ring for her or Dr. Power's French Preventives for her husband?"

"The lady where she works gave her some advertising circulars," I said, a bit taken aback by Isabelle's forwardness. "Mattie threw them away."

Isabelle stayed in the doorway a few moments more, watching me.

"What shall you wear to the wedding, Nan?" she asked.

"I have but one good dress. You've seen it—the brown challis. I thought to trim it with new white collar and cuffs for the occasion."

"Just wait a moment," Isabelle said, and quickly left the room.

When she returned several minutes later, she had draped over one arm a dress of lemon yellow sateen, and in the other hand a small packet folded over with white paper as they used for dainty purchases downstairs in the shop. She kept hold of this packet and spread the dress out on the table. It was a little behind the latest fashions, with a train and a tied-back skirt to pull the fabric in folds close against the wearer's legs, huge funnel-shaped sleeves, and a fitted, high-necked bodice embroidered with red silk moss roses.

"You may have it," Isabelle said, with an encouraging smile. "I'm sure you can remake it into something suitable."

I lifted one of the sleeves tentatively. The fabric shone, even in the soft lamplight. Though it was certainly not a ball-gown or evening dress, it seemed incredibly grand to me, who had never worn a dress nearly like it.

"And take this to your friend," Isabelle added, shyly handing me the wrapped packet.

When I unfolded the paper, I found it contained a chemisette of white English linen intricately embroidered in white linen thread with swirls of satin-stitch flowers and trails of leaves and delicate ferns; there was cutwork, too, and needlepoint fillings.

"This is much better as a gift for a bride than tucked into the wardrobe of a long-used wife like myself."

"Are you sure? The labor . . ."

I turned the exquisite garment in my hands. The sewing was so fine, it looked just as good on the reverse side. If Isabelle had had to do such whitework steadily, for employment, as some poorer women must, her eyes would probably fail, as many of theirs do.

"As you know, Edwin does not appreciate my work. And though I strive against vanity, one does like to have notice taken. . . . So, if you think it'll please Miss Morrison, I'd be more than glad for her to have it."

"Oh, it's certain to. None of us could have managed the time or the skill with a needle to turn out such a piece. Thank you for it, and for the dress, too."

Moved by Isabelle's generosity, I impulsively leaned forward and briefly embraced her, laying my cheek lightly against hers. The move must have startled her, for she turned her head abruptly, and her mouth brushed my face; I felt the moist warmth of her breath and caught the signature scent of roses arising from her throat. We parted, and in case I had embarrassed her, I kept my eyes down, busy at gathering up the dress and the chemisette and the nightgown I'd been sewing. She laid a hand on my wrist, and I looked up.

"Just be sure to bring me a slice of the cake," she said. "For luck."

I nodded, though I couldn't think what kind of luck she'd want or get from a wedding cake.

THE DAY before the wedding, which was scheduled for late afternoon, I went out to my father's house to clean and decorate. Mattie came the next morning to help us prepare the celebration supper that was to follow the ceremony, and she was as amazed and tickled with what Elsinore and I had wrought in the old house as a child beholding her first Christmas tree. We had gleaned the hillsides and begged from neighbors' gardens in order to adorn the house with fresh flowers. Banks of daisies framed the front door, inside and out; the cold fireplace was filled with ferns; the creamers on the mantel spilled over with pink clover; jars of roses stood on the table. Elsinore had draped ivy, honeysuckle, and other trailing greenery over the specimen boxes on the walls and across the deep windowsills.

"Oh," Mattie exclaimed, "it's like a magical garden. How shall we ever tear ourselves from regarding it to go and cook?"

"Despite appearances, the garden didn't spring up by magic, and neither will the food," I said, laughing, happy to see the good effect of our labors.

"There's not many tasks left," Elsinore said. "Sippy and I have already dressed the ducks, and the white beans are soaking. We did the tipsy cake and the iced apple pudding last night."

Mattie looked from Elsinore to me, then around again at the decorated room, and when her gaze came back to me, there were tears in her eyes.

"We have time for a walk, I think," I said, taking her arm.

Mattie nodded, and we turned to the door. We passed through the yard, which had been cleared of chickens for the day, and around behind the house. My father was there washing down his cart; he had carried manure this morning, and tomorrow he was to move someone's belongings to a new home. He stopped to watch us walk by, but he did not greet us. Perhaps our faces showed something that warned him off. After we had gone some yards beyond him, I heard the scrub of his bristle brush on the wood bed of the cart resume, but with a slower rhythm than earlier, a thoughtful rhythm.

I led Mattie down the back side of our hill and along the stream that marked the edge of our plot to a stand of trees, mostly birch and fir, but some sassafrass and elm and others. As a small child, I had thought it a forest as deep as any in a fairy tale, and I was always relieved when, heart pounding, I burst out of its shadows into the open meadow on the other side.

I stopped at a horse chestnut tree and sat down, pulling gently on Mattie's hand so she'd sit down, too. She picked up a fallen chestnut and dug with her fingernails at the soft spikes on the fleshy green casing.

"I'm glad you liked our decorations," I said after a few minutes.

"Liked? Oh, that's not a big enough word. They're beautiful . . . glorious. . . . It's only . . ."

"What?"

Mattie tossed the chestnut into the stream, where it turned twice in a small eddy before being taken away by the slow current.

"You'll think me horribly ungrateful."

"Come, Mattie, what?"

"The house is beautiful, but it makes me sad to see it." She took a deep, steadying breath. "It makes me sad to see you, too—doing for me, turning a smiling face to me as if there's no change coming between us."

"We'll be meeting less often, I know, Mattie, but there'll be no change in our feelings for each other, I hope. I'll be the same person tomorrow as I am today."

"But I won't be, Hanna. I won't be, and somehow I never thought of it until I saw the house, decked out so grand and welcoming just when I must be abandoning it."

It was something I had not thought about, either, or if the thought had arisen, I'd pushed it aside, like a housewife returning a particularly bothersome mending job to the bottom of her workbasket. But it could be ignored no longer. In a few hours Mattie would become a wife, and thereafter, her first energies and best loyalties would be due Paolo, her husband, and their children, when they came. That's the way the world worked. What did the tender feelings of two green girls count for in the face of all that? Of course, Mattie would not really abandon me, but she was right to use the word. A forfeit was being exacted from our friendship. As much as it tore at my heart, I was gratified that Mattie had not shied from putting it so plainly. It was a mark of her caring for me, and I would not tarnish it by trying to reassure her or by making promises that circumstances would not allow us to keep.

"I shall miss you, Mattie Morrison," I finally said.

Mattie then fell sobbing against me, and wrapping my arms about her, I gave way to tears as well. We made a scene as might be described in a novel, which is not to belittle it—for I have found novels do honest justice to human life in a way no other writings can. Even in those days, I did not countenance the dire warnings of the experts who declared that novel reading caused uterine congestion and painful menstruation, nervous disease, and morbid mental states. (Excepted from these dangers were religious novels like *Ben Hur* and *The Gates Ajar*.)

Mattie and I stayed in the woods a half hour, reminiscing about our times together as if we were two old ladies with decades of acquaintance. Mattie spoke a bit, too, of the future, of how she would have me to Sunday dinner sometimes, and of how our daughters would one day be fast friends. Then we walked to the meadow, where we lay down among tall stems of silky oat grass and switchgrass.

"Look," Mattie said, pulling a silver medallion out of her skirt pocket and holding it up for me to see.

"It's a miraculous medal," she explained. "I got it for Paolo instead of a wedding ring. I had to save for months."

"Why not a ring?" I asked.

"He's got only three fingers on his left hand. From an accident with a revolving square saw in the planing mill where he used to work."

She slipped the shiny medal back into her pocket, and we both closed our eyes and dozed a while in the warm sun.

When we returned to the house, the ducks were roasting, the beans were cooking, and the pudding had been unmolded. Sippy was studding the cake with flaked almonds, and Elsinore was slicing celery, which was to be boiled and served with a sauce of mace-seasoned cream. They were working outside on the small back porch to avoid the heat thrown off by the busy cast-iron range.

Mattie and I laid the table. There would be eight of us in all: the bride and groom, the groom's brother, my family of four, and the priest. Then I went upstairs to my old sleeping loft to get our wedding clothes. We had to get dressed downstairs in Sippy's room, for our skirts would not have allowed us the physical freedom to climb down the ladder.

Mattie wanted a wedding costume that could be used again, so she had decided against white as impractical. We had made a double dress, copied from an engraving in *Godey's Lady's Book*. Out of pale blue chintz, we sewed a modified polonaise. We saved expense on the underskirt by making it plain calico and patching in pieces of coral silk only where it showed through under the cutaways of the polonaise. There were little white bows at the wrists; Elsinore had fashioned these. The overskirt of the polonaise was bunched with soft pleats at the back, like a pretty waterfall, and draped at the hips; the close bodice had a fitted waist, the front forming a point below the waist. This design, plus a small horsehair bustle hooked to the waistband of the crinolette, flattered Mattie's natural shape so well, no corset was needed. All the edges of the polonaise, including the high, square neckline, were trimmed in braid of coral and white silk. Mattie had brought orange blossoms from a city florist; I set some in her hair, and the rest she fashioned into her bouquet.

I had cut down the wide sleeves of Isabelle's yellow dress into coat sleeves with reversed cuffs, which helped tame the elaborate design. I had also removed the train, and Sippy had cleverly made it into a Zoave jacket for Elsinore, which perked up her white poplin Sunday dress and gave us the look of a matched pair.

When I slipped on the remade yellow dress, I could not help but think of Isabelle. I wondered when she had worn it, if it had been before or after she succumbed to being disappointed in her marriage. I wondered, too, given that disappointment, how she maintained such a lively interest in true love. She reminded me of Elsinore with her insects, studying their habits, cutting into their tunnels and hives, and searching, always searching, for a rare one. But perhaps, I thought, as Mattie fastened the buttons down my back, it is only that weddings excite sentimentality in Isabelle in the common way they do most people, even cynics, the link between the ceremony and the life thereafter being somehow temporarily ignored.

Together, Mattie, Elsinore, and I were a colorful spectacle. Sippy teased that we needn't have bothered with all the flowers, for just our standing in the room transformed it. Even my father approved us.

"Very nice, girls," he said, circling around us as if we were mares at a sale. "Very nice work."

Paolo and his brother and the priest arrived together. The

brothers had brought Father Monaco from town, as there were no Catholic churches in our area. The Catholics, mostly Irish, German, and Italian immigrants, settled largely in the cities then, even though many of them had been country people in their homelands.

Mattie had hidden herself in Sippy's bedroom, so we waded into introductions on our own, and during the tangle, I took quick stock of Paolo Testa. He was tall and thin and had a pleasant, broad face, velvety brown eyes being its best feature. He kept a serious expression throughout the greetings. I put it down to nervousness, as I was sure a man little given to smiling could not have won Mattie. The looks of the younger brother, Lorenzo, were similar, though his frame was a bit shorter and more developed. But by some ingenious permutation of nature, where Paolo's face was merely agreeable, Lorenzo's was disarmingly handsome, with dark, thickly lashed eyes, a strong Roman nose, and a wide mouth.

We all grouped ourselves before the fireplace, Father Monaco standing with his back to it. The mantel had become an altar of sorts by means of a large lithograph of a Madonna and Child that the Testa brothers had brought for the occasion and propped up amid the creamers and clover. My father knocked at the bedroom door, and when Mattie answered, he led her to Paolo's side. It was a short distance, and we had no music, but no bride could have had a fonder audience.

The priest spoke Latin, and Mattie and Paolo and Lorenzo all took Communion wafers and wine, but otherwise it was much like other weddings I'd seen in our neighborhood. It ended in the same flurry of kisses and handshakes, the same strange feeling of sinking joy.

Besides the Madonna, the brothers had brought three bottles of red wine, and Lorenzo Testa insisted on glasses for us all, even Elsinore, whose portion we watered down. He made toasts to the newlyweds; to the newlyweds' parents, distant or deceased; to the priest; to Italy and to America. Lorenzo had come to America as an infant, and his English was as clean as a bell, but a few small turns of phrase marked him as someone who thought in another language as well. Before he got to the national tributes, Sippy and I went to the kitchen, as prudence suggested the food should soon appear.

As we were carrying out platters, we heard my father break into song, as he was wont to do at local weddings. I had thought he'd be too shy to sing before strangers; perhaps the wine or Lorenzo's hearty manner encouraged him. At any rate, it was a surprise that took everyone well. He began with "I Know That My Redeemer Liveth," which quieted the festive energies of our guests, then he dipped them into sentiment with "Silver Threads among the Gold," and expertly returned them to lighthearted merriment with "Comin' through the Rye" and "The Swapping Song."

The supper was a success, and everyone complimented us, especially on the ducks and the cake. In a quiet moment afterward, Mattie told me that she was glad the first meal she had shared with Paolo as his wife had come from my hands. After the cake, we lingered over strong coffee, the men sipping brandy, too, from a dusty bottle my father had pulled out from a blanket chest by the cellar stairs. The lowering sun threw bars of light across the table. The crumbs on the ironed cloth cast tiny, jagged shadows; the blade of the cake knife gleamed, as did Mattie's gold band when she lifted her cup to her mouth.

Isabelle's dress began to feel heavy in the accumulated heat of the day. The narrowed sleeves, though loose enough to allow air up my arms and permit a comfortable bending of the elbows, nevertheless seemed confining. My lower body was certainly confined. As I sat at table, I was aware of the folds of cloth around my legs, as close as an infant's swaddling blanket, and when I walked, I was limited to short, careful steps. Isabelle's dress felt suddenly like Isabelle herself, as if she were sitting on my lap, placing herself between me and my family and guests. I realized I had been, all day, gathering impressions for her, answers to anticipated questions. I had at times stepped outside a scene to watch it with her eyes, imagining what she'd notice and fail to notice, what meanings she'd taken from it. I looked, then, at Mattie, engrossed in a story Lorenzo was telling about Paolo as a boy, her face turned away from me so I could see only part of her profile. I resolved not to tell Isabelle about Mattie and me in the woods. I would not feed her my friend.

THIRTEEN

AS THE evening shadows lengthened, the vigor of our little wedding party waned. Elsinore replenished the coffee and my father the brandy, but our conversation dipped like a kite in a dying, directionless wind. Still, we sat on a bit longer; the day had engendered enough fellow feeling that no one wished to break the circle. When we city dwellers finally began to make ready to meet the coach to take us back, my father offered to carry us instead.

"Won't have all the comfort of the coach, but there's the advantage I can take you to your doors," he said.

"You do so much for us today already, *signore,*" Paolo said, shaking his head and putting up his hands in protest.

"I need to be in the city early in the morning anyway," my father said, "so I may as well go in tonight and stop over."

"You can drop me at the Testas'," said Father Monaco helpfully. "My rectory is just a few blocks from there."

The first part of the ride was quiet. My father had spread fresh hay in the bed of the cart, and Elsinore had thrown clean blankets over, so we were comfortable enough that the priest lay back and soon fell asleep, and Mattie, her head against Paolo's shoulder, followed. Paolo, though at the opposite end of the cart from me and Lorenzo, could have conversed with us, but he didn't, keeping his own thoughts, which I imagined to be serious and far-reaching, by the nature of his gaze over the passing scenery, his eyes fixed so steady that they could not have really been seeing what was physically before them. There was a full moon—I wondered if it would still be framed in my little skylight by the time I reached home—which gave Paolo's face and, indeed, the forms of all my companions and the whole slow-moving landscape an otherworldly quality, as if we were figures in a stereopticon rather than breathing beings. Perhaps it was this effect of light that prompted Lorenzo's remark—the first since our departure an hour earlier—when Father Monaco snorted and rolled over suddenly in his sleep.

"He wrestles the devil in his dreams," Lorenzo said, shifting his position to avoid a kick by the unmindful priest.

"Or the hay dust is tickling his nose," I replied.

Lorenzo studied me with a curious expression, as if he had a question in his mind and could not decide whether to ask it.

"No more than that?" he said at last.

"An old man snoring." I shrugged.

"Is an ordinary thing, yes, but if you don't find mystery in ordinary things, you don't find it anywhere."

I thought about my ordinary days. Where in cleaning, cooking, sewing, rising at dawn, and lying down at night could mysteries be found? My life was eminently workaday. Even my daydreams were practical ones. At nineteen, Lorenzo was younger than I, but even at his age, I'd been more flat-footed than fantastical.

"Do you often have such fancies?" I asked Lorenzo. "Or is it the moonlight and the wine that inspire you?"

"The night is soft, and we are with a man of God and two fresh-made lovers beside us. But even at less times, I look for magic."

I had never heard anyone speak thus. I'd marked the charm of the moonlight myself, it was true, and it had seemed a lovely gift, more marvelous because it was unearned and fleeting, but I had not thought to tell of it, nor to search for other such gifts that might surround me unnoticed.

Lorenzo's life had been no less hard than mine. He and his older brother, Paolo, had been raised by an aunt in New York after the deaths of their parents in Italy. He worked in a factory and lived with Paolo in a tiny apartment that now he'd have to share with Mattie, too, though I expected Mattie would sweeten his life as much or more than she cluttered it. Such living could breed a thoughtful man, of course, even an inquiring man, but how had he turned out inventive and conjuring? My own life experiences had only made me observant, pensive in a down-to-earth way. Romantic natures, I'd always felt, came with privilege, or, at the least, required leisure.

"Your view is appealing, Mr. Testa," I said. "But it is not one I could follow easily. My nature is too practical."

"Your sister with her bugs," Lorenzo said, "there is an appreciation of mystery."

"Yes, but I hope she will make it more someday."

"More?"

"She ought to study further. Become a scientist or a teacher."

"A woman scientist?" Lorenzo laughed. "A teacher, perhaps, but a scientist?"

"I see your imagination does not extend as far as it might, sir."

Lorenzo merely smiled at my sharp words.

"Yes, that may be," he said. "But I find yours goes farther than you say."

"It's not a matter of imagination," I protested, deliberately ignoring his mild repentence. "There are colleges for women now, and study clubs."

"For highborn ladies."

"I know the obstacles are many. But Elsinore must set herself against them."

We had entered the city by then and were passing through narrow streets lined with narrow, two- and three-story row houses. The windows all were dark. Like me, the occupants would be rising early to set off for work. A short tier of white stone steps led up to each door, their repetition down every block like the foamed tongues of exhausted horses.

"Perhaps it is you who wish to battle obstacles," Lorenzo said quietly. "Is this fire in young Miss Willer?"

I had no answer. Certainly, my desire to see Elsinore enrich her mind and broaden the scope of her life was my own notion. She had never spoken of such hopes. I told myself it was because she was still so young and because she was much influenced by my father, who, like most men, did not think a woman's mind (or life, for that matter) needed or was capable of much enlargement.

"If ever you do enter battle," Lorenzo continued, "for yourself or for someone else, I think it is well you are practical. You'll see what needs to do, and you will do it."

I could not tell for sure in the darkness if Lorenzo might be mocking or upbraiding me. His tone did not hint at either; nor, however, did he sound admiring. There was a touch of regret, I thought, in his voice, as one might use when speaking of a talented person who had died young. If Lorenzo had said about a man the very same thing he had just said about me, it would be heard by anyone as complimentary. But I am not a man, and so it was, in my case, a kind of lament, an accusation of some basic failure, or, at least, a prediction of one, should I let my inclinations carry me forward to their logical and unfeminine conclusions.

I LET myself in to the Martins' apartment as quietly as possible. I had never returned so late before, and even though I had been away with their full knowledge and did not owe them any service until the next morning, still it felt stealthy to be coming in while they were abed, as if I had something to hide. Added to this strange feeling were emotional and physical weariness, and a mild melancholy, which was due probably to a trace of effect from the wine and the conversation with Lorenzo Testa.

I lit the lamp I had set by the door yesterday for just this purpose, and slipping off my shoes, I carried them, the lamp, and the string bag holding the wrapped piece of wedding cake for Isabelle through the apartment toward the back stairs. When I entered the kitchen, I found Isabelle sitting there staring at a lone, thick candle in the center of the table. Her presence so startled me, I let out a high-pitched gasp. She, in turn, stood up suddenly, gripping the edge of the table as if she needed to steady herself. She was in her nightdress, her thick hair plaited down her back, her face freakishly lit from below by the dancing yellow candle flame.

"What's wrong?" I said.

Isabelle relaxed her grip on the table and stepped away from it. Her mouth shaped a tentative smile.

"I wanted to see you in your finery," she said.

I set the lamp and the string bag on the table and my shoes on the floor and stared at her in amazement. Melancholy and tiredness, pushed aside abruptly by the surprise of finding her there, now returned, and I longed to be free of my vaunted finery and curled up in my private bed.

"You waited up for that?" I said.

I could not keep irritation out of my voice. I did not even try.

"And to hear of your day while it's still fresh in your thoughts," she said timidly.

"There's nothing fresh about me at all just now, Isabelle," I said, nevertheless sitting down, for I knew I could not escape so easily.

Isabelle sat down, too, and folded her hands on her lap like a schoolgirl and waited patiently for me to begin. Refraining from prompting me was her one concession to my obvious weariness. I do believe she would have sat there indefinitely waiting for me to speak. After all, how long had she been waiting already in the dim, silent kitchen? But before I could gather myself to start, in walked Mr. Edwin, holding high a lamp as if he were signaling a ship to shore. Apparently, his dressing gown had been hastily thrown on, for the belt was not tied, and I could see his flapping nightshirt and his skinny, hairy ankles below, the whole adding to my impression of a man responding to an emergency at sea.

"What's wrong?" he said in alarm, but this time Isabelle did not rise to meet the question.

"We're only talking, Edwin," she said calmly.

"At this hour?"

Though it was not a question that strictly required answer, I expected Isabelle to respond in some way. But she did not. Instead, she turned her face toward me again, and Mr. Edwin began to look quite foolish standing there waiting for her to continue with her explanation. He must have realized that he was looking foolish, for he put on a fierce scowl, and all his next words were spoken harshly.

"Willer, you may go," he said.

I picked up my shoes and the lamp and made for the stairs. I was not across the kitchen before I heard Isabelle's chair scrape loudly on the linoleum. Venturing a glance over my shoulder, I beheld Isabelle risen from her seat and Mr. Edwin gripping her upper arm, his face jutted near to hers.

"You get back to bed like a decent wife," he was saying, trying to keep his voice down. The word "decent" came out as a fierce hiss.

"You cannot rule when I may come and go in my own kitchen," Isabelle replied angrily.

I reached the door to the stairs, opened it, and put my foot on the first step.

"Is this really the place you'd choose, my dear?" I heard Mr. Edwin say, with no tenderness to the endearment.

There was a clamor then as the chair fell against the metal front of the pie safe and Isabelle cried out—such a piteous sound, like the yelp of a chained dog—and without thinking, I turned full to look at them. Mr. Edwin had pulled Isabelle against him; he held her tightly around the waist with one arm, his other hand still holding high his lamp in that curious way. His head was lowered, roughly nuzzling her throat and breasts; the vigor of his activity unloosened the drawstring of her nightdress so that one white shoulder and breast were exposed, the nipple dark and forlorn looking, like the scar of a brand. For a brief instant, Isabelle locked her wild gaze on me. She broke away from Mr. Edwin then and pulled her clothing straight. He did not oppose her.

I entered the stairwell quickly, before Mr. Edwin had time to follow the line of Isabelle's sight and turn around to find me. As I slowly ascended, I heard sounds that were the chair and table being righted, and Isabelle sniffling, Mr. Edwin telling her in a remarkably mild voice, "That's enough of that, now," as if she were a spoiled child who was making too much of a skinned knee.

I rushed up the remaining stairs to the second floor, then up the stairs to my room and stood frozen just inside my door, my heart thudding. The room seemed to spin around me. As the dizziness subsided, I dared to move to my bed. I lay down and stared at the indifferent moon in the skylight above me until my eyes burned with not blinking. I had meant only to calm myself for a few minutes, then get up and undress and wash my face before retiring in earnest, but suddenly all that seemed an insurmountable task, so I groped for my blankets and pulled them up over Isabelle's yellow dress, up to my chin and into my mouth, where I bit down on them and moaned. To my surprise, sleep, which I had feared would be a long time coming, instead dropped down upon me like a velvet hood.

FOURTEEN

SUNDAY WAS not a day at liberty for me, but the household tasks then were far lighter than on other days, so I always looked to Sunday as a day of rest. It afforded me more leisure, at times, than my Thursday afternoons, which I often spent discharging personal errands.

The Sunday morning after Mattie's wedding ran as usual. I served the Martins a simple breakfast of coffee, tomato omelette, and rice muffins, and they went off to church. They were largely quiet during their breakfast, as they had been at every meal since the cruel scuffle in the kitchen, and it appeared to me the reconciled quiet of truce rather than the smothered quiet of a feud. I especially thought so because of how Isabelle had tried, on the day after, to shave down the meanness of Mr. Edwin's forced embrace.

"You mustn't think, Nan," she had said as we worked in the kitchen, "that my husband has at all a rough or thoughtless nature."

While she spoke, she was saturating cotton flannel cloths with oxalic acid; she meant to lay the soaked cloths over the white piano keys to bleach them. I was sharpening knives. For safety's sake, both tasks required we did not turn our eyes away from the activity of our hands. I chose not to set down my work for conversation, besides, because I did not really want to talk about what I had witnessed between Isabelle and Mr. Edwin—the scene still made me shudder when it came unbidden to mind—and I most certainly did not wish to learn what had transpired when they left the kitchen, however mollifying it may have been.

"Mr. Edwin," Isabelle continued, "has had some business worries lately, and his temper is short because of them. He holds me in the highest esteem. It would distress him—and me—if you thought otherwise."

"I know it's not my place to judge," I replied, keeping the stroke of knife against whetstone regular and strong. The soft, scraping noise effected a kind of music, like the Salvation Army tambourines that make the grim story of saving souls sunk in poverty and despair sound like a merry party.

"Judgments form, whether it is one's place or not," Isabelle said tartly. "Only remember, Nan, the truest judgments do not look only at one deed, but at the whole landscape of what is done and not done, of what is possible and not possible."

Then she carried her wrung-out flannels into the parlor to clean the piano keys.

That day went on normally, with no more discussion of Wednesday night. I did not have the afternoon free, as I had taken all Wednesday instead because of the wedding. Thursday was odd-job day, when I did chores left out elsewhere in the week, and Isabelle went shopping at Wanamaker's, often lingering in the ladies' writing room to read, occasionally lunching with Mrs. Cox, the wife of Mr. Edwin's partner. The following days, too, kept to routine—Friday for housecleaning and Saturday for baking. So, on the Sunday morning, after the Martins had left for church and I had washed up the breakfast things, I found myself, as I did every Sunday, with three hours open to my own devices. Most of the Sunday dinner had been prepared the day before: the clam pie and boiled ham, the blackberry crumble. Doing the lettuce and the mashed potatoes and string beans would take up only a short time right before the meal.

It had been understood when Isabelle engaged me that my Sunday mornings would be given to matters of the spirit. It had taken me only a month to translate that from "attending a church of my choice," as Mr. Edwin had phrased it, to walking in Fairmount Park, a place so large and various that I repeated my route no more often than every six weeks. I had even invested in new flannel for a walking skirt and made it with gores and a shortened length just above the ankles for easy striding.

On this Sunday, I chose to walk along the Schuylkill River, past the rowing clubs of Boathouse Row, down to the formal gardens and classical buildings of the Fairmount Waterworks, to Spring Garden Street Bridge, which was my turning-around point. It was a fine day. The river, ruffled by breezes and gleaming under the sunlight, was populated with scullers, both singletons and teams, their small narrow boats gliding along with the grace of water striders. A touring steamer was just taking off from the waterworks landing stage, its paddle wheel lazily churning the water white. None of the pleasure seekers on the river or beside it seemed to mind the river's smell, the combined effect of discharges into the Schuylkill from tanneries, dye works, slaughterhouses, and city sewage. Or perhaps the odor was simply accepted as an immutable fact of life better ignored.

A group of bicyclists passed me, several men on Ordinaries, miraculously balancing atop the huge front wheels, two women on demure tricycles, which they could ride without resorting to the controversial bloomer costume, and one man on the new Victor, a bicycle with two equal-sized wheels and a dropped frame with no crossbar. It was the first Victor I'd seen, and it occurred to me as I watched it pass that it was a design suitable to women, too, for there was no chance of skirts getting entangled in wheels. Though it was said, I knew, that reputations could.

I sat for a while on a bench in the shade of a majestic old elm and observed some children feeding wild geese. The pretty weather and the cheerful activity all about me succeeded in dispelling the hobgoblin thoughts that had been shadowing me since Wednesday night. If Isabelle could philosophize away Mr. Edwin's behavior, why should I dwell on it? I felt so disburdened, in fact, that on my way home I gathered some dried leaves for Isabelle. She liked to spend Sunday afternoons in artistic pursuits, and she had lately taken up the challenge of making leaf skeletons. She'd soak dried leaves in water until they were pulpy, then scrub them with a brush until only their skeletons remained. Finally, she'd dry the fragile leaf skeletons, arrange them with ribbons and with dried grasses and seeds or perhaps some small seashells, cover the creation with a glass dome, and place the finished shade on a table in the parlor. Making a successful shade took much dexterity and a good eye for the artificial arrangement of natural materials. Isabelle's parlor displayed a number of these glass-encased beauties.

As it turned out, Isabelle, too, had found in that bright Sunday morning a source of fresh energy. Her renewal did not come from a walk in the park, however. It came from a man.

She located me in the dining room, where I was setting the table. Mr. Edwin was in the parlor communing with the *Sunday Inquirer,* whose editorials he often answered aloud. Some news items, too, if they were agitating enough, could bring forth clucks and harrumphs and telegraphic words of approval or dismay.

"Oh, Nan, I wish you'd been with us today," she said breathlessly. "We had a wonderful sermon from a visiting minister, the Reverend George Dale. He's newly ordained, but he speaks so much more movingly than our pastor, who's been preaching fifteen years or more."

"What was his subject?" I asked.

"Death. And heaven."

"A logical pairing, though not very original," I said, teasing her a little, as her state of transport was so exalted as to appear silly.

"Ministers are rarely original," Isabelle conceded amiably. "It was Reverend Dale's turns of phrase and the roll of his voice that were so bracing."

"What did he say?"

"Let me see," she said, sitting down and taking a sweet gherkin from the pickle dish. This she alternately ate and gestured with as she tried to summarize Reverend Dale's sermon.

"Death is God's way of calling us home, he said. And though we cry when someone dies, really it is not something to mourn but a glad thing for that person, a release from imprisonment."

Isabelle paused to recollect more.

"Heaven is a place where families are reunited in a perfect human society," she said.

"I was taught more of hell as a child than heaven," I said.

"So was I. When heaven was mentioned at all, it was very unclear: floating clouds and hymns being sung."

"But Reverend Dale knows more?"

"Oh, it isn't just *his* thinking, Nan, though his words are his own, of course." Isabelle began on a second gherkin. "All the best preachers say heaven is like Earth, only much grander and happier. Why, that Reverend Henry Ward Beecher goes so far as to say there is no hell!"

"That would be news in my neighborhood," I said.

"My father and I can be together in heaven in a beautiful home," Isabelle continued, "and my little baby, too, for there are nurseries in heaven for children who die before their parents. And there will be no jealousies there among men and no recriminations."

"And who keeps the houses in heaven?" I asked, noticing a spot of pickle juice on the white damask tablecloth.

Isabelle shrugged, annoyed perhaps at such a mundane consideration.

"Don't you see, Nan?" she insisted. "Eternity will be woman's sphere, just as the commerce and politics of this life are man's sphere. The greater power is ultimately ours."

"Reverend Dale said that?"

"Not precisely. But he said that piety would be eternally victorious and that women had a natural gift for piety. He said that our homes are churches and we are priestesses in them."

"And the congregation?"

Isabelle stood up, looking a little crestfallen. She went to the sideboard and poured a sherry to take to Mr. Edwin, a regular before-dinner custom on Sundays.

"The children are the congregation," she said quietly, placing the glass of sherry on a small silver tray.

Turning to go, she added, "But a wife must bring her husband to the domestic altar, too, and influence him to be a civilized man and a good Christian."

"Don't worry, Isabelle," I said. "There will be more than enough mothers in heaven, I expect. Surely they will leave room for the rest of us as well."

THE MARTINS were so impressed with the Reverend Dale's preaching, Mr. Edwin instigated a special collection in their church to pay Reverend Dale's fee and bring him back to preach there again. The Saturday evening before, they took him to the outdoor restaurant at Kiralfy's Alhambra Palace, a rare outing for the Martins, since Mr. Edwin was fussy about how his food was prepared, always mindful of the possibilities of dyspepsia and constipation. The meal was a kindness I'm sure the young minister well appreciated for he had not got his own church yet and so, probably, could not often afford restaurants.

The first time Reverend Dale was to come to the Martins' home, Isabelle was more aflutter than she had been before the disastrous luncheon for Mr. Frederick Martin. That gentleman seemed to have lost his special place in Isabelle's heart. Except for one thin envelope sent to Isabelle shortly before his departure, letters from him now came addressed only to his brother. Isabelle had tossed the single page from the thin envelope into the fire box of the kitchen stove.

"My brother-in-law has decided to attempt being a prudent man," she'd said to me, though I hadn't asked. "It doesn't become him."

Part of Isabelle's excitement about Reverend Dale's visit was due to the fact that it came on short notice. When Mr. Edwin stopped home at midday, he told Isabelle he had met Reverend Dale on the street and had asked him to supper. The Martins' suppers were usually light, their noon dinner being the substantial meal of the day. Mr. Edwin had kept the habit of taking dinner at home, which he'd begun to do when Isabelle was far advanced in her pregnancy.

"Reverend Dale will not expect to be impressed," Isabelle said. She was pacing the parlor while I awaited her instructions on supper. "But we must set a good table nonetheless and make him feel welcome and valued."

"There's the cold lamb," I offered.

"Yes, that'll do. And some sliced beef heart. Rice batter cakes, perhaps? Or toasted rusk. Sliced tomatoes . . ."

"We've some ripe currants and cream for dessert."

"Good, and go downstairs for mint jelly for the lamb and some young onions and peas."

When Reverend Dale rang at the door, Mr. Edwin had not yet arrived home, but Isabelle was dressed and waiting, and the meal preparations were well in hand. Reverend Dale was a thin, fair man with unremarkable features that could have been handsome in someone with a little more color and weight. His hair was strawberry blond, and I think he was vain about it, for he wore it rather long; one loose wave was forever falling over his brow and into his pale blue eyes, and he had developed, therefore, a graceful habit of repeatedly combing his hair back with his slender fingers, of which I think he was also a bit vain. He gave me a shy smile when I opened the door to him, and I saw he had good teeth. I had taken to noticing men's teeth since coming to work for the Martins.

I led Reverend Dale upstairs and into the parlor, where Isabelle was at the piano playing. She did not stop until her piece was finished, though she must have seen from the corner of her eye that we were standing by. Even after the last notes, she sat still a moment or two, her gaze downcast at her hands resting on the keys, as if calling herself back from some enchantment the music had carried her to. Reverend Dale did not seem to mind the delay, perhaps because ministers are used to distracted people lost in prayer. Isabelle had a beguiling enough profile, in any case, to make the study of it pleasant, and the crisp white shirtwaist she'd chosen to wear, though tailored in a masculine fashion, paradoxically called attention to her decidedly unmasculine attributes.

"Reverend Dale," she said smiling, as she slowly turned her head toward him and started to rise.

"Please," he said, indicating the piano with a dandified sweep of his hand, "if you would go on, Mrs. Martin. I'm a great lover of music, and I seldom get to hear it in such intimate surroundings. It was Chopin you just played, wasn't it?"

"Yes, a nocturne," Isabelle said, resuming her seat.

She sorted through some sheet music and finally selected one. I spied a blush on her cheeks; she was pleased to have someone appreciate her talents. As I left the room, she was beginning to play again, the Reverend Dale stationed behind her and a little to one side, ready to turn her pages.

Reverend Dale must have been quite taken with Isabelle's playing, for I heard the piano continue, with only brief breaks, until Mr. Edwin arrived. Most of the pieces sounded like the Chopin, but I recognized some popular tunes, too, like "She Never Blamed Him, Never," and "The Baseball Waltz." Later, as I cleared the table before dessert, Reverend Dale praised Isabelle's playing to Mr. Edwin.

"Mrs. Martin is an accomplished pianist," he said. "You must take great pride in her."

"Yes," Mr. Edwin beamed. "My wife is an educated person, you know. Reads poetry and science. Knows enough chemistry to concoct tonics that soothe me more than anything a pharmacist has ever sold me. I can't keep up with her in some things. But my mind is needed for important matters, anyway, business affairs and so on."

"My husband exaggerates, Reverend Dale," Isabelle said. "I have had some education, but my experience is spotty at best. The classics, for example. I have read only some of them and none, I'm afraid, in the original Greek."

"The classics were my specialty in divinity college," Reverend Dale said.

"Well, then," Mr. Edwin exclaimed. "You might tutor Isabelle. Would you like that, my dear? Then I shall not have to hear how marriage has confined an inquiring spirit, eh? A wife with some education does a man credit, I say, as does having a man of letters as a visitor in the home. Of course, I mean to pay you, Reverend."

Neither Isabelle nor the minister replied for a moment, both being taken by surprise. Then they spoke at once, over each other.

"Edwin, Reverend Dale is a busy man—"

"Sir, there can be no question of payment—"

They stopped and looked across the table at each other, and Mr. Edwin glanced back and forth between them like a benevolent father.

"I could come on Monday afternoons, if that's convenient," Reverend Dale said. "But only if the terms are friendship, not hire."

"That would be most convenient," Isabelle agreed. "But only if you will stay each time and sup with us."

I left the dining room then, and when I returned with the currants and cream, the conversation had turned to news of the surrender of the Apache, Geronimo.

I saw Reverend Dale again when I brought him his hat two hours later. They were all three standing in the entrance foyer to take their leave.

Reverend Dale shook Mr. Edwin's hand and made Isabelle

a small bow, to which she responded with a smile and a pretty nod. Mr. Edwin opened the door for Reverend Dale, and as he did so, Isabelle caught her husband's free hand and held it as a girl of sixteen might do with a sweetheart. They stood, hand in hand, at the top of the stairs and watched their guest descend.

I was sure that Mr. Edwin knew the stirring of Isabelle's affection was a direct consequence of his engaging her a tutor and that, in fact, the expectation of her gratitude had spurred his act. But I wished, for both their sakes, that it went deeper—that the husband was learning a wife's mind needed useful activity, and that the wife was learning a husband might see into her heart even if he didn't speak of it.

FIFTEEN

ISABELLE'S SESSIONS with Reverend Dale began the first week of July. In the second week, the reverend supplemented her lessons at home with a trip to a picture exhibition, and in the third, with a lecture at the Franklin Institute and a meeting of the Science and Art Club of Germantown. By the middle of August, I was setting a place at supper for Reverend Dale two or three times a week.

Once, Isabelle and her tutor went roller skating, necessitating a hasty trip beforehand to Wanamaker's for an appropriate outfit. When Reverend Dale brought Isabelle home from the rink, Mr. Edwin lifted his eyebrows at the length of her full, loose skating dress, which was well above the ankles, but looking up from her skirt hem to her glowing face, he declared skating must be a healthy and suitable sport after all.

"You're as rosy as a peach, my dear," he said. "Perhaps I should take her skating myself some time, eh, George?"

I don't believe Mr. Edwin really meant to go skating with Isabelle—it would not have fit his reserved, diligent nature. But I do think he was pleased by the effect Reverend Dale was having on her. She came in from most of their outings rosy in temperment as well as in complexion, and when Reverend Dale was present, she allowed Mr. Edwin liberties she would have shrunk from had she and her husband been alone in the house—a caress over her shoulders, a pinch of her cheek, and once (after the skating jaunt) a kiss on the mouth. On that evening, the door had barely closed behind Reverend Dale before Mr. Edwin had slid his arm around his wife's waist and I had been dismissed for the night.

"Leave the clearing up till morning, Willer," he'd said to me, though it was rare he took any notice of what I did, let alone when I did it. I surmised he wanted me away upstairs. The parlor and the kitchen, where I would have been doing the clearing up, were on the same floor as the Martins' bedroom.

Mr. Edwin was not so openly amorous with Isabelle again. He contented himself with lesser intimacies, like a finger traced along the side of her neck or the request of a sentimental love song. The August doldrums were telling on his health; he claimed vapors from the river and the wharves made him feel sluggish and queasy. Isabelle's summer tonic of rum steeped with saffron and aloes did not revive him, though he dosed himself daily, convinced he'd be feeling even more dulled without it.

At Isabelle's suggestion, Reverend Dale kept a lounging jacket at the Martins', which he donned after supper while he listened to Isabelle play and Mr. Edwin sat reading the evening newspapers. She embroidered a pair of slippers to match the jacket. As Reverend Dale had already given Isabelle small tokens—a pencil drawing he'd made of the city skyline from the Belmont mansion, where they'd taken tea one afternoon; and on another occasion, a velvet-covered keepsake album with a brass clasp—she was free to reciprocate without impropriety, especially since her gift came from her own needle.

A stranger entering the Martins' parlor on the evenings Reverend Dale was there would have been hard-pressed to say which was the husband, both men looked so relaxed and at home. Isabelle gave them equal deference, so her behavior would have provided no clue. Her age placed her closer to Reverend Dale, who was only two years younger than she, but

Mr. Edwin, ten years her senior, was certainly well within range to be her spouse.

The portrait of a family circle that the three of them formed struck me as odd, however, and I did not believe that it could last. I recalled how three is a troublesome number with children—two children will make happy playmates, and four or more a lively crew of companions, but put three children together, and a pair will form to close out the third, with cruelty and lamentations or anger and petty violence the inevitable results. Of course, these three were not children, but still I felt theirs was not a situation of natural balance and that, though all looked tranquil, there was movement beneath, like the shimmy in a pot of water before the first tiny bubbles of boil start.

"Why do you worry?" Mattie said when I confided my observations. "It's nothing to do with you."

We were strolling through Society Hill on a humid Sunday morning, Paolo and Lorenzo a few hundred yards in front of us. They had gone to an early Mass, Mattie said, just to make the time for our walk, as Paolo knew how much she wanted to see me. She told me this with pride, and I knew I was meant to think him generous and thoughtful, but instead my contrary mind wondered why he would not let her walk out alone with me.

I wiped my sweaty face with a handkerchief—perhaps the heat was making me irritable. I was certainly glad to meet Mattie again, and reacquainting myself with Paolo and Lorenzo might prove enjoyable enough if I let it. I was in need of company. Isabelle's schedule with Reverend Dale had left me a great deal on my own lately, and though I was never idle, my activity felt heavy and slow because it was done so much in silence. I had become gradually accustomed to Isabelle's attention and conversation, and I felt her diminished presence more keenly than I cared to admit.

"I'm not worried, exactly," I replied to Mattie, unbuttoning my high collar and turning my head to catch a light river breeze coming from the Delaware. "I'll be sorry to see Mrs. Martin disappointed is all, as I'm sure she must be someday. She has a way of living in her fancies."

"She is foolish, then, and spoiled, too, I bet."

"Yes, she's foolish sometimes, and Mr. Edwin does indulge her on occasion, but I can't call her spoiled. She's aware there is something she does not have, perhaps cannot have, and she wants it, wants it with all her heart."

"Wants what?" Mattie asked.

"I don't know. I don't think even she knows. She's much taken with true love, though."

"But she's a married woman!"

I laughed then, to hear Mattie, a bride, sound so like a long-settled matron. There was nothing for it but to laugh, though a part of me wanted to take Mattie by the shoulders and look deep into her clear, blue eyes and tell her that she need not close every door just because she had acquired a new name and a wider bed. After a second, Mattie laughed, too—she was always able to take amusement at her own expense. I was sure I heard a ring of regret in the laughter, too, so I felt that though we were apart now, we still walked some common plain of understanding. This belief comforted me, because I knew that there would come times when her loyalty to Paolo and my respect for that loyalty would require me to hold my tongue.

"Well, anyway," Mattie continued, "I hope Mrs. Martin isn't expecting true love from a minister who is, besides, a friend of her husband."

"No, no, I misspoke," I said. "She is merely enjoying his notice and appreciation, maybe more so because she is safe from its becoming a romance. But she will still feel spurned, I fear, when he goes."

"You ought to leave service, Hanna," Mattie said earnestly.

"But, Mattie, you've said how hard your work is at the box factory, on your feet ten hours a day in a dusty room with no windows, a few minutes snatched for dinner, one bathroom to sixty women. And not making any more than you did as a maid."

"I'm tired at night, certainly, but when I leave that building, my time is my own until I enter it again. I never had that peace as a servant. Perhaps Mrs. Martin is different, but every domestic girl I ever talked to had the same complaints. They were treated as machines or as slaves, even, liable to interruption and ordering at any time; and those in small houses like yours always said how lonesome and left out of the world they often felt."

I had no answer for Mattie. There was much truth in what she said. And yet, I had come to think of Isabelle's house, if not as my home, then as a close likeness to it. In the kitchen I had my own chair that no one else used, and my little room upstairs. Though Isabelle could be imperious when it suited her, she acted more frequently like a sister to me—either an older sister supervising my doings in the household, or a younger sister seeking my comfort. I did not expect to stay in service indefinitely, but it was not clear to me how or why I would leave. When the time came, I would recognize it, I thought. And somehow I knew it would not be to go on to another house, nor, like other girls, to a factory or store or sweatshop. Nor, I was beginning to fear at the very secret bottom of my heart, to a husband.

As if she had read my mind, a mischievous smile reshaped Mattie's face, and she linked her arm in mine and leaned toward me conspiratorially.

"You know," she said, "Lorenzo often speaks of our wedding afternoon and how delightful the company was and how pretty we all looked."

I took advantage of the day's heat to wipe my face again and hide the blush I felt spreading there. In spite of myself, I glanced ahead to the two men and took Lorenzo's measure, even though I knew proper girls considered men's characters above their appearances. It was a caution with which I heartily agreed in principle, but just at the moment, I found myself pleased that Lorenzo's shoulders were broad and his waist and hips narrow and that the waves in his black hair gleamed in the sun like a raven's back. Then Lorenzo turned to look for us, and I noticed that even though the bright sky was causing him to frown, he remained winningly handsome. I was complimented to have been well remembered by such a man.

The men stopped, and when we caught up to them, Mattie traded my arm for Paolo's, and Lorenzo and I fell in behind them. Of course, I did not take his arm, nor did he offer it, since we were neither married nor engaged, but I was nevertheless acutely aware of his physical presence beside me as we went on. I was aware, too, of my own body in an unusual way. It was not just a busy object to hustle around, nor merely a prompt for food or rest. I noticed, all of a sudden, its separate, distinct parts and how they were moving, and with a start I realized that my figure and features were open to the same kind of examination and judgment I had just given Lorenzo's. I found myself hoping—palpitating, almost—for a favorable appraisal from him, and wondering if there were some more advantageous way to walk or to hold my head, and what topics of conversation might interest him.

I didn't like having such concerns, as they made me feel nervous and awkward, so I was glad for the diversion when we reached the bustling square at Second and Pine, near the Head House of the market sheds, where we came upon a small, birdlike woman engaged in pressing leaflets into the hands of passersby. Most took her papers passively enough, though some people stared a bit warily at the little woman, as if she were a stray dog that might nip them if they let her too close, and two men actually backtracked to return the leaflets to her, one declaring loudly that she should be arrested as a public nuisance.

The woman flitted busily up to Paolo and Mattie as they passed; Paolo took a leaflet from her and stopped to read it, Mattie leaning over to see, too. The woman approached me and Lorenzo next. I purposely gave her an encouraging smile because she looked at close quarters so earnest and overheated and anxious. I could tell by the quality of her dress and her grooming that she was a woman like Isabelle, that is, not a working woman nor the wife of a plain-working man, though she was not as fashionable as Isabelle, nor did her appearance give off that aspect of frailty conveyed by Isabelle's dainty poses in front of company. It was a curious contradiction that Isabelle, who so ardently pursued robust health through careful diet, good ventilation of the bedroom, salt rubdowns, and Indian club exercises, should wish to nurture an impression of fragility. I suppose she thought it boosted her credentials as a true lady, and perhaps it was an aid in keeping Mr. Edwin's carnal demands somewhat at bay.

"That woman must be a discontented spinster to be wasting her Sunday afternoon and spoiling other people's enjoyment of it with this," Paolo said in disgust as we came up to him.

He wadded up the leaflet and tossed it in the gutter.

"She was wearing a wedding band," I noted, though I winced as I said it, not knowing exactly why, but feeling there was somehow as much unfairness in my defense of the woman as there had been in his criticism.

Paolo snorted.

"Then her husband must be a sorry sort not to be able to keep her in," he said. "Or else her tongue-lashing's driven him to the saloon and he doesn't care anymore what she does."

Lorenzo, head bent over the leaflet, laughed at Paolo's last remark, but I had not read the leaflet yet and so could not appreciate his brother's wit. Paolo and Mattie walked on.

I looked at the leaflet and saw it was from the Women's Christian Temperance Union. "We are engaged in splendid warfare against the Republic's greatest problems", it read, "and we shall not retreat from the white fields of reform until every saloon and every pleasure palace is shuttered, and every drop of beer and whiskey in these United States and beyond has been mingled with the salt tears of the sea." The leaflet went on to descry the damage done to families and to society by the twin vices of alcohol drinking and prostitution and to call for citizens' petitions against them. The language was stirring, and I thought the pamphleteer and the others in the union very brave.

"Did you get to the end yet?" Lorenzo said.

He tapped the paper with his thumb, which was thick and hard looking, like my father's. Where he pointed, "Do Everything!" was printed in large letters, followed by the signature of Frances E. Willard, president of the WCTU.

"They're not content with denying a man's thirst, they want the vote, too," Lorenzo said in a tone of outrage.

"And why shouldn't women vote?" I said quietly, so as not to inflame him more. "We pay taxes and we are subject to the law, just like men."

"What's the use of it? Women will only vote as their husbands or fathers tell them."

I folded the leaflet and used it to fan my face.

"I don't think I would," I replied.

Lorenzo stopped walking and stared at me as if he expected to find something in my appearance he'd not noticed before, a humped, obstinate forehead, perhaps, or a wandering, crossed eye. I had to stop also, of course. Under his scrutiny, I felt childish and had a child's desire to hide my face in my hands or duck behind a tree. Instead, I forced myself to face him squarely and to disguise as best I could the effort it was costing me. The disapproving brown gaze that met me turned gentle so quickly as to seem affectionate, and suddenly we did not seem combatants, as I had thought we were becoming. Lorenzo smiled softly, and I smiled back, not knowing why and not needing to know.

"Don't you trust us, then, to look out for you?" he said, adding after a pause, "Wouldn't you trust me?"

"It isn't that," I said.

The intriguing idea of trusting Lorenzo was distracting me

from marshaling a defense of female suffrage, which, in any case, I felt inadequate to undertake. Though the suffrage battle was already decades old, I myself possessed, at that time, no reasoned arguments or ready answers, but only the instinct that it was a necessary and right thing. I had another instinct, as well, and that was to refrain from speaking where there was feeling but no logic, particularly to someone who was prepared to contradict me and who, besides, was causing such a disturbance in my senses. It turned out that Lorenzo, too, was disinclined to continue. I don't know if it was because he'd decided his point had been successfully made and needed no further buttressing or because he, like me, felt diverted toward more pleasant considerations. I suspect it was, at least in part, the former, but basking in that summer moment, I was aware only of a happy, mutual confusion.

"Look," he said, pointing ahead. "My brother's found a *granita* man. What could be better on such a day?"

"Not a thing," I said, absurdly glad to agree, and we resumed walking toward where Mattie and Paolo, eating lemon water ices, stood waiting for us to join them.

WHEN I returned home, the Martins were already there. I hurried past the closed parlor doors into the dining room, which I had set up that morning, then through the kitchen, and upstairs to my room to change. No matter what the weather, Mr. Edwin insisted on a hot midday meal, so the kitchen and the closed spiral stairwell to the second floor were thick with the steamy aroma of roasting beef. I had arrived too late to bake squash, as Isabelle had wanted, so I decided to boil and mash some white potatoes to accompany the beet salad and the asparagus, already washed and waiting to be cooked.

I rapped on the parlor doors and slid them open at Isabelle's reply. I found the Martins seated as they often were, Mr. Edwin with the Sunday papers spread about him on the sofa, his face hidden behind the open financial pages, and Isabelle across from him, in a chair adroitly angled to enable her to converse comfortably if he desired it, but not positioned so forthrightly that an absence of conversation would reflect critically on him. Despite the usualness of the scene, I sensed immediately upon entering the room an air of strain, as if the Martins had hastened into these typical postures upon hearing my rap and would hold them only until my exit. Isabelle, especially, appeared tense. When she sat in the parlor with her husband, Isabelle invariably occupied herself with embroidery, or with browsing ladies' magazines like *Godey's* and *Peterson's,* or some other easily interrupted activity, but today her hands were uncharacteristically folded tightly on her empty lap.

"Dinner will be a little delayed," I said.

"And why is that?" Isabelle snapped.

"I only need to boil the potatoes."

"I didn't order potatoes."

"It's instead of the squash. I didn't leave enough time—"

"I make menus to be followed, Nan, not altered to suit the whims of your private schedule."

Mr. Edwin rattled his paper loudly as he turned a page.

"Let the girl be, Belle," he said. "I like potatoes better than squash, anyway."

"I've asked you not to call me that, Edwin."

Mr. Edwin lowered his paper and looked at his wife.

"But it means 'Beauty,' my dear, and in your own tongue."

"No one here knows my tongue. Here, Belle is a name for an actress. Or worse."

"Then I shall use it only in private, where there can be no doubt as to my meaning, and no one to overhear and misinterpret."

Mr. Edwin directed a wink and an amused, close-lipped grin at me. Not waiting for an answering smile, he lifted the newspaper in front of his face again and resumed reading. But he would not have got a smile from me, however long he waited. For I had seen Isabelle's blush as he spoke, and the nervous opening and closing of her clasped fingers, and her sudden pretended interest in the view from the window, which was of the top of the same gingko tree always visible there, its delicate fan-shaped leaves and drooping yellow fruit.

Isabelle turned her head toward me. She looked quite sad at that moment, sad and weary, as if she were a much older woman caught within a much harder life.

"Potatoes will be fine, Nan," she said quietly.

"My sherry?" Mr. Edwin spoke from behind his paper.

"Do you think you should, Edwin?"

"And why not, for heaven's sake?" The paper came down. "I only said my health was not up to a train journey and a stay in a damp seaside resort, not that my whole regimen must be altered."

Isabelle stood up to go to the dining room for Mr. Edwin's sherry, and I returned to the kitchen. Now I knew that disappointment was the cause of Isabelle's mood. The Martins had been planning to go to Ocean Grove in New Jersey to hear Reverend Dale preach at the Methodist camp meeting. They were to be away nearly a week. Isabelle had been quite looking forward to the trip, and so had I, as she'd said that I could have three whole days as my own while they were gone, and even the days I'd be at the house would have half the work in them. Mr. Edwin's fussy notions about what his health could tolerate would deprive us both. I gave the potatoes a good mashing.

I observed Mr. Edwin closely while I served dinner. He seemed no more sallow than usual. He'd had one of his phlegmy spells about a week ago, coughing and moaning that he felt cold and weak. Isabelle put him to bed with hot water bottles and mixed up a syrup for him of horseradish root and sugar and had him inhale the steam from scalding hot vinegar, and after a day and a half of such attentions, he was back about his rounds. He had had no relapse that I'd heard of, and Mr. Edwin was not one to be quiet about illness. I concluded that either he simply did not want to go to Ocean Grove or that he truly believed the sea air would be bad for him. He had joint complaints in winter that he often linked to dampness.

"We may lose some money on our cottage," Isabelle was saying when I brought in the chocolate pudding and coconut cake. "We will be canceling late."

Apparently, she had not yet completely given up hope that the trip might go forward. I slowed in my cutting of the cake.

"Perhaps," Mr. Edwin said. "I'll send off a telegram to George today. He may know someone who'd like to take over our place."

"George will be sorry not to see us."

"Ocean Grove hosts hundreds of thousands of visitors every summer. We won't be missed."

"I really would like to go, Edwin," Isabelle said. "I'm sure you'd feel quite well there, and I'd bring my medicine chest just in case."

"There's always next year, Isabelle," Mr. Edwin said, thrumming his fingers on the table edge, which meant his patience was wearing thin.

I didn't know whether it was Isabelle's pestering or my slowness with the cake and pudding that was annoying him, but I hastened to serve his dessert. As I set Isabelle's plate down in front of her, she gave a little start, and looked quickly back and forth between me and Mr. Edwin.

"Edwin, why don't I go to Ocean Grove on my own? And take Nan along?"

"Me?" I said, surprised.

"Willer?" said Mr. Edwin.

"George can shepherd us about and be my escort when needed, and Nan will be a companion for walks and in the cottage. It's a perfect solution."

"My dear, I don't think—"

"You can eat in restaurants or at your father's. Nan will leave the icebox full of cold meats and vegetable salads, and baked goods in the larder. One of the boys from the shop could sweep up. And we won't stay as long as you and I had intended."

"How long?"

"Four days. Three."

Mr. Edwin ate a bite of cake and thought.

"I suppose I can be a temporary widower for the good cause of your meditation and worship at camp meetings."

"Oh, Edwin, thank you."

"And will the two of you pray for me?" Mr. Edwin joked, waving his fork back and forth at us.

"Certainly," Isabelle replied just as cheerfully. "And we shall bring you a box of saltwater taffy, too."

Neither of them asked if I wished to go to Ocean Grove or not, just as they would not have asked their luggage if it was inclined to travel. I was vexed to have my promised days evaporate before I had even fully daydreamed them, but I was more vexed at being so unconsidered. Yet later, over the dishes in the sink, I began to take hold of the unexpected journey and feel pleased about it. I was going to touch the ocean.

SIXTEEN

I FIRST saw the ocean in the rain. But cloudy skies could not diminish the majesty of the sight. The beach was devoid of people, except for a few resolute seashell hunters. I stepped cautiously onto the damp sand pitted by raindrops, half expecting to hear a policeman's whistle shooing me off. This sense of illegality came not only from the emptiness of the place, but also from the fact that I was supposed to be on an errand and had taken a deliberate and unsanctioned detour.

Isabelle was unpacking in our little clapboard cottage and had sent me for some simple groceries. We'd be taking all meals except breakfast at the communal eating tents or at the Osborne House, so we didn't need much, but Reverend Dale was expected for a late supper that evening after his attendance at speeches by some ministers from the African Methodist Episcopal Church.

I had set out down Pilgrim Pathway honestly enough, but when I got to the corner of a wide avenue and looked down its length, I saw, at its end, an empty reach. Guessing it led to the ocean, I turned down the avenue and headed for the open space. I passed several large boardinghouses; their scrollwork porches were occupied by ladies writing letters at bamboo tables and children playing jackstraws on the floor or gazing longingly out to the wet sidewalks.

I had meant to stand on the plank walk beside the beach

for only a few moments, but the sound and smell and the heaving sight of the gray-green ocean drew me down onto the sand. I went right to the edge of the water, where it rushed up and back, up and back, like something alive. It was an awesome thought to know that nothing short of the end of the world would ever stop it, nothing men did could ever tame or change it. Even Mr. Verne's Captain Nemo had not learned all the sea's secrets.

I should have felt humbled walking beside the ocean, so close to so much power and mystery, yet instead I felt expanded, as if its immenseness were entering my heart, as if I, too, were a creature of depths and mystery. I didn't think any camp meeting would stir me as much, not even the Sunday evening surf meeting. The hem of my skirt and my shoes were encrusted with wet sand, and Isabelle might be cross at my long absence, but I had no regrets at having surrendered to the lure of the sea.

The rain worsened on my way back, and just as I came up the steps of the cottage, there was a loud crack of thunder, which disguised the sound of my arrival. Balancing my closed umbrella, a bag of groceries, a folded copy of *The Ocean Grove Record,* and a box containing one of Mrs. Wagner's fresh fruit pies—an Ocean Grove specialty—I pushed the screened door open with my back and turned around to find Isabelle and Reverend Dale in the small sitting room. He was in one of the two wicker armchairs and she was seated on the straw rug beside his chair. I was not sure—it was a fleeting impression— but I thought that her head had been resting on his knees.

"Willer, you're soaked," he said, coming to take the umbrella and parcels.

Isabelle watched us, not moving from her place on the floor. Reverend Dale had handed her a book when he stood up, and she held it loosely now in her lap. Apparently he'd been reading to her. Perhaps she'd been reading it herself before he came. I could not imagine she'd expected the minister. Her hair was loose and damp, and I recalled she'd meant to wash it while I was out. She was wearing a dimity wrapper, pale pink printed with mauve rosebuds. The pastel color darkened her eyes and hair. It was modest apparel, especially since Isabelle was sure to have underneath pantalettes, a chemise, and a petticoat, but it was an unusual costume for receiving a visitor, even one who had surprised her and was a close family friend.

"Did you find all we need, Nan?" Isabelle asked.

"Yes, ma'am."

"Reverend Dale stopped by to say he can't be here for supper after all."

Neither of them elaborated. They stayed quiet, both facing me, as if they were players on a stage awaiting a cue.

"I've seen the ocean," I said.

"You must go bathing tomorrow," said Reverend Dale. "It's supposed to be a fine day."

I had taken off my hat and rubber coat. I reached for the parcels. Reverend Dale, seeming lost in thought, perhaps about sea bathing, kept hold of them.

"I'd like to get out of my wet shoes, sir," I said.

"Give her the groceries, George," Isabelle prompted, getting up at last.

"Oh." He laughed mildly at himself.

When I returned to the sitting room ten minutes later, Reverend Dale was gone.

The rain persisted, so we could not stroll the plank walk that evening, but we braved the weather to attend a chautauqua where a world traveler, using a gas-fired stereopticon projector, showed pictures on a large canvas screen of the Holy Land and Alaska and California. Isabelle had not wanted to go to the sermons in the auditorium yet.

"Reverend Dale's preaching tomorrow. We'll go then," she said.

I found it difficult to fall asleep that night. My mind was busy about our train journey and the ocean under rain and the illustrated lecture. Also, across a space of only three feet, Isabelle lay in an adjoining bed, and I was hard put to relax, with her so near in such intimate circumstances. I felt it would be a great embarrassment if I snored, or if she did, or even if I simply rolled back and forth, as I often did before settling into a comfortable sleeping position. These foolish worries kept me still and awake.

"Nan? Do you hear it?"

"The ocean?"

"Like the slow heartbeat of a dying giant."

"Not so melancholy as that, I think. A great heartbeat, but not of something dying."

We listened together for a few moments to the muted slap and hiss of the waves.

"Reverend Dale says he must speak to Edwin when we are all back in town."

There was a tremor in Isabelle's voice that put me on alert. I turned my head and could just make out her profile in the darkness. She was staring at the low ceiling; her hands were folded over her chest. She looked almost corpselike.

"He says that he is attracted to me, that thoughts of me disturb him in his work, and that Edwin should know this. He says he will ask Edwin if it would not be best for him to discontinue his friendship with us."

Isabelle's words came out clearly and strongly, and I realized the tremor I had detected was due to anger, not sorrow, though I suspected sorrow, too, was there.

"What will Mr. Edwin do?"

"I don't know," Isabelle cried, suddenly sitting up. "Beware of men who say they want only to secure your happiness, Nan. In the end, it's they, not you, who decide what it is will make you happy."

I wondered if she were referring to Mr. Edwin or Reverend Dale, or perhaps to her lost father, who had engineered all the conditions of her life.

"Why must he play at chivalry?" she went on. "It's already been agreed."

"What has?"

Isabelle turned her face toward me. A breeze from the open window at her back lifted strands of her hair and rippled her thin batiste nightgown so that she looked, for a moment, the portrait of a madwoman.

"Edwin has given me to George," she said.

"Given you?" I asked, startled.

"I'm as good as promised to him. For the future." She lay back down. "It's the same thing."

With a decided flounce of her cotton blanket, Isabelle turned on her side, away from me, so I didn't feel I could ask more. I didn't think I'd get satisfactory answers, anyway. I was sure this must be some misconstrued fancy of Isabelle's rather than bare truth, but it was an idea that could lead her into trouble, and so I worried for her.

I thought about Edwin Martin and George Dale; both men seemed pale and tedious beside Isabelle's fervor, however groundless it might be, though Reverend Dale, at least, shared some of her interests. I thought of Isabelle as a girl with a doll-house, moving play figures about. But they would not stay, they toppled over in place or fell out of windows because their feet were not broad enough, their legs not spread sufficiently to bear the weight of her grand plans for them.

꧁ THE NEXT day was fine, as Reverend Dale had predicted. Sunlight poured in at the windows, and with it a citrus scent from lemon geraniums in window boxes. The air was humid like the river breezes in Philadelphia, but with a sharp tang the rivers never had, and I knew it must be air that had passed over the ocean and that carried the ocean's text, as the Bible carries the meaning and promises of God.

Reverend Dale arrived early to take us exploring. Isabelle greeted him warmly with no hint of rebuke or even recall. She jollied him into eating some Sally Lunn, even though he protested he'd already breakfasted. He'd looked apprehensive when I left him in, but under Isabelle's attentions he eased. I saw that if he had not taken the tea cake nor shown himself at ease, Isabelle would not have left the cottage that day. Perhaps he saw it, too.

We walked some of the same streets I had traveled the day before, but now all was bright and gay. The dust on the dirt roads was held down by a lingering dampness from the rain. Reverend Dale explained it would have been so anyway because water wagons sprinkled the streets daily.

We did not traverse the whole of Ocean Grove, as the resort covers two-hundred sixty-six acres, but we saw one of the twin freshwater finger lakes that border it on either end, the grove of Jersey oak and pine that gave it its name, and one of the two ocean bathing grounds. We took footbridges across and back over Wesley Lake, on which floated close to a hundred little boats decorated with flags and colorful canvas tops and Chinese lanterns. Some of the boaters were playing mandolins and guitars, and there was a charming argument of melodies in the air.

We passed a fair sampling of the hundreds of summer cottages, some like our own and some larger; and scores of boardinghouses and hotels with wide verandas and festoons of gingerbread woodwork; and along the lakefront, row upon row upon row of peak-roofed tents with little front porches shaded by striped canvas awnings. The tents had short picket fences and gardens in front and small wooden kitchens attached in back.

"There are families who've rented these tents every summer for years," Reverend Dale said.

He was walking between Isabelle and me, and he carefully directed all his remarks at both of us. Despite this courtesy, I felt a bit nervous being part of our threesome, as if I were committing an indiscretion. However light Isabelle and Reverend Dale kept their conversation, a rigidity showed through, like the luster of dark wood through a lace tablecloth. And, against expectation, the familiarity Isabelle and I shared at home helped make the present situation more rather than less uncomfortable.

"Finally, we come to the heart of things, ladies," Reverend Dale said as we approached the resort's center, the park around the great outdoor auditorium.

"Do you always prefer such a roundabout route, Reverend?" Isabelle asked.

"I find the effect to be better. Have I tired you?"

"No, I have great stamina. Nan, are you tired?"

"No, ma'am. It's all been very interesting."

"You see, George," Isabelle drawled. "We're content to have reached the heart gradually. Show it to us."

Reverend Dale, seeming a little flustered, began in a loud, teacherly voice to name the purposes of the buildings we now found ourselves among. He pointed out a bookstore, a small chapel, the town clock on Association Hall, the Bishop Janes Memorial Tabernacle, Beersheba Well, a large dome housing a scale model of Jerusalem, the Young People's Temple, and, of course, the huge auditorium, which alone covered nearly half an acre.

The auditorium was surrounded on three sides by more tents, and a wide grassy boulevard led from the auditorium to the beach and plank walk two hundred yards away. The proximity of the boundless ocean gave the auditorium complex an atmosphere at once festive and holy. Reverend Dale told us proudly that the concrete sidewalks down Ocean Pathway had been laid just last year and that the Camp Meeting Association was encouraging private landholders to put in concrete walks, too, and to curb corners with ship timbers.

"The association is always vigilant to beautify and improve Ocean Grove," Reverend Dale said. "They own a hothouse for cultivating flowers to adorn the buildings, and every April, they plant trees. One hundred were set out this spring."

The strains of a choir practicing a particularly martial hymn drifted out of the open-sided wooden tabernacle. There were people everywhere, sitting on benches and settees or hurrying by on their way to Bible class or other meetings. Reverend Dale said we would see even more people at the preaching service. We planned to go to the third and last main service of the day.

When we went up Ocean Pathway to the plank walk, it was busy with strollers: fashionable ladies and gentlemen, tradesmen, farmers, whole families. There was great variety in the throng, and also a sameness. I saw a few Negroes, and people who appeared prosperous and many who were less assuming, but there was no one looked like Lorenzo and his brother. In Ocean Grove, the Christian life was a Protestant life; Catholics did not fit.

"You can follow the plank walk all the way in to Asbury Park. They have concessions and pack peddlers and organ-grinders there," Reverend Dale said. "There's none allowed in Ocean Grove, of course."

"Perhaps Nan would like that," Isabelle said.

"The ocean is amusement enough for me," I said, though I was curious to see Asbury Park. If Isabelle wanted to go, however, she'd have to say it directly. I'd not play her excuse.

We turned onto a pavilion adjacent to the boardwalk to watch the ocean for a while. Isabelle and Reverend Dale sat on a bench, and I stood at the rail, longing to get closer to the spray and rushing noise of the breakers.

"Do you think we might find a souvenir gift for Edwin in Asbury Park?" Isabelle asked Reverend Dale.

"Most likely."

"Then we will go."

A small boy near us was lining up bits of bread along the top of the railing. Scores of gray-and-white gulls swooped down out of nowhere, screaming and flapping their wings, repeatedly dislodging one another from the railing as they fought over the food. The boy laughed and flung pieces of bread up into the air, drawing more gulls and inflaming them to aerial squabbles and acrobatic feats as they attempted to catch the bread in flight, plunging after it as it dropped. Two pieces landed on Isabelle's lap, and she was immediately targeted by three large herring gulls, their wings beating around her head, webbed pink feet and long hooked bills pushing at one another and inadvertently at her shoulders and legs.

She jumped up with a scream, Reverend Dale chasing away the birds with his cloth cap. The boy's mother, who had been in conversation with another woman, looked over at the commotion and hurried forward, pulling the boy away by his ear. She gave him a twisting pinch on his bare arm, which made him yelp, and then picked up the unfinished sentence with her friend as if she'd been interrupted by no more than a noisome horsefly. It was like a trained performance, her movements were so quick and smooth.

We left the pavilion, Reverend Dale supporting Isabelle by her elbow and tenderly brushing unseen debris from her shoulders and back. She herself brushed the front of her striped seersucker dress, which indeed did show a few crumbs and fluffs of down.

"I could take you to Asbury Park tomorrow, if you like," he was saying. "You and Willer."

Isabelle smiled tolerantly at him.

"It won't pull you away from spiritual matters?"

"Not at all. I had been thinking of going to a band concert."

"Could we do both, do you think? I have the time and energy for both. Unless that's too much of our company for one day?"

Her voice was sweet and offhand, as if his answer, or even her own suggestion, were of no more than passing interest to her. I pitied him.

"Why, no. That is, yes, I think that's a fine arrangement. I'll just walk you home now and then go for tickets."

"Nan and I can make our own way. Feel free to go about your business."

This, too, was delivered with a smile. Poor Reverend Dale hesitated, seeming to ponder if there was some puzzle within the simple phrases. Then he bade us good day, shaking Isabelle's hand and nodding at me. We went home to get our bathing costumes, Isabelle prattling on about the loveliness and gentility of Ocean Grove and the possibility of taking a whole month at the resort next summer, as if she were a woman of independent means hemmed in by no one.

SEVENTEEN

ISABELLE HAD bought herself a bathing costume for the trip, and she hired one for me at Lillagore's Bathing Ground. We were almost as covered as in our street clothes, but without all the layers; we were in no danger of being fined for improper bathing suits. Reverend Dale had told us the police would even take people out of the water if they were indecently attired. Still, I felt quite shy coming out of the bathhouse.

Isabelle's costume was of soft serge the color of red grapeskins, and mine was navy blue mohair. Both consisted of kneelength drawers and a short-sleeved tunic; we wore, as well, full-length stockings, bathing shoes, and ruffled caps. As we walked down the sand to the water, I felt I was being stared at, but probably I wasn't, since there were many women attired like us, and most people were busy with picnics or conversation or children. A good number of women wore walking dresses or Garibaldi shirtwaists and sat with parasols on benches or wooden folding chairs and looked out to sea. The beach was as brillant and clean as if it were giving off its own light.

Isabelle and I stood a long while letting the cool water wash around our ankles, feeling it carve out soft nests around our feet in the sand. Other women and children stood or sat around us; some of the children were running back and forth on the slope of packed wet sand with an energy as ceaseless as the briskly moving waters. I spotted several men swimming out in the deeper water, their arching white arms hitting the water rhythmically, like machines. I wondered how it must feel to be loose and unfettered like that, in a strange element, in such command of one's body.

"Let's go," Isabelle finally said, entering the water with determination.

I heard someone behind us say the ocean was calm today, and I was grateful for that, though to me it appeared quite spirited. Holding on to a lifeline attached to poles, we slowly waded out. Isabelle didn't stop until we'd reached the point where the water was lifting in swells about waist high. At low ebb, the water was still above our knees. There were only a few people beyond this spot. I marveled at Isabelle's bravery, and I made a brave show myself, though I still gripped the rope tightly, and my heart fluttered when the water climbed up my chest, which it did a time or two.

We stood in the bracing water, our bodies turned toward the open ocean. Rows of waves, coming sometimes in quick little groups, sometimes as lone billows bracketed by pauses of flat water, sucked us first toward the beach, then in the opposite direction, out toward the sea's very bosom.

Though I did not shed all my timidity, gradually a turbulent kind of pleasure was added to it. Everyone around us was merry and squealing, and soon my fear itself became part of my enjoyment. As each wave passed, I eagerly scanned the next to see how large it was and where it might break. I loved how the walls of water would rise and rise and then hover a moment before they curled over and fell. Most exciting were the ones we caught at the crest. The thin top edge of the wave splashed and reached, and we leaped to keep our heads up, and the water, like an enormous soft hand, lifted us off the sandy bottom and gently floated us down again, before crashing over just behind us.

I learned from our neighbors on the lifeline to back up or move forward in response to the shapes of the incoming waves. I even became bold enough a few times to let go of the line momentarily in order to move around someone and meet a wave farther out. Isabelle was no longer beside me, but I didn't mind. I was in the ocean, and it was grand.

Then a great, tumbling wave reared up unexpectedly like a recalcitrant horse and broke right on top of me. It ripped my hands from the lifeline and sent me wildly rolling, whether landward or seaward I couldn't tell. Buffeted about in a churning world of no air, no light, deadened sound, I could do nothing to right myself. My cap came off and was lost, my bare arms scraped along the coarse sand.

Suddenly, I was thrown into the sunlight again, near the edge of the waterline. A little girl was squatting next to me, her mouth agape with surprise. I had washed up right beside where she was digging for sandcrabs, and she could not have looked more amazed at me than if I had been a mermaid.

My heart pounding, I laughed out loud, relieved to be alive and in one piece and thrilled by my small adventure. Isabelle came over. She had seen me go down and run to fetch a dragger to pull me out. He gave me his hand and helped me up. The wet bathing costume, in which my limbs had felt so free when dry, was now heavy, and the drawers and shoes had collected large clumps of sand. It was cumbersome to walk with all that sodden weight, and I thought that even if I knew how to swim, I would surely have sunk from exhaustion after only a few strokes in those clothes.

Back at the bathing pavilion, we soaked in hot saltwater baths, and then Isabelle wanted a nap, so we dressed and went home. While she rested, I swept the sitting room, rinsed out our bathing costumes, and made up some cucumber-and-lettuce sandwiches on Graham bran bread. I thought our attending the preaching service might interfere with taking supper at the boardinghouse. None of these tasks took much time, and, indeed, I rather enjoyed them, the cottage was so cozy and neat.

Isabelle had said I could still have three days to myself when we got back to Philadelphia, just as I would have if the Martins had made their trip as originally planned. Now, however, with Isabelle and Mr. Edwin at home, I would have to take my days away from the house, which meant I must spend them at my father's place. This was agreeable enough—I had not spent time with my family since Mattie's wedding—but it would not provide the feeling of liberty I had been counting on, and so I was a little disappointed. I was pondering this as I sat on a cushioned rattan bench on the cottage's tiny porch, when it occurred to me how to make my visit home more of a holiday.

I retrieved paper, pen, and envelopes from Isabelle's writing supplies and prepared two letters, one to Mattie and one to Sippy, proposing that Mattie, Paolo, and Lorenzo spend a full Sunday with us walking in the country and sharing a meal. I sent a separate note to my father, for courtesy's sake, though I knew he'd have no objections to company as long as his dinner was on time. I suspected, in fact, that he'd like seeing the Testa brothers again, as he'd seemed to have taken to them at the wedding, and I thought he might even include them in the horseshoe pitch he and his friends often arranged on Sunday afternoons.

I wondered if there was any game like that in Italy. Certainly, Lorenzo and Paolo would not have encountered it in the city streets of their New York boyhoods. Boyhood. Lorenzo was barely out of his, yet he impressed me thoroughly as a man, making me feel, in fact, younger than he, when actually I was four years older. He knew more of the world than I did, I thought; his ideas and actions had as a backdrop places and persons foreign to me. He had been but a baby in Italy, but I was sure it had marked him indelibly; his aunt and uncle had raised him to be an American but to cherish the language, food, and faith of his homeland. Almost as unknown to me as Italy were the streets of Philadelphia. Nowhere was closed to Lorenzo. Mattie, with her factory job and her husband, was now able to penetrate more of the city, but I was still untried in the world beyond shops and public parks.

I scolded myself to be more honest. It was not only Lorenzo's wider experience that made him seem older and manly. It was the flash in his eyes, the confident roll of his gait, the winning charm of his private smile. Lorenzo seemed a man because I took him for one. He stirred a current in me as in iron keys set near a magnet, and because he was the first to have had that effect on me, I credited him with virtues and abilities of which I had no sound proof.

These new feelings were at the same time unsettling and delightful, and I wished, alternately, to be rid of them and to have them increased. Was this the state Isabelle sought? Had she finally despaired of maintaining it within her marriage? Had it ever been there? I sighed sympathetically, and I confess to harboring a feeling of superiority. However confused my emotions, they seemed then far less complicated than Isabelle's.

𝒮𝒳 THE OCEAN Grove Auditorium was filled to capacity for the preaching service, as Reverend Dale said it always was. It held seating for five thousand and room for one thousand standees, and every space was taken. There were more women in the audience than men, an expanse of bonnets. Seventy-five preachers sat on the octagonal platform, though not all were slated to speak. Isabelle soon identified Reverend Dale, finding him by his thick yellow hair and his sky blue silk cravat.

The auditorium was roofed, but it had no walls, giving free play to the ocean breezes and, through the wooden Gothic arches at the auditorium's rim, allowing views of the surrounding park and resort buildings. The meeting started with a hymn, "I Yield, I Yield, I Can Hold Out No More." The Silver Lake Glee Club kept us on tempo, if not on pitch.

Reverend Dale was third to speak. First came a white-whiskered fellow preaching abstinence from alcohol, tobacco, riding vehicles on Sundays, dancing, and card playing. This man was an old-time revivalist, zealous and dramatic. I remember once as a child going to a camp meeting with my mother and grandmother and witnessing such preaching. The meeting was no more than a collection of tents around a rough wooden stand in a forest clearing, but I recall it as bristling with activity, like an anthill under attack. Preachers paraded and shouted, while listeners barked and leaped, jerked and fainted. Of course, nothing like that happened at Ocean Grove, queen of religious resorts. The Methodists had tamed the raucous outdoor meeting. But there was still fire in the old evangelist, and the crowd, though sedate, was still stirred, some even to the shedding of tears, and I expect many a private resolution to improve was made.

A lady preacher was next on the bill. She spoke on perfectionism, calling the individual conscience the supreme moral standard.

"The Christian character is granite at bottom and lily beautiful at top," she said. "Look at what strong Christians have accomplished. They made the air in this country too pure for slavery to breathe in, and soon it will be too pure for the inebriate and the polygamist as well."

Reverend Dale was milder in manner than his predecessors, but he exerted no less a grip on the audience. There was a sounding board above his head, but he was still required to speak loudly to reach all parts of the auditorium; even so there was a quietude about him that was mesmerizing. People had to sit still and hush their inner thoughts and ignore the passing insect or the odorous person in the next seat to attend to Reverend Dale, and they did.

"Do my eyes deceive me?" Reverend Dale began with genuine consternation. "I look around me . . ."

He paused, turning his head and shifting his blue eyes toward half a dozen different places in the audience.

". . . and I see . . . I see . . . angels!"

He spread his arms wide.

"Angels!" he repeated in a hoarse whisper, as if dumbstruck with awe. "Angels."

"Is it happpenstance that this great auditorium today is filled with more ladies than gentlemen? Pick up the membership register of any church—any church anywhere in this nation—and you will find female names in the majority. Is this a mistake? Go to a Christian prayer circle or to the meeting of an aid society for the needy and distressed, and you will find the same. Is this unnatural?"

Reverend Dale began walking slowly up and down the platform, again casting his piercing glance here and there. I once felt, with a start, that he fixed right on me, peered right into my eyes, though we were at a distance from him that made that impossible. Besides, he didn't have his spectacles, and I knew from seeing him use them at the Martins' that we were all probably a blur to him. Still, he gave a powerful impression of looking into you from up there. I began to see the minister's appeal for Isabelle. His being so comfortably in command on stage magnified him somehow.

"No, my friends," he finally said, answering his own questions. "God does not make mistakes. This phenomenon is the very height of Nature. It is the soul's work, the soul's doing."

Reverend Dale's voice had risen with each word as if it were climbing stairsteps. Isabelle leaned slightly forward, entranced.

"It is the soul that shapes women so they are gentle and pitying and pious," he continued. "A feeling of dependence is native to the female heart and leads it properly to the two spheres in which it will be happiest and most useful: in the church and in the home."

Reverend Dale went on to say that women were the light of the home and that a woman's first duty was to provide a happy, well-run home for her husband, who needed rest and sanctuary.

It was a pretty picture. Reverend Dale portrayed a place that I would certainly have been pleased to enter when I was feeling tired or discouraged. But Isabelle and I were on the other side of that picture, the side where the hooks and wires and nails were, where spiders nested and silverfish scurried.

Reverend Dale closed by describing a man, at the end of a long day of struggle in the godless realm of commerce, returning to his home and finding clean and handsome rooms, the aroma of wholesome foods, and his guardian angel, a welcoming, inspiring wife.

". . . seated, perhaps," Reverend Dale rhapsodized, "at a piano, face illuminated by candles, eyes vacant, innocent fingers conjuring deep emotion from some simple ballad. What garden would this not be? What heaven on earth?"

Isabelle gave a deep sigh of satisfaction as Reverend Dale took his seat.

The next preacher might have punctured her serenity, but I don't believe she listened very closely to him. Isabelle had a great talent for selecting just the elements that suited her from what she heard or read. It's a common human proclivity, but in Isabelle it had attained a rare refinement.

This final preacher built upon Reverend Dale's theme, adding motherhood to the scene. He proclaimed that a woman could not reach the highest development of her noble nature until she had children. Children were her "moral and physiological destiny." The childless wife risked becoming a pet or plaything, though admittedly she could save herself from this by visiting the poor and sick.

"Happily for society, women are little troubled with amative feelings," the minister intoned. "Love of home, children, and domestic duties are a woman's only passions."

He smiled benevolently, gratefully it seemed, at us, and

touched the fingertips of his hands together, making the shape of a peaked roof in front of his heart.

"Your purity, ladies," he said, "is the everlasting barrier against which the tides of man's sensual nature surge. It is your holy work, your exalted station in life, to shape the characters of your children and to soften and civilize your husbands."

He was not the theatrical speaker Reverend Dale was, and his pinched, pockmarked face was not as easy to look at, so he did not enthrall his listeners as thoroughly, but I saw assenting nods in the audience, nevertheless, especially when he shifted from morality to patriotism. He railed against apartment living, contraception, and abortion nostrums and claimed they were damaging the health of the nation.

"For if the good native stock of America continues their current trend to small families—having only four children or three or even none!—and the hordes of fertile women coming to our shores from southern and eastern Europe continue to produce large broods, I ask you," he wailed, "who will rule America's future?"

I looked at Isabelle to gauge the effect of the preacher's arguments on her. Her unfocused stare told me that, purposely or not, she was benignly ensnared in her own thoughts. I envied her self-government.

The meeting closed in the traditional Ocean Grove way, with the audience waving white handkerchiefs in the air to thank the preachers and praise the Lord. Isabelle was roused from her dream weaving by this lively display, but she fell back into herself on our walk home, so we shared no discussion of the ideas we'd heard in the auditorium.

REVEREND DALE had been able to secure only two tickets for the band concert next afternoon, so I did not go. I was very content to spend the time among the crowds on the plank walk and in the park. I stood for a short while at the back of a small meeting hall where a woman was talking about the African missions, but I had had enough of lectures, so I slipped out before she was done and went to see the camera obscura.

The camera was installed at the north end of the beach, near Ross's Bathing Ground, in a small wooden building topped by a fat, funnel-shaped tower. I entered a darkened room and joined a group of other people staring at the surface of a round table on which appeared panorama reflections of all that was going on outside. A man explained that a lens in the top of the tower was scanning the surroundings in a full circle. When he moved a lever, the scene changed, so that we saw, first, bathers in the sea, then the deck of a passing ship, then passersby on the plank walk, then loungers on hotel porches, then wagons and carriages in the streets. It was a curious experience to take in so many sides from one location, a hidden place, and to be watching people who did not know they were being observed. I wondered if they'd have behaved differently if they'd known we could see them, though none of them was doing anything remarkable or particularly private. I reminded myself that they were stout Christians and so believed they were always under observation, and by more important Eyes than mine.

After securing myself a cooling treat at Day's Ice Cream Garden, I met Isabelle and Reverend Dale at the crosswalk near the Webb Avenue Pavilion, as we had designated earlier, and we moved north up the plank walk to Asbury Park, in company with thousands of other vacationers. Reverend Dale informed us that the Ocean Grove planking was all new, it and two pavilions and the flag mast all having been swept away in a fierce storm last November.

Reverend Dale was in high spirits. He'd received many compliments on his preaching last night, Isabelle told me, and I could see that things were smooth between the two of them, whether because they had reached an agreement or because

Isabelle had conquered her dismay, I did not know. In any case, they were so truly lighthearted, I was able to forget the oddness of our combination and enjoy myself.

Asbury Park had been founded by a Methodist, but it was not a religious resort. Its plank walk was bright with amusements and concessions, its air lively with rollicking music, the nasal calls of barkers and hawkers, the gamboling of street performers in motley, and the shouts of children. Reverend Dale walked between me and Isabelle, steering us first to one attraction, then another, like an indulgent uncle.

We rode the carousel; we watched jugglers and a little dog that danced on its hind legs and a contortionist who stood on her hands and folded herself in half so that her buttocks touched the top of her head and her feet were set on her shoulders, with her toes next to her chin. We ate fried clams and corn muffins and rock candy and frozen custard.

I was glad we had not come to Ocean Grove during the ten days of the Annual Camp Meeting, as then such an excursion would not have been possible. The association not only discourages pleasure outings during the season's culminating meeting, it also asks that there be no sea bathing, no boating, no croquet, nor even private amusements, but only prayer, hymn singing, and attendance at as many services as one's strength will allow. Reverend Dale said a record number of conversions and sanctifications were expected at the Love Feast this year; one hundred ministers were to administer the Lord's Supper at the closing meeting.

Reverend Dale bought us each a souvenir of the evening: for me, a star-shaped pincushion with Asbury Park spelled out on it in glass beads, and for Isabelle, a little polished-cotton purse, with Asbury Park and the design of a rose also worked in beads. Isabelle bought a box of saltwater taffy and some postcards for Mr. Edwin, and I got Elsinore a clever little bouquet made of seashells.

After watching a fireworks display over the beach, we walked back to Ocean Grove. The quiet there was welcoming and homey. Reverend Dale and Isabelle fell silent in a comfortable way. The strollers around us spoke in lowered tones; the sound of their shoes on the wood planks was louder than their voices. Some of the men were carrying sleepy children. The beach stretched ghostly white off to our left, and beyond it the dark ocean, beating, beating like a colossal heart.

EIGHTEEN

WE HAD been home a week when Mr. Edwin fell sick. I postponed my three days off, as I had never seen him as bad before and I didn't like to leave Isabelle when she was so fatigued and worried from nursing him. Mr. Edwin's illness coincided with Reverend Dale's return to the city, but Isabelle turned the minister away at the door when he came to call, saying her husband needed absolute quiet and uninterrupted rest.

I had grown used to Mr. Edwin's exaggerations of headaches and lung congestion, his attacks of hives and indigestion, which occurred regularly despite Isabelle's and my best efforts to feed him carefully. But this time he appeared truly sick.

He said his arms and legs ached. He had diarrhea and a low appetite, and though he professed he could not get out of bed, still he was restless there and twitched in his sleep and twisted about while awake. He complained about the light so much Isabelle had me hang the heavy winter drapes.

After two days of no improvement, Isabelle ordered the single bed brought up into the apartment again. She had it set up in the parlor so that Mr. Edwin would have more interesting surroundings when he was awake and so that she could more easily sit with him, which she did most of the day and well into the night. He told me once when I was putting clean linens on his pillows that he could only achieve restful slumber when he knew Isabelle was nearby, and he swore that even in the deepest sleep he could feel her hand holding his foot, a tenderness he asked for repeatedly.

As usual when he felt out of sorts, Mr. Edwin relied on Isabelle's knowledge of medicines and did not even consider consulting a physician. He had absolute faith in her remedies, and, indeed, they were usually effective. Even in this more extreme illness, he enjoyed periods of relief, but nothing she gave him seemed able to restore him to active health.

I'm not sure of all she used, as she often bade me stay with Mr. Edwin in the parlor while she concocted mixtures in the kitchen. I know she gave him citric acid for headache, and spoons of ashes stirred in cider for nausea, and castor oil boiled with milk and West Indian molasses as a cathartic. She sent me to the apothecary for Lydia Pinkham's Vegetable Compound, Dr. Jayne's Carminative, Dover's Powder, and Baker's Stomach Bitters and tested them all out on Mr. Edwin to see if their varying compounds and the different amounts of alcohol and opium in them would help him. She had her own recipes, too, and when she'd finished in the kitchen, bitter odors lingered behind her of paregoric, vinegar, myrrh, and other less definable substances.

Isabelle had me keep a pot of blackberry tea always hot for Mr. Edwin because, on top of everything else, he was suffering from sore gums. While we were in Ocean Grove, Mr. Edwin, as a surprise for Isabelle, had gone to a dentist, had all his blackened teeth removed and been fitted with plates. The plates irritated him, however, and his sudden illness had kept him from returning to the dentist, which he was reluctant to do in any case. His gums remained tender even after he'd had the plates out for several days, drunk quarts of tea, taken calomel, and applied ginger poultices.

After a monotonous week of nursing that must have felt more prolonged to Mr. Edwin than it did to Isabelle and me, I came into the parlor one morning to find him sitting up in bed with tears streaming down his face. Isabelle was at the end of the bed massaging his feet and hushing him and crooning at him as one does with a fussy baby. She told me to set down the Dr. Kellogg's Granola I'd brought, and from the briskness of her tone, I understood that I was to leave the room at once.

I had no desire to linger anyway, as seeing Mr. Edwin in such a state was disconcerting and embarrassing. I believe men have as much right to tears as women, but they seldom exercise it, so to see a man cry is always alarming. Mr. Edwin had never been a robust man, but he had his own brand of force and presence, and the surrender to despair that I had just witnessed filled me with a strange dread.

As I was sliding shut the parlor doors, the bell from the street rang. I hurried downstairs to answer it, wondering who it could be so early in the day. I expected Reverend Dale or Mr. Cox, either of whom might stop to inquire about Mr. Edwin's health, so I was quite taken aback to open the door on Mr. Sylvester Martin. The fierce scowl on the old man's face did nothing to restore my poise.

"Sir," I said stupidly.

"Is my son at home?" he asked, peering around me up the stairs.

"Yes, but—"

"Well, let me by, girl," he growled.

I turned quickly and went upstairs. He followed close on my heels and stayed tightly behind me right up to the parlor doors. Apparently he wasn't going to let me give Isabelle even a moment's warning. I opened the doors, and we entered together like two maple leaves borne on a gust of wind.

I was relieved to see Mr. Edwin had composed himself and was now calmly eating his cereal. Isabelle was not in the room. Perhaps, having heard the doorbell, she'd gone to arrange her hair or wash her face. She'd looked as if she'd spent the night in the parlor.

"Edwin," Mr. Martin thundered, sounding joyful, angry, and worried all at once.

Mr. Edwin set his bowl on a small table next to his bed and stared at his father. He looked for a moment as if he might begin to cry again, but then he managed a wan smile. The old man went to the bed and laid a large hand on his son's bony shoulder.

"I went to your shop on Race Street," he said. "They told me you hadn't been by all week. I checked at the Spruce Street shop, too. Same story."

Mr. Edwin nodded and spread his hands helplessly.

"What's she done to you, my boy?" The old man bent over his son and spoke in a sorrowful whisper.

"Good morning, *Père*," came Isabelle's voice from behind me. "Have you had your breakfast yet? Just tell Willer what you'd like."

Mr. Martin looked up guiltily, clearly wondering if Isabelle had heard his last remark. But his face quickly darkened.

"I demand to know what's happening here," he said.

Isabelle walked over to the bed and stood on the side opposite Mr. Martin. I saw she had, indeed, tidied her hair and put on a fresh blouse. The blouse was sheer, pale yellow nainsook, very girlish with its puffed sleeves and scooped neck, and it showed off Isabelle's rounded arms and the smooth skin over her collarbone. She would not have worn it out on the street, nor even at home if she were expecting formal calls. It was well suited to the chores of a sickroom, however, as it gave her arms free movement.

"Edwin is ill, as you see," Isabelle said.

"And why wasn't I informed?"

"We were waiting until we could report a change for the better," Isabelle replied evenly.

Mr. Edwin was watching the conversation as if he were at a tennis match.

"I'm his father. I want to know his condition at all times.

It's a parent's natural feeling that perhaps escapes your under-standing."

Isabelle took hold of one of Mr. Edwin's hands in both of hers, but kept her gaze on his father.

"I am his wife. It's my duty to safeguard his condition by keeping all disturbing influences away from him."

"Isabelle has been the best of nurses, Father," Mr. Edwin said.

Mr. Martin sat down heavily in a chair near the bed.

"What does the doctor say?" he asked quietly.

"I've had no doctor," Mr. Edwin answered.

"What?" Mr. Martin roared, his outrage revived.

"Edwin doesn't trust doctors. You know that, *Père.*"

"I'll have a doctor in no matter what either of you say. It's obvious whatever Frenchy hocus-pocus has been going on here has done no good at all."

"Nan," Isabelle said, "bring my father-in-law some juice and coffee; then vegetable hash on toast and cottage cheese. Bacon, too."

"I'll have a doctor here this very afternoon," the old man repeated as I left the room.

MR. MARTIN kept his word. Isabelle and Mr. Edwin must have made an agreement with him because there was no trouble from either of them when the doctor and Mr. Martin arrived at about three o'clock. Isabelle had had a nap by then and had changed into a skirt of cream-colored bunting trimmed with three deep ruffles and a polonaise overdress of the same fabric. The sleeves of the polonaise ended demurely below the elbow and were finished with standing and falling frills of lace. The rectangular Pompadour neckline was also trimmed with a ruche of lace. She looked remarkably com-posed and quite lovely.

I brought the gentlemen into the parlor, where Isabelle was reading aloud to Mr. Edwin from the best-selling novel

The Prince of the House of David. She finished her sentence before closing the book, and when she did look up, I saw the doctor straighten his posture and dart one hand up to adjust his neckwear, which was a jauntily checked Glendale tie. He was a man of about the same age as Mr. Edwin's father, but he obviously still appreciated an attractive woman. The doctor had the misfortune of tripping slightly over the edge of a rug when he stepped forward to take Isabelle's outstretched hand, but she pretended not to notice. I went to the kitchen to set out the tea sandwiches and petits fours Isabelle had ordered for the men's visit.

I served the refreshments about twenty minutes later in the dining room. Mr. Edwin was not there, but he was the only topic of conversation.

"Your husband presents a somewhat bewildering array of symptoms, Mrs. Martin," the doctor said, opening a small notebook of well-worn calf leather and running his finger down a list scribbled in pencil. "I gather he often has physical complaints but usually not this serious."

"That's right, Dr. Cornelius."

"What about electricity, Doctor?" asked Mr. Martin. "I've heard electrical treatment can cure any number of ailments. My neighbor, Mrs. Rudley, bought an electric flesh brush from a catalog, and she swears it cured her rheumatism and didn't even hurt."

"It's true electricity is the germ of all life," Dr. Cornelius said patiently. "I myself have in my office four types of galvanic batteries and forty-four electrodes for different parts of the body: the nose, the larynx, the rectum, the ovaries, and so on."

Mr. Martin seemed flustered by the doctor's frankness. He swallowed two petits fours in one gulp and handed me his plate to be refilled.

"I wouldn't go into such details," the doctor said, noticing the old man's discomfort, "except that Mrs. Martin seems so well informed medically."

"Thank you, Doctor," Isabelle said.

"In fact," the doctor continued, bending over to retrieve something from the black valise at his feet, "I have here a version of Rockwell and Beard's *Practical Treatise on the Medical and Surgical Uses of Electricity, Including Localized and General Electricalization,* which may interest you, Mrs. Martin. Abridged, of course, and couched in popular terminology."

He laid a thick pamphlet on the table. Below the lengthy title on the pamphlet's yellow cover appeared a sort of coat of arms showing a powerful fist grasping a bunch of jagged lightning bolts. The fist's muscular wrist thrust upward out of an entwining ribbon lettered with *VENI, VIDI, VICI.*

"Well, are you going to use electricity or not?" Mr. Martin pursued.

"Electricity is very effective in treating neurasthenia, and your son does have some signs of that: dyspepsia, sensitivity to weather changes, an occupation requiring a lot of mental activity, headaches, insomnia, and by his own admission, feelings of hopelessness. But . . ."

"But? But?" Mr. Martin fumed. "Don't tell me what he *hasn't* got, man."

"He also shows some signs of hysteria," Dr. Cornelius went on, unperturbed, "chiefly—if you'll excuse a hasty judgment—suffering caused by imaginary pains and ills."

"Imaginary? My son wouldn't stay away from his business this long for imaginary pains."

"Edwin does dwell on small ailments overmuch sometimes, *Père,*" Isabelle reminded him gently. "And he worries about threats to his health and sometimes even thinks he is dying when it is only a bad case of gas."

Mr. Martin frowned. The consultation was clearly not going the way he had expected.

"Even so, I doubt your husband is an hysteric," said Dr. Cornelius. "Hysteria is largely a female disease." The doctor shook his head in woeful contemplation. "Too many women these days are indolent and overindulge themselves in the excitements of reading, social gatherings, and religious enthusiasms," he said. "Even ladies fashions—I refer, of course, to the corset, which squeezes blood to the head, putting pressure on the nervous system and thus the personality, and to high-heeled shoes, which compress and deform even the daintiest feet and make the exercise of walking so unnatural and uncomfortable that—"

"What do you propose for my son?" Mr. Martin said, trying to steer the doctor to some solid conclusion.

"Two things. First, he must go to a dentist."

"He refuses," Isabelle interjected. "He fears the pain."

"Not to the same one who made his plates. That incompetent merely sawed off his teeth at the jawline and left the roots to rot. He needs full extractions."

"I'll convince him," Mr. Martin said. "What's the other thing?"

Dr. Cornelius looked at me.

"I hesitate to say . . ."

"You can speak in front of Nan," Isabelle said. "She helps me care for Edwin, sees to his food. It will be useful for her to know his complete condition."

The doctor looked unconvinced, but as the old man made no objection, he shrugged acquiescence and placed his hands palms down on the table, as if at a seance.

"I fear Mr. Edwin Martin has been poisoned," he said.

Old Mr. Martin jumped up.

"I knew it!" he cried, glaring at Isabelle, whose face had flushed very pink.

Dr. Cornelius raised a cautioning hand.

"I must ask you both a very personal question—one you may not be able to answer, but one I hope you *will* answer if you can. I would have asked the patient himself, but he seems in too morbid a state of mind, and I didn't want to upset him."

We all stared at the doctor.

"You're sure you won't excuse your maid, Mrs. Martin?"

"No, no," Isabelle replied irritably.

Dr. Cornelius took a celluloid mercantile pencil from his

pocket and screwed it open. He held it poised over his little notebook.

"What we may be seeing in this patient is mercury poisoning from overuse of a medication for venereal disease. Do either of you have reason to believe Edwin Martin would be taking such a medication?"

"Absolutely not," Mr. Martin said immediately. "Come with me and ask him yourself. He's not so weak he can't defend his good name."

Mr. Martin strode around the table and looked like he would lift the doctor out of his chair and carry him bodily into the parlor.

"I'm sure my father-in-law is right, Doctor," Isabelle said coldly. "Could Edwin be sensitive, perhaps, to the calomel I've been giving him for his sore gums?"

"It is a mercury derivative, and overuse in children can cause pink disease, but the doses you've administered are slight. It's possible our patient has a special sensitivity, as you suggest, though it will be the first case I've encountered in an adult."

"There, the woman's got more sense than you, Cornelius."

The doctor ignored Mr. Martin's jibe and continued to study his notes.

"If the dentist finds necrosis in the jaw, that could account for the general illness. Partially, at least."

"Now you're being reasonable," Mr. Martin said. "Come on, then, and talk to Edwin."

"You still want me to confront him?"

"I want you to hear a firm denial straight from his lips," Mr. Martin nodded.

"So do I," added Isabelle. "Don't feel you must spare his feelings of delicacy any more than you did mine."

Mr. Martin glanced at her with approval. For once, they were allies.

When the two men left the room, I was surprised to see Isabelle lean her head in her arms on the table and begin to cry. Not that I didn't think it wasn't warranted. It had been a long week and a hard day, and she had moved through it all, until that very moment, with the stoicism of a soldier. I stepped forward and rested my arm across her shoulders. She sat up and pressed the side of her face against my belly, wrapping her arms around my waist.

"Oh, Nan," she said. "Was it only two weeks ago we were so happy at the seashore? Did it really happen? Can you even remember it?"

I could remember. It had happened. But for Isabelle, it might have been better if it hadn't.

MR. MARTIN bullied Mr. Edwin into going to a new dentist the next day. He had eighteen extractions done and proudly declared he had not even felt nervous because Dr. Cornelius had used hypnosis to calm him that morning.

"I sat back, and the teeth flew out," Mr. Edwin beamed.

The hypnosis had been Isabelle's suggestion; she'd been reading about mesmerism, and she told Dr. Cornelius she thought Mr. Edwin would be a good subject. The doctor, who considered himself a man of forward-looking science, was happy to try it. I thought that if hypnosis worked at all, it would certainly work on Mr. Edwin, who liked to believe in unusual remedies.

Within two days of the extractions, Mr. Edwin was remarkably improved overall. Isabelle had eliminated most of her potions, giving him only motherwort tea for sleep and cajeput tree oil on cotton wool for his gums. On the third day, with Dr. Cornelius's approval, Mr. Edwin took a half day out making the rounds of his shops with his father, and on the fourth day, I began my holiday.

I left the Martins' early in order to get a full day in the country. I sat with Sippy a while in the shade of the front yard, helped Elsinore with her housework, and then took a long walk with her across the woods and meadow behind our house and then along the edges of neighbors' fields of tall rustling corn and buckwheat and spreading squash vines. Elsinore had her butterfly net and a jar; we came home with two butterflies, a black-and-orange viceroy and a fritillary spangled with silver spots, and a huge tile-horned prionus beetle with long, red-brown antennae of sharp, overlapping plates.

It was an afternoon of simple amusements. The world around us seemed bursting with ripe life, the humid air hung with smells of turned earth, green plants, and distant cows. Living in the city, I had nearly forgotten how Nature fleshes forth in late summer.

My father came in at supper. He smelled of sweat and ale. He was glad to see me, though he didn't smile or have much to say. He is a man who needs to be read, and I had learned long ago how to do so. He poured water into my glass before pouring his own. He lingered at the table after Elsinore had taken his plate away, and asked a few questions about Ocean Grove. By these things, I knew he was pleased to have me there and perhaps even missed me.

Mattie and Lorenzo came the next day, and we took another long walk. Paolo had been out late the night before and wanted to stay home and rest.

"There's a dance hall he likes," Mattie said. "A respectable place," she added quickly. "He took me there once."

"What's it like?" Elsinore asked.

"A big, noisy place. Groups of girls come in together and workingmen, too, and dance and talk together."

"On their own?" Elsinore said.

"Oh, yes."

"Girls aren't brought up like they used to be," Lorenzo put in.

"It's not the girls, nor their upbringing, Lorenzo; it's the times," said Mattie. "Think of that boardinghouse on our street, how many single women live there crowded up, away from their families, come to Philadelphia to be typists and shopgirls and factory hands. They just want something different from work sometimes, something gay and pretty."

"Look, a Baltimore," Elsinore cried, running to a small spring in the wood we were passing through.

She squatted over a patch of mud where a checkered butterfly rested. I don't know how she had picked out its brown, yellow, orange, and black wings from among the shadows and old leaves on the mud.

"There's a hotel near that dance hall with rooms had by the day," Lorenzo said, now that we were out of Elsinore's hearing.

"How do you know that?" Mattie demanded.

"I saw a sign."

"Well, most of the girls in the dance hall looked just like me or Hanna. Not like the streetwalkers that hang about the men's saloons."

"No, they're not streetwalkers," Lorenzo admitted. "But some of them do lose themselves sometimes."

"Come see before it's gone," Elsinore called, and Lorenzo went over to admire her find.

"I'm sure he must be right," Mattie said, sighing. "There's girls at the factory who talk about flirting, about what they'll let a man do and what they won't. Some are only a few years older than Elsinore."

"I find myself still thinking of Elsinore as a child," I said.

"That's because she still lives like one," Mattie said. "But by her next birthday, she'll be old enough to keep company."

Elsinore and Lorenzo had left the spring and were coming toward us. She threw back her head and laughed at something he'd said, and he grinned at her delight. Before the two reached us, Mattie took my arm and steered me ahead on the path.

"Have you given it any thought, Hanna?"

"What?"

"Keeping company yourself. You'll soon be on the shady side of thirty."

I quickened our pace. I didn't want Lorenzo and Elsinore to overhear us.

"I have thought of love, Mattie," I confessed. "But not of marriage. It seems a tangled thing."

"Oh," she said, drawing the syllable out slowly, "it's not so difficult really, if you don't think about it too much."

"Thinking is my secret vice." I smiled.

"Perhaps you should come to the dance hall next time Paolo takes me. Don't let Lorenzo put you off."

Mattie stooped to pick a lily of the valley growing low on the forest floor. When she spoke again, she did not look at me, but at the flower, seeming to address it.

"Though I don't know when I might be going to the dance hall again, now that I must watch my health more."

"What's wrong, Mattie?" I said, thinking of the newspaper editorials I'd seen about factory workers with consumption from poor ventilation or general ill health from too brief meal breaks, the terrible and constant noise of machinery, and the long, long hours.

Mattie threw down her flower and took my hands in hers.

"Hanna, don't sound so grim. It's a baby. I'll be having a baby in the spring."

She was so obviously pleased by this announcement, despite her shyness in making it, that I gave her a hearty hug of congratulations.

Lorenzo and Elsinore had come to a halt some distance behind us. We turned and saw Elsinore pointing at a tree trunk, her nose almost against the bark. Presumably she'd been intrigued by another insect. Lorenzo was looking not at the spot where Elsinore pointed, but at Elsinore herself, at the side of her round-cheeked face. She stepped sideways suddenly and collided with him; he grasped her arm to steady her. She nodded thanks at him, then ducked away.

"Hanna," she shouted, and ran up to me. "It's a walking stick, back there on that locust tree. That's why we stopped."

She slipped her arm about my waist and we walked on, Mattie on my other side, and Lorenzo next to her.

"We could go to Wissahickon Creek in town, Miss Willer, and see what creatures we can harvest there for your sister," Lorenzo said. "I know I can get some big cockroaches down at the docks."

"No need to go that far." Mattie laughed.

We came out of the woods and followed a dirt road uphill a while, crossing an apple orchard to get back home. Lorenzo went off with my father to play horseshoes while Elsinore and I prepared supper. Sippy and Mattie gave us some practical help, but mostly they made the work light with their conversation, Mattie sharing amusing and scandalous gossip about the people in her factory, and Sippy giving me news of deaths, births, marriages, and fights in my old neighborhood. And, of course, Sippy had much to say about how Mattie should take care of herself now and later.

At the table, it was the men who held forth. Lorenzo told us of his hopes for getting a job at Dentzel's making carousel animals. He said it was mostly Germans, but a man he knew who worked there had promised to bring him in to meet a supervisor.

"Lorenzo's forever drawing horses and tigers and camels, all with faces of strange little men peeking out from under the fancy saddles," Mattie said.

"Gargoyles," Lorenzo explained. "It's my mark. A man likes to distinguish himself from the rest."

"He carves, too," Mattie said. "Any block of wood he can get his hands on."

"My uncle was a cabinetmaker. He taught me. I've got a few of his chisels and planes."

"There's some log ends out back you're welcome to," my father offered.

Lorenzo couldn't have grinned more happily or thanked my father more heartily if he'd been given bars of gold.

My father is easily embarrassed by any display of emotion. Lorenzo, seeming to sense this, deftly turned the talk to the afternoon's horseshoe pitching. Bringing an outsider's eye to the game and the players, Lorenzo described the men and their various reactions to winning and losing with great flourish.

My father's bent for storytelling was thereby encouraged, and he set off on a string of entertaining tales. He ranged all over, telling with equal color about a faithful old horse he'd had long ago who loved fried doughnuts and about seeing Buffalo Bill Cody's Wild West Show last year, where Annie Oakley shot out candle flames while racing past standing on her horse. By the time the evening sun was angling bars of deep yellow light into the room and we were finishing the plum cake dessert, he had drifted into a portrait of his younger brother, killed at Gettysburg.

"Bill wasn't a well liked boy outside the family," he said. "Bit of a bully, you know. Worst kind, too. He'd not be content just to best someone in a fight, he'd make 'em plead and cry before he'd stop. Once, he made young Silas Dorr down the way thank him for lifting his foot off his neck and letting him get his face up out of the mud."

"He wasn't so bad later," Sippy put in.

"No," my father said. "But it was more because folks took care not to cross him than that he mended his ways. Billy Goat they called him behind his back, because he got mean for no reason and because you didn't dare turn your back on him or even let him catch you in the corner of his eye."

"Did he know they called him that?" Elsinore asked.

We'd heard of our uncle Bill before, but not this detail. It was typical of my father's stories that each telling added a little more flesh, like a hog slowly fattening for Christmas ham.

"Sure he did," my father answered. "He liked it."

He paused to eat the last few mouthfuls of plum cake on his plate. Lorenzo and Mattie probably thought he was done telling about his brother, but the rest of us knew he was only trolling his mind for an appropriate ending. Despite the random, homespun character of my father's narratives, he always managed to pull some bit of philosophy out of them. I don't believe he ever set out to teach a moral or make a point with a story—he was too enamoured of pure tale spinning—it's just that he was a natural fable maker. I think he surprised even himself sometimes by where a story had led him. It is the one way in which he and I are alike—if such a trait can be inherited—for I, too, can rarely let events rest as naked facts, but must clothe them with meaning.

"The funny thing is," my father began again. "Bill's remembered around here not for a bully, but as a hero. And it's only because he died in the right place for it."

"But if he was as mean as you say, how could people forget that?" Mattie said.

My father shrugged.

"People need heroes wherever they can get them, I guess," he said. "Helps them understand big things better. There was forty-eight thousand boys killed or wounded at Gettysburg, counting both sides. Having one of our own among them brought the slaughter home, made it real; and if he wasn't a hero, well, then, what was it all for, anyway?"

I went to my room that night filled with stories and awed at how every one, humorous or tragic, had its own remarkable features and how, taken together, they bore witness to the tenacious vitality of people and the complexities and surprises in even the most ordinary-looking lives.

"What is it you want for yourself?" I asked Elsinore as we sat on our bed before putting out the lamps.

I was brushing and plaiting her hair. It was pale and fine, like cornsilk, unlike mine, which is dark and thick, with stubborn waves.

"Some surah for a dress," Elsinore answered promptly. "There was some listed in the new Bloomingdale's catalog."

"That's a fancy fabric."

"It's only a silk," she complained, adding amiably, "All right, then, some cotton percale or Swiss muslin."

I stored away her wish. Isabelle frequented a draper who sometimes gave her a special price because she was a regular customer. Perhaps he'd have a surah remnant I could afford, or some China silk. I glanced down Elsinore's back to estimate the yardage she'd need for a dress. Even in her nightgown, her body's promise was evident. She'd have my mother's full-hipped figure, I could see already.

I thought of the girls Mattie and Lorenzo had talked about, girls who had been like Elsinore once and who had taken on city living without the guidance of husbands or parents. I myself had done it, though domestic work provided more shelter than other jobs in some ways. In other ways—chiefly when girls faced the insistence of seductive masters—it was more dangerous, but I had not had that problem.

Many said cities were unhealthy and immoral, but even critics saw them as necessary to the economic growth of the nation. That was why the refuge of the home that Reverend Dale had preached about was so important. I was now accustomed to Philadelphia's noise and dirt and smells, its crowded streets and squares, its stores and street vendors and waifs, and I traveled its main thoroughfares confidently—though I moved through only certain parts of town and rarely went out at night. But I couldn't picture Elsinore in the city. It was not that I thought of my little sister as less adaptable than I, only that in my imagination she was always protected in the country with Father and Sippy. Though it was never a precise thought, having Elsinore in the back of my mind in that green, quiet place kept the ugly scenes I sometimes encountered in the city from touching me too sharply.

"I didn't mean what *thing* did you want," I continued with Elsinore. "What do you want to do?"

"When?"

"When you're more grown and through with the school here. It will be sooner than you think."

I meant to start more of a rote game than a true conversation with Elsinore about her future, as if I were beginning the once-upon-a-time of a favorite fairytale. I expected her to pick up the next part, then I would take the following part, and so on together to the mutually known end.

"I suppose I shall meet someone and marry and have children," she said.

"Later, of course."

She lifted her shoulders in a shrug.

"Until then, I shall stay here and keep house for Sippy and Father and make my collection better and better and take walks like we did today. . . ."

It was not the reply I was looking for. She had trailed off, not turning to face me, though I'd finished with her hair.

"But Elsinore, what about college?"

She shifted around and looked at me. Her face was more serious than I'd ever seen it.

"I know it's what you want," she said.

"Yes. Because I want a good life for you, one where you can use your mind."

"No, Hanna, it's what you want for *you.*"

I didn't know what to say. At first, I was angry and thought Elsinore ungrateful and frivolous. But I knew in my heart she was neither of these, so I swallowed my anger and hurt. Then, under those feelings, I became aware of a tiny bead of awful recognition. Did Elsinore know me better than I knew myself?

"But your insects. . . ." I mumbled.

"I'll still collect them and draw them and study about them," Elsinore said eagerly, laying her hand on my knee.

"I thought you wanted this, too, Elsinore. . . . When you answered my letters, you—"

"I *do* want it, in a way. But not enough, you see. You yourself said it would be a great fight for me to find a college and get in and stay in. I don't want it enough to fight, Hanna, and you can't make the fight *for* me. It wouldn't be a happy footing for either of us if you did."

When had my little sister grown so wise? She had always

been a sober, watchful child. Perhaps that came from losing her mother young. Of course, it was her ability to notice and conjecture and classify that had made me think she ought to carry her education as far as possible. I had not been prepared for her to turn her skills of observation from insects to human beings.

NINETEEN

EVERY MORNING after breakfast, before going out to his shops, Mr. Edwin spent an hour on what he called "expansionist thinking." He used an alcove off the parlor rather than his downstairs office for this activity because he said better ideas came to him there.

The alcove was furnished more simply than the rest of the house, with a mahogany desk of clean lines, a wide leather Eastlake chair, and a small fawn-colored rug. A dark-stained wood easel near the wall held a framed lithograph of Independence Hall. The single window was covered by a plain white holland shade whose bottom edge Isabelle had stenciled with a delicate design of acorns and oak leaves. Mr. Edwin liked calling this nook his "brown study," a remark whose clever wit Isabelle invariably smiled at, no matter how often she heard it.

Usually Mr. Edwin left pulled aside the velvet portiere that curtained the alcove off from the parlor. Often, as I tidied the parlor, I'd see him leaning back in his leather chair and staring up at the embossed tin ceiling. Other times he was bent over his desk sketching out designs for window displays and advertising flyers or making ruled diagrams for rearranging the goods in his shops. When the morning mail arrived early enough, I brought it to him in the alcove. I had done this one morning shortly after my holiday and then proceeded to dust the parlor, a quiet activity that would not disturb Mr. Edwin. Isabelle came in to water the houseplants, and Mr. Edwin waved an envelope at her.

"Isabelle, here's a letter from George. Postmarked Philadelphia. I didn't know he was back from Ocean Grove."

Isabelle put down her watering can and went to him with her arm outstretched.

"Let me see," she said in a chirpy voice.

"But my dear, it isn't addressed to you."

Isabelle stopped, but she did not return to her watering.

"He came by while you were ill," she said.

"Perhaps he's written to inquire after my health, then," said Mr. Edwin, slicing open the letter.

Isabelle watched him intently as he read, with the same expression of fierce concentration she'd worn when she'd watched his labored breathing in sleep during his illness, as if she were waiting for something she both expected and feared.

"Well, well," Mr. Edwin said, folding the letter and putting it in his jacket pocket. "I knew our friend was a serious young man, but the extent of his earnestness impresses me. I shall answer him today by messenger and suggest he stop by this evening for a talk. Would that suit you, my dear?"

"Yes, if you wish it. What did he say?"

"As I mentioned, Isabelle, the letter was not addressed to you."

Mr. Edwin turned back to the papers on his desk, and after she had studied him for a few moments, during which time he never looked up, Isabelle left the room. I finished watering the plants for her.

Isabelle had planned that we would cut and hem new drapes for the dining room, but she decided instead to go buy a hat, leaving me on my own for a good part of that day. I was surprised at the change, since the drapes were a project Isabelle had talked about before I took my three days away. She had even warned Mr. Edwin the night before that the dining room would be in an uproar all day, and he'd said he'd take dinner out with his father.

There was, as always, a bag of mending needing attention, so I was kept busy in Isabelle's absence, though I did take time to read about the unveiling of the Statue of Liberty. The newspapers had reprinted every speech and song from the dedication ceremonies, which included President Cleveland, a million spectators, and a parade of twenty thousand. The only thing marring the grand spirit of the day, the papers said, was a boatload of suffragists who circled the great statue's island and shouted at the six hundred dignitaries gathered there because only two were women.

"Do you like it?" Isabelle asked me, modeling her purchase late that afternoon. It was a toque of purple satin decorated with two pairs of white dove's wings.

"I like the color," I said.

Isabelle took it off and looked at it thoughtfully, then replaced it in the hatbox.

"I walked and walked today, Nan."

"To show off your hat?"

"No, just to walk. In truth, it's why I went out. The hat was only an excuse. I couldn't be still today, nor stay home and make drapes."

I picked up the hatbox to take to the wardrobe in the bedroom.

"You needn't make excuses to me, Isabelle."

"But if Edwin had come home, I wouldn't want you to have to lie, and he'd never understand my needing to walk, to keep moving until all I could think of were my tired legs and feet."

I nodded at her. My work often sent me out on errands, but there were days on end that Isabelle didn't leave the apartment, and though it was spacious and comfortable, it must seem to her almost a cage at times.

"It was the letter this morning set me walking. You know that, don't you, Nan?"

"I hadn't thought of it," I said honestly. "You think Reverend Dale's done as he said he would in Ocean Grove?"

"Undoubtedly. It was his intent when he came by that once. But, of course, Edwin was too ill for visitors."

"Did you expect him to give up the idea?"

"The passing of a little time can dull a notion formed in an impetuous moment," Isabelle said.

"Not always," I pointed out.

"No, not always," she agreed.

Isabelle walked to the windows, then to the bookcase, then to her writing desk and back to me, standing near the sofa. At each place, she lightly touched something: the leaf of an African violet, a book spine, the inkwell. She reminded me of one of Elsinore's butterflies, alighting briefly, then fluttering on, marking an irregular, nervous path through the heavy summer air.

"He *gave* me to him," she said emphatically, looking at me defiantly, as if I had contradicted her.

"What do you mean, Isabelle?"

"Once, when Edwin was finding fault with me over having forgotten to order in his favorite marmalade, George said if I ever came under his care, he would have to teach me differently. Edwin said I'd do well to be a minister's wife and he'd no doubt that George would take good care of me."

It sounded to me like conversational froth, even though Isabelle was relating it with overwrought seriousness.

"But, Isabelle," I said, "couldn't they have been joking? Weren't they smiling and teasing?"

"It was no joke to me."

THE MOOD in the Martins' parlor that evening was subdued. Isabelle wore a brown-and-black plaid dress of simple lines with no train, almost as if she were in mourning. Of course, it did flatter her dark coloring, and the absence of gathers, ruffles, and pleats eliminated distractions from her figure. Reverend Dale, too, looked funereal, in face if not in attire. He was a bit of a dandy and wore that night a pearl gray lounge suit, a style newly popular among educated young men, with a short, high-buttoned jacket, long narrow trousers, and a red tie. Mr. Edwin looked even more Reverend Dale's senior than he was, since he still wore the older style of a dark jacket hanging to the middle of his thighs, baggy trousers of a lighter color, and a high collar with a wide black cravat.

Coffee and brandy were already set up in the parlor, so I had no reason to be there after I let Reverend Dale in. I did see Mr. Edwin greet him warmly, however, and I was very curious about what the outcome of this meeting would be and how it would be arrived at.

Saturday was our baking day, so while the unknown business in the parlor progressed, I busied myself in the kitchen getting things ready for the next morning. I combined yeast, sugar, water, and flour to make the sponge for white bread and set it to rise overnight, and I cut up and stewed some rhubarb stalks with plenty of sugar for pies.

After a while, Isabelle poked her head in.

"Nan, we need you inside a moment."

She turned away, and I took off my apron and followed her. Halfway across the darkened dining room, she spun about and grasped both my hands in hers.

"He's commended his honesty," she whispered excitedly.

"Who?" I asked.

"Edwin," she replied. "Edwin said a man who dares to be frank to a husband about such feelings as George has confessed can be counted on to keep the tightest rein on them. Daylight kills the dankest mushroom, he said. Or something like that. . . ."

"Then Reverend Dale is still welcome?"

Isabelle nodded. I thought she should have been pleased by this turn of events, and perhaps she was, but her expression was serious and unsmiling.

"Of course, I must keep up my part," she said.

"Your part?"

"As a loving wife, Nan," she explained with some irritation.

She let go my hands but made no move to continue on to the parlor. The men must have been wondering at our delay, perhaps even bristling over it, but I knew neither of them would come seeking us.

"It *is* easier being a good wife with George around." She gave a short, strangled laugh. "You could say Edwin and I are both beneficiaries of George's friendship!"

Isabelle smoothed her skirt and the sides of her hair, as if she'd just come inside from a windy day, and turning resolutely, she made for the parlor once more.

Mr. Edwin gave a sharp look as we entered, but he made no other comment on our laggardness. Isabelle went to stand behind her husband's high-backed armchair, and I stopped beside the étagère. As the Martins' home museum, the étagère occupied prime position in the room, so by placing myself next to it, I faced both the Martins and Reverend Dale though they were on opposite sides.

"Really, Edwin, this isn't necessary," Reverend Dale said with a weak, nervous smile. He was sitting on the sofa, toward the front edge of the cushions.

"It will indulge me," Mr. Edwin replied.

The minister's hands made a small gesture of reluctant surrender.

From the corner of my eye, I could see most of the contents of the étagère. I knew them well from having dusted them. On the shelves sat a few elegantly bound volumes of poetry; vases of Murano glass and handpainted porcelain; a whimsical beehive-shaped bottle from the famous Whitney Glass Works in New Jersey; a jade figurine of a Chinese lady; a large piece of coral; and several small frames in which Isabelle had arranged dyed goose feathers and butterfly scales to look like wreaths of flowers. The human scene before me suddenly appeared as carefully composed as the display in the étagère, where each thing declared its own merits yet also gathered rank from the company of the other things set around it.

"Willer, I called you in here as a kind of witness," Mr. Edwin said. "You know, like at the signing of a will or wedding license or other important document."

"You want me to sign something, Mr. Edwin?"

"No, no, nothing so formal as that."

He reached up without turning around, and Isabelle put her hand in his. He slid his fingers to her wrist and held it, as if he were taking her pulse.

"I just wanted to repeat before an honest, impartial witness that Reverend Dale's tutelage of my wife has had nothing but good effects on her mind and spirits, which, in turn, has made our home life together more harmonious; and that I have confidence in their fellowship and look on Reverend Dale with the affection of a true friend."

Mr. Edwin, still holding Isabelle's wrist, tugged her forward and obliged her to perch on the arm of his chair, where he was able to put his arm around her waist and rest his hand on her hip.

"Yes, sir," I said, not knowing how to respond to the strange situation.

Mr. Edwin turned his gaze from me to Reverend Dale.

"Now, George, give Isabelle a kiss to let her know you don't feel as sour as you look."

"Edwin, I don't think—" Reverend Dale stammered.

"Come, come, even men of the cloth may give a chaste kiss now and then," Mr. Edwin chided.

Reverend Dale stood up slowly and crossed to Isabelle, who made no move to meet him. Indeed, Mr. Edwin's hand still cradled her hip, and she would have had to break his embrace to stand up.

"That's all, Willer," Mr. Edwin said, glancing at me again.

As I left the room, Reverend Dale was leaning forward toward Isabelle's upturned face, and Mr. Edwin was absorbed in watching him. I did not look back to see if the kiss fell on Isabelle's brow or on her lips.

The next day, both Mr. Edwin and Isabelle arose uncharacteristically late. After he'd left, she and I spent the day baking, speaking only of flour and butter, and of the turn in the weather toward fall.

☙ THREE WEEKS later, we were, indeed, well into autumn. The sun was still hot on my back when I swept the sidewalk, but the air was crisp, and you had only to step into the shadow of a building to feel a cape of coolness descend over your shoulders. The trees around Rittenhouse Square and along the Schuylkill were changing from green to red and yellow and orange, and when it rained, a dark chill that was never the companion of summer rains crept into the Martins' rooms, making the stove-warmed kitchen at once a cheerful refuge and a confinement.

It was raining the day I visited Mattie in her little apartment. I'd gotten a note from her saying she'd had to leave the factory after having fainted there twice. It was not in her nature to complain, but she sounded worried and lonely, so I wrote back that I'd come to see her on my next half day.

As I mounted the stairs to the fifth-floor flat, I thought about Mattie having to negotiate the steep climb later in her pregnancy or when she was carrying a heavy, wriggling baby. It is the small things, I think, like a long flight of stairs when you are tired, that accumulate imperceptibly to wear down optimism and patience.

A grimy skylight provided pale illumination for the hallways and stairwell. The skylight leaked, and a chipped graniteware bowl had been set on the bottom floor to catch the fat, grayish droplets that fell steadily from the roof to the street level. There is something mournful about the sound of dripping water. It speaks of forlorn places and irreducible ills.

Mattie's tall, narrow building was unusual for the area and, indeed, for the city; it had been a chair maker's establishment in colonial days. Most residential blocks in Philadelphia had three-story, single-family row houses end to end, though in working people's neighborhoods, half the families took in boarders.

Mattie must have been listening for footsteps on the stairs, for she opened her door before I had reached the final landing and came to meet me at the top step.

"Hanna." She smiled, embracing me with a sigh, as if she'd not believed I would come.

She was wearing a loose, high-waisted dress of flowered blue-and-orange calico. Though her pregnancy was not yet obvious, apparently her middle had thickened enough that she could no longer take close-fitting bodices. Mattie had very fair skin, but her complexion today was unnaturally pallid; even her numerous freckles seemed faded. She looked drawn and edgy, like a child who has had too much of the school-room and too little sun.

"No one troubled you on your way up?" she asked.

"No, why?"

"Oh, there's a man below who's often the worse for drink. When his wife locks him out, he'll accost anyone that passes, either to curse and push at them or to cry and moan about his 'hard life.' He prefers to stop women and children, anyone who looks like they'll not fight back. He's never bothered Paolo or Lorenzo."

"What do you do when you see him?"

"If I'm alone, I wait for someone to walk up with me, or I make a dash to rush by him. He'll usually stumble on the stairs if he tries to follow. There's others in the building will shout to his wife and make her take him inside, but I don't like to do that, as there's often terrible screaming and yelling afterwards, and sometimes, next day, she's got bruises and cuts on her. The children, too."

We had entered Mattie's front room. In the center of the

room, two overstuffed wine red chairs faced each other, and between them stood a table draped with a long, fringed cloth. There were, also, three mismatched plain wood chairs, two along the wall, and one near the pair of tall windows. At the foot of the window chair was a large willow basket. The only new pieces were the overstuffed chairs; Paolo was buying them by installments, Mattie said proudly, and they would own them completely in twenty-five months.

"He let me pick them out," she said. "And, of course, I added all the fabrics to the house, and the tissue flowers. Two men together don't think of things like that. Not even curtains!"

The walls were papered with a floral pattern, and along one wall were pictures, their gilt frames touching to form a kind of linked chain: illustrations cut from magazines and merchants' calendars; prints of country scenes, shepherds and water carriers and hay makers; and of saints, including a striking one of a beautiful young man, barely clothed and cruelly studded with arrows.

A thick curtain hung diagonally across one corner of the room. Mattie pulled it back to reveal a narrow iron bed, where Lorenzo slept. A tiny round table beside the bed held an oil lamp and a china dish with a few coins, some matches, and two or three drawing pencils on it. He had put a row of nails in the wall as clothes hooks; the Madonna and Child they had brought to the wedding hung from the nail nearest the bed. A sheaf of papers tied with string protruded from under the bed, more pencils beside it. I saw the space for only a few seconds before Mattie closed the curtain again—we were both feeling, I think, a bit like trespassers—but I came from it with a strongly physical sense of Lorenzo, as if I had crept up behind him while he was daydreaming and he had turned suddenly and touched me.

Mattie took me to the kitchen, which had a small stove, a chest-style icebox, a wooden table and chairs painted white, a wood sink, and curtained shelves for holding dishes and food-stuffs. My kitchen at the Martins' was luxurious by comparison, with its large upright icebox and Sterling range, two tables, easy chair, granite sink, glass-fronted cabinets, windows, and a separate pantry. But Mattie had two canaries in a cage, and their bright songs enlivened the place considerably. And it was, as well, her very own kitchen, however humble.

A madras curtain hung over the doorway to Mattie and Paolo's bedroom, which was simply furnished with another iron bed, larger than Lorenzo's, and a heavy old bureau.

Because of the grayness of the day, Mattie and I sat in the front room, where the most daylight was. I had brought her a peach pie—Mr. Edwin said it was likely to be the last fruit of the season the city shops would get—but she didn't want to cut into it until the men came home. Fortunately, I had also brought two cinnamon sugar turnovers I'd made from the pie-dough scraps, and we ate those with a pot of tea and felt we were treating ourselves well.

"How are you feeling?" I asked, when I saw, at last, she was not going to bring the subject up herself.

"Fine, mostly."

"But you fainted, you said."

"It was the heat. And not having a place to sit down," she said, as if protecting herself from an accusation.

"Don't they know you're pregnant?"

"No one can sit down, no matter what. The Knights of Labor got them to put in a few stools, but the foreman won't let us use them."

"So you only get a break when you eat?"

Mattie's face twisted into a wry smile.

"There's a men's dining room where they can get a hot dinner for ten cents, but we girls have to dine at our work stations on cold food brought from home. Standing up."

Pulling aside the gauzy muslin curtain at the window, Mattie gazed out at the sky.

"Rain's stopped, but it won't be clearing today," she said, sighing.

"Can't the Knights do more about your conditions?" I asked.

Mattie turned her attention from the cloudy sky to me. For a moment, bright fury flashed from her eyes, like a glint from a diamond ring in sunlight, then it was gone, and she looked only tired and unresisting.

"Hanna, the men earn nine to fifteen dollars a week, while for the same work and the same eighty-four hours, the women earn three dollars a week. If the Knights can't change that, what difference does a stool or two make?"

I reached over and patted her hand.

"It's better you're out of there," I said.

"I wanted to put aside some money for the baby," she said. "We can't manage to with only Paolo's pay."

"A baby needs a healthy mother more than anything else, Mattie."

She nodded, then pointed at the large basket near her feet.

"I'm doing piecework now," she said.

I leaned over and saw that the basket was filled with buttons, thousands of buttons.

"I sort and string them. Sometimes I sew them on shirts. There's a woman downstairs, Mrs. Litvak, who gives me the shirts she and her girls can't finish on time. They're paid by the day, but they have to do a certain number of shirts a day, and they're not paid until they're done, and it's always too many shirts, so each day's work laps over into the next. Before they started sharing with me, they worked six and seven days, sixteen to eighteen hours each day, and got only four days' pay."

"But if they give you work, don't they get less money?"

"Yes, a little, but Mrs. Litvak says at least now they don't have to wait for their pay so long, and her girls can take some hours to stretch and think and go outside. They'll do with less food, she says, but survival mustn't be the only thing in their lives."

"It's not right," I said. "People shouldn't have to choose like that."

"But they do, Hanna."

Mattie reached down and dug into the mound of buttons, sliding them through her fingers as if they were pirate doubloons. She lifted two fistfuls and let them drop back into the basket one by one, and I felt as if I were watching minutes dropping out of her days, days out of her years. I don't know what distressed me more—Mattie's plight or her acceptance of it.

"Mattie, I read that a woman who works in a collar factory in New York just started a Working Woman's Society."

"What for?"

"To back women strikers and to inform the public about women's working conditions. That could happen here, too, don't you think?"

Mattie stood up and rubbed the small of her back with the heels of her hands.

"Maybe things will be different someday," she said. "But Mrs. Litvak has to think about today, and about the nearest tomorrow. And so do I."

She turned and walked to the kitchen, and I felt I would be no friend if I kept on at her about the unfairness of her situation. She had a baby coming. She was not as well as she ought to be. She had to select where she put the strength left to her. I would not make her feel any of it was her own fault simply because she did not spend herself in protest.

"Would you like to stay to supper?" Mattie said, turning at the kitchen doorway.

Behind her, first one canary and then the other began to sing, their sweet trills tumbling over one another like clear waters over smooth stones. Mattie smiled, and the tiredness and pallor fell away from her face.

"You mustn't worry about me, Hanna," she said, still smiling. "I'm well loved here."

"And here," I said, touching my hand to my heart.

Her smile broadened. We stayed a moment looking at each other; I felt a surge of energy and connection, as when I was a girl running relay races in the schoolhouse yard, pounding ahead of my competitors, my arm straining forward to meet the outstretched arm of a waiting teammate who was calling me in with shouts and whistles. Then Mattie cocked her head toward the kitchen, as if to say, now I must get busy.

"I won't stay, thanks, anyway," I said. "I want to get home before dark."

"All right," she said. "But you'll come again?"

"Of course."

"You know, as hard as it was, I miss going to the factory. I miss the other girls."

While I was pinning on my hat, Mattie retrieved my umbrella from the kitchen sink, where she'd set it to drain when I came in.

"Will you drop off some shirts to Mrs. Litvak on your way out? She's on the third floor."

I assented, and Mattie gave me a large canvas bag firmly stuffed with shirts.

"Mattie, I wish you didn't have to do this work."

"It's not absolutely necessary, I suppose, and I expect after the baby comes, I'll be busy enough with him. But I do feel easier spending money when I've brought some of it in."

"Perhaps I can carry the Martins' mending over one day, and we can sew together."

"I'd like that."

We embraced and made our farewells. Mattie leaned over the landing and watched me descend until I reached the third floor and had to walk out of her sight to the back of the hallway to reach the door to the Litvak apartment.

My knock was answered by a little girl of about five.

"Is this Mrs. Litvak's home?" I asked.

The child nodded yes and opened the door more widely. She was thin and small and didn't look strong enough to manage the heavy canvas bag, so I took it into the front room my-self. There I found a large woman seated in a rocking chair, surrounded by four girls ranging in age from fifteen to seven. The girls were seated on straight-backed chairs or on the floor, and all were busy sewing buttons on shirts. Piles of shirts stood around the room like soft, misshapen pillars. The air smelled of clean cotton and bleach.

As soon as she closed the door behind me, the five-year-old took up a spot on the floor near the woman's chair and began pulling bastings out of shirt hems. It must have been a task very familiar to her, because she was able to do it without looking at her hands. Instead, she fixed her gaze on me, as if I were an exotic zoo animal. Indeed, all the girls were looking at me, though none of them had stopped working.

"I brought you these from Mattie Testa," I said to the woman.

"You can put them there," she said, indicating a large ham-per already quite full of shirts.

"Don't think us rude, miss," she added after I'd deposited my burden. "But if we stop, it's just that much more time put on to the end of the day, and my two girls here that are still at school have a hard time getting up in the morning and staying awake in the classroom. I'm Mrs. Litvak. I guess Mrs. Testa told you."

"Yes. I'm Hanna Willer, Mrs. Testa's friend."

"She's a nice young woman. Clean and self-respecting. Not like some sweaters."

"Yes."

The girls continued to watch me, and their hands contin-ued to keep busy. Their faces all had a pinched, spiritless qual-ity; even the younger ones showed none of the rosiness or buoyancy you'd expect to find in a child.

"Mrs. Litvak," I said, struck by a sudden idea. "Do you think you could send one or two of your girls upstairs to work with Mrs. Testa once in a while? I know she'd value their company, though she'd never presume to ask for it."

Mrs. Litvak frowned, considering the suggestion. The girls, I noticed, had now turned their attention fully to their mother. And still the hands kept on.

"We couldn't have any slackening of the work. We barely manage now. I'm a widow, you know."

"No, I didn't know. I'm sorry."

Mrs. Litvak raised her eyebrows and gave an almost imperceptible shrug of her fat shoulders.

"It's been over four years," she said quietly. "My Rachel don't even remember him."

She nodded her head toward the little girl who had answered the door.

"I'm Rachel," the child piped up, seemingly proud to have been singled out from her sisters, even for the dubious distinction of ignorance of her father.

"I'm sure Mrs. Testa wouldn't slow the girls down," I said.

"Well, we'll try it," Mrs. Litvak said. "I'll talk to Mrs. Testa next time I bring her shirts."

I thanked her and turned to go. I had to let myself out, as Rachel did not seem willing to abandon pulling out her bastings a second time, and no one else moved to get the door for me. Perhaps each one was hoping to earn a chance to work upstairs with Mattie, though it would be only a small relief. After I shut the door behind me, it occurred to me that not one person in that room had smiled the whole time I'd been there.

I was pondering this and other things as I walked slowly down the hall, and though I had heard heavy footsteps coming from below, I was still surprised when two men rushing up the stairs rounded the last step and converged upon me on the narrow landing. Recalling Mattie's story of her drunken neighbor, I knew a moment's fright, but in the next instant I recognized Paolo and Lorenzo, and there were loud and cheerful greetings from both of them.

When they discovered I was on my way out, Lorenzo insisted on walking me home. I said there was no need, but I didn't argue much. I was glad for an excuse to avoid my own thoughts, and I was, I admit, more than a little intrigued by the idea of a private time with Lorenzo, the first of our acquaintance.

Contrary to Mattie's prediction, the weather had cleared, and though there were still clouds, there were also sizable patches of blue-white sky visible. It promised to be a lovely sunset. Already the larger clouds were edged with a deep yellow, and the wispier ones were completely pinkish orange, like tufts of dyed alpaca. I felt a longing to be at my father's hilltop house in the country, where I'd need to take only a few steps outside the back door to have spread before me an unimpeded and spacious view of the setting sun, where I could spy out rabbits and bats and other creatures of early evening, and, later, shooting stars.

As we walked, Lorenzo and I talked about the people we had in common. He asked after my father and grandmother and Elsinore. He told me how pleased Paolo was about the baby, how he was taking on extra work shifts every few days to get ready for the new expenses.

"Are you in a hurry to get home?" he said after we'd exhausted these topics and walked a block in silence.

"Well, I'd thought to get back by dark."

"Will you let me treat you to supper? There's a place I know. Simple food. But good. Italian food."

We were waiting to cross a busy intersection. The noise of passing carriages and trolleys and the bustle and jarring of pedestrians around us allowed me to hesitate with my answer.

"Is a celebration," he said.

"For what?"

"Dentzel's took me on today. Apprentice carver—sanding, sharpening tools, and so on—but is a beginning. I'll make my own designs someday."

He was as flushed as a child before a birthday cake.

"If they're good enough," he added modestly.

"I'm sure they are," I said.

He grinned hugely. He needed that little to hold on to his confidence.

"Supper?"

"Yes," I decided. "Supper."

The restaurant consisted of three small, interconnected rooms below street level in what must have once been living quarters. The kitchen lay behind, close enough that we could hear the clang of pots and, occasionally, the raised voices of the two cooks demanding, Lorenzo translated, that cheese be grated or platters supplied or vegetables washed. Two dark-eyed girls about Elsinore's age hurried in and out of the dining rooms to take customers' orders, serve food, and clear tables. It was they, I presumed, who also answered the needs in the kitchen. The restaurant was hot, humid with aromas of tomato sauce and garlic and wine, and each time the swinging doors of the kitchen opened, a new wave of heat and smells emerged like a sigh from a summer oven.

The coarse cloth on our table was stained with splashes of red wine and drips of olive oil, but our serving girl swept it clean of crumbs and spread fresh, starched napkins before us as place mats. Lorenzo spoke to her in Italian. There was no menu; he didn't ask me what I wanted. The amount of discussion seemed lengthy for just the ordering of a meal, but I liked the sound of the language and the way they gestured at each other, as if they were sculpting the air. I noticed similar hand movements elaborating conversations at other tables.

Our meal was delicious and all new to me. We had gnocchi, which are small potato dumplings, in a creamy sauce Lorenzo said was made with four kinds of cheese; and chicory, a bitter green, cooked in oil and doused with lemon juice. Lorenzo also had baccala, salted dried cod, which he thought too strong for me. After a small taste, I agreed. There was panzanella, a salad of torn bread, tomatoes, and onion in red wine and olive oil; and glasses of Chianti; and for dessert, fresh pears with chocolate melted over them.

Lorenzo was well known there. Several men stopped at the

table to greet him. Each time, I felt myself surreptitiously appraised. But soon, the warmth of the room, the comfort of the food, and the softening effect of the wine eased me out of my awkwardness, and it seemed an eminently hospitable and pleasant place to be.

Lorenzo was full of his ambitions for designing and carving carousel animals. He wanted his creations to terrify and amaze, to be admired as art, not just used as seats on an amusement ride. He proposed to make animals with lifelike muscle tone, expressions, and poses; the fantastical would enter in the saddle trappings.

"Even if it's dragon or griffin, should look real," he said earnestly. "The smallest details must be watched."

He was full of questions about the carousel in Asbury Park, and I was sorry I hadn't been a better observer of it. But the scantness of my replies never deterred him from yet another question. He reminded me of Elsinore, in the tirelessness of his curiosity and the knowledge of animal anatomy he'd acquired simply by studying horses on the streets of New York and Philadelphia.

"You won't get impatient working on other men's carvings, following other men's plans?" I asked.

"Maybe." He laughed. "But there will be so much to learn, too. And I want to talk to the painters, see how they do—I have the idea to spread colored glaze over silver leaf so the animal gleams and looks made of moonstones."

"I wonder if your new employers know what they've taken on," I kidded him.

"Is a place where a man can grow," he responded seriously. "If the company wants to stay ahead, it will have to make better marvelous figures than anyone else, and when they start looking for that, there I am."

He spread his arms, as if offering himself, and he looked so handsome and energetic, so alive, I could not imagine anyone declining him.

It was dark when we left the restaurant. The streetlamps

had been lit; the wet sidewalks and cobblestones looked polished beneath their glow, and the shadows huddled outside their reach appeared impenetrable. I was glad to be walking with a man, so that I could feel relaxed enough to enjoy the whole pattern, both the circles of light and the niches of darkness. Rejecting my earlier wish for the country, I concluded that the city was a perfectly pretty place to be on a damp autumn evening. No doubt my new preference owed something to the lingering effects of the wine.

The nearest streetlamp to the Martins' was in front of the dry goods store next to Mr. Edwin's grocery. I stopped there to search in my reticule for my house key. Of course, Lorenzo stopped, too, and out of the corner of my eye, I saw him look up and down the street, perhaps charting which way he'd take home. Just as I found my key, Lorenzo put his hand on my arm and gently pulled me into the deep doorway of the dry goods store, which was shadowed by a large awning.

There was an indescribable second during which I was both mystified by his action and clearly aware of his intentions. Before I could sort out this contradiction, his arms were around me, his face close to mine. He paused then and looked into my eyes. I saw that he would desist if I gave a sign that was what I wished, but I found it was not what I wished. I could smell wine and chocolate on his breath, and on his hair a sweet oil, and I wanted to move into those smells, to taste them, to mix them with my own smells. Above all, I did not want him to release his hold on me, to leave me standing confused and chilled in the cold, puddled doorway. So I let him kiss me. After, he kept his arms loosely about me.

"A full pleasure. As I always thought," he whispered.

"You've thought before of doing this?"

"Of course." He smiled.

He brushed his fingertips over my mouth.

"And you?" he asked.

"No," I said, flustered. "I've thought . . . not exactly this."

"No matter," he said, lowering his mouth over mine again.

Again I let him. He lingered longer that time, and as naturally as water overflowing a tub, I began kissing him back. Together, we slowly made a third entity that was simply and intricately a kiss, an independent being with a brief but fervent life span. When we parted, my breathing had quickened and my head was dizzy. This was pleasure, to be sure, but it was a bit frightening as well.

Lorenzo took my hand and held it as we walked the short distance to my front door. He squeezed my fingers gently before he let go. I opened the lock but remained irresolutely on the sidewalk.

"You'll rest easy?" Lorenzo said.

"Yes," I replied, though I wasn't as sure as I hoped I sounded.

"*Buona sera,* then," he said, taking a few steps backward. "Good night. And *grazie.*"

"Good night," I said, and passed into the house.

I couldn't manage to tell him he was welcome. That automatic phrase had suddenly loomed so much larger than the innocent courtesy it usually was.

TWENTY

I DIDN'T see Lorenzo again for two weeks, but he was often in my thoughts. I never set out to think about him, nor about what had happened between us. My mind wandered with a will of its own, and once on that path, it would not be turned back.

Actually, there were two paths. Down one lay review. I would visit, in imagination, the feelings that had swept over me in the doorway of the dry goods store—a doorway I passed almost daily and that, every time, made my heart race— not so much to relive them, though that had its appeal, but to discover my known, ordinary self within them. I had been surprised by passion, and now I was surprised at my ability to recapture it in my mind so readily and so vividly in the absence of the man who had provoked it. Did this mean I was begun on my way to ruin?

The other path led to Mattie. Though she seemed anxious for me to have a suitor, that he might be her brother-in-law who lived with her seemed fraught with jeopardy. In any case, was Lorenzo my suitor? Did I want him to be? I suspected, even through the lingering glow of those moments in the doorway, that neither Lorenzo nor I yet meant anything so serious, and might not ever. Where, then, would that leave Mattie and me, and Mattie and Lorenzo, and Mattie and Paolo, and on and on? Already, a distance had crept between me and my friend. Fearful of meeting Lorenzo and appearing to pursue him, I had not gone to sew with Mattie, and in the brief note I sent her excusing myself, I said nothing of him, not knowing what he might have said of me.

Perhaps because I was, in my own life, trying to order affections and desires which were dividing over rough terrain like rivulets from a melting snowbank, I became aware, in those two weeks, that Isabelle, too, was struggling to locate a point of balance. On the surface, her dilemma as a favorite between two men had been neatly solved by Reverend Dale's honesty and Mr. Edwin's tolerance. She could enjoy the minister's company with an easy conscience—though, truthfully, she had never shown herself bothered by guilt—and she had a new reason to treasure her husband. In addition, the men's friendship had been preserved; it may even have been augmented by the recognition of their shared appreciation of Isabelle. The trio in the parlor no longer appeared destined to splinter and disintegrate.

But Isabelle was not happy. Reverend Dale still came by to tutor her, but they did not take outings, as they used to, despite the fact that we were having a glorious fall, with day after bright, crisp day. Their meetings were more sedate than in the past—perhaps Isabelle had reached a level in her studies that did not lend itself to gaiety. I didn't hear as much laughter coming from the parlor when they were at work there, nor as much piano playing.

When Reverend Dale left in the evenings, after supper, Isabelle let Mr. Edwin see him out, whereas before, she had always done it. I'd go into the parlor to clear away the men's brandy glasses and cigar stubs and find Isabelle sitting listlessly, wearing the bored, peevish expression of a person in a stalled train at the start of a very long journey. She'd stay there until Mr. Edwin called her to their room, then she'd rise slowly and leave. Often, she didn't even say good night to me. And the next morning, she'd come to breakfast looking tired and drawn, as if she'd not slept well.

Mr. Edwin, by contrast, was jollier than I'd ever seen him. He seemed to be always smiling, mostly at Isabelle, but also, sometimes, at me. Once, I saw him standing by a front window smiling down at the passing street scene.

He'd had new dental plates made by White's, the city's finest firm for such things, and the dentist Dr. Cornelius had recommended made sure they fit comfortably. That alone might have accounted for his more frequent smiles, and the smiles, in turn, for his appearing so jovial, but I sensed there was something more to it. Of course, his health was holding steady, and that must have pleased him. And his business was thriving, in large measure because he'd figured out a way to build refrigerated rooms to store fruit. I heard him tell Isabelle business was so brisk, he and Mr. Cox were considering calling Mr. Frederick back from Australia to manage one or two of the shops for them.

But despite all this, I conceived the odd notion that Mr. Edwin's happiness was somehow connected to Isabelle's unhappiness. Not that he was happy because she wasn't, but that both frames of mind sprang from the same source. The exact nature of that source was beyond my full grasp, as if, catching the movement of a shadow at the edge of my vision, I had turned to find no one in the room and nothing out of place. I don't believe Mr. Edwin was aware of Isabelle's discontent, her behavior in his presence was so unchanged. Even with me, she was largely her usual self, only a little less talkative.

She began writing letters again. In two weeks, she wrote three. I assumed Mr. Edwin's recent talk of his brother had inspired Isabelle to ease whatever crossness she'd felt toward the younger Mr. Martin and to revive their correspondence, but I couldn't know for certain because she carried the letters to the post office herself.

In this same period, Isabelle made several shopping expeditions, coming home with knickknacks or scarves or perfumed talc, always something unnecessary, and seemingly not especially coveted, since she put each purchase—after showing it to me and to Mr. Edwin—back in its wrapper or box and set it on the floor of the hall closet. Amazingly, Mr. Edwin, a careful man with money, bestowed on these trifles an indulgent smile, as if nothing Isabelle did could possibly perturb him.

She took me with her one time to Wanamaker's Grand Depot at Thirteenth and Market. I stood behind her as she sat on a stool in front of a glass case and tried on pair after pair of gloves, not buying any. Then she moved on to hair ornaments, looking at velvet bows, combs of jet and gold, pink satin roses, and ostrich feather tips. She also tried on capes of various fabrics and lengths, and a number of hats.

Though she did finally make a purchase—a tea apron of sheer white gossamer trimmed with lace, ribbons, and embroidered peacocks—Isabelle appeared more interested in the act of examining the goods than she did in the goods themselves. She took obvious enjoyment in seeing herself in the mirrors the salesgirls and salesmen provided; she studied her reflection as a hungry man might look through a bakery window at a cake mounded with whipped cream and sugared fruits. She also seemed to enjoy watching us watch her. It didn't matter whether I said an item was becoming to her or not; what mattered was that I was a witness to the display of her private pleasure in her appearance.

As we walked down our street after this shopping trip, we both noticed a man standing outside our door. We were still more than a block away, and it was early evening, with the sunlight nearly gone and the streetlamps not yet lit, so we could not make out his face, but we knew it was not Mr. Edwin because he was scheduled for a late meeting with Mr. Cox. As we got closer, we could tell by the man's dress that he was not a gentleman. I guessed he might be someone from one of Mr. Edwin's shops, sent with a message. In the next instant, I recognized Lorenzo, and my face flushed with heat. I felt bands of perspiration form beneath my collar and my bonnet.

"*Buona sera,*" he said, pulling off his cap as we came up.

He glanced at Isabelle, then turned to me as if she were not there.

"I'm waiting half an hour," he said. "I was leaving in a few minutes."

Isabelle was looking back and forth between me and Lorenzo with undisguised curiosity.

"This is Mr. Testa, my friend's brother-in-law," I said to her. "Mr. Testa, this is Mrs. Martin."

Isabelle smiled and inclined her head becomingly, but Lorenzo appeared unimpressed. I confess to being pleased at that.

"I have news," he told her.

"Has something happened to Mattie?" I said, suddenly frightened by his strange manner.

"She needs you," he answered. "You can come right away?"

"What's happened?" I insisted, grabbing hold of his sleeve.

"It's Paolo. There was an accident. . . ."

Lorenzo turned his face from us, staring out into the street. A round-bellied West Philadelphia omnibus rattled past, but I don't think he saw it. His shoulders lifted and fell in a deep sigh whose slow sound was masked by the noise of wheels and horses' hooves on the uneven paving stones.

"He's not dead," he said gruffly, still facing the street.

He set his cap firmly on his head again and stared at me.

"Mattie didn't ask, but if you can spend this night with her, I know it would give comfort. And I can feel I did the best for her by bringing you."

"Where do you have to go?" Isabelle said.

"South. Near to Seventh and Catherine."

She opened her purse, extracted a few coins, and offered them to Lorenzo.

"For the horsecar," she said.

He didn't take the money.

"Nan will want to get there as quickly as she can, Mr. Testa. You've spent enough time already coming to fetch her."

He took the coins from her gloved palm and put them in his pocket.

"A loan," he said. "I don't take—"

"I'm sure you don't," Isabelle said. "But this is an emergency, isn't it?"

Lorenzo nodded his gratitude, and when Isabelle put out her right hand, he paused only a second before shaking it.

"I hope your brother will be all right," she said warmly.

"We must wait to see, *signora.*" he replied.

Lorenzo and I walked the three blocks to the horsecar line in silence. The tightness in his face checked any questions. All sorts of horrible possibilities were flooding my mind, but I felt a kind of excitement, too, to be hurrying urgently along the street with Lorenzo, and a renegade happiness managed to slip in beside my dread.

Entering the horsecar before me, Lorenzo led the way to seats in the rear, away from the other riders, and when the car jerked forward on its tracks, he began, finally, to talk in a low voice.

"He was trying to help another man," he said. "Paolo always has a quick heart."

Lorenzo shook his head and chuckled to himself, but his smile was so pained, the sight of it chilled rather than encouraged me.

"Once, when we were boys, he jumped into the river after a little one who fell in; but Paolo can't swim, so someone else had to jump in and get both."

The car made a stop, and more passengers boarded. The seats near us were no longer unoccupied. It was not an agreeable place for relating—or hearing—difficult news.

"Lorenzo, you can wait to tell me. . . ."

He looked at me, startled, and his bright eyes stopped my speech. I felt as if he were regarding me from a distance, through the memory of his brother in the river and his knowledge of the circumstances in which his brother now lay.

"You call me Lorenzo."

I kept my gaze steady despite my embarrassment. I had spoken without calculation, yet somewhere in my mind I must have known that to use his name would subtly extend the kiss in the doorway, would nudge it away from being the impulse of a moment, like the striking of a match in the dark, and toward being a new point of view, like the break of day. I wondered, too late, if Lorenzo would think me selfish and coldhearted to have done it at such a time.

"That's good," he said after a few seconds' silence. "One good thing on this black day."

We spoke no more during the ride. I occupied my nervous mind by observing the people who got on and off the horse-car and by peering out into the darkening streets. When we disembarked, we were still some blocks away from the Testas' place. Lorenzo wanted time to talk before we met Mattie. Scores of tired, dirty workingmen passed us on their way home to supper, and a few factory girls, but I didn't take note of any of them in detail. We might as well have been walking between stripped, immobile winter trees as among living, pressing human beings. All my attention was on Lorenzo, who was telling his story as starkly as if he'd been sending it by telegraph.

"A hand truck of iron bars was going fast down a ramp. Too fast to control. A fifteen-ton load, and no brakes. With another truck stopped below . . ."

Lorenzo turned up his collar and shoved his hands into his pockets, as if he were trying to ward off what he must say next.

"There was a man in the way. Paolo tried to grab him. His arm was caught between the trucks. His arm . . . it's gone."

"Paolo's arm?"

Lorenzo looked at me as if I were an imbecile. Then he realized my confusion, and his gaze softened.

"Yes, Paolo's arm. His good arm."

Lorenzo rubbed one hand roughly over his forehead.

"The man he tried to save is dead. Pierced as by a hundred spears, the foreman said."

I must have cried out, though I don't remember it, for Lorenzo stopped walking, took my elbow, and moved me out of the stream of trudging pedestrians. What I do remember is a sickened feeling in the pit of my stomach and around my heart, as if I had a live fish flopping about inside me.

"Take a breath," Lorenzo said.

I obeyed. His voice and the touch of his hand were the only solid things in my universe at that moment.

"Again," he said.

We stood there, I breathing as deeply and slowly as I could, he watching me do it. It took several minutes before I was calmed.

"This is not how I thought for our next meeting," he said softly then. "But I'm glad for it, anyway."

He let go of my elbow and, frowning, lowered his gaze to his boots.

"God forgive me, Paolo is lying in the almshouse hospital, and I can feel gladness."

"I know, Lorenzo," I said. "I have the same feelings."

"Let's go," he said abruptly.

He walked briskly down the street. His face was so grimly set and his stride so strong that people moved aside to let him by, as if he were the prow of a ship parting the waters. I, on the other hand, had to dodge around people and around the cellar doors and front stoops that jutted out into the sidewalk; I only just managed to keep up with him. I did notice, however, that though he never looked over at me, he did shorten his stride now and then to let me catch up.

"Get Mattie to sleep," he said during one of these moments of slower pace. "She needs strength for Paolo when he comes home tomorrow."

"Has she seen him?"

"No. I made her stay back. The neighbor women told me

Blockley is a dangerous place for carrying a baby. People get typhoid there, they said."

We'd reached the corner of Lorenzo's block. He stopped. "Can you go alone?" he said.

"Yes," I answered.

"I want to see Paolo's friends from the steelworks. And they say that man's widow wants me to come by."

"It's awful what happened to your brother," I said, "but at least you and Mattie aren't having to receive calls like that."

Lorenzo appeared little comforted by the thought. There was a tension in him like that in a jack-in-the-box right before it pops. I had the sense he was not only like the jack, straining to escape, but also like the child slowly turning the crank, wanting to delay the jack's release. I waited, not wishing to dismiss him by moving away.

"Have you ever been to a factory?" he said at last.

"No, but Mattie's told me a little about the box factory."

"They're all the same—some worse, some better. They all have ways to make you die for your living."

I knew he was speaking of more than threats to bodily health, and I knew, despite my lack of direct experience, that he was right. Still, thinking of him having to walk into a factory tomorrow, and the next day, and the day after that, I wished heartily that I could contradict him.

"Don't let Mattie look for me to come home tonight," Lorenzo said as he turned to go.

I watched him stride the length of the block and round a corner, his hands again jammed into his pockets, his shoulders drawn up as if against a cold wind. I felt a tightness in my own back to see him so armored.

೨೭ I FOUND Mrs. Litvak and her little Rachel with Mattie. The woman had sent her daughters around to the neighbors to glean contributions of food, and Mattie's kitchen table was spread with breads and jars of preserves, and a rich soup was simmering on the small stove, filling the apartment with a welcoming aroma. I guessed Mattie was not yet ready to be cheered by good smells or neighborly generosity, but I believed that somehow, beneath her notice, these things were holding her up, and I was sure Mrs. Litvak knew it, too.

Mattie was amazed to see me. Lorenzo hadn't told her he was going for me. He didn't want to disappoint her if I wasn't able to come. But Mattie's amazement at finding me at her door lasted only a second; her distress washed it away.

"Hanna," she cried. "Paolo . . . Paolo's hurt . . ."

"I know," I said, taking her into my arms. "That's why I'm here."

"Hello, miss," said Mrs. Litvak, coming out of the kitchen.

Rachel followed right behind her mother. The child was gnawing on a heel of pumpernickel bread, and when I smiled at her in greeting, she made no sign of recognizing me, but kept at the bread with the gusto of a teething baby.

"Maybe you'll be better than me at getting her to eat," Mrs. Litvak said, pointing at Mattie. "I've been here for hours, and she hasn't taken a thing."

"Mattie, you must eat," I said gently.

"I'm not hungry."

"Well, I came away without my supper. Will you sit with me while I eat?"

Mattie said yes, and we went to the kitchen. Mrs. Litvak nodded encouragement at me behind Mattie's back. Pushing Rachel in front of her, Mrs. Litvak let herself out.

"Send downstairs if you need me, Mrs. Testa," she called before she shut the door. "The girls and me will be up late tonight sewing."

I cleared some space on the kitchen table and set two places. Then I cut four slices of pumpernickel and quartered an apple, and served up two bowls of hot soup. Mattie watched the simple proceedings, but she wasn't really paying attention. A blind person would have shown more interest.

I sat down and began to eat. Mattie just kept folding and

unfolding the edge of her napkin. I put my hand on top of hers to stop her, and she looked up into my face.

"I keep thinking about the pain," she said. "And how he might be afraid, and I'm not there with him. And I think of crazy things, too, like where is his arm? We have to bury it, you know; the Church says we have to bury it."

"Let Lorenzo take care of that, Mattie."

"Where is Lorenzo?"

"He had people to see," I said. "But he's bringing Paolo home tomorrow, and you have to be ready."

"How do I get ready, Hanna? How do I do that?"

"I don't know, Mattie. But I think eating some soup would be a good start."

She picked up her spoon.

"Lorenzo said when Paolo lost his fingers, he wouldn't talk for a week and wouldn't take his hand out of his pocket for three more weeks after that."

"Mattie, dear, you need your strength. There's the baby to think of, too."

She began, dutifully, to eat, and though she took no pleasure in the food, she finished the bowl of soup and a half slice of bread. Mention of the baby had made Mattie docile; she made no protest against drinking a large mug of chamomile tea, which I hoped would relax her enough for sleep. I sincerely wished I had one of Isabelle's nostrums with me.

We retired together in Mattie and Paolo's bed. Mattie insisted she'd not be able to sleep lying in it alone. The only other bed available to me was Lorenzo's, anyway, and I felt an acute shyness at even considering using it. Mattie and I lay side by side on our backs, as we had done in the meadow on her wedding day. She was quiet for such a long time, I thought she'd fallen asleep. The unfamiliarity of the room and the agitation of the evening were keeping me awake.

"Hanna," Mattie said, surprising me. "I wonder if it will be different now for Paolo and me."

"It must, in some way."

"But it will be all right?"

It was a question, but I don't think she really expected an answer. She scooted closer to me. I turned a little toward her and lay my arm across her waist; I could feel the small, hard swell of her abdomen, where the baby was growing. She put her hand there, too.

"It will be all right," she said.

TWENTY-ONE

❧ "HOW DID he look? Did he put on a brave face or was he gloomy? Was Mrs. Testa crying? Oh, Nan, it must have been like a stage melodrama."

I sat at Isabelle's kitchen table as she stirred about making coffee and sandwiches. In somewhat the same way, Mattie had let me officiate in her kitchen, wanting simultaneously to be left alone and not to be left alone. I accepted Isabelle's caretaking and felt a grudging gratitude for it, even with the accompanying chatter. I had spent a restless night and had arrived at the Martins' at midday feeling, in body and heart, as untidy as a scarecrow. Isabelle herself had had almost as little sleep as I because Mr. Edwin had been up and down with stomach complaints, brought on, he said, by the requirement that he suddenly switch from my cooking to his wife's, but she was, nevertheless, in a pleasant and collected frame of mind.

The scene Isabelle wanted me to recount, of Paolo's homecoming, was still vivid in my mind—indeed, nothing could have distracted me from it—but I resisted talking about it all the same, as if describing it would give it more staying power, both in my memory and in Mattie's life. I wanted to believe that Paolo's accident and his moody homecoming were singular, boundaried events, like bricks. Two bricks could not build a wall; two bricks could be stepped over or moved aside, chipped at or kicked away.

"You know," Isabelle continued, blithely ignoring my silence, "Mrs. Cox is a friendly visitor to the worthy poor for the Union Benevolent Association. Perhaps she could arrange to see your friends, bring them some food. . . ."

"They're not poor," I objected.

"But they will be, won't they?"

Isabelle had been spooning pickled walnuts from a jar; she stopped a moment to look at me. Her expression was one of sympathy and regret, as if I were a child and she had just inadvertently revealed the fact that Santa Claus does not exist.

"Maybe not *poor,*" she amended, "but needy. Now that Mr. Testa's no longer able-bodied."

She set before me a plate with a few walnuts, cold ham on two biscuits, and cabbage in mayonnaise. She was having only a bowl of rice with sugar and cream. Isabelle liked sweet things when she was acting nursemaid.

"Mr. Testa—the one who came for you—he seemed very upset."

"Of course."

"The other Mr. Testa, who was hurt, did he? . . . What is his name?"

"Paolo."

"And your Mr. Testa—what's his name?"

I felt a quickening in my throat like fear, and yet unlike it.

"He's not *mine,*" I said.

"I only meant it as a figure of speech, Nan. To distinguish the two Mr. Testas."

I studied her a moment. She returned my gaze with clear-eyed serenity, and I didn't have the will to challenge her. Besides, I realized with a saving insight, further protest would only inspire more inquisitiveness.

"Lorenzo," I answered simply.

"Lorenzo," she said, nodding, as if I had supplied her with the most gratifying news.

"Now, Paolo and his wife? . . ."

"Mattie."

"Oh, yes. Paolo and Mattie. What was it like with them?"

"I stayed only a short while after he arrived. We . . . Mr. Testa and I . . . Lorenzo, that is . . . we wanted to leave them private, so he walked with me several blocks to see me out of the neighborhood and well on my way home, then he went back in case he was needed."

"It must have been a sorrowful meeting. Yet glad, too, since he could have been killed, couldn't he? Or gotten septic at the hospital."

"It was mostly glad," I said, remembering how Mattie had rushed to Paolo out on the landing and embraced him and passed her fingers all over his face, as if that were the part of him that had been disfigured, and how she'd kissed him and lifted his hand with the old wound of the missing fingers and pressed the back of it against her cheek.

But I couldn't remember Mattie's actions without recalling Paolo's, too, and that my mind shied from, because Paolo had not really made any actions. He'd stood as straight and un-moving as a tobacconist's Indian, letting Mattie fuss around him but not warming to her, seeming, even, not to notice her, just as a man carved of wood won't notice a fly crawling over him. Paolo did look into Mattie's face once, though, and when he did, I almost wished for the return of his blank ex-pression, because in that look was such mourning, you would have thought he was beholding Mattie in her coffin instead of Mattie alive and loving right against him.

"He needs time to get used to it," Lorenzo told me as we walked down the street.

That made sense to me, and I determined to hold on to the hope that in time Paolo would come all the way home to Mattie.

"When you hear of such a tragedy," Isabelle said, "it makes you think of your own life a little differently, doesn't it?"

"You mean being thankful for what you have?"

"Yes, that. But also, being reminded of how unexpected life

can be—anyone's life—and how brief. Hesitation seems a sin in the face of that."

"Hesitation?"

"Oh, you know," Isabelle said, getting up to put her empty bowl in the sink. "Putting things off. Finding excuses. Waiting instead of laying hold."

"I suppose," I said, too tired to talk philosophy. While I finished my food, Isabelle fixed a tray for Mr. Edwin, who was still in bed, having felt too unrested to go out to his shops. He'd sent a boy from the store below to Mr. Cox to ask him to drop by in the late afternoon and fill him in on the business of the day. I saw Isabelle was giving Mr. Edwin strong green tea, dyspepsia bread, and a shot glass of purplish liquid that must have been one of her home remedies.

"I'd like a nap if I could, Isabelle," I said before she left the room with the tray.

"So would I," she replied testily, letting the strain of her night show for the first time.

"Don't mind me, Nan," she added in the next breath. "Take a nap, by all means. I'm just bringing Edwin something to make him sleep, so I shall be resting on the sofa myself soon."

I sat quietly alone in the kitchen a while, feeling relieved to be back home, realizing with a mild start how much I did consider Isabelle's home my own. Parts of it, at least. The kitchen, my bedroom, the sewing room where she and I had sat long afternoons before her baby was born and before she'd met Reverend Dale. Sometimes we'd even had tea and cookies there and watched the weather over the rooftops, like two little girls squirreled away in a secret treehouse. As Reverend Dale's visits became more frequent, however, our times in the sewing room had diminished and changed, until we were using it merely as a workroom where we efficiently completed tasks with no extra time given to lazy conversation or cloud viewing. I wondered if we'd be returning to the earlier habits of the sewing room now that Isabelle seemed to have lost her enthusiasm for the cautious minister.

The doorbell called back my wandering mind. I decided to answer it as a last task before my nap. Though Isabelle probably wouldn't have minded so much if I ignored the bell, I found it too hard to do so.

"Have I caught my son at dinner?" Mr. Sylvester Martin said in greeting. "I've brought happy news."

"Mr. Edwin's indisposed," I answered.

The old man frowned.

"Just a small stomach upset, sir."

"She had you making those rich Frenchy desserts again? Never mind, this'll perk him up," he said, waving a telegram envelope at me.

I left Mr. Martin in the parlor and went to let Isabelle know he was there. She told me to bring him into the bedroom, as it would be too much trouble for Mr. Edwin to get out of bed now that he'd had his sleeping draught and was beginning to feel drowsy.

"Look, Edwin," Mr. Martin shouted over my shoulder as I led him into the bedroom. "It's Fred. He's coming back. And he says there's a good chance this time he'll stay."

Mr. Edwin's eyelids were half-closed, but he managed to smile and nod at his father.

"Yes, we knew," Mr. Edwin mumbled. "I'm glad you're pleased."

"How are you, Edwin? A stomach upset, the girl said. But you're looking sort of weakish."

"He's just sleepy, *Père,*" Isabelle said.

"Well, all right, I'll clear out and let him rest."

Isabelle got up to accompany Mr. Martin out of the room. I waited so I could close the curtains and adjust Mr. Edwin's blankets after they'd left. At the doorway, Mr. Martin turned and looked back at Mr. Edwin. The old gentleman appeared worried, and I could see he was struggling not to convey his worry to his son.

"You take care, Edwin," he said loudly. "You want to be up

and about by the time Fred gets here. That won't be many more days now."

"Yes," Isabelle said. "Fred will make us a deadline."

⁂ THE FOLLOWING several days are blurred in my memory, which is surprising because I've often since thought over them, examined them for clues to things that happened later whose seeds might have been contained there. I used to ponder whether I could have altered the course of events if I'd noticed those seeds in time. But I've come to believe that portents are only spied in hindsight (if they are ever found at all), perversely illuminated by the shadows stretching back over them, as if, like phosphorescent sea creatures, they need darkness to be discovered.

Isabelle's cooking was not to blame for Mr. Edwin's ill health, for my return to the kitchen brought him no lasting improvement. His sickness was not unlike the one he'd suffered after our return from Ocean Grove, both in the similarity of many of his symptoms and in the unyielding hold the illness had on him. He went in and out of aches and complaints, sometimes rallying a few hours toward wellness, only to slip away from it again in some new direction.

Spiritually, Mr. Edwin was steadier. He was uniformly morose. Mr. Sylvester Martin had Dr. Cornelius in, and the doctor declared that Mr. Edwin's state of mind was the worst enemy of his recovery. Though Mr. Martin was still advocating for electric treatments, he followed Dr. Cornelius's advice to soothe Mr. Edwin's frayed nerves by having him look at pictures. Mr. Martin had the American Art Union send Mr. Edwin a full set of their reproductions of country scenes for dyspeptic businessmen.

Isabelle, of course, had a regime for Mr. Edwin, too: sponge baths with cold water, fresh air from the open windows, and various tisanes, bromides, and bitters, all of her own design.

The odors of some of her mixtures were downright nauseating, but Mr. Edwin obediently downed every one. If faith in his nurse could have cured him, Mr. Edwin would have been dancing a jig by the second day.

I was kept running. There was the house to manage without Isabelle's assistance, and I had to cook differently for her and for Mr. Edwin, he requiring milky foods and bran cereals and breads, she wanting vegetables, a little fish, and sweets. Sometimes there was Mr. Sylvester Martin to do for, too, and he was a prodigious and diverse eater, favoring organ meats and pot pies.

I squeezed time to send Mattie a brief note every evening. I didn't expect answers, and told her so to keep her mind easy, but after three days, I decided to take a few hours to go see her and judge for myself how things stood in her household. Mr. Edwin had had a moderate night and a quietly cheerful morning; Dr. Cornelius was much encouraged, as was Mr. Edwin himself. He even ordered me to secure oysters for his breakfast next morning. Mr. Sylvester Martin, who had come with Dr. Cornelius, was delighted at his son's color and verve.

"Oysters!" he rejoiced. "My boy, when you turn face, you don't do it by halves. Better look sharp, Isabelle, he'll be getting back a taste for more than oysters before you can say cock robin."

The three men laughed, old Mr. Martin loudest, Mr. Edwin with shy glee, and Dr. Cornelius politely chuckling while casting an apologetic glance at Isabelle, who remained stony faced. Unfortunately, Mr. Martin's rude humor had spoiled Isabelle's sense of relief, so much so that she seemed, in fact, not relieved at all, but more anxious than she'd been when Mr. Edwin was showing no response to the efforts being made to cure him.

The two gentlemen did not stay for midday dinner. Indeed, Isabelle did not invite them. When she learned I wanted to visit Mattie, she excused me even from preparing food for her and Mr. Edwin so that I might have full use of the afternoon.

"I'll get the oysters on my way back," I said.

"Don't bother. I can send a boy from downstairs. Stay to supper with your friends if you've a mind to."

"I don't know how long I'll want to stay. It depends on how Mr. Testa is feeling."

"Lorenzo?" Isabelle said with a sly smile.

I blushed.

"Paolo," I answered.

"Come, Nan, there's more than one temperature wants taking in that house."

"Isabelle, I wouldn't think you'd find such remarks in you after having been so recently made uncomfortable yourself by like teasing."

Now it was her turn to blush, and she turned away to hide it from me. We were in the sewing room. Isabelle had gone there, she'd said, to straighten up. The room had been left with yardages strewn about, some pinned with pattern papers, some draped together over chairs to give the effect of various combinations of fabrics. We'd started on winter dressmaking days ago, but Paolo's accident and Mr. Edwin's illness had intervened and kept us from returning to our work. I think, though, that Isabelle had come to the room not to tidy it, but as a retreat; its disarray was pleasant and comforting, all soft folds and auspicious beginnings. Now she looked out the window and idly twisted and untwisted a length of moiré ribbon around her fingers. I noticed frost in the upper corners of the windowpane, and I knew I'd have a cold walk ahead of me in spite of the day's sunshine. I was eager to be on my way.

"I'm sorry, Nan," Isabelle said, her back still to me.

She sat down on the armchair closest to the window and leaned back with a sigh, disregarding the panne velvet and wool challis hung over the chair's back. She looked at me and smiled. It was a penitent smile, not a mischievous one, and it softened my annoyance with her.

"Perhaps I am jealous," she said.

"Jealous?"

"To be as you are, on the bright edge of love, sought out by a handsome young man. . . ."

"Isabelle . . ."

"No, don't contradict me. Let me believe it. I'm not teasing you now. I'm simply indulging myself. Courtship is such a happy time for a woman; she's not expected to be cheerfully obedient in all things, as a wife is. In fact, when a woman is being courted, it is *her* will that dictates."

"You give it too much importance," I said.

"Your romance?"

"Any romance."

She stood up.

"You *are* sensible, Nan. I would trust your reasoning in any situation, I think. But you won't begrudge me a little dream weaving, will you?"

"I couldn't stop you in that. No one could. Nor should they."

"No, no one could," she said and, starting to hum softly, she turned to fold up fabrics. I took it as my permission to leave.

LORENZO AND Paolo were not at home, but Mattie was, and though I roused her from a nap, she appeared very glad to see me. I regretted my intrusion nonetheless, for I saw by the dark circles under her eyes that she was badly in need of rest.

"Spending time with you will revive me more than a few moments' sleep, Hanna," she said generously.

"By the look of you, you need more than moments, Mattie."

"Moments is all there is for me just now. Even when Paolo's out—which isn't often—or when he's sound asleep himself, I can't seem to stay down longer than an hour before I'm awake and roaming the house or staring at the ceiling."

"Worries?"

She nodded.

"Money?"

"For one."

We heard footsteps, and Mattie immediately went out to the hall landing to lean over the bannister and look down at who was coming. But it turned out to be someone for the floor below, so she came back inside.

"Lorenzo's taken Paolo to the House of Industry over on Catherine Street, in case they can find a trade to train him in that he could manage," she explained.

"Do you think they will?"

She stared at me glumly, the droop of her features accentuated by the apartment's dimness. The sun was close to setting, and we'd not lit any lamps yet. Studying my friend in the ordinary obscurity of that early winter's dusk, I imagined that even in full light, Mattie would look gray and clouded.

"I know it's wrong of me not to feel hopeful," she said.

"Lorenzo must think there's a chance, or he wouldn't have—"

"Lorenzo wants a chance so badly that he won't see the truth," she said with uncharacteristic bitterness.

"The truth?"

"That Paolo wouldn't take a chance, even if one could be found. Paolo doesn't want anything now. Or anybody."

She began moving around the room lighting lamps, her hands quavering. I came up behind her and put my arms around her shoulders to make her stop. She didn't turn into my embrace, but she didn't pull away, either.

"Mattie," I said, "It's still early days. He won't stay like this."

She looked at me with something like pity in her eyes.

"You don't know that, Hanna. No one does."

She leaned her head on my shoulder then, and I felt her body soften and grow heavy against me, like a baby's does when it has done crying and has fallen asleep in your arms.

"He's like a stone, Hanna. He'll eat what I put in front of him, and he lets me dress him, and he'll listen to the visitor from the St. Vincent de Paul Society or to Father Monaco and will kneel down to receive Father's blessing, but I think he only does it all so we won't bother him with more. At night, he sits in the kitchen drinking wine until I come to take him to bed. He won't let anyone sit with him. I know he's ready for sleep when he starts singing. I never would have thought singing could make me afraid, but his does."

There was nothing I could say. Mattie didn't seem to expect an answer anyway. Probably she wanted just the reverse, and that's what I gave her. I remembered Sippy saying that one of the chief things a woman in labor needed was a good witness, and that careful witnessing could be more soothing and fortifying than any medicine. It seemed to me Mattie was in a kind of labor, wrapped in pain and fear, caught in something whose end could not be hurried. So I did with Mattie what I'd seen Sippy do so many times. I held her hand and listened to her. Later, after supper, I helped her into bed and stroked her brow until she was asleep.

I left a note on the door to the apartment so that the men would be quiet as they came in. Down on the street, I was so dispirited that I felt physically exhausted, so I decided to splurge on the horsecar to get home. Despite the bumpy, start-and-stop ride, I dozed most of the way. It was the only rest I was destined to get that night.

TWENTY-TWO

AS IT WAS nearly ten o'clock when I arrived home, I expected the house to be dark and quiet. Quiet it was, but the parlor doors, which were slid half-open, showed that room was still lit, and glancing down the hall, I noticed light coming from the doorways to the dining room and kitchen, too.

I looked into the parlor. Mr. Edwin was asleep on the couch, set up as usual with lots of pillows and crocheted throws. A hurricane lamp on a tall table behind him shed a saffron glow on the crowd of little glass bottles that always followed him from room to room when he was ill. A tray with dirty supper dishes sat on the floor. Isabelle was in the parlor, too, sleeping slumped in a chair at the end of the couch, her hand loosely grasping Mr. Edwin's right foot, which protruded from beneath his covers. I thought she must have been very tired to have fallen asleep thus. Her awkward posture appeared exceptionally uncomfortable, both because of the stiffness of her chair and because of how she had angled her body in order to keep hold of her husband's foot.

As I softly approached them, I watched Isabelle's face for any signs of wakefulness, not wanting to startle her. I was sure she was only lightly asleep; I knew from our stay in Ocean Grove that Isabelle snored when she was in deep sleep. But to my surprise, I had to call her name several times and shake her shoulder to rouse her. When at last she opened her eyes, she smiled to find me bending over her.

"Nan," she whispered. "I've been waiting."

"Waiting for me? Did you need something?"

She looked at me quizzically.

"What?" she said, with the soft frown of the newly wakened.

"Never mind. Come, you should get to bed now," I said, putting my hands on her arm to help her stand.

"But Edwin . . . He's so cold," she said worriedly. She had yet to let go of his foot.

"His foot's been out in the air of the room," I said, turning away. "Tuck it under, and I'll get a quilt from the bedroom for him."

I had only got halfway across the room when Isabelle screamed. I swung around. Isabelle was leaning over Mr. Edwin, cupping his face in her hands and tilting it up so that the light from the lamp fell full upon him. One of his arms had slid out from under the afghans; it hung with unnatural stillness off the edge of the couch, his fingers bent straight by contact with the floor. All this I saw in an instant. In that same instant, I knew what it must mean, but my mind balked at the knowledge, and I stopped, unable to move or speak.

Isabelle let Mr. Edwin's head drop back against the pillows. She wiped her hands on her skirt as if they were wet or soiled.

"He's dead," she cried out. "Nan, he's dead!"

I came forward then. I lifted Mr. Edwin's arm back onto the couch. The heaviness of the arm and the coldness of his hand erased all doubt, but I felt for a pulse anyway. Behind me, I heard the rustle of Isabelle's skirt as she paced up and down.

"Dead," she was saying over and over. "Dead. How can it be? Dead, dead."

I linked arms with Isabelle and led her to the dining room, where I sat her down and poured her a large glass of brandy.

"No arguments," I said firmly, though she was showing no inclination to protest.

She shuddered at the first swallow, but she held on to the glass tightly and continued to sip at it. I poured myself a smaller glass and downed it quickly, as I would medicine.

"He must have gone peacefully," I said.

"What makes you say that?"

"Because his dying didn't wake you."

"Oh. Yes."

We lapsed into silence. There is not much to say in the presence of death. Isabelle stared into her brandy as if it were a pond reflecting leaf shadows, and I gazed out the window at sharper shadows defined by an electric arc light on a tall, red iron pole. By contrast, the gaslight inside seemed yellow and sickly. But perhaps it was just my temperament at the time.

"Mr. Edwin's father is bound to be hit hard," I said, noticing two white-haired gentlemen passing on the street below.

"I won't think of that until morning," Isabelle replied.

"But, Isabelle, you must send for him tonight."

She looked at me with pleading, frightened eyes.

"Really, you must," I repeated. "You know you must."

"Bring me paper and pen and ink," she said flatly. "I'll compose a note. The boy who sleeps at the dry goods store can carry it."

It took a good deal of banging on the door to summon the boy at the store. He finally came hurrying forward, stuffing his nightshirt into his pants, his hair tangled and dusty, as if he'd been lying on the floor in a cobwebby corner, which perhaps he had. He was only twelve or thirteen. Given his scrawny size and his heavy sleeping habits, I wondered how effective he was as a watchman. He couldn't be expected to do more than call the alarm if a fire or a thief appeared. He probably only earned breakfast and a place to sleep for his efforts; that wouldn't buy heroism. He was good-natured, though, and made no complaint, nor even displayed any curiosity at being called on as a messenger in the middle of the night, but took Isabelle's note with a cheerful nod, and slipping on his shoes and a jacket, was off down the street before I had gotten back inside our front door.

While I was at my errand, Isabelle had straightened the parlor a bit in preparation for Mr. Sylvester Martin's arrival. The tray of supper dishes and the little glass bottles had been moved to a table on the other side of the room from the couch; Mr. Edwin's covers had been smoothed and his hands arranged demurely on his chest; more lamps and a few candles were lit; and, despite the night's cold, windows had been opened to freshen the air in the room.

Isabelle was in the bedroom changing out of her foulard wrapper. I stood over Mr. Edwin and studied his face. If I had looked more closely at him earlier, I would not have needed Isabelle's cry to alert me to his condition. There is a profound difference between the face of a dead person and the face of someone asleep, however much the two states seem to mimic each other. In death, the face is empty. It isn't just the color change or the immobility, though these are part of it. It's almost as if a scent is given off that our animal selves detect, the scent of difference, the scent of absence. Mr. Edwin had been present in this house even when he was out at his shops; we were his proprietary colony. Now he was no longer here, even though his body still reclined in the center of the parlor.

"Nan, best go roast some coffee beans and start a shortcake. Canned peaches . . . whatever else you can think of," Isabelle said, coming into the parlor.

She was wearing a long-sleeved, high-necked gray cashmere dress patterned with widely spaced white dots and puffs of white tulle at the cuffs. The narrow waist of the boned basque bodice was accentuated by a wide girdle. A long, slender bustle gave the pleated back drapery a graceful shape. There was an understated prettiness to the costume. Perhaps, I thought, even old Mr. Martin would soften under its influence and feel the urge to protect its wearer.

I was just taking the shortcake out of the oven when the bell rang. I found not only Mr. Sylvester Martin at the door, but also Dr. Cornelius. The two men followed me upstairs and into the parlor. At the sound of their entry into the room, Isabelle slowly raised her gaze from a thick book on her lap.

"You," Mr. Martin growled at Isabelle. "For once, you could have met me at the door like a proper daughter."

"Sir," said Dr. Cornelius, laying his hand on Mr. Martin's shoulder.

The old man sagged as if he were a marionette and one of his strings had been cut. But it was not the doctor's touch that had affected him. He had taken the first full sight of his son laid out on the couch. A moan escaped him, and he rushed forward and knelt on the floor near Mr. Edwin's head, taking one of the dead man's hands in his own and kissing it tenderly.

"I was reading the Bible," Isabelle said, standing up, though Mr. Martin was no longer paying her heed.

"Of course, dear lady," Dr. Cornelius said. "But you, above anyone, can understand your father-in-law's feelings, I'm sure. Grief can make us abrupt, can make us say things we do not mean."

"I don't need you making excuses for me, Doctor," Mr. Martin said, getting up. "I brought you here for one reason. As a witness. A medical witness."

"I confess, Mrs. Martin," Dr. Cornelius said gently to Isabelle, "I was rather staggered to learn of your husband's death. He was so chipper only this morning. I'd made remark on it in his record."

"I know, Doctor," Isabelle said, clutching the Bible to her chest. "That's what makes it all the harder."

She turned away from the men with a stifled sob and crossed the room to stand beside me. I put my arm around her waist. Dr. Cornelius looked decidedly ill at ease, as if he were worried it was something in him and not just the pure situation that was so upsetting to her.

"Don't be fooled by those crocodile tears, Dr. Cornelius,"

Mr. Martin said. "My son was, and look what happened to him."

"The doctor is right, *Père*," Isabelle said. "Your grief is making you speak thoughtlessly. But for Edwin's sake, I forgive you."

"Mr. Martin, I caution you to—" began Dr. Cornelius.

"Forgive? Caution? To blazes with both of you. I stand on my rights as Edwin's nearest blood relative, and I demand an autopsy."

"An autopsy?" Isabelle gasped. I felt her back stiffen against my arm.

"Under the circumstances, Mrs. Martin," Dr. Cornelius explained, "a postmortem exam is a reasonable idea. A patient on the mend suddenly takes a fatal turn. . . . I have no suspicions of foul play, of course, but as your husband's physician, I'd like to know what happened. Wouldn't you?"

"Forget her, Cornelius," Mr. Martin snapped. "We don't need her permission."

"She's the widow, sir," Dr. Cornelius returned with equal ire. "And she was a brave and faithful nurse to your son. There's nothing to be gained by incivility."

"You're wrong there, Doctor. Engaging in incivility is the only thing's keeping me from striking the woman down."

As boorish as Mr. Martin was being, I did feel sorry for him. It was apparent he found it nearly unbearable to be in Isabelle's company and yet he could not leave her without also leaving his son. If he could only have some time alone with Mr. Edwin, I thought, perhaps he'd calm down.

"Dr. Cornelius," I said. "I've got coffee and cake and fruits ready, and Mrs. Martin hasn't had anything but some brandy since supper. . . ."

"So right," the doctor said, understanding my purpose. "Mrs. Martin, if we could withdraw into the dining room?"

Isabelle nodded and pulled away from me. She led Dr. Cornelius to the dining room. I closed both sets of parlor doors so that Mr. Sylvester Martin could have privacy, and then went to the kitchen to get the food and coffee.

An hour later, Mr. Martin left, not stopping in the dining room to announce his departure. We knew he was gone only because we heard the door shut behind him. Dr. Cornelius gave Isabelle a sedative and sat at her bedside a half hour until it took effect. Then he spent some time in the parlor, sniffing and poking at Mr. Edwin and at the dirty supper dishes and the medicine bottles, and between sniffs and pokes, tapping his teeth thoughtfully with his mechanical pencil and jotting notes in his creased leather book. When, at last, the doctor was taking his leave, the windows were beginning to pink up with dawn.

"They'll be around for the body later this morning, Willer," the doctor told me. "Your mistress shouldn't be alone. Is there a sister or other family member you can call on? A friend?"

"There's Mrs. Cox," I said, "though she and Mrs. Martin are not close friends. And Reverend Dale. He's been a friend to both the Martins."

"A woman friend is always good at such times, even one who's not especially close, but a man of the church who is also a family friend would be even better. Send for the Reverend Dale."

"Yes, sir," I said.

"Better yet, give me his address, and I'll stop on my way home," Dr. Cornelius said. "Ministers are like doctors—they're used to callers at all hours."

After the doctor left, I went into the kitchen, looked around at the unwashed bowls and plates and the flour on the table and walked out again. By postponing cleanup, I might get in an hour's rest before Reverend Dale arrived. I went into the parlor next. Mr. Edwin was there alone, and I felt a little guilty not sitting with him. I pulled open the curtains, and the room lightened with the pale beginnings of a new day.

"No need for you to be in gloom, sir," I said.

But gloom tarried in the room yet. It was a trick of my tired eyes, I suppose, but I had to turn away from the sight of Mr. Edwin, for he, who had been master here, was now defeated, and he seemed, suddenly, to show in his waxen face some alarm at that.

TWENTY-THREE

IT'S NOT only doctors and ministers who work all hours, but housemaids, too. Two men came to collect Mr. Edwin's body before seven in the morning; I had to wake Isabelle up so that she might see Mr. Edwin one last time. I asked the men to wait in the hall while she took her final leave. I would have waited there, too, for it seemed a most intimate business, but Isabelle insisted vehemently I stay with her in the parlor, so to pacify her, I did.

Isabelle sat a while beside the couch and stared at Mr. Edwin, her hand resting on his chest. She spoke to him with great feeling in French. The strange words were pretty sounding, even though her voice was strained with emotion. Finally, she stood up and made a sign with her hand that I should let the men in.

They had a simple stretcher draped with a winding sheet, and when they'd lifted Mr. Edwin onto it and wrapped him tightly, he looked a bit like a large cocoon. The sight must have impressed Isabelle with the extremity of her situation, for she began to weep, holding a large white handkerchief over her face. The men didn't even look at her. They were intent on maneuvering the stretcher out of the rooms and then balancing it down the long flight of stairs to the street, as any men would be who had to move a heavy, awkwardly shaped burden.

Isabelle stayed at the top of the stairs watching their slow descent, but I went back into the parlor to look out the window. On the street below a covered buggy waited, and standing next to it was Mr. Sylvester Martin. He wore a black armband on his coat sleeve, and though I couldn't see his face, I was sure it was incubating sorrow. I knew the men had made it to the sidewalk before I saw them because Mr. Martin took off his hat and stepped forward with an outstretched arm, as if he were offering to escort a lady across a busy intersection. Making feeble gestures of assistance, which the men ignored, he shuttled to and fro beside them as they loaded his son's body into the buggy. Then they went up front, and Mr. Martin climbed into the back with the body.

As I watched the buggy pull away from the curb, I wondered if Mr. Sylvester Martin was talking to Mr. Edwin, as Isabelle had just done in the parlor; I wondered if he was begging his son's pardon for subjecting him to a postmortem after Mr. Edwin had so avoided doctors in life.

Isabelle managed to eat a good breakfast, knowing the day ahead would be a strenuous one. She spent time at her desk writing telegrams to people who needed to be informed of Mr. Edwin's death; assembling details for the newspaper obituary; and listing related chores, such as ordering mourning stationery, selecting a casket, and setting up an appointment with a seamstress for her widow's wardrobe. Then she went down the street to get a salmon, wanting to do the chore herself to have a few minutes' fresh air and exercise.

When she returned, we packed away all her jewelry and clothing except the gray dress she'd worn the night before and was wearing again, and a relatively plain day gown of brown merino wool. It had a shirred inset of white chiffon down the front, but it and the gray dress were the plainest outfits Isabelle owned and would have to do until her first black gown was done. She'd need to wear black for one year, easing into gray and purple during the following year, in dresses of severely simple design.

"If I am fitted today," she said, "at least one dress ought to be ready by day after tomorrow."

By noon, Isabelle's energy was flagging. Understandably, she had no taste for going through Mr. Edwin's things, though she did clear away his toilet articles from the top of his bureau in the bedroom, and she drew the velvet curtain closed in front of the alcove off the parlor to hide from sight the desk where he had toiled faithfully every morning. She made herself a tea from the dried petals of roses and violets and borage flowers. She said it was a blend meant to cheer a glum heart.

We'd had no word from Reverend Dale, and though Isabelle didn't mention it, I imagined she was perplexed by his absence. When the bell rang as I was getting ready to bake the salmon for Isabelle's midday meal, I expected the missing minister, but found Mr. Cox instead. Mr. Edwin's partner was a small, thin man of nervous habits. His face was perennially pinched and worried, but under the affliction of Mr. Edwin's death, Mr. Cox appeared even more than usual like an ill-fed rodent.

"Mrs. Martin," Mr. Cox groaned on being admitted to the parlor.

"Mr. Cox," Isabelle answered demurely, turning away from her contemplation of a tintype of herself and Mr. Edwin that sat on the mantle.

"My greatest sympathy to you in this tragedy," Mr. Cox continued. "Why, only yesterday Edwin sent me a sketch for the most ingenious Christmas displays, and now when I see our windows, I'll feel such . . . Unless you think it inappropriate to use his plans? I don't wish to cause you further grief. . . ."

"Of course you must use them, Mr. Cox. Edwin would have wanted that."

"Thank you. I think so, too."

"Nan," Isabelle said, "Bring Mr. Cox some coffee and shortcake. Quince preserves and whipped cream for your cake, Mr. Cox?"

Mr. Cox nodded and gave me a weak smile, implying, it seemed, that we must conspire to agree with whatever the new widow might suggest. When I returned some minutes later, Mr. Cox was making a more substantial attempt to console Isabelle.

"You mustn't concern yourself with the business, Mrs. Martin," he was saying. "I'm happy to run it on my own as long as is required. Then, when you're up to it, I'll explain what you need to know, we can draw up papers. . . ."

"Edwin made provisions," Isabelle replied.

"No doubt, no doubt."

"There was a new will. In April."

Mr. Cox's eyebrows lifted in surprise.

"A new will?" he said. "But, of course, his father and his brother are still the main—"

Isabelle stood up suddenly and wrung her hands.

"Mr. Cox, I can't really hold my mind to anything today. There's so much to consider, and yet I keep returning to Edwin stretched out there on the couch, Edwin gone. . . ."

Mr. Cox, who had been unwittingly leaning back against the very pillows Mr. Edwin had last lain his head on, started up from the couch and went to Isabelle, covering her clenched hands with his own.

"I'm sorry. I didn't mean to tax you," he said. "If there's any service my wife or I can perform, please don't hesitate to ask."

"Well," said Isabelle. "If Mrs. Cox is free this afternoon, perhaps she could accompany me to the seamstress? For my mourning garments."

"She'll be sure to come," Mr. Cox said.

"Three o'clock," Isabelle told him. "And now, if you'll excuse me, I must lie down. Willer can show you out."

"Yes, certainly," said Mr. Cox, a little confused. With a backward glance at the untouched cake and cream, he followed me out of the room.

After seeing Mr. Cox to the street, I remounted the stairs slowly, my mind busy with new questions. Mr. Cox's concern for the grocery business had pushed me into assessing my own future. Would Isabelle be keeping the apartment or moving elsewhere? If she moved, would she stay in Philadelphia? Would she still need me? I didn't like the idea of having to find another place. Should I try factory work? A store or office? Mr. Edwin's death had been such a shock, I hadn't thought past it, except to pity Isabelle that her life had been so suddenly and irreparably fractured. Now I saw that my life, too, was liable to be disrupted and that I might soon be required to turn some unexpected corner. What I couldn't predict then was that the corner, when it came, would have no guidepost and permit no doubling back.

MRS. COX called at three o'clock as promised, carrying a hatbox. Knowing Isabelle's penchant for frivolous hats, she'd brought her a black crape bonnet she'd worn when in mourning for her mother.

"Just for the next few days," she told Isabelle. "I thought you'd find it useful."

"How considerate," Isabelle said, rotating the bonnet in her hands. "Perhaps we should stop at a milliner's today, too?"

"If you think you're up to it," Mrs. Cox answered.

Alcesta Cox was as sturdy as her husband was thin, and she was unlike him in manner, too. They were both practical people, but where he was a worrier, and, like most worriers, naturally alert to hidden pitfalls, she stayed with the surface of things and did not look for trouble.

"It's easier to keep busy than to stay here fidgeting," Isabelle said.

"Yes, there's always a surge of energy after a death. Nature's opiate, I suppose. And there is so much to attend to, isn't there? Though I imagine Mr. Martin senior is helping with all that."

"Nan," Isabelle said, "where did I put my list from this morning? I'd appreciate it, Alcesta, if you'd look it over. To be sure I haven't neglected anything."

I brought the list, which I remembered seeing on the dining room table, and waited while Mrs. Cox read it slowly, nodding over each item. From observing her on other occasions, I knew she liked to give advice.

"Be sure on the mourning stationery," she suggested, "that you order some with a full quarter-inch black border for this year, and then some with a narrower black border for next year."

Isabelle took the list to her desk and made a note of this.

"It's not written there, but you'll want some hair jewelry made, of course," Mrs. Cox said. "A bracelet or brooch. I know a woman very skilled in it."

"Oh, I forgot," Isabelle said in dismay.

"Send your girl here round to the funeral parlor. They'll clip some hair for you."

"Edwin's not at the funeral parlor yet."

"Where is he?" said Mrs. Cox, looking disconcertedly around as if she might have overlooked Mr. Edwin laid out somewhere in the room.

"I'm not sure," Isabelle replied timidly. "There's to be a postmortem. Very routine, the doctor said. Because of the suddenness of the death."

"Oh," said Mrs. Cox, shrugging. "Well, send round to the doctor, then."

After the women had left, I ran the carpet sweeper over the main-floor rooms and then dressed myself to go to Dr. Cornelius. At the street door, I encountered Reverend Dale.

"Willer," he said, all out of breath. "I just received the doctor's message. I was away on church business overnight, in Prospectville."

"Why, sir," I said, "that's near to my father's home."

"Yes? A lovely area. But what's this news of the Martins, Willer? Edwin dead?"

"Yes, sir. Last night."

"If I'd known he was that ill, I'd never have gone away overnight."

"It wasn't expected, sir."

"And Isabelle? How is she?"

"Bearing up well. She's out now with Mrs. Cox."

Reverend Dale looked up at the third-story windows, as if he might spy Isabelle peeking from behind a curtain. I don't think he doubted my truthfulness; it was only that, having rushed to the house to comfort her, he was at a loss what to do with the momentum of his good intentions.

"And where are you off to, Willer?"

"To Dr. Cornelius. To fetch a lock of Mr. Edwin's hair for Mrs. Martin."

"Let me do the errand," Reverend Dale said.

The November afternoon had turned gray and sharp, with a quick wind, and it looked as if a fog or rain might be in by the time I was on my way home, so I was glad to transfer my chore to the solicitous minister. I gave him Dr. Cornelius's address and explained Isabelle's request. He said he'd call again at seven or eight that evening.

I went back inside and made myself a cup of Isabelle's glum-heart tea and put lots of honey in it.

⳨ REVEREND DALE did not return until eight-thirty. Isabelle waited for him, though I could see she was very tired. Mrs. Cox had told her that accepting sympathy was one of the most wearing tasks of bereavement, but that it was the chief one by which most people judged a family's true feelings for the deceased.

Isabelle surprised both me and Reverend Dale by opening the parlor doors to greet him as soon as we had entered the hall from the stairs.

"George," she said, coming quickly forward.

It was clear by her tone of voice and the lean of her body that she expected him to embrace her, and he did, but rather meekly, I thought, considering she was a newly made widow and he was both a friend and her spiritual advisor. After only a moment, he held her shoulders and pushed her gently away, as if she were hysterical and he must settle her down. In fact, of the two, it was Reverend Dale who appeared more agitated. Fearful, I would have said, if, at the time, that hadn't been so unlikely. Isabelle, too, noticed his strange state and drew him into the parlor, sliding the doors shut behind them.

I went to the dining room to put away some linens. I dawdled over the task, stopping occasionally to peer out the window at the fog curling around the streetlamps. I was sleepy, but I couldn't retire until Isabelle did. Earlier, she'd promised she'd keep Reverend Dale's visit brief. The door leading from the dining room to the parlor was ajar, and I half listened to the sound of the voices within, waiting for the cadences that would identify a farewell. Very soon, the voices grew louder, and I could hear every word without trying.

"But the doctor said there was a strong smell of chloroform when they opened Edwin's stomach. And that was just the preliminary exam," Reverend Dale was saying.

"Dr. Cornelius should not be relaying such details," Isabelle countered.

"When I bought it for you, you said it was for his pain," Reverend Dale pressed her.

"I never said that."

"You did!"

There passed some muttering between them I couldn't make out and some apparent moving about the room.

"Of course I must care what people think," Reverend Dale shouted. "I could be defrocked. If it can be proved you gave Edwin cholorform that I purchased, how will I look?"

"Oh, damn the chloroform!"

Again the voices dropped and, in a few minutes, I heard the hallway door open and shut. Reverend Dale had left. Isabelle came into the dining room, looking momentarily startled to find me there. Her cheeks were flushed.

"I won't need anything else tonight," she said calmly.

"Very well," I said.

"He didn't even bring the hair," she said.

"Why not?"

"Edwin's body wasn't there. They've taken him for an official autopsy."

"What does that mean?"

Isabelle sighed.

"We must wait and see," she said. "We must sit at home and wait."

Twenty-Four

IT WAS a full month before we learned the results of the autopsy, as the doctors decided to send the contents of Mr. Edwin's stomach and other parts of him to a toxicologist for study. Isabelle passed the time largely as she had said she would, waiting at home. The first month of widowhood must be spent at home in any case, excluding visits to church. But widows may receive callers. A few church ladies came by in the first week, and Mrs. Cox established Thursday afternoon as a habit, necessitating a shift in my half day off. Dr. Cornelius also came by once a week, though he had no set day.

Reverend Dale was conspicuous for his absence, except for his attendance at a prayer service held for Mr. Edwin at the Martins' church. Mr. Sylvester Martin, too, stayed away from our house, both men apparently waiting for the coroner's report to guide them in their future dealings with Isabelle. I suspected the two men of hoping for quite different outcomes.

But the only caller who made any difference in Isabelle's spirits—the only one, perhaps, capable of making a difference, by either appearing or failing to appear—was Mr. Frederick Martin. He had arrived in New York one day short of a week after Mr. Edwin's death and was in Philadelphia the next day. This Isabelle learned from a note he sent her. It was nearly another week before he came, unannounced, to the house. That meeting was remarkable, and like the confused period around Mr. Edwin's last illness and Paolo's accident, it has caused me much reconsideration.

After I led Mr. Frederick upstairs, he refused to enter the apartment, but told me to go bring Isabelle to the threshold. As soon as she appeared, he lifted his hand in warning to stifle any words or gestures from her.

"Isabelle," he said seriously, "I'm here against my father's wishes, but I can go no farther until I'm convinced he's wrong about you."

"You were always your own man, Fred," Isabelle said. "I don't fear your judgment."

Unable in this strange situation either to shut the door or to take Mr. Frederick's hat, I started down the hall toward the kitchen.

"Willer," Mr. Frederick called, "I want you to stay. This won't take long."

I stopped, but I didn't return to the doorway. The Martin men might favor witnesses, but I resolved not to take a greater part than absolutely necessary. To stand and watch and listen, to make a record in my mind of another's life should be my choice and no other's; if I did not always have such freedom, at least I could choose the outward forms of my docility and the inward meanings I put on what I witnessed. There is more than one purpose to every action, and involuntary actions can come to have purposes, too.

From my vantage point down the hallway, Isabelle and Mr. Frederick looked as if they were on a stage. Sunlight from the parlor windows struck their area, while I was in shadow. I could see Mr. Frederick full on; he never looked away from Isabelle's face. His gaze was as relentless as the summer sun. I think I would have cringed under it, but Isabelle stayed as steady and straight as a sunflower.

"Edwin was my brother," Mr. Frederick said, making the obvious fact sound like a reluctant confession.

"As he always was," Isabelle said.

Isabelle's back was to me, but I could imagine her large, un-

221

flinching eyes as Mr. Frederick was seeing them, made darker and more affecting by her black dress and the simple arrangement of her hair, which she now wore pulled back in a low bun with no ornaments or curls.

"My father accuses you—"

"He is an old man bent low with grief. Now you're here, things will go softer."

"Don't count on me to soften him in this, Isabelle. He is immovable."

"And you, Fred? Can you be moved?"

Mr. Frederick seemed to wince, though he neither shifted his position nor altered his expression. Not only must the sunflower ceaselessly face the sun; the sun cannot divert its light from the sunflower.

"A sincere word from you could move me," Mr. Frederick replied after a moment. "I've always been susceptible to that."

Isabelle stepped forward and reached for Mr. Frederick's hat, which he held at his side. But she did not dare yet to touch it or him.

"I was a good wife to Edwin," she said.

"Were you?"

"Never forget, Fred, I did not choose him on my own. Ours was not a marriage of kindred spirits."

"Few are, by my observations."

Isabelle put her fingertips on the brim of Mr. Frederick's hat. He let her take it.

"And by your observations," she asked, "would you say Edwin was happy in his marriage?"

"I think he was well satisfied. Even as a boy, he liked having what others admired."

She walked slowly to the hall stand and hung up his hat.

"Will you come in now?"

"I need an answer, Isabelle."

Isabelle kept her back to Mr. Frederick. She stared down the hallway at me, as if I had been the one who'd asked for an answer.

"I nursed Edwin carefully, as I always had," she finally said. "I fell asleep at his bedside, and when I awoke, he was dead."

Isabelle turned to face Mr. Frederick again. He stayed at the threshold, waiting for her to go on, but it was soon apparent that she had done with explanations for now.

"Did I give you what you wanted, Fred?"

Mr. Frederick contemplated this a moment.

"Not completely," he said.

"Is there room in you to be your father's son and your brother's brother and still be a friend to me? I am alone now, you know."

Again Mr. Frederick thought; then he stepped hesitantly into the hallway.

"Nan," Isabelle said. "Fix us something nice. Mr. Martin's made a long journey to arrive here."

They passed into the parlor, and I was left to close the door.

ONE DAY in mid-December, I went to Mattie's to help her move. Snow was falling lightly on my way there; it was just beginning to stick to tree branches and stair railings. I had to tread carefully along the slippery sidewalks.

I had not seen Mattie since the evening of Mr. Edwin's death, but she and I had developed a correspondence. It's odd how letter writing seems to come easier to a troubled heart than to a contented one. Mattie claimed to have hated school, and she usually stayed away from writing and reading as too close to being a student, yet she wrote to me at length and begged me to write back.

"It's almost like having you here," she wrote, "whether I'm putting my day down on paper for you or reading about your day (again and again) and what you do and think in it."

In her letters, Mattie told me Paolo had found neither work nor training for work and that he remained secluded into himself. Lorenzo's new job at the carousel company brought him less money than his work at Stetson Hats had, and Mattie's piecework went up and down, which is why they were moving to cheaper quarters. I was sure cheaper must mean smaller and rougher, though Mattie didn't say so. Sorrowful sentences regularly broke through Mattie's news, but she always followed them with bids at hope, as if she were catching herself by the collar to avoid the brink of self-pity.

"Paolo would not even get out of bed today," she had written in one letter. "It seems to me at such times that it's his heart not his arm that was chopped away. The baby kicked when I was in the kitchen and when I got to Paolo in the bedroom, the child was still again. Paolo didn't believe me or didn't care, but I'm sure if he could feel it once, it would change his mind. Isn't that what babies are for?"

For my part, the news I sent Mattie was mostly Isabelle's news—the death, of course; her father-in-law's suspicions; the various visitors. In describing these things for Mattie, I was laying them out for myself, too. It was as if I'd been receiving picture postcards from a traveler whose itinerary I didn't know; not until I'd spread all the cards on a table and consulted maps and a calendar would I be able to plot out the traveler's course. Isabelle was my traveler, affording me quick, contained glimpses of mysterious landscapes. But my own mind was a traveler, too, and sometimes the places it went were just as surprising.

When I wrote Mattie that Mr. Sylvester Martin's accusations grew out of spite and grief, I was, in part at least, trying on that belief as I might have tried on a pair of shoes, walking around in them to see if they fit comfortably or if they pinched, or if they fit now, but promised to pinch later. I didn't tell Mattie what I'd overheard about the choloroform because I hadn't understood what it meant. Nor did I relate the details of Mr. Frederick's first visit, though I did say he was coming around every few days, which showed he was confident his father was mistaken about Isabelle. Fragments. Suppositions. Gaps. These are the materials out of which knowledge of another person is built. These and what we know of the desires and hopes of our own silent selves. And there is precious little more on which to build that personal knowledge, either.

When I reached Mattie's street, I found Lorenzo outside with a cart on which a few pieces of furniture were loaded. He was looping a rope around the legs of a table and through the slats at the sides of the cart. A skinny horse wearing a thin plaid blanket was hitched to the cart. The animal wore blinders, but he looked as if he wouldn't have bothered to look around at what was happening anyway. There was a spiritlessness about him that told more about his life than if I had tagged after him through a day of arduous tedium and seen his dirty stall or his mealy oats.

"Hanna!" called Lorenzo, jumping down from the cart when he caught sight of me.

He took off his gloves and pushed them in his pockets and reached toward me, grasping my own gloved hands with his bare hands. I was too shy to remove my gloves—following his action, it would seem an extravagant gesture—but I wanted to.

"Mattie said you'd try to come," Lorenzo grinned.

"I hoped my company would help her today."

"It will," Lorenzo said, letting go of my hands. He seemed embarrassed that he was still holding on, and his smile faded. "We all welcome a fresh face around."

"I'm glad to see you again, too," I said, feeling very daring. I was rewarded by the return of his smile.

"I'll walk you in."

The staircase was too narrow for two abreast, so Lorenzo went ahead and I followed.

"We don't have so much," he said, speaking over his shoulder to me, "but it takes the devil's own time to get us out of here."

He was climbing quite slowly, and at first I thought he was tired from having made several trips down with furniture and boxes, but I soon decided he was lagging because he wanted a chance to talk.

"It's Paolo," he said.

"Because he's not able to carry?"

"Not just that. That's only a little."

"Mattie wrote me that he's the same as he was when he came home from the hospital. But you did say it would take time."

Lorenzo stopped and turned to me.

"He's not the same. He's worse."

"Maybe if he could find work . . . if there was something he could still do with his one hand that would . . ."

There was a hard look in Lorenzo's eyes that stopped me. I'd never seen it in him before, and though I could not claim to know him so well that I was versed in all his moods, I felt instinctively that it was something new to him, a combination of anger and futility and abhorrence.

"He can open a bottle and lift it to his mouth well enough," he said bitterly.

"Mattie wrote me—"

"Did she tell you the two different nights he didn't come home?"

His voice was a hoarse whisper, in part to keep the neighbors from overhearing and in part, I think, because his own distress alarmed him.

"We were afraid he was dead somewhere. And when he came back, instead of relief, I was blind angry. You know what he said?"

"What?"

"He said being dead somewhere wouldn't be so bad. For any of us."

"Oh, Lorenzo."

"And Holy Mary forgive me, Hanna, sometimes I almost think so, too. I don't want him dead, but there's nights I want to stay away from home myself, just to breathe free and forget his pain. And hers. To not have it in front of me all the time."

Because I couldn't find any words, I put my hand on Lorenzo's arm to comfort him. He took up my hand and pulled me to him and held me; it was not a lover's embrace, but it made me feel more tenderly toward him than I ever had. The shoulder of his jacket was wet with melted snow, and the stiff wool felt scratchy against my cheek, yet even through our heavy winter clothing, there was a giving and receiving between us that was sweet and candid.

When we heard a door open behind us, Lorenzo dropped his arms from around me and I stepped away from him. We were on the landing near Mrs. Litvak's apartment, and turning at the sound of footsteps, I saw her two oldest girls coming down the dingy hall toward the stairs. They were bent forward, carrying thick bundles on their backs. As they passed single file between me and Lorenzo, they greeted us politely. I saw that their bundles were tied-up stacks of shirts. It made my own back ache to see them.

The girls' passing broke the spell between me and Lorenzo. Or perhaps he regretted revealing himself so. In any case, he said nothing more the rest of the way up, and when we entered the apartment, he spoke not a word to Mattie, only hefting a wooden box of dishes packed in straw and going back downstairs.

"Oh, Hanna," Mattie said when he'd gone, "these men and their silences are like to drive me mad sometimes."

She quickly erased her frown with a resigned smile.

"But getting a man to speak when he doesn't want to is as profitless as looking for pears on an apple tree," she added.

"I've come to work," I said cheerily, taking off my coat and hat. "What's left to be done?"

"Not much," said Mattie looking around the bare room. "Just this basket to go, a sack or two in the kitchen. And the big mattress. Lorenzo's cross about it, but we had to leave it to the last."

"Why?"

"Paolo's still asleep. He came in late last night."

"Does he do that often?"

"Often enough."

Mattie stopped and unnecessarily rearranged some small things in the large basket at her feet. I saw the subject of Paolo was done for now.

"I'm getting him up," Lorenzo said, coming into the apartment.

He spoke forcefully, as if expecting Mattie to protest, but she didn't even look at him. Instead, she went to the kitchen for the two sacks.

"We'll put these on the cart and start walking," she said to me, setting down the sacks to put on her coat. Then she went quickly into the kitchen again and came out with the canaries' cage covered by a heavy wool shawl.

We could hear moans coming from the bedroom, presumably Paolo objecting to being awakened, then Lorenzo ordering his brother to stand up and help him with the mattress. Next, some muttered Italian from Paolo, with the unmistakable inflection of curses.

"Paolo's the oldest," Mattie explained. "He doesn't like being told to."

"I doubt Lorenzo likes doing it," I said.

Mattie gave me a quick, assessing look.

"Let's go," she said. "It's better to leave them alone."

Before we'd reached the ground floor, we could hear the men lumbering down above us, more curt Italian words flying between them. Just as we got to the outside door, there was a loud stumbling noise, and Mattie turned anxiously to the stairs.

"He's all right," Lorenzo shouted down, anticipating Mattie's response.

Mattie hesitated, listening. Paolo's and Lorenzo's footsteps resumed their slow, regular beat. I gently guided her to the door; she led the way out and didn't look back, but it was obvious her mind was still with the men on the stairs.

Our walk was under a mile, but it took us into a different world. Mattie's new home was a "father, son, and holy ghost," which is the name given to a kind of small house made of three rooms, piled one atop the other, connected by a narrow spiral staircase. The house stood in a small courtyard packed close with nine other such homes, off an alley behind a street of taller row houses that kept it always in shadow. Not only light was blocked, but also the movement of air; a steady wind had been blowing during our walk, but when we entered the courtyard, the wind abruptly dropped away.

There was a woodpile in the courtyard and a dead rat near it. Next to the woodpile was a privy, which Mattie said was for the use of all the courtyard's residents. A hydrant in the center of the courtyard was, likewise, for everyone's use. Large tin washtubs leaned beside several doorways; I guessed laundry, and perhaps, in summer, even the bathing of children occurred outdoors, though in summer, the airlessness of the closed-in place would not have been very pleasant. Even then, on a cold winter day, the unmistakable smell of the privy hung in the courtyard, as if, like mildew, it coated the very walls of the houses.

Trinity houses were meant, of course, for single families, ideally small families. But Mattie, Lorenzo, and Paolo would be sharing their house with a family of five, the Dolans. The Dolans had shifted into the two upper rooms so they could let out the first floor.

"We're not as cramped as we could be," said Mrs. Dolan after she'd opened the door to me and Mattie. "Across the way, there's three families, one on each floor. A bandbox tenement, the Guardians of the Poor call it. But common sense and plain need is what it is, as I see it. I know Mr. Martorelli over there. He keeps goats in the cellar; sometimes I get milk from him. His daughter's living over to Rittenhouse Square. She's a wet nurse."

Mrs. Dolan eyed Mattie up and down.

"You might consider it, Mrs. Testa, when the time comes," she said. "I know a doctor is always looking for clean, moral girls for his ladies that are too delicate or too fashionable. It's good money, and they pay to board your own baby out, too. They won't have other babies in those fine houses it seems."

Mattie shook her head. "I don't think so," she said.

"No, Sofia Martorelli doesn't like it either," Mrs. Dolan said, sighing. "She's apart from the servants, but she's not in the family, either, is she? And they make rules over what she must and mustn't eat, for the sake of keeping her milk good. She worries over her little Delia, too, that she'll get sick at the baby farm or be neglected."

"That's the part I couldn't bear," Mattie said.

Mrs. Dolan lifted her eyebrows and, lowering her voice, she confided to us that she'd heard only one in ten babies in infant boardinghomes survived, seeming to forget that just moments ago she'd suggested Mattie send her baby to such a place. Then she made a little grunt and resumed her normal speaking voice.

"Sofia says they've started her mistress's baby on Mellin's Liquid Food to wean it, so she'll soon be home. With Delia. And with empty pockets again."

Mrs. Dolan gave us a meaningful frown and left, walking slowly up the stairs. She was a bulky woman and nearly filled the width of the sharply twisting staircase. Watching her go, it suddenly struck me that the Dolans would be continually passing through Mattie's one-room apartment on their way in and out of the house.

"She's talkative, but she's tolerable. I've met them all. They're a decent family," Mattie said, as if reading my mind.

We set to work sweeping the floor and wiping down the baseboards and the window. It didn't take long, as the room was not very big, and Mrs. Dolan had obviously done some cleaning before us. I brought in some wood from outside, and Mattie put it in the stove, which was to serve them for both cooking and heating. Because of Paolo's injury, they were receiving wood relief, so she knew she'd be able to replenish what I'd taken. We sat down on the floor to wait for the men.

"Well, you've gotten away from those stairs, anyway," I said.

Mattie nodded. She was facing the window and watching the softly falling snow. The flakes were larger and coming more thickly than they had during our walk.

"You mustn't drink from that hydrant," I warned her.

"I'll boil it good."

"Mattie, you can't afford to get sick."

She turned slowly to me. In the gloom, her face looked older, as if her youth had worn away long ago.

"I can't afford bottled water," she said.

I took hold of her hand and held it. She shifted her position a bit and leaned her head on my shoulder. We both gazed out the window across the room, as if we were riding on a train together into some unknown land and were straining to take in what it looked like even though it was too dark to see properly.

The voices of the Testa brothers in the courtyard roused us, and we went to help them unload the cart. I greeted Paolo as we passed, and he returned my hello, but grudgingly, as if he were not pleased to see me. I didn't take offense, for Mattie's sake, and also because I suspected these days Paolo had few good words for anyone. With four of us working, it didn't take long to empty the cart. There wasn't much on it, in any case, as they'd sold off some of their furniture, including the upholstered chairs Mattie had been so proud of.

Mattie found her kettle in a box and put on water for tea, but I excused myself from staying. Lorenzo was able to offer me a ride before he had to return the cart only if I came right away. I gave Mattie a hug and she put on a brave smile, and we made promises to keep writing and to see each other again before too long. I looked through the window as I passed outside and saw Mattie standing by the stove staring at the kettle as if it were a crystal ball and Paolo lying on the mattress on the floor, his face turned to the wall, perhaps also staring, in his mind's eye, into some clouded future. I understood what Lorenzo had said earlier about wanting to flee from the sorrow in Mattie and Paolo.

Snow was still falling, but I was comfortable on the cart, as Mattie had given me a blanket for my lap and I had had the foresight to grab Mr. Edwin's big black umbrella from the hall stand as I left home. Lorenzo declined to share the blanket, but he let me sit close enough to hold the umbrella over both our heads, on the excuse that it let him see better to drive. I found his shyness charming.

Lorenzo directed the cart through streets of row houses and past small alleys also crowded with houses. I often glimpsed, through dark archways, enclosed courtyards like Mattie's. Finally we entered wide Washington Avenue, where we traveled along the railroad corridor. We headed toward the waterfront, passing textile plants and coal yards, then turned north, past Sparks Shot Tower and the South Second Street market. It being neither Wednesday nor Saturday and no farmers in town, the market was quiet, but the shot manufacturers were going.

"How does it work?" I asked, looking up at the hundred-fifty-foot tall brick tower.

"They pour hot lead through screens," Lorenzo said, pointing to the top of the tower, "The falling shot cools and gets hard, and then cools more in water at the bottom. They polish and pack it in those buildings next door."

"Funny to think of lead shot starting out as something like spring rain," I said.

Lorenzo looked at me and smiled.

"You tumble things up, don't you?" he said.

"When we first met," I replied, "you judged me woefully practical and, sadly, not given *enough* to tumbling thoughts."

"When we met," Lorenzo said, still smiling, "I judged you very agreeable. In the thoughts and in the face. And nothing has disappointed."

His flattery embarrassed me, even though I savored it, and I wished we were in a situation where I could move away from him or at least hide my face from his amused gaze for a moment or two. Mercifully we entered a crowded intersection and he had to shift his attention to the traffic. Once through the tangle of carriages and wagons and pushcarts, Lorenzo took up conversation again, but in a different vein.

"There's a carver's job coming up at another factory, Looff's," he said. "I think I could get it."

"Lorenzo, that's wonderful."

"It's in Brooklyn, New York."

I felt as if someone had thumped his fist against my chest. From the inside. Suddenly all the troubles and perplexities of recent weeks loomed larger, and I found I was unexpectedly discouraged and weary.

"Are you going?" I managed.

"I don't know."

"What about your brother? And Mattie and the baby?"

"What about? I can send money—there's nothing more I can do. Maybe without me here, Paolo will stand on his own."

"Do you really believe that?"

Lorenzo was silent a few minutes.

"You know that shot tower?" he said at last. "First, a Quaker owns it, and the shot was for hunting and sport. But when they start selling for soldiers, the Quaker sold out to Sparks. He wouldn't be part of something that could kill someone."

"Washing your hands of something is not always honorable, Lorenzo. Remember Pontius Pilate."

Lorenzo pulled up on the reins so hard the poor old horse reared and neighed in surprise and pain. The cart skidded into the curb and stopped. Grabbing hold of the edge of the seat to keep my place, I dropped Mr. Edwin's umbrella into the street. Lorenzo turned to me and gripped my arms. His eyes were angry, yet the overriding impression his face gave was of despair.

"When I walk into a room, my brother turns away. When I talk to him, he looks at me like he hates me, like I'm his enemy."

"He can't think that," I said.

"Maybe I *am* his enemy, Hanna. Maybe seeing me whole keeps Paolo down."

"You don't know that for certain. And you don't know what your leaving would mean for him."

Lorenzo let go of me and leaned forward, putting his elbows on his knees and his head in his hands.

"I'm sorry for what I said, Lorenzo. I was being selfish. I was thinking what your leaving might mean to *me.*"

He sat up and looked at me. Snowflakes caught on his thick lashes.

"I hope it makes you sad," he said.

"That's not a very friendly wish," I said, trying to sound light.

"It is if I am a certain kind of friend."

He jumped off the cart to retrieve the umbrella, and when he'd climbed on again, he clucked to the horse, and we were on our way once more.

"I haven't decided yet," he said quietly after we'd gone a block.

"You'll tell me if you do?"

"Of course."

We rode in silence the rest of the way, which was not far. Lorenzo was helping me down from the cart in front of the Martins' when the front door of the house opened. We looked up and encountered the alarming sight of Isabelle in the company of two men in bowler hats, one on each side of her holding her arms in a very proprietary way.

"Nan!" she cried when she saw me.

"Who is this?" one of the men said gruffly, pointing at me. He had a bushy mustache and looked like a man in an ad for hair oil.

"This is my friend," Isabelle answered.

"I work here," I said at the same time.

"I am Lorenzo Testa," Lorenzo said, though no one had asked him. "I'm bringing Miss Willer home."

"What's happening, Isabelle?" I said.

"Mrs. Martin is under arrest," said the hair-oil man.

"Arrest?" Lorenzo was incredulous.

"For the murder of her husband, Mr. Edwin Martin. By poison, I believe."

Without further ado, the hair oil man and his companion steered Isabelle to a waiting buggy. I stared after them, stupefied, half expecting them to turn around and come back, full of apologies for their mistake. Instead, the buggy rounded the corner and disappeared. Even before they were out of sight, the soft, remorseless snow had begun to erase the marks of their wheels.

TWENTY-FIVE

WITH THE house empty, I could not ask Lorenzo to come in, though I know he was chilled and could have used a cup of beef broth or cocoa. I didn't regret it. Propriety was my ally; I couldn't have tolerated anyone's company just then, not even his.

The parlor fire was low when I went in, so I stoked it, out of habit, I suppose, but also with some lingering, half-formed presumption that Isabelle would soon be brought home. And though on the street I'd wished to be alone, once inside, I found the solitude eerie. The furnace provided sufficient warmth, but keeping the parlor fire lit gave the house a semblance of fuller occupancy.

I went through to the kitchen and made myself some cocoa. I was about to sit at the table to drink it when, on a sudden whim, I put a saucer under my cup and carried it into the parlor.

I had never sat down in the parlor before. I surveyed the choice of seats nervously. Not the couch—it had been too recently a bier. There were a number of chairs. The Martins had never had so many guests at one time that all the chairs were filled, but, of course, a proper parlor could not do with fewer, since there must be cool seats available for the ladies. Gentlemen always stood up when a lady entered a room, and no lady would sit in a chair still warm from a man.

I moved toward the matched pair of chairs that had been the customary places of Isabelle and Mr. Edwin. Both chairs were of mahogany with dark green horsehair upholstery, but Mr. Edwin's was shaped like a throne and Isabelle's like a perch. His had arms and a high back for resting his head—indeed, I'd often seen him leaning back comfortably in this chair with his legs stretched out before him or resting on a hassock and his elbows braced on the chair arms while he read the newspapers. Isabelle, by contrast, always sat up straight in her armless chair, her body not touching the chair's low back, her hands in her lap, busy with stitchery or holding open a small book or simply folded together. Though I had to overcome a momentary sense of wickedness, I sat firmly down in Mr. Edwin's chair.

The familiar room seemed different when viewed from a seated position, less grand somehow, a bit cluttered and closed in. I thought, incongruously, of Mattie's tight, airless courtyard, and then, with a shudder, of where Isabelle might be spending the night. I had never seen a jail cell, but I imagined it must be, at the least, cramped, barren, and cheerless. I looked across at Isabelle's chair. When would she be home again? Would she ever come home? What had really happened in this room the night Mr. Edwin died?

Poisoning is a very private crime. I did not want to believe Isabelle had killed Mr. Edwin. I didn't want to believe she had even wanted him dead, but if she had, poisoning would have appealed to her, would even have allowed her, perhaps, to feel she had not done anything quite so terrible as murder, but only a different kind of remedying.

I took my cup and saucer back to the kitchen and went into the pantry for the dust pan to sweep up some cocoa I'd spilled earlier. I noticed Isabelle had set out the nutmeg grater and the bottle of brandied orange and lemon peels and had brought down a dozen apples from the sand jar in the cold half of the attic. We'd planned to make seed cakes and nut breads tomorrow for Mrs. Cox's Christmas baskets for the needy in

Northern Liberties, and one or two for ourselves as well. Finding Isabelle's small preparations sent a great rush of desolation through my heart. We always assume a future. Life would be unbearable and unworkable without trust in a future, but it's inevitable this trust will be betrayed from time to time. The nutmeg grater and the fruits were evidence of such a betrayal.

I picked up the grater and put it back in its drawer. I didn't know what things I might have to do tomorrow, but baking Christmas breads was not likely to be one of them. And beyond tomorrow?

A few days after Mr. Edwin's death, Isabelle had told me not to worry about my place with her, that she was Mr. Edwin's sole beneficiary and that he had even removed the odious clause from an earlier will that had said she would receive an allowance from the estate only as long as she remained unmarried. But now Isabelle was gone, plucked out of her ordinary life like a pit from a cherry. What need had a woman in jail for a maid? I'd better write to my father, I thought, and let him know that my Christmas visit might extend indefinitely. It was not only Isabelle who had been plucked.

☙ "WHAT'S ALL THIS?" Mr. Frederick said when I let him in the next day, midmorning.

Not knowing what else to do, I had searched out his address in a little book on Isabelle's writing desk and sent word to him by the draper's boy. By the time Mr. Frederick arrived, several policemen were there combing all the rooms, even mine, for "criminal artifacts," and the house was beginning to look as if a great wind had swept through it.

I'd tried, at first, to follow behind them righting things, but I couldn't keep up, and, besides, the one in charge, a Mr. Hauser, said I must sit in one place so they might keep an eye on me. He set a man to watch me lest I try to sneak away and conceal something from them, though even if I'd had that impulse I wouldn't have known what needed hiding. There seemed little pattern to the things they were putting aside to take with them: medicine bottles, a drinking glass, books, a packet of letters.

"Do they have to be so careless?" Mr. Frederick asked when I'd explained what the men were about. "Who's in charge?"

I took him through to the Martins' bedroom, where we found Mr. Hauser at Isabelle's bureau. He paused when we entered. In one hand he held a pale blue, ruffled petticoat and in the other a combination chemise-drawers of pink satin.

It was disconcerting to see the policeman digging through Isabelle's lingerie. At best, it seemed rude, at worst, a violation of her person, as if he'd sidled unnoticed to her bedside and was caressing her while she slept. I blushed to think of the man searching my own room, ferreting through my few belongings, stirring the ashes in the little coal stove, pulling the chamber pot out from under my bed. The pot was clean, but still and all a personal item that none but me ever handled, and I wondered, for the first time, about how Mr. Edwin could have been so indifferent about my emptying his every morning. The Martins had a water closet, but Mr. Edwin had not liked walking down the hall at night; he said it interrupted his sleepy frame of mind too sharply and made a labyrinth out of a simple business.

"Sir, what are you doing?" Mr. Frederick demanded, outraged.

"Who are you?" replied Mr. Hauser, unabashed.

"I'm Mrs. Martin's brother-in-law. I understand you have a job to do, but is this really necessary?" Mr. Frederick pointed to the silky garments in Mr. Hauser's hands.

"The deceased was your brother?"

"Yes."

"Then you ought to want us to get to the bottom of this."

"Of course, but to think that Mrs. Martin could ever . . . or that you'd find anything among her intimate . . ."

"We're neither judge nor jury, Mr. Martin," Mr. Hauser said, throwing the clothes in his hands onto the bed and opening another drawer. "You might say we're like sieves. Sieves with brains."

He looked up from the drawer and tapped the side of his head with his finger.

"And if we don't sort through everything . . . why, we just might miss the one nugget of ore that would make all the difference. You'd be surprised where people hide things, what they keep that they should have thrown away, what innocent-appearing item turns out to be the final nail, as they say."

He gave Mr. Frederick an unpleasant smile.

"Or," he added, "that gets them off the hook, if that's your concern."

He tossed a corset, two embroidered crepe de chine night-gowns, and a pair of lace-trimmed knickers onto the bed.

"She liked luxury, didn't she, your sister-in-law?"

"As you yourself said," Mr. Frederick replied icily, "it's not your place to judge."

"Nor yours to interfere," Mr. Hauser growled. "If you intend to stay, I must require you to wait in the parlor with this young lady while we finish."

"No need, I'm leaving."

I accompanied Mr. Frederick to the front door.

"You were right to send for me, Willer," he said. "I'll go round to Edwin's lawyer. Mr. Fisk, isn't it? And to see Mrs. Martin if I can. Will you manage here?"

"Certainly, sir."

Managing turned out to include fixing sandwiches and coffee and baked apples for the lot of policemen. Mr. Hauser presented it as a request, but we both knew there was no question of refusal. It gave me something to do, anyway, and helped quiet the flutters in my stomach, though they were not totally gone even by late evening when all the furniture and whatnots had been put to rights again and I had climbed trembling into my bed at the top of the silent, forsaken house.

I WENT down the block next morning to buy green coffee beans, the policemen having depleted our stock. I didn't want to go into Mr. Edwin's shop below for Sanborn coffee, as I usually did, for fear of being peppered with questions. My instinct turned out to be right, as Isabelle's arrest was front page news. I picked up copies of *The Item, The Call, Philadelphia Record* and *The Star,* in case one had information the others didn't, and hurried home to read them.

I learned nothing I did not already know, in the way of facts. The news writers called Isabelle a "mysterious, dark-eyed beauty" and Mr. Edwin a "respected businessman." There was nothing inaccurate in these descriptions, but something in them shaded both the Martins in ways that made them seem a bit different from what they actually were. My feeling sprang, no doubt, from the fact that I knew them well, from many sides, and that the news writers did not, and, moreover, that they had had to condense what they did know.

I tried to think what opinions strangers might form from the articles. Was it a bad thing for a woman to be mysterious? For a widow to be beautiful? Or was it only bad when that woman got herself in the papers as a suspected murderess? And was Mr. Edwin's death more tragic because he was respected and in business? Suppose my father or Lorenzo or Paolo had died under suspicious circumstances? Would such a death be less shocking than Mr. Edwin's? I had no answers for these problems. I resolved to keep up with all the papers as long as this affair went on. I decided, too, to visit Isabelle that very day, if they'd let me, to see what she had to say for herself.

Isabelle was being held at the central police station in old City Hall at Fifth and Chestnut, easy walking distance. I would have walked in any case. There was money in the house—I knew where Isabelle kept her household allowance—but I would not have spent any on carfare, as I didn't know when or if other money would be available. There was a biting wind that hurt my face, and my toes ached despite my quick pace.

The windows of the businesses I passed were decked with spruce garlands and parsley bunches tied with red ribbons, and shop windows were spread with attractive displays of gifts. Many of the big buildings along Bankers' Row had wreaths on their doors.

This was no day for side trips, but I was reminded of the better-class residential streets Isabelle had told me about where lattice window blinds were left open in order to show off large evergreen trees inside decked with gilt papers and glass balls and little pictures. Isabelle had said some households allowed passersby to come in to view their trees and the scenes laid beneath them. Last year, she'd visited one house with a model steamboat three feet long with fifty passengers cut from colored paper and a sea of blue bunting, and another that had a perfectly accurate miniature fire-hose carriage with doll firemen. She'd promised to take me knocking on doors with her this year, but, of course, that was before Mr. Edwin died.

The police station was a dreary place, despite the holly sprigs someone had pinned around the tall receiving desk. The walls were painted a yellow that looked more like an accidental stain than a true color. Still, it was well heated, and I was grateful for that. I thought I'd sit on one of the splintery benches a while to warm up before walking home if it turned out they wouldn't let me see Isabelle.

There were already a few pitiable creatures on the benches— an old man, asleep and snoring, with rags tied around his shoes to keep the soles and tops together; two women, one youngish and one of indeterminate age, both with bright orange hair and painted red lips and tired eyes; and a skinny boy of about twelve, who kept wringing his cap worriedly in his hands and twisting it round and round and round.

The policeman behind the high desk was hugely fat. I could not picture him running down the street after a thief or wrestling a ruffian in an alley. They probably never sent him out, except for parades.

"Excuse me," I said, "I'd like to see Mrs. Martin?"

"A prisoner?" the fat policeman said in a bored voice.

"Yes."

He shuffled through some papers on his desk and read bits from a couple of them.

"Relative?" he asked, looking down at me from his tall stool.

"No."

He leaned over and pulled a large black ledger from under the desk. The stool creaked as he shifted his weight from one haunch to the other.

"She's already had a visitor today," he said, his gaze on the open ledger.

"I'm her maid," I said. "I thought there might be something she'd want me to bring her from home."

"She'll have to make do. Just like everybody else."

"There's only one visitor allowed a day?" I said.

He nodded, and his jowls shook like turkey wattles. I'd have to get there earlier tomorrow.

"Says here she's in for murdering her husband," he said, leaning forward as if he had some secret information for me. "If it was up to me, she wouldn't get no visitors at all."

"That hasn't been proved yet," I said, indignant, "and you don't know that it will be."

"People don't get themselves arrested over nothing. She's guilty all right. Of something."

He leaned back, settling into his flesh again, and I saw there was no use in arguing with him. I went and sat on the bench beside the two women, who slid aside to make me room. The fat policeman peered over his desk at us, seeming to gloat over our anxieties. While I waited for the cold to seep out of my feet, I indulged in imagining myself giving him a great shove, toppling him backward off his stool onto the floor, where he'd probably squirm as helplessly as a huge caterpillar.

Just as I was thinking I was ready to leave, another policeman came through a door behind the desk. The fat one looked over the papers the new policeman had brought him; then he said something to him in a hushed tone and pointed at the benches. The new policeman looked right at me, nodded to the fat policeman, and left, going back through the door he'd come in by.

"Was that *Isabelle* Martin?" the fat man called to me, as if the jail were full of Mrs. Martins accused of murdering Mr. Martins.

"Yes," I said, standing up.

He beckoned me forward.

"Her other visitor was a lawyer," he said. "That don't count."

"I can see her?"

He jerked his head to the side, indicating a door to my right, by which I guessed he meant I should go through it. Then he made himself very busy with papers on his desk. I didn't want to ask him anything more, for fear he'd change his mind about letting me see Isabelle, so I went through the door and into a short, narrow hall. There was another desk just inside the doorway, but of normal height, and the man seated at it was of normal girth and bulk. There were two shut doors in the hall, one in each wall.

"Name?" said the policeman at the desk.

"Mine?"

He looked at me with disdain.

"Hanna Willer," I answered.

He wrote it down.

"Prisoner?"

"Mrs. Martin. *Isabelle* Martin."

He wrote that down, too.

"Wait in there," he said, and pointed to the door in the left-hand wall.

I entered a small room furnished with a scarred wood table and two bare wood chairs. A tiny barred window high up in one wall provided the only light, which, owing to the overcast day, was gray and feeble. Unlike the heated entry room of the station house, this room was cold and damp, like a dirt cellar. I took the chair facing the door and sat down to wait. After about fifteen minutes, the door opened and Isabelle came in. Someone behind her closed the door. I heard the turn of a key. We were locked in.

She said nothing, but stood there staring at me with those great dark eyes of hers. If she was surprised to see me, she didn't show it. Her hair was unkempt, stray pieces having pulled out of her bun at the sides and back, but otherwise her appearance was as usual. I don't know what I had expected—a smeared, tear-stained face, a disarrangement of her clothing— but there was none of it. Of course, she'd only been in jail two nights.

"Isabelle," I said, standing up. "How are you?"

It seemed a dull question and also a profound one. I hadn't known I was going to ask it, nor what else, exactly, I was going to say to her, but there had to be a start somewhere, and Isabelle was not offering one. I realized then that she must be more disarranged than showed on the outside.

"Oh, Nan, I'm so glad you came," she said, moving forward and taking both my hands. Her fingers were icy, and when she drew close to embrace me, I could smell her unwashed body and other, fainter odors—cooked cabbage and sour milk.

I drew the chairs away from the table so we might sit nearer each other and soften a bit the hard simplicity of the locked room.

"I have no mirror," Isabelle said, tucking her loose hair behind her ears.

"I don't carry one," I said, digging in my purse, "but I do have a brush."

Isabelle pulled the pins out of her bun and let her hair fall heavy down her back. Without her asking, I stood behind her and began brushing with long, leisurely strokes. As I was a housemaid, not a personal maid, it was not something I was used to doing. I had brushed Isabelle's hair for her one other time, however—the day after the birth of Agatha Yvonne, when Isabelle was weak in both body and spirit and there was no real comfort words could provide her. I did it unasked then, too.

When I'd finished, Isabelle repinned her hair and seemed more in control of herself. She sat up straighter and even managed a smile when she thanked me that was truly pleased, not a sad or sham smile, as some can be.

"Will they let you keep the brush?" I said, holding it out to her.

"I expect they will," she said, taking it. "There was a lawyer here this morning—a very high-priced lawyer sent by my father—and he told me it had been arranged I could have certain things—writing paper and cologne and such—if I wanted. I can even send out for meals."

"Really?"

I thought of the fat policeman and how he'd dislike Isabelle's privileges. I hoped he'd have to deliver her food personally, though I thought it unlikely. But he'd probably have to register its arrival and watch it go in.

"Yes, really," Isabelle said, a trifle put out. "Haven't I always told you my father is an influential man? You don't think he'd leave me in these circumstances without some offer of assistance?"

"Will he come to see you, do you think?"

Isabelle looked up at the little window and frowned.

"Certainly not," she said quietly.

I regretted my curiosity. It had overrun discretion.

"Isabelle, I'm not sure what to do about the house . . . about staying on. . . . I thought I'd best move back to my father's, and then, later, if you still need . . . I mean, when you return . . ."

"Oh, no, Nan, I want you to stay at the house. I'll send word to Mr. Fisk that your pay is to be kept up and that you're to have food and fuel allowances, too. I should feel abandoned if you left. You wouldn't abandon me, Nan, would you, just when I most need a friend?"

I shook my head no, though I couldn't think how staying on at the Martins' as a hired servant proved friendship.

"I didn't mean to unsettle your mind," I said. "I only wanted some guidance about the house. I expect your situation is unsettling enough."

Isabelle's eyes widened a bit, and her cheeks flushed with color.

"The first night was terrible, of course," she said. "Unsettling, as you say. But now—and I know this might sound strange—I'm almost peaceful."

"Peaceful?"

"Resigned, perhaps, is a better word. Or suspended. Yes, suspended. As if this is a necessary pause between two halves of my life, Edwin's time and the time after Edwin. It's a bit like being at a water-cure retreat. Strict, slow, purifying."

I was amazed at this description. Did it signify the attitude of an innocent person or a guilty one? Isabelle seemed to be saying it only required patience on her part and she'd be freed. Because she had done no wrong? Because she sincerely believed she had done no wrong? Or because she had confidence in the skills of her father's expensive lawyer?

"Isabelle, have you told all there is to Mr. Edwin's last illness and his final night?"

She stared at me, her expression lively with thought.

"You mustn't ask me that, Nan."

She stood up and paced the little room back and forth once. Then she stood still, gently slapping the back of the hairbrush against her open palm, while regarding me with a calm, frank look.

"The lawyer says I'm not to speak with anyone about what happened. I'm not even going to testify in court. It will be a trial of medical experts, he says. Medical evidence is his specialty."

"But, Isabelle—"

A key sounded loudly in the lock, and the door opened. A man stood waiting in the hall to take Isabelle away. She obediently turned to go, but she looked back at me over her shoulder as the man gripped her elbow.

"I have said before what happened. You must decide for yourself, Nan," she said.

And then she was gone.

TWENTY-SIX

AFTER MY visit to Isabelle, there were only four more days until Christmas Eve, when I was expected at my father's. Though my duties in the Martin house were greatly abbreviated with both Isabelle and Mr. Edwin absent, the season kept me busy. I sewed a simple blouse for Elsinore out of a remnant of figured India silk Isabelle had given me for myself. I took some of my savings and spent a day of careful shopping, coming home with a meerschaum pipe with a turkey-bone stem for my father, an ivory piecrust jagger for Sippy, and for Mattie, a tiny bottle of scent.

Mrs. Cox came by to ask that I bake the promised breads and cakes for the poor in Northern Liberties, as she didn't want Isabelle's misfortune to be multiplied by stinting on the baskets for hungry mothers and children. This chore took a full day and permitted a second visit by Mrs. Cox to pick up the baked goods, which opportunity she used, as she had the first, to press me for information. As I'd not gone to see Isabelle again, I could tell Mrs. Cox nothing new, and she seemed dissatisfied with me because of that and because, I suspect, I wouldn't venture any opinions about Mr. Edwin's death or the Martins' marriage.

Mrs. Cox had a maid with her to carry the breads and cakes, and as they were leaving, she asked the girl wouldn't she like to have such a convenience as to work in a house with no master or mistress and all the cupboards unlocked. I knew she meant it as a barb to me, and though I restrained myself from showing her, I did feel it as one, especially since, unknown to her, I had put away two loaves and two cakes to take to my family for Christmas. Isabelle would almost certainly have let me have them if she'd been there, but Mrs. Cox made me feel a bit of a thief anyway—though only for a short while, as later I thought it was she, in a way, who had come looking for unlocked cupboards, hoping to spy out some tittle-tattle on the Martins.

I blamed Mrs. Cox for the visit from Mr. Fisk the next day, as I'm sure she told her husband I wasn't to be trusted and he passed it on to the lawyer. It could have happened that way. Sometimes the roots of matters are never fully dug out. Mr. Fisk said it was Mr. Sylvester Martin who had concerns, and it could have happened that way, too.

"I know Mrs. Martin wishes you to stay on," Mr. Fisk said, standing in the entrance hallway. Neither of us felt right about using the parlor. "But it is a delicate situation. Mr. Martin senior has entered a caveat against his son's will—indeed, Mrs. Martin's arrest alone would have thrown the terms of the document into question—and it is not clear in whose camp you abide, so to speak."

"I abide in my own camp, sir, as it's not my place nor my desire to take sides," I said, "and I don't see how dusting furniture and sweeping floors can be seen as taking sides anyway. Surely Mr. Martin doesn't expect to come do it himself."

"There's no need for insolence," Mr. Fisk said crisply. "I mention this for your sake as much as for anyone's."

"For my sake?"

"You need to be sure of your earnings, I suppose? How long they will last?"

"Yes, sir."

"And if you're called to give testimony, you don't want people thinking what you say is colored by who has bought your dinner."

"No, sir," I answered, alarmed by the thought of appearing in court, which possibility had not occurred to me.

"Very well, then. I'll speak to Mr. Martin and to your mistress. I believe I can arrange that for the time being you are provided for out of the estate, so that neither one of them can be seen as your benefactor. However things turn out, it would be well to have someone looking out for the house in the meanwhile. They don't agree on much, but I think they can agree on that."

"Thank you, sir."

Mr. Fisk nodded, acknowledging the appropriateness of my repentance and gratitude. Then he narrowed his eyes at me, which was a feat, as he had narrow eyes naturally, almost as tapered as the eyes of the Chinaman on Race Street who laundered our sheets.

"Take care that things are kept as they should be," the lawyer said ominously.

"Of course, sir," I said.

He put on his hat, and I stepped in front of him to open the door. He went out, but hesitated on the small landing at the top of the stairs to the street, one last thing on his mind.

"You understand, Willer," he said, "that you won't get your full wages. After all, your work is much less."

"If you say so, sir," I replied, knowing there was no point in disputing him.

❧ I SLEPT poorly the night before my departure; I was worrying about the future, near and far, both mine and others'. Also, a dog somewhere was howling through most of the night, and I remembered Sippy saying that was a foreboding of calamity.

A month and a half ago, the Christmas holiday had presented itself as a bright spot on the horizon; I'd imagined all the pretty things Isabelle and I would do to decorate the house, and the grace of two whole days away from work, and

I had looked forward to the homey pleasures of sitting by my old fireside and sleeping in my old bed with Elsinore and sharing Christmas dinner with the Testas. Now, despite my satchel of gifts, I was going home more petitioner than provider, and my friends were as likely to bring gloom as gaiety to our Christmas table.

I'd arranged weeks ago to take the train to Hatboro, where my father was to meet me, and though I should have changed the plan due to my newly reduced circumstances, I did not, holding stubbornly to a wish for some comfort. I took a trolley down Market to the Broad Street Station, whose tall clock tower and spires and arched windows and entryways made it look more like a cathedral than a railroad terminal. But unlike the statues of holy men and Bible scenes I'd seen on European churches in books, the facade of the station was sculpted with history lessons on the progress of technology.

There was a jollity to the bustle of people moving through the grand spaces inside, owing, I guess, to holiday expectations, but instead of cheering me, the atmosphere only made my worries seem heavier. I settled myself on the train, put my parcels and my ticket on the empty seat beside me, and was asleep before the train had left the elevated tracks along the Chinese Wall viaduct. I didn't wake fully until one stop before mine, not even when the conductor came by collecting tickets, though I heard his voice singing out the stations and the all-aboards as if from far away across a snowy weed meadow.

It was dusk when I arrived at Hatboro, but I quickly picked out my father's wagon from among several others. He gave me his customarily reserved greeting, but he'd thought to bring some heated bricks wrapped in a blanket for me, so I had a warm footrest and a warm covering to put over my lap and hands, and no hullabaloo salute could have made me feel more welcomed or valued.

As we rode silently through the darkening countryside, past shorn fields, grist mills, and quarries, the defeating grip that what-ifs and hows had had on my spirits during the previous night at last loosened. I was not thinking any more clearly, but somehow the cold, clean air made the need for clear thinking seem less urgent. I became aware of a place within me as still as the winter night, a tiny place, like the germ in a wheat kernel, but like the tiny germ, potent. Out of it would come answers when answers were required, if I let them and if I listened. The full sureness of this feeling soon evaporated—impermanence was in its nature, like the skin of a soap bubble—but I retained from it a new sense of strength.

We stopped in Horshamville, where Elsinore's school was. The Friends meetinghouse was lit, but that was not our destination. One of the stores was still open to supply the housewives of the village's twenty homes with any last-minute needs. We took our bricks inside to reheat them on the store's stove, and my father bought a vial of oil of peppermint Elsinore wanted for making pulled candy. Prospectville and Davis Grove, villages nearer our house, were both much smaller than Horshamville, and their lone general stores didn't carry such niceties as oil of peppermint, though you could order it in.

"I've watched in the papers about your lady," my father said when we were on the road again.

"I went to see her," I said.

"In jail?" My father's voice was both horrified and intrigued.

"Yes. But not in her cell."

"Did she show remorse?"

"No."

My father harrumphed.

"It's got so few know how to feel shame anymore," he said.

"Perhaps she has nothing to be ashamed of," I replied.

"How can you believe that?" he asked. "With the new will and the secret medicines."

I made no answer, as I didn't know precisely what I believed. Appearances certainly weighed against Isabelle. Additionally I was aware of things others were not, such as Isabelle's general unhappiness and her specific dislike of her husband's physical attentions. But were these enough to lead her, or anyone, to cold-blooded, calculated murder? If such feelings naturally bred murderous intent, wouldn't there be many more dead husbands about?

I had read numerous editorials both praising and descrying the "new woman," who sought to exert influence on matters beyond her own home, to lead a life useful to society and not just to her own family. From the ranks of the "new women" came suffragettes, housing reformers, home economists, advocates for child laborers, and prohibitionists. I remember Reverend Dale once objecting to ladies' moral reform associations on the grounds that they debased ladies' minds by making them too familiar with vice.

Perhaps the "new women" were simply discontented wives and mothers who had accepted their private lots and turned their discontent outward to remedy social ills. But what of women like Isabelle, who had no larger interests? How did they make their lives work? Surely not by murder.

"You wrote you might be finding yourself between positions for a while," my father said as we turned off the main road onto the long track that would take us home.

"That was just settled yesterday," I replied. "A lawyer came by and said I was to be kept on through the trial."

"I don't like you staying in a poisoner's house."

"That's not been shown to be true, yet, Father, however bad you think it looks."

My father made a low growling noise as he used to do when he came up against my mother's will and knew it couldn't be changed. That was usually in small things, like how she might spend a bit of her egg money or excusing the children from chores for a church picnic.

"You're to leave not an hour past that woman's conviction," he said sternly.

I didn't dispute this, letting him claim the easy victory. If Isabelle were convicted, I'd have no choice but to leave. All that was left for me to do, it seemed then, was wait.

Our last miles were under a huge, starry sky. In the city, with its congestion of buildings and sooty, odorous air, the sky was obscured, broken into pieces, almost forgotten. Yet the sky was half the world. My heart swelled with awe to see it, despite my mind's somber turnings.

⤭ EARLY CHRISTMAS morning, we all went to a service given by a traveling minister in the hall at Prospectville, and I was gladdened to meet many of my old neighbors there and to hear news from relatives of those who had moved away and to see how children I'd help Sippy birth had grown.

A number of my former schoolmates already had husbands and one or two babies; Elsinore asked me if that didn't make me feel restless, and I could honestly say it did not. I wondered at her remark though, as such inquiries often tell on the questioner.

The biggest part of the rest of the day was spent preparing Christmas dinner, and though the work was similar to what I was required to do every day at the Martins', it gave deeper satisfaction because it was done in a place I belonged to, with and for people who belonged to me.

Sippy and Elsinore had designed a grand meal, as befit the holiday. We were to start with cream of onion soup and fried smelts with tartar sauce. Then would come roast pork loin, potato balls, roast apples, hominy croquettes, and celery salad, and for dessert, mince pie and deep apple pie, cheese and nuts. We'd gone into my baked goods for breakfast, and brought one cake to the minister, and still had some left to send home with Mattie.

We expected the Testas about three o'clock. At two-thirty, we heard the crunch of footsteps coming up the frozen path, but when I opened the door, I found only Lorenzo there.

"Paolo didn't want the trip," he explained as soon as he'd stepped inside. "And Mattie won't leave him on Christmas."

I made no answer, but my face must have given away my consternation.

"I shouldn't come alone," Lorenzo said haltingly.

"Of course you should," Sippy called from her place by the hearth. "Give Elsie your things and come here to the fire."

Elsinore hurried forward to take Lorenzo's scarf and jacket.

"Yes, come in," I said, recovering myself. "I'm glad you felt you could come on your own."

"*Grazie*," Lorenzo answered.

"Some hot cider, now," my father boomed. "You've had a cold walk from the coach."

I longed to take Lorenzo aside and ask him more about Mattie and Paolo, but having made him doubtful of his welcome, I wanted to leave the subject be for a while. So the evening progressed warmly, with feasting and well-wishing, and even some singing. After dinner, Elsinore read us the Christmas story from Luke, which is longer than the one in Matthew, but my favorite because it has so much of Mary in it. I like how she converses with the angel Gabriel, and how the baby John jumps inside Elizabeth's womb when Mary comes to visit, and most especially, how after everyone has come to see her baby in the manger, it says that Mary "kept all these things and pondered them in her heart."

Elsinore recited "Twas the Night Before Christmas," too, and Lorenzo said she could be an actress, she did reading and reciting so well and was pretty enough, besides. My father protested that he expected Elsinore to find more honest uses for her talents and her prettiness, and Lorenzo said she surely would, and hadn't she already done so right by our fireside tonight? Elsinore was wearing the new blouse, and she did look very pretty, with the firelight casting a gleam on the silky fabric and on her pale hair and making her cheeks pink from its heat.

The Testas had meant to spend the night with us, and my father insisted there was no reason to alter this plan. He was taking me and Elsinore to Philadelphia first thing in the morning, anyway, and Lorenzo could easily ride along. I'd decided to close up most of the rooms at the Martins', and though it took some doing, I'd convinced my father to let me bring Elsinore to town for a few days to help me with the heavy cleaning.

As everyone separated to prepare for bed, I invited Lorenzo to walk outside and look at the stars. The sky was as dazzling as it had been the night before, and I saw by Lorenzo's expression that he was as moved by it as I had been. But tonight, I could not shake my earthly concerns.

"You couldn't convince them to come?" I said after we'd gazed at the stars a few moments in silence.

"I try, Hanna," Lorenzo said.

"I'm sure you did."

"And I bought them a chicken and some turnips and onions. Mattie was happy to make the private Christmas dinner."

"Are things any better with Paolo?"

"A bit. He found work."

"Really?"

Lorenzo hung his head and frowned.

"It has money, so he feels better, not so useless. That's good, I guess, but it's not . . . he shouldn't have to . . ."

"What?"

Lorenzo looked at me.

"He is doing, but he feels ashamed, too. It's a low use of any man, but Paolo . . . he was always so full of pride . . ."

"What work is it?" I said.

"Collecting for a dog pure loft."

"A dog pure loft?"

"To go around the city picking up dog wastes, then take it to the loft to dry out. They sell it to tanneries for the leather curing. He wants drying shelves in our own house so he could sell direct, but I wouldn't let him. The smell . . . and Mattie could get sick. We fight about it."

"Surely Mattie backed you."

"She's a good wife. She stayed out."

Why is it, I wondered, that men think quiet wives are good wives? Why shouldn't Mattie have a say about living with shelves of drying dog feces? Perhaps, if their situation were grim enough, she'd even agree it was a necessity, but Lorenzo seemed to think her opinion should not be heard either way.

"You're getting cold," Lorenzo said. "We'll go back in."

"Actually, I'm enjoying the cold," I lied, not wishing to be bossed.

"For me, everything this evening has joy," Lorenzo said, making me feel sorry for my crossness.

He took his hand from his pocket and reached toward me, and I brought my hand from beneath my wrap. His warm, hard fingers closed around mine. He peered at me in the darkness. We had been outside long enough that I could see details fairly well, and I was sure by the cast of his eyes that he wanted to kiss me. We were in sight of the house, however, and he may have been made timid by the closeness of my father. At any rate, we did not kiss, but only stood looking at each other, with a kind of fierceness fermenting between us, so that, in the end, I felt I *had* been kissed, and very thoroughly, too.

ELSINORE WAS excited to be going for a stay in the city, her first, and her high spirits dominated the ride to Philadelphia. She was full of questions and soon had us describing our favorite places and various interesting sights. I was surprised to realize, at one point, that she'd elicited a promise from Lorenzo to take us both to a cricket match come spring. Millhands from Kensington regularly played college men from Haverford, and there were four gentlemen's cricket clubs, besides, and a team that traveled to England to play. Elsinore had solicited the invitation so skillfully and modestly that I could not recall, even when I tried, a specific request on her part, though it was clear to me the idea had been hers. I wondered if Lorenzo had noticed the details of the transaction, or if he was under the impression that he himself had originated the plan.

Father took us to the Testas first because Elsinore wanted to deliver the basket of food we'd brought in person and wish Mattie a happy new year. I worried about her seeing the dreary courtyard, as I knew she hadn't encountered anything like it before, but I finally concluded she was old enough and sensible enough to manage it. And I wanted to visit Mattie, too.

Because Elsinore was so busy taking in everything around her on all sides, she was the first one to spot Mattie standing on the sidewalk outside the alley leading to her courtyard. She was clutching a shawl tightly around her and standing very still, only turning her head now and then to look up and down the street. When Elsinore pointed her out, Lorenzo jumped off the wagon and ran to her. Just to watch him hurry like that made my heart stop with fear. By the time our wagon reached Mattie, Lorenzo had left her and was rushing down the alley.

"Mattie, what is it?" I said.

She was shivering when Elsinore and I came up to her.

"How long have you been out here?" my father said, joining us.

Mattie looked round at all three of us. She showed no curiosity at our arrival, though we hadn't been expected.

"Where's her place, Hanna?" Father asked me. "We've got to get her inside."

"No!" Mattie shouted, still shivering.

"Mattie," I said softly. She looked at me, as if just recognizing me.

"Paolo," she said, starting to cry.

I put my arm around her shoulders, and she leaned into

me. When I turned her toward the alley, she walked with me a few steps, then stopped short.

"No, no," she wailed, and would go no farther.

"Elsie," Father said. "Get a couple of blankets from the wagon. If she won't go in, at least we can wrap her up."

Elsinore ran to the wagon and back. We draped the blankets on Mattie, using the end of one to cover her bare head. I told my father the turns to take to get to the Testa home, and he set off to see what was the matter. Mattie was so upset, I didn't want to press her for answers. We waited for what seemed a long time, none of us speaking. Passersby looked questioningly at us, but no one stopped to ask if we needed help. I could see Elsinore was frightened by Mattie's strangeness. She stood close to me and linked her arm through mine.

Finally, we saw Father come around the corner of the alley. He beckoned to me, and I went to him, leaving Mattie with Elsinore.

"Her husband's dead," he said.

"What happened?"

"Hanged himself. Mattie found him this morning when she got in from the market. She went screaming outside, and the neighbor lady from upstairs came to see what was what. She got her mister to cut him down and lay him out on the bed, but they couldn't get Mattie to come back in. She's been out on the street about two hours, they say. Waiting for Lorenzo, they figured."

"Lorenzo's with him now?"

My father nodded.

"He wants her to come in and wash the body," he said, looking over toward Mattie.

It was Mattie's place to do this, of course, but I didn't see how she could in her present state. If she weren't pregnant, I might have tried to cajole her, but I feared for the baby's health if Mattie became any more distraught. Digging in my reticule, I drew out my house keys and held them out to my father.

"Take Mattie to the Martins'," I said. "Elsinore can get her

260

something hot to drink and put her to bed. My room's at the top of the house. There's a coal fire already laid. If you light it while they're in the kitchen, the room will be warmed when she gets to it."

My father shook his head and refused the keys.

"I'm not going into a stranger's house," he said.

"I'll come along as soon as I can. I just want to help Lorenzo with his brother. I think Mattie would want me to, if she were more mindful."

"It's not right."

"What?"

"None of it."

I sighed. No, none of it was right. It wasn't right that Paolo lost his arm and another man his life because the factory owner hadn't fixed the carts with brakes, as the foreman had asked repeatedly. It wasn't right that Mattie's baby would be born without a father, and that Lorenzo would probably harbor the belief he could have saved his brother if only he'd stayed home. It wasn't right that Mr. Edwin was dead, however it had happened, nor that Isabelle was being paraded through the newspapers as a cold, disdainful, unnatural wife when not one word of official, court evidence had yet been given for or against her, and she was not, in any case, to be tried on her fitness as a wife but on the possibility of murder.

"It may not be the wisest solution to take Mattie to the Martins'," I said to my father, "but I can think of nothing else right now. You did say we should get her inside."

"I meant into her own place."

"You've seen it—you've seen *him*. Do you really advise sending her in there?"

My father looked pained. I know he was strongly opposed to using Isabelle's house, perhaps even fearful of it, though he'd never say that. Yet Mattie, who had been married in his home and who was my friend, was crying out, silently but plaintively, for protection, and he found it hard to turn away from that.

"Very well," he said at last. "But I'll just drop the girls off and come straight back for you."

I gave him the keys, but no thanks, as I knew he would have found thanks an insult. He was only doing what appeared necessary, and of his own free will, not to accommodate me.

I watched them depart, wanting to be sure Mattie went along quietly, which she did, without even a backward glance. Then I walked down the alley, across the fetid courtyard and into the Testas' one-room home.

Lorenzo was standing over Paolo's body, which was stretched out on a double bed. I saw a curtain across the room's opposite corner, as there'd been in the front room in the old apartment, and I guessed Lorenzo's bed was behind it. The room was cold. The stove must have gone out while Mattie was standing on the street. There were footsteps overhead—the Dolans moving about. They were probably trying to be soft about it, but in the chilled silence of that horrible chamber, any outside sound would have seemed clamorous and obscene, mocking with its intimations of life still going on elsewhere.

Lorenzo looked over his shoulder when he heard me come in, then turned his gaze again to Paolo. A narrow leather belt hung from Lorenzo's hand; it was buckled into a noose.

"It was still around his neck," he said.

"I sent Mattie away," I said.

"Away?"

"She'll be back later. Or tomorrow. I'm sure she'll want to, as soon as she's had time to recover a bit."

He looked at me, his face dark with many emotions.

"My brother can't wait on her sour stomach," he said angrily.

"Lorenzo, she found him. Think what that was like."

He walked to the table in the middle of the room and threw the belt onto it. The loud knock of the buckle against the wood seemed to deflate him, as if his anger were a toy balloon collapsed by a pinprick.

"It must take him a long time to fix it like that," he said quietly. "He must really wanted . . . I wonder how long he knew he will do it."

"Will you let me clean him up?" I said softly.

I'd worked with Sippy a few times on the bodies of tiny dead babies and new mothers, and, of course, I helped lay out my own mother. It was a hard chore, but it gave a reprieve of sorts from immediate grief, and that was all I could offer Lorenzo, as there would never be answers to his wonderings.

"Hanna, last night, I was happy. I saw a chance for happiness outside this room. And all the time, Paolo was . . . What was Paolo seeing last night?"

"I don't know, Lorenzo, but I don't think he'd have begrudged you happiness. Not even in his darkest moments. Would he?"

Lorenzo shook his head no and kept on shaking it, fighting against tears, I thought. I put my hands on his cheeks to still him. He covered my hands with his own, then turned his face and held his mouth against first one of my palms, then the other, in kisses that hungered and grieved. Then he pressed my hands together as if he'd just put something in them he wanted me to hide and keep safe.

"We'll need to put him on the table," I said.

Lorenzo nodded, gently lowering my hands to my sides.

"Dolan from upstairs can help me lift," he said.

Mrs. Dolan came down, too, and it was she and I who did the work on Paolo, though Lorenzo did build a fire in the stove for us and went outside and filled a kettle of water to heat. He stood watching us a while, staring mostly at his brother's face, which was easier on him, I guess, than looking at the poor stump of Paolo's arm, or his soiled trousers, or the mangled hand that must have fumbled so with fixing the fatal belt loop. For me, the hardest thing to see was the miraculous medal around Paolo's bruised neck, for it brought to mind his and Mattie's wedding and his joy and pride that day.

Before we were done, Mrs. Dolan told Lorenzo he ought

to fetch Father Monaco, and he went, though he was nervous about what the priest would say. Mrs. Dolan informed me suicides couldn't be buried in consecrated ground, but they could be prayed over, and there was the widow and the little, innocent orphan baby needing prayers and blessing, too. I was glad she'd thought of it because when my father came for me, Lorenzo wasn't left alone. From the courtyard I looked back through the window, as I'd done on the day Mattie had moved in, and I saw Lorenzo and Father Monaco kneeling together with rosaries in their hands.

"How's Mattie?" I asked my father when we were on the wagon.

"Quiet," he said.

He picked up a folded newspaper from the seat beside him.

"Your lady's made the front page again."

Despite the strain of the last few hours, I was curious. I opened the paper. There was a picture of Isabelle, the same one they'd been running from time to time, a partial profile, as if she were just turning her head toward someone calling her name, her eyes wide and expectant, her mouth serious. Next to it, where they'd sometimes put a picture of Mr. Edwin, was a photo of Reverend Dale, looking startled; underneath, it said he'd been arrested that very morning as an accessory before the fact to willful murder.

TWENTY-SEVEN

FATHER MONACO said a funeral Mass for Paolo the very next day. He wasn't supposed to, but since he'd known the Testas from their first arrival in Philadelphia and had married Paolo and Mattie, he agreed to it, provided it was done right away and no one but Lorenzo and Mattie attended.

Lorenzo returned Mattie to the Martins' late that night. Elsinore and I were just getting ready to go to bed; I hadn't expected Mattie back.

"I can't stay in that room," Mattie said. "Even one night. We went by there, but I just couldn't stay."

"She's got time coming—rent's paid for end of January," Lorenzo said, wanting me to know, I think, that he'd tried to take care of her.

"I'll look tomorrow for a place, Hanna," Mattie said.

I couldn't bear the pleading sound in her voice, the look on her face as if I might turn her out.

"You'll look only if you feel up to it," I said. "You did right to come here."

"But your job . . ."

"My job is already in hazard's way. I've got beds to spare and you need one, and that's the end of it, as I see it," I said, though I didn't feel quite so cocksure as I made out.

Elsinore came from the kitchen. She must have recognized

the voices and interrupted her bedtime preparations. Her hair was down and her blouse had been hastily put on—one edge of it was pulled out from her skirt. She greeted Mattie with a hug free of surprise, and I saw my friend relax at last into the safety I wanted to give her.

"Mattie, you can share the guest room with me," Elsinore said. "I expect you'd like to go right up?"

Mattie nodded, and Elsinore led her away, going again to the kitchen and up the back stairs, though the main staircase was right there in front of us. It was a habit I'd been keeping even while alone in the house, and Elsinore had picked it up, but it was not until I saw her and Mattie bypass the front stairs that it struck me as ridiculous.

It's funny how people hold on to things like that and how simple, innocent digressions from routine or custom or others' expectations can seem bold or even dangerous. Yet truly bold acts—acts where one follows one's own guidance, however uncertain, however maverick—often grow out of small turnings. Or die unborn because such turnings are not considered.

"Your sister has the gentle touch," Lorenzo said, watching the two depart.

"Yes, she does."

"How long you can keep her?"

"Elsinore?"

"Mattie."

"I don't know."

We stood irresolutely, he reluctant to go out of company on the very day he'd buried his brother, I unsure whether delaying him would hearten him or make his leaving later that much more difficult.

"We've just had some cocoa, and the things are still out," I ventured. "Would you like a cup?"

He smiled and nodded, and we went to the kitchen, where he sat down at the table and I set to work heating some milk.

I imagined I could feel him watching my back, and I felt a warmth spread through my body from the pit of my stomach, as if I were pressed up against him and not across the room from him. This feeling had the strange effect of making me clumsy, so that I splashed hot milk when I was filling the cup and put in too much sugar and then dropped the spoon and had to get another, but Lorenzo made no remarks on my ineptitude. Indeed, he said nothing at all, except *grazie* when I brought him the drink, and his silence and his dark gaze on my face as I sat down opposite him made the warmth spread again. I was relieved when he glanced down at the cup as he drank, and then around the room, appraising it.

"It's getting time I have a home, I think," he said.

"You won't be staying at the Dolans' either?"

He shook his head.

"I'm at a boardinghouse near the factory," he said. "I got it right away because Mattie and me couldn't keep on living together. That Dolan place was never home, anyway."

"Nor is a boardinghouse."

"No, you're right. "The boardinghouse is mostly birds of passage."

He sighed, stretching out his arms and legs as if he'd been cramped in a small, cold space a long time.

"Birds of passage?"

"Laborers who come from Sicily to make fortunes and then go back to their villages like big men. They don't want homes here. They don't even stay in Philadelphia, if the *padroni* find them places in coal mines or with the railroads."

"Have you ever lived on your own without Paolo?" I asked.

"No, never. But it's not just Paolo being gone."

He leaned over the table toward me and regarded me with a searching expression.

"Don't you want a home, Hanna?"

I was afraid to answer. Was he leading up to the suggestion

that he and I make a home together as man and wife? If he wasn't and I responded as if he were, it would be terribly embarrassing for both of us. On the other hand, if he did have that in mind, my reply might be taken either as a promise—which I wasn't clear I wanted to give yet—or, if I feigned ignorance and answered only in general terms, as a dismissal of him. Or could he wish to hear the private hopes that had formed before I knew him? I'd never told them to anyone, and I found myself superstitious about uttering them, in case by doing so I invoked a curse and canceled forever, even from fantasy, that small kingdom of a few rooms of my own.

"Yes," I finally said. "I want a home. Someday."

"Maybe soon, Hanna. You have changes put on you quick, too."

"Temporarily," I said, standing up and carrying his empty cup to the sink.

He made no reply. I stayed busy rinsing the cup and spoon and milk saucepan, drying them, putting them away.

"So," he said, and his voice had a different quality, hearty yet strangely empty, all intimacy gone out of it. "I guess this is where she mixed the poison. Here in the kitchen. It's more horrible, no? The kitchen is like the housewife's heart."

I turned to face him.

"This is my kitchen, too."

"*Bene.* Could I be here if it's not?"

He got up and pushed in his chair.

"I can say good night?"

I gave the smallest nod of my head. He walked over to me and put his hands lightly on my shoulders. He gave me a brief kiss on the mouth, as if he were tasting me. Our bodies did not touch.

"Don't think so hard," he said softly, as if he were making the tenderest of farewells.

I wasn't sure what he meant, but I didn't ask him, nor did he elaborate. He only turned and went out, leaving my head crowded with possibilities.

MATTIE STAYED four days. The first two, she slept a lot, lying down only when I insisted but then dropping off quite quickly, and in between she helped me and Elsinore with the house, though we wouldn't let her do any heavy cleaning. On the third day, she went out looking for work and shelter and would not hear of us going along. I didn't like it, but she became so agitated when I objected, it seemed better to let her have her way. By the middle of the fourth day, she had a place in a boardinghouse in Southwark where there were mostly single young women, and a job wrapping cigars in a loft on the top floor of the same building. At least she was able to do this work sitting down, and she didn't have to go out into the winter streets to get there.

I was expecting Isabelle's lawyer late that afternoon, so when Lorenzo came to accompany Mattie to the trinity house to get the rest of her personal things and take them to the boardinghouse, I sent Elsinore with them. Though the lawyer was not with Mr. Fisk and so was not concerned with how the house was being kept, I judged it better not to propagate questions in his mind by making my houseguests obvious. The lawyer, Mr. Clark, arrived right on time, a scant fifteen minutes after the others had left, and he had Mr. Frederick Martin with him.

Feeling familiar in the house, Mr. Frederick headed directly for the parlor when I let them in. Mr. Clark motioned me ahead of him, and I followed Mr. Frederick, but despite the lawyer's manners, I knew I wasn't meant to play the hostess, so I stayed standing while the two men sat. Neither of them suggested I do otherwise. Just lucky for them, Elsinore and I hadn't covered the furniture in the parlor yet, though we had begun covering the pictures on the wall.

"I came along to take Mr. Clark through the house, Willer," Mr. Frederick said.

"I find that in order to mount a thorough defense, it's invaluable to personally examine the scene of activity whenever possible," Mr. Clark explained, and I gathered from how he said it that Mr. Frederick maybe didn't agree it was necessary or seemly.

"Will you need to see the upstairs?" I asked.

"Perhaps," Mr. Clark said. "But I understand the Martins lived mainly on this floor?"

"Yes, sir. It's just, sir, that I've been working through the rooms giving them a good cleaning, and the upstairs is a little awry. Especially the guest bedroom."

"Oh, I don't expect I'll need to see that, Miss Willer."

Mr. Clark had brought a slim leather case with him, and now he opened it and pulled out some loose papers with handwriting on them, not done too neatly from what I could see. He read through them, asking me a question now and then, never looking up, but writing down some of my words at the margins of his papers. I was forced to speak to the bald spot at the top of his head. He asked how long I'd been at the Martins', was I satisfied there, what were my duties, what were Mr. Edwin's health and habits, how often had Reverend Dale visited.

"That rabbit!" Mr. Frederick exclaimed at the mention of the minister's name. "Do you know he actually told a reporter that Isabelle had been the ruin of him? The gall of the man! The vanity! As if Isabelle would have bothered to ruin a rabbit like that. He was restful to have around, she told me. Can you imagine having a woman call you restful? I hope I may be spared such compliments."

"Such outbursts, Mr. Martin, will not help your sister-in-law," Mr. Clark said. "In criminal proceedings, the less said by the accused and his sympathizers the better. Words can be twisted to fit many meanings, believe me."

"It's only Willer here," Mr. Frederick complained. "She's on our side, aren't you, Willer?"

"The point is, Mr. Martin," the lawyer continued, "that in minds keyed to a certain pitch, your support of Mrs. Martin could be counted against her, especially given your father's insinuations."

"My father!" Mr. Frederick groaned.

"I will work to discount him on the witness stand, but you must not place yourself at cross-purposes to me by hovering about my client and protesting her innocence on street corners."

"That's a bit of an exaggeration."

"I'm just trying to make my point."

"It's made." Mr. Frederick sighed.

"What do you think, Willer? I'm to be shipped off again," he said to me, for all the world like a little boy appealing a father's harsh sentence to a doting mother. "For appearance's sake."

"Does Mrs. Martin know?" I asked.

"Yes, I've seen her. She was damned calm about it, actually."

"That's because she trusts me," Mr. Clark said. "She knows her innocence must be constructed carefully, with attention to every detail that's entered in as well as to every detail that's omitted."

"Constructed? You don't need to construct Isabelle's innocence. She *is* innocent."

"Of course," Mr. Clark said soothingly. "But, you see, in my business, both innocence and guilt are always treated as constructions. It helps us strategize more clearly."

"God save me from lawyers."

Mr. Clark smiled.

"If we should meet on Judgment Day," he joked, "perhaps you'll want to reverse that wish."

He put his papers away then and turned serious attention to me.

"Now, Miss Willer, I want to hear everything you can recall about Mr. Edwin Martin's last day, and what you found when you came home that night. You've been called for the prosecution, but I'll be asking you questions in court, too."

So I gave him my recounting as simply and directly as I

could, reasoning that simplicity was best under the circumstances. After all, Mr. Clark had said himself that excess information and opinions only made meanings more susceptible to being twisted. I showed him where Mr. Edwin had lain and where Isabelle had sat and where the medicine bottles had stood, and he seemed satisfied and only asked a question or two more.

The men were gone an hour before Elsinore returned. She came up alone, as Lorenzo had left her at the street door, saying he had the early shift next day. She told me about Mattie's new place, which she said was drab but clean, and she thought she'd send Mattie one of her boxed butterflies to brighten her tiny room.

"She had to leave the canaries with that Mrs. Dolan," Elsinore said.

"The boardinghouse won't allow them?"

Elsinore shook her head. "I hope she'll be all right."

"So do I," I said.

"What will she do when the baby comes?"

"She said she needed to get further past what happened to Paolo before she could begin to figure that out."

"Lorenzo's worried about her."

" 'Lorenzo'? "

Elsinore blushed.

"He said I was to call him that since we've all been through so much this week, and he feels our family has been such friends to him. Do you mind, Hanna?"

"Why should I mind?"

"Well, you do like him, don't you?"

"Yes," I said cautiously, "I like him."

"I can see why. He's very nice."

I felt a twinge in me that I guessed was jealousy, but it was not as biting or shackling as I thought jealousy would be. It felt more like a warning, as when extra seagulls on the river herald a storm at sea. It often struck me eerily when I'd see the river glutted with those arguing flocks of gulls come inland for shelter. The idea of wild, wind-lashed waves and beating gray rain and ships in mortal danger would fill my imagination, and I'd feel small and vulnerable, as if the ocean might prove capable of rushing into the city and washing my life away.

"Elsinore," I said, deliberately shaking my unreasonable apprehension, "tomorrow is New Year's Day. We won't work, but go instead to see the mummers, and then the next day, we'll work in the morning and go to the Pennsylvania Academy of the Fine Arts in the afternoon. You must take in some of the city before you go back home."

Elsinore responded with a wide smile and an enthusiastic hug.

"But, Hanna," she said suddenly, "didn't you say Mrs. Martin's trial starts on January second?"

"Yes, but Mr. Clark told me the first day was mostly legal business and speeches, and I didn't need to be there until the third day."

So Elsinore and I had our outings, making our way on New Year's Day through the rowdy masqueraders, singers, and comic dancers along Second Street and down by the Delaware River, men wearing inside-out coats decorated with ribbons and cards or widespread collars and capes so large they needed boys in back to carry them. Other men made pairs, one dressed as a girl with a braided wig and short skirts that showed her pantaloons, and the other with a top hat and cane, both having their faces darkened with lampblack. There were real dark people there, too, costumed, dancing a kind of strut and singing "Oh, Dem Golden Slippers."

The next day, we had a quieter taste of Philadelphia, looking at paintings by Mr. Thomas Eakins and Miss Cecilia Beaux. But in another respect, the day was far from quiet. On the way home from the academy, I bought a newspaper and was stunned to read that at the opening of the trial, all charges against Reverend Dale had been withdrawn. Isabelle now stood alone. I resolved I would not miss another day in court.

TWENTY-EIGHT

THE SIDEWALK outside the brick courthouse on Sixth Street was thronged with people, and I was surprised to notice that more than half were ladies. There was such a press and confusion, I believe Elsinore and I would not have gotten inside except that we caught the eye of Mr. Clark as he was making his way through the crowd, and he took us, one on each arm, up the steps with him. Even with so formidable an escort, we were almost not admitted because we had no tickets, but Mr. Clark glowered at the officer at the door and said I was an important witness and was not to be impeded, today or any day. To be safe, he procured a pass for me good for the duration of the trial and noted on it that my sister was to be let in, too, if she came along.

I was glad for Mr. Clark's help, but I hoped he was exaggerating when he called me an important witness. I was very nervous about testifying and had been calming myself by holding to the idea that what I'd be asked about was of minor significance to the final verdict, more scene-setting information than evidence capable of tipping the scales one way or the other.

It is always tempting, in mazy situations, to stand apart and keep one's own counsel, to pretend that one is outside fate and circumstance and association. But, of course, only the dead have that luxury—though even they may be turned to the purposes of the living—and inaction is every bit as definite a choice as action. I do not think there really is such a thing as a thoroughly unwitting act, nor a thoroughly innocent person, with the exception of young children. I date this belief to Isabelle's trial.

"Excuse me, sir," I said to Mr. Clark as we walked down the hall to the courtroom. "I was wondering if Reverend Dale's dismissal was a good thing? For Mrs. Martin?"

"I plan to make it a good thing."

"How is that, sir?"

"There may not be enough, in a legal sense, to carry through on charges against Reverend Dale, but the good minister has undeniably put himself in a very awkward position in this business, and I won't let the jury forget that. These are modern times, Miss Willer. People are less and less inclined to apply a double standard."

He stopped just outside the door to the courtroom and looked earnestly at me.

"I will treat Reverend Dale in a friendly manner to keep him away from damaging statements, yet I will associate his actions with Mrs. Martin's actions as much as I can. The jury will be reluctant to send her to her doom while he passes unrebuked to freedom."

"It seems a slender chance," I said.

"Certainly it will be a delicate operation, but that's only one piece of my strategy, Miss Willer. Watch closely. I trust you'll find it instructive."

Mr. Clark left us then, and Elsinore and I hurried to find seats. We had to sit along the wall, but the spectator pews were on raised flooring, so we could see the whole room well enough. The lawyers' tables and the dock were in full view.

The courtroom was large, with a high ceiling and tall windows, but apparently it was not big enough to accommodate all those who wished to be spectators, for a two-tiered platform had been constructed at the rear of the room and outfitted with chairs to make more seating. I could tell the platform had been a hasty job because the lumber was unfinished and unpainted, with nail heads, splintery cut ends of boards, and scuff marks from the carpenters' boots all plainly visible. I was glad Elsinore and I had secured seats in the pews, as the chairs on the platform looked flimsy and unsteady. Indeed, one day I saw a stout woman nearly fall when she did not sit down squarely enough; it was only a quick grab from another matron beside her that prevented her from toppling with her chair off the platform's upper level.

I recognized several people in the audience—if that is the proper name for all of us come to listen in on Isabelle's story and work it into our understandings of the world—and I pointed them out to Elsinore. There was Mr. Sylvester Martin, and beside him Mr. and Mrs. Cox. I also spotted Dr. Cornelius, Mr. Fisk, and the policeman, Mr. Hauser. I'd read in the papers that Mr. Hauser had caused a mild sensation when testifying yesterday about what his team discovered in the Martin house. Among the articles he listed were condoms, found in the pockets of a pair of Mr. Edwin's trousers, and a copy of Squire's *Companion to British Pharmacopoeia,* which "naturally fell open," he'd said, to the page on chloroform.

Reverend Dale was present across the aisle from us. He was flanked by two white-haired old gentlemen wearing clerical collars, and he looked very pale and worried, not at all as I would have expected a newly freed man to appear. His companions had stern demeanors and stared straight ahead at the judge's massive stand, though there was no one there yet to be seen. They seemed to me like duty guards, and I wondered if they'd come to encourage Reverend Dale or to reprove him.

There were other vaguely familiar faces in the crowd; I guessed they might be people who had attended Mr. Edwin's funeral. But the bulk of the spectators were total strangers to me and, I suspected, to Isabelle and Mr. Edwin. What had drawn them? There had not been a day since Isabelle's arrest that some mention of her had not been in the papers. Was mere awareness of the case enough to bring people out? I noted again the preponderance of women in the audience. There'd be many a late, cold supper served in town tonight, I thought.

At last, the room was filled. Without announcement, the trapdoor to the dock opened, and Isabelle was led in. The loud, undefined jumble of voices in the audience dropped to a purr. Isabelle was in black, of course, but it was not heavy mourning. There was a flush to her cheeks, and I wondered if she might be a little feverish, but she looked strong and collected, so I guess it was just excitement. She was the only woman in the room not wearing a hat, and despite her calm demeanor, this strangely branded her, making her appear unprotected, like a young animal.

She made a quick scan of the crowd, but she made no sign that she had picked me out. I had a good look at her eyes, though, remarkable as ever, and I fancied they were clear of guilt, though it occurred to me they might only be, as my father had complained, clear of remorse.

"I wonder which would be worse," Elsinore whispered to me, "being on trial when you are guilty or when you are not."

"I suspect it's a trapped feeling either way," I said.

"But Mrs. Martin doesn't look like she feels trapped, does she? I mean, she doesn't look frightened at all."

I recalled Isabelle's comment that being in jail was like being at a water-cure, and I wondered if she still felt that way. She was no longer at the station-house jail but at the Philadelphia County Prison in Moyamensing. I'd read there were benevolent lady visitors who went into the women's building there, but that otherwise prisoners were isolated with only their consciences and the Bible for company. How many, criminal or no, could comfortably endure that for long?

Yet, as Elsinore had said, Isabelle did not seem distraught. There was a stillness about her, as though she had settled things in her own mind and was only waiting stoically for the rest of us to catch up. Over the following days, I often studied her as witnesses spoke. She listened intently enough, but she gave no sign whether or not she agreed with what was being said. It was almost as if she considered they were talking about someone else, a person about whom she was curious but who was not herself, not any longer.

A man standing to one side of the judge's bench told us all to rise, which we did, with much rustling of fine skirts and some scraping noises from the chairs on the platform at the back. A tall man in black robes entered, looking like a disgruntled old military man because of his erect bearing and a passing resemblance to the fierce Stonewall Jackson. Judges, indeed, are like generals in that they preside over battles and sometimes must dispatch men to their deaths using cold reason. And the outcomes of trials, despite the marshaling of facts and crisp rules about fairness, seem to me to owe as much to messy chance and irrelevant emotion as do the results of skirmishes in war. I suppose there is nothing human beings do that is not tinged by the vagaries and histories of our hearts. We deceive ourselves to think that we are in any wholesale way orderly, predictable, or explainable.

The first few witnesses were doctors. Under questioning by the prosecutor, two who had done the autopsy on Mr. Edwin described their grisly procedures and told of the conditions of his brain and organs, all normal except for the stomach, which gave off strong smells of garlic and chloroform and showed signs of inflammation characteristic of a local irritant, quite possibly liquid chloroform. The intestines, too, the doctors said, smelled of chloroform, though less so. They found pieces of undigested mango chutney in the intestines, and of all the detailed medical testimony, this one scrap made me feel squeamish because it forcefully reminded me that this was not a collection of laboratory specimens they were discussing, but the remnants of a person I had known.

"Doctor," Mr. Clark said to the second physician when it came his turn to ask questions, "what was the condition of the jaws?"

"There was necrosis—destruction of the tissue."

"And are you aware that the deceased, Edwin Martin, used chlorodyne on his gums and rinsed his mouth with it in order to relieve the pain of this necrosis?"

"Yes, I believe his physician, Dr. Cornelius, mentioned that."

"If he had accidentally swallowed some, couldn't this have accounted for the smell you found?"

"I don't believe the smell would have been as strong. When we opened the stomach, it was as if a bottle of chloroform had been unstoppered."

"But chlorodyne does smell of chloroform, does it not?"

"Yes, it does. Slightly."

Mr. Clark walked to his table and referred to some papers there. Then he addressed the doctor again.

"And the irritation you found in the stomach. Could it have been due to a chronic gastritis rather than to a local irritant?"

"It had the look of a recent inflammation."

"Can inflammation due to irritation and inflammation due to chronic disease be definitely distinguished?"

"Not always, but to my mind—"

"Not always. Thank you, Doctor."

The judge scowled at Mr. Clark.

"Go on, Doctor," he said. "To your mind . . ."

"To my mind, Your Honor," the doctor replied, "the inflammation was very characteristic of a local irritant and was certainly recent. And the inflamed patch was in the area of the stomach where liquid would flow if a person were on his back."

"One other matter, Doctor," Mr. Clark said, seeming not to care about the judge's interruption. "What are the symptoms of poisoning by liquid chloroform?"

"It is a very rare thing, I believe."

"But what are the symptoms?"

"I have no personal knowledge, never having encountered it in my practice."

"Have you performed other autopsies where death by ingestion of liquid chloroform was suspected?"

"No."

"Have people ingested chloroform and lived?"

"I believe so."

"How much would be needed to cause death?"

"I expect a person couldn't survive four ounces."

"But that is an estimate?"

"Yes."

Mr. Clark paced alongside the jury railing as if deep in puzzled thought.

"Don't you think then, Doctor, that someone bent on murder might choose a more reliable poison, like arsenic or digitalis—the tried and true, so to speak?"

The prosecutor, Mr. Holland, protested that question, so the doctor was not required to answer it. Again, Mr. Clark did not appear perturbed, even though the case for death by liquid chloroform still seemed strong. Indeed, it was definitively confirmed by the next doctor, the toxicologist who had analyzed the contents of Mr. Edwin's stomach. Later, after days of watching him, I saw the shape of Mr. Clark's intentions. He was a sower of doubts. He must have known that certain of his suggestions would be dismissed outright or weakened by subsequent testimony, but he kept at it anyway, hoping, perhaps, that his listeners, awash in possibilities, must let some doubts parade through their minds as facts and some facts degrade into doubts.

I'd read in the newspapers, on the first day of the trial, about Mr. Clark's examination of Mr. Sylvester Martin. Mr. Martin had repeated the accusation I'd heard months ago that Isabelle and Mr. Frederick had once run off together. Mr. Clark, brandishing Mr. Martin's notarized apology, had deftly turned the accusation against Isabelle's character into an exposition of Mr. Martin as a jealous, selfish, vengeful old man worried about the continuance of his son's financial support.

Mr. Clark even brought out that Mr. Martin had not attended his son's wedding, for which he gave the pallid excuse that he had been "regrettably too busy."

At least one reporter was clearly convinced that Mr. Martin avidly disliked Isabelle and, consequently, would say anything to discredit her, in the eyes of both his son and the larger world. In another paper were two letters to the editor, both from married women who commiserated with Isabelle's plight as an ill-treated daughter-in-law trying to maintain a congenial home in the face of spite and suspicion, though neither of them went so far as to propose she had not murdered her husband.

At the midday break, Elsinore and I went home for a meal, and she decided to stay there, having found the court proceedings less interesting than she'd expected. I returned to court, where Reverend Dale began his time on the witness stand. Only Mr. Holland examined him that day. Examination by Mr. Clark was scheduled for the next day.

The prosecutor elicited from Reverend Dale how long he'd known the Martins, how often he'd seen them, and what he knew of Mr. Edwin's health.

"Before the episode in August, he appeared in good health usually," Reverend Dale reported.

"That would be after Mrs. Martin's visit to Ocean Grove?" Mr. Holland said.

"Yes, directly after."

"This was a sudden affliction, then?"

"It appeared so. Though I had in the past sometimes seen Edwin clutch his side after eating, and he once confided in me he suffered severely from dyspepsia."

"And did this affliction in August subside as suddenly as it had appeared?"

"Yes, it did."

"Did any event precede this rapid recovery?"

"Well, I was not allowed in the Martin home at the time,

but Edwin's health did seem to take an upturn right after his father brought in Dr. Cornelius."

"In other words," Mr. Holland said, "right after Edwin Martin's condition came to the attention of other people who might suspect his wife was slowly poisoning him."

Mr. Clark strenuously protested this remark. Mr. Holland smiled at him with false contrition.

"What do you mean, Reverend Dale, when you say you were not allowed in the Martin home?" the prosecutor asked next.

"Mrs. Martin felt it would be too much of a strain for her husband to have visitors."

"Did you have particular business you wished to take up at that time with Edwin Martin?"

Reverend Dale shifted uneasily in his seat. He looked worriedly toward the two elderly ministers who'd come with him.

"Yes, I did," he said softly.

"What was your business?"

"I intended to tell Edwin that I wouldn't be calling on them anymore because I . . . because my feelings for Isabelle were . . ."

"Reverend Dale, were you in love with Isabelle Martin?"

Reverend Dale snapped his gaze away from his companions in the audience and looked with alarm at Mr. Holland.

"No, sir," he said emphatically. "But I knew my fondness for her was moving in a direction it should not, and I wanted to be honest with Edwin and to remove myself from . . . well, from temptation."

A storm of whispers surged through the audience. The judge rapped his mallet sharply and called for silence.

"Did Mrs. Martin know of your plans to speak to her husband?" the prosecutor asked Reverend Dale when quiet had resumed.

"Yes, she did. When we were in Ocean Grove, I told her I meant to see him as soon as I returned to Philadelphia."

"But his sudden illness prevented you in that."

"Yes. Well, it was only a postponement, really. Eventually I wrote to Edwin with my concerns."

Mr. Holland nodded at Reverend Dale, as if commending him for his virtue, and Reverend Dale managed a modest smile. But the smile faded at the next question.

"Did Mrs. Martin believe you to be in love with her?"

Mr. Clark objected to the prosecutor's language, and the judge agreed to his objection.

"Did you ever write letters to Mrs. Martin?" Mr. Holland asked.

"We exchanged letters from time to time. As friend to friend."

"Did you ever write poetry for her?"

As before, Reverend Dale moved about uneasily in his seat. "Yes," he replied with some reluctance.

Mr. Holland then read a short verse into the record as an example. It was embarrassingly poor poetry, and when I saw it reproduced in the newspaper that evening, I confess I pitied the foolish man.

> *Who is it that hath burst the door*
> *Unclosed the heart 'twas shut before*
> *And set her queenlike on its throne*
> *And made my homage all her own?*
> Ma tres belle *Isabelle.*

"What conclusions, Reverend Dale, do you expect a woman might draw from such missives?"

Again Mr. Clark objected to the prosecutor's asking Reverend Dale's opinion of what Isabelle could have thought.

"Did you ask Mrs. Martin to return these 'friendly' writings to you?" Mr. Holland asked instead.

"Yes."

"When?"

"After Edwin's death."

"After the preliminary postmortem?"

"Yes."

"In other words, Reverend Dale, after it appeared foul play had occurred?"

"I suppose so."

"Didn't you ask for the return of your letters and poems because you feared they might implicate you?"

"Well, I was perplexed. And . . . I was . . . alarmed at the possibility that she . . ."

"Didn't you want to retrieve your letters precisely because you believed Isabelle Martin had murdered her husband in order to free herself to marry you—a man she had plentiful reasons to presume loved and desired her?"

"I was duped!" Reverend Dale leaned forward and gripped the edge of the wooden box around the witness seat. "Duped by a wicked woman!"

"You're not the first man for that, sir, nor will you be the last," the prosecutor remarked drily.

"You'll keep your social observations to yourself," the judge scolded him.

Mr. Holland bowed his head courteously. Reverend Dale was excused, and the whole proceedings adjourned for the day. The judge noted that Reverend Dale would be called to continue first thing tomorrow, a reminder the shaken minister received with a pained expression.

There was a quiet pause in the audience before people began talking among themselves and gathering their things to go. Looking around me, I felt the pause emanated from the women. Whether they leaned slightly forward in their seats or held themselves straight, there was a tension in them that needed a moment to subside. I have seen such tension in children when they've been listening to an absorbing story, when they've ridden on the storyteller's voice and words into a realm both familiar and fantastic; they, too, sit silent and still for a minute after the storyteller stops, as if they are waking up.

When I got home, Elsinore had supper ready, so I was able to walk into the house and sit down at once to a set table and a hot meal. While we ate, I told her about Reverend Dale's performance. Then we talked about the doctors we had heard in the morning, and we both marveled at the oddness of hearing a story told by way of a string of answers to painstaking questions.

"How far did you get on the walls?" I asked Elsinore when we had tired of talking of the trial.

The papered walls in the parlor, dining room, and master bedroom needed cleaning, and Elsinore had agreed that afternoon to begin the job without me. I'd been saving stale bread to rub on the walls to take off the dust.

"I only got the bedroom done," she said sheepishly. "I went out."

"Out?" I said, surprised.

"Lorenzo Testa came by. We went to drink a coffee down the street."

"Oh?"

"Well, I couldn't have him in with you not at home."

"No, you couldn't. And whose idea was the coffee?"

"I don't know. His, I guess. Was it all right, Hanna? I'll finish the walls tomorrow."

Unexpectedly, I sighed.

"It's not the walls, Elsinore."

"He came looking for *you,* Hanna. He'd much rather have had his coffee with you."

Elsinore sounded so distressed, I repented of my jealousy, for that is where my sigh had come from.

"It's all right, Elsie," I said, none too convincingly, I'm afraid.

"I won't do it again, now that I see it makes you unhappy," she promised. "It was thoughtless of me."

"And I am giving it too *much* thought," I said. "There's no need to say more about it."

Relieved, Elsinore got up to clear the table. I went into the dining room and spread that table with newspapers. As had become my habit since Isabelle's arrest, I'd bought copies of all the papers on my way home. I skimmed the news reports, interested by what quotes had been chosen to represent the day's court proceedings, but of greater interest were the editorials, of which there were many. One impugned Isabelle for being a foreigner. After all, the writer said, the very designation "French" implied immorality. Just think, he said, of French postcards and French novels, to say nothing of French letters, which was a common name for condoms. More serious editorials used Isabelle's case to argue against loveless, arranged marriages and to despair of the declining influence of family and neighbors in city living, where the advice of doctors, ministers, and lawyers had replaced the wisdom of parents and grandparents and the force of local custom.

I was folding up the papers and thinking over what I'd read when the doorbell rang. It was Reverend Dale, looking no less nervous than he had on the witness stand. He asked if he could come upstairs and speak to me for a few moments. I took him into the dining room, and we sat down across from each other.

"You look as though you're keeping well, Willer," he began.

"Quite well, thank you, sir."

"Despite the cold weather of late?"

"The house is snug."

He nodded thoughtfully, as if we were in the midst of a profound discussion.

"I myself will be free of cold weather soon. I've been called to the African missions."

"Yes, sir?"

"The church elders felt . . . There's a great need for ministers in Africa just now, you see. I'm honored to have been chosen. . . ."

"Congratulations, sir."

He cleared his throat noisily and sat slightly taller in his chair.

"You're to be a witness, I understand, Willer," he said.

"Yes, sir."

"And what will you say?"

"I don't know, sir, exactly, until I hear the questions."

"Of course, of course."

He looked wistfully about the room, and I had the impression he was reminiscing. After all, he and the Martins had shared many meals in that room, and they had manufactured a kind of happiness for themselves, for a time.

"I have been worried, sir, though," I said. "I wouldn't want to say anything that might be taken wrongly."

"You must say what you know, Willer. It's what I shall do, too. If Mrs. Martin is innocent, we'll do her no harm. The truth can never do harm."

"But what of the others?"

"The others?"

I tapped the pile of folded newspapers.

"The women reading about the trial," I said. "And the ones in the courtroom and outside the courthouse."

"I don't understand. . . ."

"If Mrs. Martin is not set free, how will those women keep hold of any true complaints they have in their own lives? How will they shout down those who say Isabelle is naught but unnatural?"

"But, Willer," Reverend Dale said seriously, "if she's done this thing, she is exactly that."

I looked down at my lap, where my hands were clenched together. I was not making him understand. How could I? I didn't completely understand it myself. Of course murder is unnatural. But couldn't it grow out of natural discontents? Should a deadly outcome be permitted to mask or cancel the rightfulness of such discontents?

Reverend Dale stood up.

"Your thinking is confused, perhaps, because Mrs. Martin has shown you kindness," he said, his voice softening. "But search your deepest heart, Willer, and you'll know what's to be done. There are duties higher than personal loyalty."

TWENTY-NINE

THE NEXT day I went to court alone, and even with my special pass, I had to stand in a long, slow line to get in. There was a harsh wind blowing. Ladies with capotes put their hoods up, and gentlemen wrapped their scarves round over their noses. Many people were stamping their feet to warm their toes, but no one left to go home. A man hawked engravings of Isabelle up and down the line, making a number of sales.

I had a closer seat that day, and when Isabelle made her scan of the audience, she found me and gave me a small, lingering smile, which I returned. As Reverend Dale had said, she'd been kind to me; whatever her misdeeds, they did not erase that. A smile was a cheap enough thing to give her in return. On this, the third day of the trial, Isabelle's survey of the room had taken on the shape of ritual; ladies raised their opera glasses in anticipation, and when Isabelle paused in my direction, not a few of those glasses were turned to scrutinize me.

The Reverend Dale was called first thing. When he got up to go to the witness stand, I saw he had the same two old ministers with him. Their white heads turned in unison to watch his progress down the pew and up to the front of the courtroom.

Mr. Clark started by asking about the chloroform. Yesterday, under questioning by the prosecutor, Reverend Dale had testified that Isabelle requested he buy chloroform for her, saying she needed it to help Mr. Edwin sleep. She'd told him, he said, that Mr. Edwin had a serious internal complaint that gave him much pain and that two doctors before Dr. Cornelius had said this complaint would be the death of him within a year. She'd also told him not to speak to Mr. Edwin about his illness as it upset him greatly to discuss it. Besides, she'd added, she was trying, with her own nursing, to contradict the medical men and extend his life.

I thought this testimony cast a bad light on Isabelle since the autopsy results showed Mr. Edwin had, in reality, no mortal afflictions. I myself never thought him a seriously ill man, but only a pampered and sometimes mopish one. His strange illness after Ocean Grove was, admittedly, a hard one, but he had recovered nicely from that, the tooth extractions seeming to work the charm. And on the last day of his life, he looked very much as if he were about to shake off the one other hard illness I'd seen him suffer.

"Reverend Dale," Mr. Clark began, "can you describe for us how you went about purchasing the chloroform for Mrs. Martin?"

"I went to one or two druggists and bought small vials and then poured the contents into a larger medicine bottle and gave that to Mrs. Martin."

"Wasn't it three druggists you went to?"

"Yes, I guess it was."

"And what did you tell the druggists you wanted the chloroform for?"

"To get grease stains out of a jacket."

"Why did you say that, sir?"

Reverend Dale looked mournfully around the room, obviously ashamed to be exposed so publicly in a lie. When his gaze passed over Isabelle, it seemed to me he winced the least little bit, like someone might do who had hit a tender spot on his hand where a stubborn splinter was sorely lodged.

"Mrs. Martin told me a druggist would be unlikely to sell her chloroform in the quantity she needed as he'd probably not believe a woman capable of the medical skill needed to administer it. Not being a doctor either, I thought I might meet with similar objections, and to explain Mrs. Martin's abilities and her husband's condition to a druggist seemed more cumbersome than simply getting the chloroform in small amounts from several places."

"I see," said Mr. Clark in an encouraging manner, as if to reassure Reverend Dale that he had acted as any reasonable man might.

"What did you do, Reverend Dale, with the three empty bottles after you'd transferred the chloroform to the large bottle?"

This sounded an inoffensive question, but it seemed to cause Reverend Dale some unease.

"I threw them away," he replied tentatively.

"When was that?"

"I don't remember exactly."

Mr. Clark walked over to his table, and an assistant there passed him a note.

"Reverend Dale, didn't you later show the police where, exactly, you threw the bottles away? Near Horticultural Hall in Fairmount Park?"

"Yes."

"Yet you can't recall *when* you threw them away?"

"Well," Reverend Dale stammered, "I suppose ... yes, I believe it was while taking a walk, on November seventeenth."

"The day after the preliminary postmortem?"

"Yes, I think the postmortem may have taken place the day before."

"Indeed it had, Reverend Dale."

The minister ran the fingers of one hand through his thick yellow hair.

"This walk you took on November seventeenth," Mr. Clark continued, "was that after Dr. Cornelius had informed you of the smell of chloroform emanating from Edwin Martin's dissected stomach?"

"I believe so. Yes."

"Is that why you threw away the evidence of your connection to the chloroform?"

"It was a nervous reaction. I wasn't thinking that clearly."

"You were afraid that your having the bottles might get you into trouble? That false interpretations might be made?"

"Yes. If it turned out that the chloroform I'd bought had been the cause of Edwin's death."

"Did you speak with Mrs. Martin before disposing of the bottles?"

"Yes. The night before."

"The night of November sixteenth, the same day Dr. Cornelius told you about the smell of chloroform?"

"Yes."

"What was the content of your conversation with Mrs. Martin that night?"

"I asked her if she had used any of the chloroform I'd purchased for her, and she said she hadn't. When I asked her if she was absolutely certain and requested to see the bottle, she became angry and shouted—pardon me, Your Honor—she shouted, 'Damn the chloroform.' "

"Was it at this time you requested the return of your letters and poems?"

"Yes. And I declined to take a gold watch she tried to give me. She said Edwin had wanted me to have it, but I'm sorry to say I no longer trusted her word."

"You were sorry?" Mr. Clark sounded surprised. "You mean until then—until the report of an ambiguous odor emanating from a corpse—you had never had cause to distrust Mrs. Martin?"

"No. She never showed me cause for mistrust."

"Nor perhaps to her husband, I submit."

Reverend Dale looked confused.

"If you intend that to be a question, Mr. Clark," the judge instructed, "phrase it as one."

Mr. Clark shook his head no. He went to his table for a drink of water, then turned again to Reverend Dale with a new line of inquiry.

"On the subject of trust, Reverend Dale," he said, "would you say Edwin Martin trusted you?"

"He considered me a close friend. And I was his spiritual advisor."

"What did he consider was your relationship with his wife?"

"The same. Friend and advisor."

"And tutor?"

"Yes."

These questions seemed to relax Reverend Dale. Perhaps he felt they were showing his nobler aspect. But Mr. Clark's next set of questions reinstated worry to the minister's brow.

"Was there a secret understanding between you and Isabelle Martin that at some future time you would become husband and wife?"

"No, there was no secret understanding."

"Was there ever any conduct between you and Mrs. Martin that could be construed as improper?"

"No."

"Did you ever kiss Isabelle Martin?"

Reverend Dale looked at Isabelle and blushed.

"Yes," he said. "But in her husband's presence."

"Did you ever kiss her out of her husband's presence?"

Reverend Dale lowered his eyes and nodded his head.

"Answer aloud," the judge ordered.

"Yes," Reverend Dale said miserably.

I noticed several men on the jury frown at this. Ministers were not meant to kiss wives. Ministers and doctors, it was generally agreed, were two kinds of men husbands could safely leave alone with their wives.

I wondered when and how often Reverend Dale had kissed Isabelle. In Ocean Grove? On their afternoons shut in the parlor studying? I wondered, too, if she had liked it, or if she had merely thought of it as the price of his attention and company, like the tokens we gave to ride the carousel in Asbury Park. I guessed it was the latter. Isabelle liked Reverend Dale because he was more refined than Mr. Edwin, not only in education but also in manner. With him, she might achieve what she struggled for with her husband, a companionship divorced from physical passion. For all her talk of romance and true love, Isabelle was no libertine. Mr. Frederick could have stirred her, I think—perhaps he even had—but she kept him, too, in a carefully imagined position, aided by the fact that he lived thousands of miles away and was her husband's brother besides.

"Reverend Dale," Mr. Clark went on, "in your capacity as trusted friend and spiritual advisor, did Edwin Martin ever consult you about the state of his marriage?"

"He spoke sometimes of his marriage, yes."

"Did he ever broach to you the idea that a man ought to have two wives?"

"Yes, he did. He asked me if the Bible was distinctly in favor of a man having only one wife."

"And your reply was . . .?"

Reverend Dale drew himself up as if to give his words more authority and to remind us that he was still, despite all else, a man of the Bible, a man of God.

"I told him that though the Bible did not expressly forbid having two wives, neither did it sanction it, so it could not be considered a proper or moral practice."

"Did he propose how this arrangement might work, on a practical level?"

"He said one wife would be for service and one for companionship."

The judge made a loud clearing of his throat at this.

"Was the man serious?" the judge asked in a tone of amazement.

"Yes, he was. He mentioned the subject on more than one occasion."

"And did he intend, Reverend," the judge continued with raised eyebrows, "for both wives to be his bedfellows?"

"I'm not certain of that, Your Honor."

"Didn't you, as a minister, find such talk unwholesome?"

"I found it odd, but Edwin Martin was a man with strange ideas."

"Not at all!" boomed a man's voice from a place several rows ahead of me. Mr. Sylvester Martin had gotten to his feet and was waving his fist at Reverend Dale. A man beside Mr. Martin, a friend I assumed, was tugging at his sleeve to get him to sit down, but the old man shook him off.

"Edwin was only joking," Mr. Martin went on, his voice trembling with emotion. "I won't have these people think he was strange!" He waved his arms to indicate the jury and the spectators.

"Sir," the judge interrupted. "Sit down and restrain yourself!"

"He's slandering my son! He's a liar—and worse! He ought never be allowed to set foot in a pulpit again. . . . He ought to be tarred and feathered. . . . He ought—"

The banging of the judge's gavel drowned Mr. Martin out.

"You will sit down or you will be barred from this court for the remainder of the trial!"

Mr. Martin threw up his hands in disgust and, shaking his head, sat down. His friend patted him soothingly on the back.

I knew that Isabelle, not Mr. Edwin, was the originator of the "strange idea" of two wives. I was amazed to learn that she had intrigued Mr. Edwin enough that he had consulted Reverend Dale about it and, apparently, had spoken to his father, too, though with more levity.

Mr. Clark next moved from the talk of two wives to Mr.

Edwin's consignment of Isabelle to Reverend Dale as some sort of vague fiancée. Again, I was surprised that this idea of Isabelle's had had some life beyond her own mind. As evidence that Mr. Edwin had contemplated Isabelle and Reverend Dale marrying at some future time, the minister offered the same story Isabelle had told me of Mr. Edwin once finding fault with her in his presence, and Reverend Dale commenting he'd teach her better if she ever came under his care.

"Surely, Reverend Dale," Mr. Clark said, "there must have been more than this one trifling and indefinite interaction to make you believe that Mr. Martin actually meant you to have his wife after he was gone."

"I hesitate to describe . . ."

"Sir," the judge said in irritation, "your testimony has long ago overstepped the bounds of decency. If the ladies present are offended by any indelicacies presented here, they had better have stayed at home." He scowled at the spectators. "In my day, a case of this nature would never have excited such interest in respectable women."

Thus prompted, Reverend Dale told how Mr. Edwin had shown him letters written by Isabelle early in their marriage, while she was away at school, in which she had declared enthusiasm for becoming a loving wife when they at last lived together. Mr. Edwin had asked Reverend Dale to use his influence to lead Isabelle back to that disposition of heart.

"I told him, of course, that I could never speak with Mrs. Martin on so intimate a topic as her . . . as their marital relations. But he seemed to think just my friendship might . . . return her frame of mind to . . . to more bridal devotions."

"Quite remarkable," muttered the judge.

"Did Edwin Martin ever make a definite statement about you and his wife?"

"He once said, 'If anything happens to me, you two may come together.' "

When court adjourned for two hours, I went home to eat and to ponder all that had been said that morning and, indeed, all I knew of the Martins. Mr. Edwin could be demanding and even overbearing, but he also, at times, succumbed to Isabelle's wishes, as when he occupied a separate bed during her pregnancy. She had used Dr. Nichols's text, *Esoteric Anthropology (The Mysteries of Man)*, to support this celibacy; Mr. Edwin was a man overly impressed by book learning. That he had continued to sleep apart from her for a while after the sad death of their infant daughter showed a compassion on his part that needed no authoritative props. By the time of the stormy luncheon with Mr. Sylvester Martin and Mr. Frederick, however, Mr. Edwin's compassion had been worn thin by a husband's natural desires. Yet even in the face of inevitable capitulation, Isabelle had managed to strike a bargain—for what else could old Mr. Martin's notarized apology be called? A woman with such skills of persuasion could have planted the ideas Mr. Edwin had presented to the minister as his own.

Was I the only person to see this? Perhaps. As the household's sole help and Isabelle's sometime confidante, I possessed bits of information and privileged observations no one else did. Which of these would I be called upon to spend and which hold? Was the choice mine or would duty preclude choice? Where, exactly, did my duty lie?

To clear my head a while, I helped Elsinore rub down the parlor walls, the last room needing this work.

"We had a note from Sippy today," Elsinore said. "Father will be in town tomorrow and will come by about midday to carry me home."

"Oh, Elsie, I haven't taken you yet to all the places you wanted to see."

"It's all right," she said, stooping to sweep up bread crumbs. "I've seen enough."

"Plus I've left you alone with the housework these two days."

She gave me a sunny smile.

"I don't mind housework," she said, adding thoughtfully, "but the time has showed me I could never abide living alone."

"Really? I think it would be a great luxury."

⁂ THE WITNESS for the afternoon was Dr. Cornelius. He wore a checked cutaway suit with a silk bow tie, and gray spats. It was a costume a younger man might favor, but the doctor was so nervous on the stand and so obviously wishing to make a good impression, one had to regard him leniently, if only out of sympathy. He had an untidy notebook with him, out of which loose pages kept slipping. By agreement of the lawyers on both sides, he was permitted to refer to this diary in answering some questions. He was a man who liked to be precise, but he had, he said, a bad memory for details. The diary helped him with that, but, alas, it also encouraged him, at times, to give so many details that the answer to a question was very nearly buried alive.

The prosecutor led Dr. Cornelius through his first meeting with Mr. Edwin and his attendance on him during the August illness and again in November. The doctor read from his notes all the medicines he'd employed, what on which days, everything from mouthwashes to morphia injections. When the judge asked Dr. Cornelius if the treatment could be summarized as soothing the stomach and providing sedatives and laxatives, the doctor agreed.

"But there were also the vermifuges—worm powders," he quickly added, leafing through his diary. "I have the mixture right here . . . the proportions of santonin and senna to sulfate of soda and Urwick's extract. . . ."

"But I thought you said Mr. Martin was suffering from mercurial poisoning and necrosis of the jaw," the exasperated judge interrupted.

"So it appeared. Though his family insisted mercurial poisoning was an impossibility. The worms were the patient's own idea. He insisted he felt worms wriggling at the back of his throat during the night."

Dr. Cornelius went on to say that Mr. Edwin often had other morbid notions about the state of his health. He also said that Mr. Edwin was a suggestible man, giving as examples the lack of pain Mr. Edwin had felt at the dentist's after Dr. Cornelius put him through hypnosis, and the effectiveness of a placebo the doctor had concocted as a sleeping draught; a "prescription for the imagination" he called it.

Next, the prosecutor had Dr. Cornelius recount the night of Mr. Edwin's death—how he'd been summoned by Mr. Sylvester Martin; how surprised he'd been to find Mr. Edwin dead when he had felt so well only that morning; what the room looked like, and the body. The only abnormality Dr. Cornelius found in Mr. Edwin was his tongue, which was very white. He smelled the body and some glasses, plates, and bottles near the body. One glass smelled of brandy, the others of mint tea, the plates smelled of supper, and the bottles of identifiable medicines.

"Was there anything whatever in the previous conduct of the deceased, in your observations of him, to suggest to you the probability of death from natural causes?" Mr. Holland asked.

"No, nothing."

"Did you say anything to Mrs. Martin that night, or she to you, about what could have been the cause of death?"

"I asked her if she could give me any explanation that would clear up the mystery, but she said she couldn't. I also asked if there were any poisons in the house, and she said there were not. I listed quite a few poisons by name, concentrating on the ones that are rapid in action, like digitalis and prussic acid, but she said no to each one. I believe I made a list of the poisons I asked about. . . ."

Dr. Cornelius rapidly turned several pages in his diary.

"That's all right, Doctor," the prosecutor said. "I'm satisfied you were thorough. I'd like to return to the condition of the body, specifically the tongue."

"It was white," the doctor said emphatically, seemingly pleased with himself for not needing to refer to his notes.

"And when you saw the deceased later, at the postmortem, was the tongue still white?"

"It was not."

Mr. Holland took a moment to clear his throat. Dr. Cornelius hastened to fill the pause.

"I did not, of course, conduct the postmortem myself," he said. "I deemed it better for impartial doctors to do it, but I was present and took notes on the complete proceedings, which is why I happened to observe the change in the tongue, as well as—"

"How, Doctor, did you account for the change in the tongue?" Mr. Holland interrupted loudly.

The doctor looked round the courtroom with a self-congratulatory smile.

"At first," he said, "I couldn't account for it. But later, I learned to interpret it by means of an experiment I made upon myself."

"What was that?" Mr. Holland asked.

"Swallowing chloroform!" The doctor beamed. "I took three and a half drams into my mouth, swallowed twenty or thirty drops, and spat the rest out. When I looked in the mirror, my tongue was very white; several hours later, the whiteness had passed away."

"Now, Dr. Cornelius," the prosecutor said, "you saw Mrs. Martin again between the time of her husband's death and the time of her arrest?"

"Oh, yes, several times."

"For what purpose?"

The doctor looked at the prosecutor with surprise.

"Why, she was a new widow, and I am a doctor."

"Yes . . .?"

"I was inquiring after her health—the quality of her sleep, her diet, the state of her spirits. All these may be greatly affected by the death of a loved one."

"And how did you find her, Doctor?"

"Quite brave and patient, as she'd been throughout her husband's illnesses."

"Not distraught?"

"Not distraught, per se, but she did require sedatives once or twice, and she was anxious, of course, to finally learn the results of the toxicologist's studies."

"I believe, Doctor, it was you who relayed these results to Mrs. Martin?"

"Just a moment, just a moment," the doctor replied, shuffling frantically in his book.

"A simple yes or no, Doctor," the judge urged.

"Yes; it would be yes, Your Honor. I was only looking for my record of that conversation. I wrote it out as soon as I got home from that visit to Mrs. Martin, as her story was so long and such an astonishing one. I wouldn't want, in repeating it to the jury, to forget any of it."

Mr. Clark stood up and addressed the judge.

"Since it is a contemporaneous record, Your Honor, I make no objection to Dr. Cornelius reading his notes on this conversation," he said.

"My learned friend cannot pick out one segment of the doctor's notes to be read, Your Honor," Mr. Holland protested. "Either all the documents the doctor has created relevant to the case must be read or none."

"Your Honor," Mr. Clark countered, "you have already allowed the doctor to refer to notes."

"Only regarding exact medical data," Mr. Holland argued.

"You will have an opportunity, Mr. Clark, to bring out what you wish about the conversation during cross-examination," the judge said. "Dr. Cornelius, you will answer counsel's questions from recollection only."

Dr. Cornelius ceremoniously closed his book and placed it gently on his lap. He glanced at Isabelle, and I fancied there was the slightest hint of apology in his look. He had always been soft with her, as receptive to her charm as a sponge to water. I saw her lower her head a moment, perhaps in response to his glance, and I wondered if the doctor would read that as forgiveness or chastisement. As it turned out, the story Dr. Cornelius told, and more importantly, the way he told it—with obvious belief and sympathy despite its fantastic claims—came to weigh, with some people at least, in Isabelle's favor.

"What was Mrs. Martin's reaction, Doctor, when you told her of the toxicologist's finding that her husband had died from swallowing liquid chloroform?" Mr. Holland began.

"Well, I began, I think, by telling her I had good news. I thought of it as good news, you see, because if the cause of death had been found to be one of those poisons that may be given in small amounts without the patient knowing it, she would most certainly have been accused of having poisoned him. Of course, she was accused anyway—arrested later that very day. I believe Reverend Dale had come forward about the chloroform before then, and old Mr. Martin had been on at the police with his suspicions from the start—"

"Doctor," the judge said crossly, "confine yourself to the question. What was Mrs. Martin's reaction?"

Before answering, Dr. Cornelius glanced at Isabelle again.

"She said, 'I am afraid, Doctor, that it is true,' or words to that effect."

There were gasps in various parts of the audience.

"Naturally," Dr. Cornelius hastily went on, "I asked her what she meant. That's when she told me her long story."

"Would it be too much to expect, Doctor," said the judge, "that you could give that story in summary, rather than word by word?"

"Without my records, Your Honor, I would be hard-pressed to do otherwise. I did intend to *try* to recall it word by word, but if you think—"

"I trust any summary from you, Doctor, will be full-fledged," the judge said.

"Thank you," Dr. Cornelius said, though he seemed unsure whether he had been complimented. I was sure he had not.

"Mrs. Martin first described her early marriage, that it had been arranged, that she was young—twenty years old to her husband's thirty," Dr. Cornelius began, picking his way carefully and slowly so as to avoid verbosity. "Her husband held peculiar views on marriage, and he insisted their relationship be entirely platonic. No sexual intercourse. Of course, Mrs. Martin expressed this to me in more delicate terminology, but that was clearly her meaning. At any rate, being, as I said, young and inexperienced, she agreed."

This was not the Edwin Martin I had known. I recalled the distressing scene in the kitchen the night of Mattie's wedding and other less ugly indications that the Martins had certainly had physical relations during my time with them. But perhaps their early period had been different, or perhaps Isabelle was referring to her two years away at school. Or perhaps, once more, Isabelle's wishes and beliefs had somehow become Mr. Edwin's, or were being made to appear so. I leaned forward in my seat, as if that would help me understand better what I was hearing.

"These terms were adhered to," the doctor continued, "with one solitary exception: when Mrs. Martin desired to become a mother. After that, the platonic relationship was resumed. Mrs. Martin asserted she was indifferent on the matter. Her husband was kind to her, and they lived together amicably."

"There was no friction over this unusual arrangement?" the prosecutor asked.

"Not over the arrangement, no," the doctor replied. "Though there was some trouble over insults by the father-in-law. I believe Mrs. Martin actually left her husband's house for a week at one time and hid from him because he did not resent his father's insults to her with enough zeal."

The judge shook his head, apparently baffled by the bizarre

portrait of Edwin Martin that had been painted by Dr. Cornelius and Reverend Dale.

"Well you might wonder," the doctor said, noticing the judge's bafflement. "Though the marriage was amicable, Mrs. Martin's position was not an easy one. Her husband liked to surround her with male acquaintances, to show off her cleverness. 'He was delighted when I gained admiration,' was what she said, I believe.

"In the last months of his life, however—which is when I knew the family—Mrs. Martin said that her husband changed. They had become friends with Reverend Dale, and Mr. Martin threw them together—'He threw us together,' she said—even asking them to kiss in his presence and seeming to enjoy it. Then, she said, her husband transferred her to the reverend—platonically, of course. 'He had given me to Mr. Dale' were her exact words. At the same time, Edwin Martin began demanding of his wife the marital rights he had never before exercised—with the one exception of conceiving their daughter.

"Mrs. Martin was confused and upset. She felt it her duty to her womanhood and to Reverend Dale to refuse her husband's advances. To aid in that, she obtained chloroform, with the idea that she would sprinkle some on a handkerchief and wave it in front of her husband's face when he accosted her, thus causing him to go to sleep and leave her alone."

"Did Mrs. Martin say how she obtained the chloroform?" Mr. Holland asked.

"No, she refused to say."

"Did she say she used it as she intended?"

"No—it's unlikely the plan would have worked anyway. He probably would have resisted, the bottle got overturned, and the pair of them been chloroformed! At any rate, Mrs. Martin said it troubled her to keep a secret from her husband, so on the last evening of his life—she not knowing, of course, it was his last evening—"

"That, sir, is for the jury to decide," the judge interjected.

"Yes. Sorry. On that evening, she brought the bottle to her husband and told him why she had it. I asked if he was cross, and she said not. She said he put the bottle aside and asked her to hold his foot so he might sleep, which she did, finally falling asleep herself in that position."

"Did you see a bottle of chloroform in the parlor when you arrived at the Martin home that night?"

"No, though I only looked around at what was in plain sight. I didn't presume to open any drawers or cabinets."

Mr. Holland glanced quizzically at the jury, as if to say, *Now, there's a mysterious point for us to remember.* Then he turned back to Dr. Cornelius.

"During this conversation you've been relating, did Mrs. Martin say what had happened to the chloroform?"

"She said she'd thrown the bottle into the river the day after her husband's death. I asked her if there'd been any gone from it, and she said she didn't know."

"Did she say why she'd thrown the bottle away?"

"No, and I didn't ask. Sad memories, I suppose."

The prosecutor said he was finished with the witness and turned him over to Mr. Clark. That gentleman drew out from the doctor a vivid and horrible description of Mr. Edwin's red, spongy gums and his decayed teeth with fungus at their roots. Then he concentrated on questions about Mr. Edwin's spirits.

"You were treating Mr. Martin, Doctor, for worms as well as for the problems in his mouth?" Mr. Clark asked at one point.

"Yes. It was only his imagination, of course, that they were in his throat, but I had Mrs. Martin save his stool for me, and, indeed, one day he did pass a worm, so I initiated treatment."

"What was Mr. Martin's reaction to passing the worm?"

"He thought it proved there was something wrong with him that I had overlooked."

"Was he more nervous and troubled after that?"

"For a day or two."

"Did Mrs. Martin ever tell you that her husband spoke about dying?"

Dr. Cornelius frowned a moment, then his face brightened.

"Yes," he answered. "On my first consultation, she remarked that he worried over small discomforts and could even imagine he was dying when all he had was a simple case of gas."

"Was anyone else present when Mrs. Martin made this remark?"

"The patient's father, Mr. Sylvester Martin, was there."

"Did he contradict his daughter-in-law about this?"

"I don't believe so. No . . . no, as I recollect—without my notes, mind—he did not." The doctor tapped his forehead gently with one finger. "Yes, I have it now. He was very interested, instead, in discussing the benefits of electricity—"

"Doctor," Mr. Clark interrupted.

". . . but his son's case didn't warrant—"

"Doctor," Mr. Clark repeated more forcefully, "despite Edwin Martin's condition not being critical, you did attend him often, did you not?"

"Yes, I did. To keep his pluck up. I would have liked to send him off on a sea trip with no one to nurse him or hold his foot or any such nonsense. If he'd been obliged to take care of himself, he'd have been all right."

"You visited Edwin Martin daily for a while? Sometimes twice a day?"

"Yes."

"And what did you observe of Mrs. Martin's nursing at those times?"

"She attended her husband with kindness, patience, and anxious affection. He himself spoke with gratitude of her devotion."

"Did she tend him night and day?"

"Yes. I could not wish for a better nurse. It's only right that I say that emphatically."

"One last question, Doctor," Mr. Clark said. "Do you have any doubts about the story Mrs. Martin told you of her marriage and her plans for the chloroform?"

"No, none. I am a doctor, you see, and I am never amazed at the strangeness of human nature."

THIRTY

COURT WAS out of session the next two days, which were Saturday and Sunday. On ten o'clock Saturday morning, Mattie came by, as we'd arranged previously by letter, which was lucky since Elsinore was to leave that day. We delayed our breakfast so that we could feed Mattie without making her feel an object of charity, which is certainly not how we considered it. The idea had been Elsinore's, and I thought how caretaking she was in a natural, unbegrudging way and how smoothly she'd nested into a strange kitchen, as if the contradictions and contentions of the city were much farther away than just outside the street door, or, for that matter, haunting the deserted rooms where Isabelle and Edwin Martin had acted their life together.

All three of us worked on preparing the meal. The activity helped our talk to flow on everyday things, putting off more serious thoughts until our energies were ready to come round to them. We made cream toast, fried liver, dropped eggs, fricasseed potatoes, and coffee. Sharing the labor let Mattie stand as friend rather than guest. It was our gift to her and she knew it, and none of us had to acknowledge it out loud.

When we were done eating, Elsinore decided impulsively to make a brown Betty. She cleared one end of the table so that she could work and still sit with us. With Elsinore's chopping and mixing as background, and later, while the brown Betty baked, filling the room with the aromas of apple, cinnamon, and melting sugar, Mattie quietly talked about her life. She didn't have much to say about cigar wrapping, except that she was sorry she still needed to take money from Lorenzo; her earnings were five dollars and twenty-four cents a week, and her room and board and necessary expenses came to five-fifty-one a week.

"He doesn't make much, an apprentice's wages. He does some work still at Stetson's for extra money. But he won't hear of me moving somewhere less costly, because where I am is safe and clean, and the food, though dull, is sufficient and properly cooked," Mattie said. "But I can't keep relying on him."

"Why not? Has he said so?" Elsinore asked with consternation.

"It's my idea, not his. I'm not his wife, after all."

"He thinks of you as his sister, Mattie," I said. "And your baby is his blood."

"I know, Hanna. But Lorenzo's life won't stay always as it is now. He'll come to have other obligations. He already has dreams. He's told you about New York?"

This last she said cautiously, studying my face for a reaction.

"Yes," I answered with equal caution. "Has he decided, then?"

"Not yet," Mattie said. "But whether it's New York or something else, change will come, and I want him to be released from me before he begins to feel me a burden."

"He'll always be tied to you," I said. "He'll want to be."

"And I want that bond. For myself, and for Paolo's child. But I don't want it to weigh him down, because then I'll feel weighed down, too, and somehow—I don't know this for sure, but I feel certain of it anyway—somehow the weight will curve back over Paolo and me like a long, cold shadow, and it will take away from my memories of our happiness. We *were* happy, you know, Paolo and I, before . . ."

I reached across the flour-dusted table and put my hands over hers.

"I know, Mattie," I said.

But really I did not. For though it is easy to identify joy in another person, and sadness or anger, happiness is not as plain. Often it is hidden and only its effects noticed; when we admire the gliding swan, we don't consider the paddling of its webbed feet. Or perhaps happiness is difficult to discern in others because so many people settle for an imitation of happiness, or are afraid to admit they are not happy, as if it were a shameful failing, or a sin. It's not that I doubted Mattie when she said she and Paolo had been happy. I didn't. It's just that I couldn't know it through my own senses. To strive for happiness, a state so elusive and skittish and personally particular, a fairy tale thing that maybe cannot be pursued at all but only found, takes a kind of bravery, I think, almost a kind of madness. If Mattie had possessed happiness, I could understand her wish to safeguard her memory of it.

"What will you do?" Elsinore said softly to Mattie, her country-girl practicality breaking into our silence.

Mattie took her hands away from mine and set them on her lap. She lifted her chin. Her melancholy look faded. I could see she was ready for this question and pleased with herself that she was.

"Paolo belonged to an Italian mutual aid society. They'll help me with expenses when the baby comes. Father Monaco has found me a family to stay with and cleaning work in Germantown at the Morton Street Day Nursery so I can keep my baby with me. If that's not enough and I have to go into a factory, Father said the Guardians of the Poor might pay a wet nurse. They usually reserve such aid for foundlings, he said, but he thought he could arrange it. Of course, I don't want to come to that."

It was a patchwork plan, one that could fall apart at any number of places, but it was a plan nevertheless, and I saw that

Mattie needed to believe it would work. I nodded at her encouragingly. Elsinore looked from one to the other of us with concern.

"But Mattie," she said before I could give her a warning nudge with my foot, "will all that really do? What if you or the baby gets sick? What if the priest can't arrange—"

"Then it's the workhouse at Blockley," Mattie interrupted in a peppery tone. "I've known some to spend a few months there every year."

"Oh," Elsinore said meekly.

"I'm sorry," Mattie told her with a sigh. "I'm not upset with you. But I must go forward, you see, without letting fears set in."

"Surely Lorenzo wouldn't let you go to the workhouse," Elsinore said.

Mattie gave her a mirthless smile.

"The possibility of his help will go against me. The Guardians offer relief only to those without family to aid them."

Mattie went to the oven to check the brown Betty. It was clear she didn't want to discuss her situation anymore. When she came back to the table, she was determinedly lighter.

"Speaking of my brother-in-law," she said, "he asked me to tell you he'd like to visit tomorrow. Will you be here?"

"I will," I said, feeling a nervous catch at the back of my throat, "but Elsinore will be gone."

"He can put up with that, I imagine," Mattie teased.

Now I wanted to shift the conversation. I told about the trial, about all that was being said and the stiff formalities of the court, about the audience and how the women listened so intently, as if their own lives and not Isabelle's were being laid out for all to see and judge.

"But why should they think that?" Elsinore said.

"They are mostly married ladies, like Isabelle; their quality of dress is like hers, even somewhat better. Perhaps they have had similar struggles to find happiness in the domestic circle."

"But surely they can't sympathize with adultery and murder?" Mattie said. "If it's proved Mrs. Martin did it."

"No," I replied. "But mightn't there be sympathy for someone's plight even while there is condemnation of the solution?"

"How do you know the women in the court sympathize with Mrs. Martin?" Mattie asked.

"The set of their faces. The way they react to what is said—with nods or shakes of their heads, with little gasps or sighs."

"I remember my mistress, when I was in service," Mattie said. "She had sick headaches all the time. The other servants, who'd been there longer, used to say her headaches came out of the sherry bottle and could be counted on to appear whenever her husband reviewed her household accounts or refused an outing or guest she wanted or crossed the hall into her bedroom too many nights in a row."

"Is it so terrible, then, being married?" asked Elsinore.

"No, dear, not terrible," Mattie said gently. "Quite lovely, in fact, at times, and quietly happy, and it gives a reassuring certainty to life. There can be disappointments, though."

"What do you do then?"

"You ignore them."

Mattie got a sad, faraway look in her eyes. She began playing with a bit of dough on the table, rolling it slowly back and forth between her fingers.

"There were editorials in several newspapers," I said, "that talked about marriage and how the trial was shedding light into its dark corners."

Mattie looked up from her dough plaything with some curiosity, though her gaze was still vague. I fetched the pile of papers from the dining room and set the stack on the floor beside the kitchen table. As I paged through a section of one,

Mattie took up another and also began searching for mentions of the trial. Elsinore watched us patiently.

"Here," I said, folding back a page of letters to the editor. "This lady says that marriage can be the vehicle to personal happiness for both man and woman only when there is an equal blend of individual tastes, wishes, and wills. And she says it's a medical fact that sexual union in marriage is healthful and contributes to spiritual love, but it must be practiced in moderation and with mutual consent."

"She put that in the newspaper?" Elsinore said.

"It seems to be quite the topic," Mattie said, spreading open a different news sheet. "In this paper, a lady writes that the Martin marriage is to be deplored for its lack of balance and self-control, because there was such an unnaturally long abstinence and then, later, Mr. Martin's unrestrained demands."

"Is it only ladies wrote in about the trial?" asked Elsinore.

"Men, too," I answered. "But they write about different things."

"Here's one," Mattie said. "A man's written to say women ought to shrink from trials as from brothels, and that even women's rights supporters shouldn't object to excluding female spectators from murder cases."

"I remember a letter yesterday something like that," I said. "where a man said he didn't understand how the ladies at the Martin trial had any interest in Isabelle's story since it was obvious that they led lives of sheltered comfort and couldn't possibly have any wrongs or tyranny to avenge."

"Give me a paper to look at," said Elsinore, bending to the floor to pick one up.

"Oh," she exclaimed after a few minutes. "Here's a gentleman calls the women at the trial 'petticoated ghouls who gloat over a fellow woman's misery.' But you didn't think they were gloating, Hanna."

"No, not at all."

"What are they afraid of, I wonder?" Mattie mused.

"Afraid?" Elsinore said.

"You're right, Mattie," I said. "I believe they are afraid, else they wouldn't object so violently."

"Maybe they think if women watch trials, they'll start wanting to be on juries."

"I wouldn't want that," Elsinore said. "I thought sitting at court was dull."

"Or maybe," I theorized, "the men who wrote those letters are worried that the interest ordinary wives are giving Isabelle might show some unspoken frustrations in their own lives."

"Do they actually worry that every wife with complaints will take to adultery and murder?" Mattie scoffed.

"No, I'm sure they're not that silly. But they want to think only a monster would betray or kill her husband. They don't want to believe Isabelle's problems and desires could be at all common."

"Oh, listen," Mattie said, pointing to a column in her paper. "This man suggests divorce be made easier so that women can have less drastic ways to escape unwanted husbands. Sensible enough. But he laments that a divorced woman who remarries would then 'have no secrets from two living men!' "

Mattie read the quote so comically, we all had to laugh. I don't know whether we'd have resumed our discussions after that or not, for just then my father rang at the door, and his arrival ended our talk, as a bounding dog will scatter hens. I invited him to take coffee in the kitchen, but he would not, clearly disapproving and ill at ease, as if the house itself and not its owners had a stain upon it. He remained in the foyer while Elsinore went to fetch her satchel, and then he took it immediately down to the street. Mattie returned to the kitchen to wrap up half the brown Betty for them to take along, leaving Elsinore and me with a few minutes alone.

"I'm going to ask Father and Sippy about Mattie coming to stay with us," she said in a low, conspiratorial voice.

"Mattie's proud," I said. "She won't do it."

314

"For even a while? For the baby's sake?"

"Maybe. If she's hard-pressed otherwise."

"I'll make it happen," Elsinore whispered urgently, hearing Mattie enter the hall.

I admired my sister's confidence in herself and in simple solutions to intricate problems. It was the confidence of youth and inexperience, which can sometimes accomplish things that daunt wiser minds. Had I ever had it? I suppose I must have, but I couldn't conjure up a recollection of it. I was not so many years beyond Elsinore, yet I felt immeasurably older, seasoned by my broader knowledge of the world.

Mattie said she ought to be going, too, as a fresh load of tobacco leaves was being brought today, making work available. Elsinore suggested Father could give Mattie a ride, so she quickly gathered her cloak and gloves, and they went downstairs together, into the rush of the streets.

THE NEXT morning I awoke, got up to build a fire in my little coal stove, and went back to bed. Except for a few times of childhood illness, I'd never before done this. Those around me wouldn't have permitted it, nor would my own ideas of responsibility and industry have permitted it.

In choosing to stay abed awhile, I was not foundering into sloth, as Mrs. Cox might have claimed, nor was I hoping to gain more sleep, though I had been up late reading. My choice was, instead, a tiny but definite declaration of myself, as when I'd answer loudly to roll call at school. I stayed in bed in order to give my mind time to roam. I had decided that I deserved such latitude simply by wanting it and that I did not need to make excuses or ask permission to take it. No one was there, anyway, to receive my excuses or asking.

It was drizzling. The skylight panes displayed an array of small puddles, like the map of a land plentiful with lakes. The pattern altered periodically as trickles of water ran over the glass. I tried restricting myself to studying one corner in order to follow the changes, but my eyes continually flitted away from the assigned spot. At one point, a pigeon landed on the skylight. It strutted in a circle, its slender pink toes wreaking delicate havoc with the map of lakeland. I wondered about the bird's feet—if they felt cold, as mine would have been had I been walking barefoot in a January rain.

While I watched the water, various thoughts traveled across my mind. I briefly held some of them, turning them this way and that before letting them move on. There was always another one following, either brought in tow behind or making its own unattended entry, like an old maid at a christening party.

Many of my thoughts were prompted by the newspaper coverage of the trial. A number of reporters yesterday had seized on the same highlights; more than one headline proclaimed "Strange Ideas of the Deceased," and one dared to lead with "D—n the Chloroform." One writer called Isabelle's story about the chloroform "marvelous," which was a circumspect way of saying he thought it was a lie.

A woman correspondent on an opinions page had harped on the double standard, and I recalled how Mr. Clark had said he was relying on such sentiments in the public to help Isabelle's case. The letter writer viewed Reverend Dale as Isabelle's lover, in attitude if not in outright fact, and asserted that he should be held to as strict standards as Isabelle. She went so far as to say that women were no less susceptible than men to yielding to "the most powerful human passions." Do not pillory Isabelle Martin for murder, she said, if the real complaint against her is immorality, not when George Dale is allowed to commit the same behavior with impunity.

I thought about the other editorials Mattie and Elsinore and I had read and about Isabelle sitting silently in the center of these streams of interpretation and advice and opinion. I thought of her daily appearance in court, of her erect carriage in black dresses cut to flatter—but subtly, so that she remained demure—and of her sweeping gaze over the attentive crowd. Almost anything could be read into that mute, dark figure, into those large, luminous eyes. There was texture enough in her looks and in the stories witnesses were telling of her to paint her as either villain or lamb. I wondered if she had become obscured even to herself. I knew she had lied about some things. Yet distorted truths seeped through those lies like moist wounds through gauze, and that made the lies convincing.

I held the power to expose one falsehood. I knew that the Martins' relationship had not been platonic. No one except Isabelle was aware that I knew it. If I came forward with that information, would her "marvelous story" unravel, the way the snip of one strand of yarn can undo a sweater? Certainly much of the story would become suspect, particularly the existence of Mr. Edwin's "strange ideas" and their purported strain on Isabelle and, more importantly, the intended purpose of the chloroform.

The more I thought about it, the more the knowledge I possessed seemed like the keystone wedged at the crown of an arch; it locked all the other pieces in place. A sweater with a hole in it can still be worn, but an arch without a keystone is just a pile of rubble. I didn't like feeling so significant. But you can never forget what you know. You can only set it aside or set it out.

My head was beginning to ache from these many musings. I got up, breakfasted, and busied myself with housework, which has the capability of either freeing the mind to wander or stopping all contemplation, depending upon how much attention you direct into it.

By the time Lorenzo arrived in the early afternoon, my head was empty and my body was nicely fatigued. I had taken off my apron and was waiting for a pot of tea to steep when he rang.

It was a mild day for the season, the rain having cleared, yesterday's wind having dropped off and the temperature risen, so Lorenzo wanted to take me walking. I suggested a cup of tea in the kitchen first.

Unlike my father, Lorenzo showed no hesitation and easily agreed to stop awhile. It wasn't strictly proper, but I felt no twinges of awkwardness about it. I supposed that was because Lorenzo was so familiar to me, but now I believe it was because I had already passed into a way of thinking and being that was a little out of the general way, an unassuming but resolute independence. I didn't see it then. It was like crossing over a county line whose boundary is marked on maps but not on the land; the unsuspecting traveler notices no break in the swell of the hills, the kinds of crops, the look of the houses. It's only when he reflects, after a time, on how far he's come that he finds he's in a new place, however alike in appearance to where he departed from.

"Your sister went home?" Lorenzo said.

"Just yesterday. She was here so briefly, but I do feel her absence."

"Because she's such a warmhearted girl."

"Yes, she is."

"I saw her one day."

"She told me."

"You were at the court."

I nodded and served Lorenzo a second helping of warmed-over brown Betty. He reached for the little pitcher to pour cream over it. I thought suddenly of my parents, how they used to engage in small unremarked movements just like that, domestic pantomimes of their long connection. I was startled to find Lorenzo and me doing the same.

"How does the trial go?" he asked, as if unaware of our subtle communion, or taking it for granted.

"It's rather confusing, actually," I said, glad to talk about something that was so occupying my mind. "Facts come out in bits and pieces and are put up against other facts that don't agree, and all are mixed in with prejudices and guesses. I don't see how a fair decision will be made."

Lorenzo looked at me with surprise.

"But the important facts are simple," he said.

"I'm beginning to wonder which are the important facts."

"*Ecco,* that the woman had poison and that her husband died of it."

I got up to fetch hot water to add to the teapot. My stomach fluttered with a nervousness suspiciously akin to annoyance.

"Those facts are so?" Lorenzo continued.

"Yes."

"Then she is probably guilty."

"How is it you're so certain?"

"You are not?"

I returned the kettle to the stove and sat down again.

"She was unhappy," I said quietly.

Lorenzo gave me a puzzled look. Indeed, I myself didn't know how that countered anything he'd said. It just seemed the necessary starting point.

"Mr. Martin married Mrs. Martin for her money."

Lorenzo waved his hand dismissively. "It's how they do, isn't it?"

"Not so much anymore."

"Well, it was for her to make the best of things. She needed babies. That would settle her."

"You see what I mean, Lorenzo?" I said, leaning forward eagerly. "How quickly the facts get mixed with outside opinions?"

I saw that he wanted to challenge me, but restrained himself. Still, he could not let the subject drop entirely.

"Elsinore said you are called for a witness."

"I've not had my turn yet."

"Perhaps things will come clearer to you then."

"Perhaps."

"Because then you will have to put aside your fuzzy pictures and tell the truth."

I felt my face flush with anger.

"What Isabelle did or didn't do is surrounded by *'fuzzy pictures,'* and not just mine," I said hotly. "And these matters—her marriage, her days, her deeds—rest on more than one truth."

"What is this, more than one truth?" he asked disdainfully.

"Maybe a wife considers her life differently from her husband, maybe sometimes what's supposed to keep her content does just the opposite. . . ."

"Hanna, you see where such thinking leads women."

"Where?"

"To murder!" He slammed the table with the flat of his hand and stood up.

I also rose. We glared at each other for a few seconds, then Lorenzo took a deep breath.

"I don't come here today to argue," he said, his voice only a bit calmer.

"But we have argued, haven't we?" I snapped back. I, too, could not calm myself so soon.

"I'm going to New York," he blurted.

I felt suddenly wounded and disconsolate, my anger deflated. I was frantic to hide the onrush of feelings, which threatened to spill out of me like rice from a burst sack. I managed one controlled syllable.

"Oh?"

"Damn it, Hanna, I'm asking for you to come with me."

The gruffness at the beginning of Lorenzo's statement had drained out of his words by the end.

"I need a wife, Hanna," he said with soft entreaty. "It's time I have a wife."

A panic seized me, such as one might feel seeing a beloved child walking precariously along a bridge railing. I wanted to reach out and pull him back—pull us both back.

"Lorenzo . . ."

The sad worry in my voice and face were obviously not what he'd been expecting. He took his cap from the back of the chair.

"I can go," he said.

"Lorenzo, I must think. . . ."

"Yes," he said solemnly. "My wife must be sure."

"You must be sure, too," I said. "About me. As I am."

He turned to leave. I didn't walk him to the door.

THIRTY-ONE

I WENT to bed early. I was not particularly tired. I only wanted the day to end. It was raining again, but harder than in the morning. Rain beat on the skylight and blew against the dormer window. My room was warm and dry, small enough that one lamp showed it all. I should have felt safe and cozy, barricaded against the weather so well, but what I felt was mortally alone, marooned. There is no solitariness like being by yourself in a small room at night in the middle of a big city.

Somewhere in me, I'd known the moment would come when Lorenzo would declare himself. I had hoped for it. I know I had. But when it came, instead of feeling myself open and swell, as I did when he was standing close to me or when he spoke my name tenderly, I felt my heart constrict, as if my pulse had stopped in fright. I ought to have pictured an expanse of bright, wide tomorrows. He was giving himself to me, offering me a future, yet I felt as if I were about to lose something instead. It wasn't just because we'd argued, though that figured in.

Much as Mattie loved me, she wouldn't understand my hesitation. Nor would Elsinore. Yet they had helped guide me to it, Mattie with her hard times and her fatherless child, Elsinore with her declined ambitions. Even Isabelle had helped. Isabelle, with her imaginings and yearnings and regrets. Her lies. If I accepted Lorenzo, what would our uneven compact be? What would I have to ignore?

Perhaps my doubts were simply commonplace nervousness and meant to be overridden. Otherwise, I thought miserably, I might never be anyone's wife, anyone's mother. The drumming rain seemed to say so.

❧ THE STREETS were still wet when I walked to court next morning. There was a softness to the day as sometimes comes unexpectedly in midwinter, as if to remind us that easy days will be met again. It had no such encouraging effect on me. I was not anguished, as I had been the night before, but I felt dulled and heavy, so the gray sky spoke more strongly to me than the mild air.

I passed the offices of *The Item* on Seventh Street. A delivery wagon was being loaded. Bundles of slender newspapers stood on the sidewalk. I noticed it was a special edition devoted to Isabelle's trial. Her likeness, those familiar eyes, peered at me from under a binding of jute twine. Today would be the final day of testimony—my day; tomorrow would be the summing up. There could be nothing new in that special edition, only review and commentary, endless commentary.

Perhaps it was my troubled mood, perhaps the mockery of kind weather when two full months of hard cold lay ahead, perhaps mere tiredness, but I bristled at the sight of those newspapers. Everyone who read them would think they knew Isabelle and what ought to be done about her. Everyone who came to court each day thought the same thing. Isabelle was not a person to them. I wondered if she were even a person any longer to those who had known her before, like Reverend Dale and Mr. Sylvester Martin and Mr. and Mrs. Cox. Isabelle was a token, her situation a *tableau vivant*. She was all wronged women, she was all women who did wrong, depending on who appraised her and what that person believed about the world. In the wall of evidence mounted against Isabelle were many stones that didn't belong—fear, superstition, and outrage; assumptions about proper place and acceptable ambitions and realistic capabilities.

There was a boy selling the special edition on the next corner. For the first time since Isabelle's arrest, I did not buy a paper.

Even for me, Isabelle's story, if not Isabelle herself, had slowly collected around it other stories. Isabelle's life was under public scrutiny, and that glaring, lonely spotlight was a formidable draw. But I kept looking into the limitless shadows around the spotlight, where so many other less sensational lives were being quietly led.

Few women any longer shared Isabelle's complaint that her husband had not been of her own choosing, though a disapproving father with means could easily prevent a wedding or delay it indefinitely. Yet even with a chosen mate, the change from solicitous suitor to authoritative husband can bring harsh surprises. Isabelle was right in one thing at least: It's hard to find contentment in a world that promises one thing and delivers another. Marry for love and companionship, the world says, but if they disappear, don't raise a fuss. Disdain sensual pleasure, but always welcome your husband's attentions. Act as your family's conscience, but don't nag. Deceive, if you must, to keep the domestic peace, but do it skillfully. Be an influence for good in society, but don't try to understand it, as its complexity is beyond you.

Isabelle was not a token, and she acted with only her own welfare in mind. Her complaints and her desires were very particular, as were her attempts at remedy. But she chafed against strictures that many others also knew. And her chafing, however wrongheaded or selfish, put those strictures in public view in a way pamphlets and editorials and strikes and rallies could never do. Isabelle was giving generalities names and faces. If she were declared guilty, so much else besides her small life would be disparaged and swept away.

I didn't have Isabelle's advantage of being able to make a difference without deliberate design. My vote must be cast with forethought. I had glimpsed those lives in the shadows. I was sure many who were living them sat on all sides of me in court every day. My testimony could protect Isabelle and her explanations, or knock them down like a tower of children's blocks. And with them would tumble reasonable objections to real conditions. Or with them, be let to stand.

☙ THE OPENING witness that day was Dr. Sewell, an expert in poisons. He was a hospital lecturer on the subject and the author of a text called *Forensic Medicine*. I spied that book and six or eight more thick volumes with medical titles on Mr. Clark's table. Several paper markers were sticking out of each book.

Dr. Sewell buttressed the conclusion of the toxicologist that Mr. Edwin had died from ingesting liquid chloroform. I wondered why this expert had been called, since the cause of death was no longer in dispute. I believed, in fact, that when Mr. Clark did dispute it, he hadn't been sincere, but had merely meant to invoke confusion, as when a stick stirred in pond muck muddies its waters. But it was not Dr. Sewell's opinion on the cause of death that interested Isabelle's lawyer.

"Doctor," Mr. Clark said, "what is the chief medical use of chloroform?"

"Chloroform," the doctor replied, "is used for anaesthetic purposes. Has been for forty years. Though it's being replaced more and more nowadays by ether."

"And in those forty years, Doctor, how many deaths have occurred through swallowing chloroform?"

"Seventeen."

"How did these seventeen deaths come about?"

"Either by accident or by suicide."

Mr. Clark strolled by the jury, skipping his glance over the jurors' faces one by one.

"Accident or suicide," he repeated, drawing the words out slowly. He turned back to the doctor.

"Has there ever been a single recorded case of murder by the administration of liquid chloroform?"

"No, there has not."

A murmur quivered through the audience, like wind through spring wheat. The judge frowned at us, and quiet was restored.

"Do you have an opinion, Doctor, as to why this might be?"

Mr. Holland objected to this question, saying Dr. Sewell was qualified only to give opinions on medical records and chemicals, not on human motives or behaviors.

"Dr. Sewell," Mr. Clark said after a moment's thought, "is chloroform a pleasant or easy liquid to swallow?"

"It would be by no means pleasant," the doctor said, "but it can be done, with determination. It has a sweet taste, yet it's a caustic liquid; there'd be a burning sensation in the mouth and esophagus."

"Could the taste and the burning sensation be disguised by dissolving the chloroform in brandy?"

"To some degree."

"But a person swallowing chloroform in brandy would still need to exercise his will to get it down?"

Again the prosecutor objected that Dr. Sewell could not provide such an opinion, and again Mr. Clark retreated.

"Were signs of irritation from a caustic agent detected in Edwin Martin's mouth or esophagus?"

"The postmortem report did not mention any."

"Since chloroform was found in the contents of Edwin Martin's stomach, how is it possible irritation of the mouth and esophagus was not present?"

"If the chloroform were bolted down quickly enough, irritation would not occur."

Mr. Clark scratched his chin, and when he spoke again, he seemed almost to be thinking aloud.

"Bolted down," he mused. "As by a man intent on taking his own life?"

"Objection!"

Mr. Clark made his opponent a small bow and went to sit down at the defense table.

"Dr. Sewell," the prosecutor followed up, "can you offer an explanation for the lack of irritation to Edwin Martin's mouth and esophagus that does not rely upon a willful act on his part?"

"The chloroform could have been introduced to the stomach by means of a gastric tube," the doctor said.

Mr. Clark raised his hand as if he were a schoolboy. The judge nodded at him. He asked his question of the doctor without standing up.

"Could such a procedure be performed by a layman, Doctor?" he said, incredulity in his voice.

Dr. Sewell smiled indulgently and shook his head.

"Highly unlikely," he said, almost amused. "It takes skill and some sangfroid. Particularly out of the scope of a woman, I should think."

The exasperated prosecutor objected once more, and the judge instructed the jury to disregard Dr. Sewell's last statement about the use of a tube being beyond the capacities of a woman not in the medical field. It seemed to me, however, that the judge's repetition of the doctor's opinion would only lodge it more firmly in the jurors' minds. I did not understand, besides, how a person could truly cleanse his memory, excising one bit and leaving all others unmarked by the discarded part. Human beings are not like paper in a typewriting machine; we do not register what we hear or see neatly and with equal impressions. Even if we did, by the time we call up a memory, even a recent one, it will have gathered about it other memories and meanings, like lint on a dark coat.

The judge started to dismiss Dr. Sewell, but Mr. Holland asked a moment's indulgence while his assistant hurriedly rummaged through a leather case at their table. When the flustered young man at last handed his superior a paper, Mr. Holland, obviously annoyed and embarrassed by the delay, took it from him with a rude snatching motion.

"Dr. Sewell," said the prosecutor, referring to the paper in his hand. "Is it possible to render a sleeping person insensible through the inhalation of chloroform?"

"I have never done it, but I know of instances where that has been successfully performed."

"Could a person who had been made insensible by the administration of inhaled chloroform be made to swallow liquid chloroform?"

"It's possible," the doctor said, thinking carefully, "if the chloroformism is not so deep as to have suppressed the swallowing reflex. I myself have poured liquid from a spoon into the gullet of an anesthesized patient and had him swallow it."

"Could it be done by an unskilled person?"

The doctor, perhaps remembering the judge's censure of his earlier opinion, paused and shifted in his seat before answering.

"The difficulties would not be insuperable," he said. "Particularly if the patient were lying on his back with his mouth open."

"Did you say 'insuperable'?" Mr. Clark called out.

"I meant to say there would be no great difficulty," Dr. Sewell amended.

"Thank you, Doctor, that is all," the prosecutor said.

"Dr. Sewell," Mr. Clark asked after the judge had recognized him again, "you mentioned difficulties. Could you specify what they might be?"

"Well," the doctor replied expansively, seeming pleased Mr. Clark was letting him show off his expertise further, "there are several potential problems. For one, if the patient were not sufficiently under the influence of chloroform not to suffer pain, the burning sensation of liquid chloroform, even disguised in brandy, might awaken him and cause him to resist, perhaps to vomit. Then, too, the liquid might be poured down the windpipe in error—though this is rare when done by a doctor."

"Can we assume, Doctor, that an unskilled person wishing to administer enough liquid chloroform down the throat of an insensible person to cause death would need some little time to do so?"

"It would not be very difficult, in some cases, to do it quickly. It is simply limited by the act of swallowing."

"If a person could not swallow or if the swallowing was slower than normal, would some of the liquid remain at the back of the throat for some time?"

"Yes."

"And in the case of liquid chloroform, would you expect to find, then, in the postmortem, signs of irritation or inflammation in the gums or throat, in the same way as when the chloroform lay in the stomach?"

"Yes, if the patient were unable to swallow."

"Yet if the medicine were taken suddenly, you would not expect to find irritation or inflammation in the mouth or throat?"

"No."

"Once again, sir, what did the postmortem report on Edwin Martin show in this regard?"

"Irritation of the stomach. No irritation of the mouth or esophagus."

As Dr. Sewell left the witness seat, I felt my body flush with heat, and all the little noises of the courtroom—people coughing or moving about in their seats, papers being shuffled at the lawyers' tables, Dr. Sewell's footsteps—grew unnaturally loud. I was apprehensive lest I be called next, and I felt as conspicuous as if I were already walking up to the judge's tall desk with all eyes upon me. I wanted to be called soon so as to get it over with, yet, perversely, I was also hoping for a postponement. So consumed was I with my agitated state of mind and body, the clerk had to call my name twice before I managed to stand up.

"Miss Hanna Willer," he pronounced. "Miss Willer, please."

As I passed the dock, I caught a whiff of roses, the scent that always drifted about Isabelle. The only time I'd been near her that she hadn't smelled of roses was when I'd visited her at the police station. Rosewater had been one of the first items she'd sent for from home after Mr. Clark had arranged she could bring such things into the jail. To encounter the soft, enchanting fragrance here and now helped calm me a bit somehow. My heart began to beat less rapidly. Sounds receded to normal levels.

As I took the oath to tell the truth, I was aware of Isabelle's gaze fastened on me. I dared a straightforward look at her just after I sat down. If she felt any trepidation about what I might say, her face did not show it. Her brow was smooth. Her slight smile seemed to say she was pleased to see me but sorry it had to be under such conditions.

It came to me suddenly that she was resigned to whatever would come—from me, from the jury, from life. Resigned not because she'd given up hope, but because she had confidence in herself and in her ability to persevere. She was her own logic. She had always been her own logic. Perhaps, like me, she'd come to see that her fate depended as much, if not more, on the passionate reactions her story evoked in people than on the evidence presented or the legal arguments made. She was letting herself be a canvas on which broad washes of color were competing for space and attention, gambling that the forces sympathetic to her would prevail—forces inclined in her favor not out of a true sympathy, but for their own reasons. My testimony, I saw, would be not only for or against Isabelle; it would be in support of one or another of the factions impassioned by her case.

Mr. Holland's early questions eased me into my role as witness. He had me tell how I'd come into the Martins' employ and what my duties were. Then he moved on to Mr. Edwin's last day.

"Were you at home the whole of that day, Miss Willer?"

"No, sir, I wasn't. Mrs. Martin gave me leave to visit a friend in the afternoon."

"Did you expect the visit to your friend to be a brief one?"

"No, sir."

"Why not?"

I didn't like the prosecutor prying into what I had been up to the day Mr. Edwin died. Wanting to know my doings in the house was one thing, but puttering into my friendship with Mattie was another. In a different setting, I could have refused to answer, but I didn't have that prerogative in court. It was an unsettling realization.

"My friend had had some troubles," I began carefully. "I expected to spend some time with her."

"And Mrs. Martin didn't object to the possibility of your visit being a lengthy one?"

"No. She said I could stay there for supper if I liked."

"How considerate of her," Mr. Holland said, though in his mouth it didn't sound like praise. "Had you asked if you might stay late?"

"No."

"It was her suggestion?"

"I . . . I don't remember. I guess so. She just knew . . ."

"She just knew, Miss Willer, that sending you off to your troubled friend would insure that you'd be gone from the house for many hours, leaving her free to act unobserved by anyone except a man who'd be dead before the night was through!"

"Objection!" Mr. Clark shouted.

"Save your speechifying for the appropriate time, Mr. Holland," the judge scolded.

"Miss Willer," Mr. Holland said in a tone of seeming friendliness that set me on edge, "why was it—beyond Mrs.

Martin's consideration for you and your troubled friend—
that she was willing to let you go out just at the time of day
when she and her bedridden husband would be requiring
supper?"

"Objection," Mr. Clark said wearily. "The witness cannot
know what was in Mrs. Martin's mind."

"Sustained."

"Very well." The prosecutor smiled at me. "Miss Willer,
why was it that *you* felt you could be spared from your usual
duties for several hours?"

"Mr. Martin was feeling better."

"Before my learned friend objects," Mr. Holland said, "tell
us, Miss Willer why you *thought* Mr. Martin was feeling
better."

"He'd been more cheerful the night before and that morning, and the doctor had been in that day and said he was encouraged."

"And didn't Edwin Martin make a request for his next
day's breakfast?"

"Yes, sir. He wanted oysters."

"Did he usually want oysters when he was ill?"

"No, sir. He ate quite blandly then."

"Before you went off on your visit, Miss Willer, did you
procure oysters for Mr. Martin?"

"No, sir."

"But if you expected to be at your friend's on into the
evening, and your master wanted the oysters for breakfast next
day, wouldn't it have been provident to get them that afternoon?"

"Mrs. Martin said she'd send a boy from the shop for
them."

"I see."

Mr. Holland stared thoughtfully at the floor a moment,
as if picturing a plate of fried eggs and oysters and toasted
crackers.

"And were there oysters in the icebox next morning?" he said with ominous gentleness.

My mind felt alarmingly empty. At that moment, I truly wasn't sure about the oysters, though I had a vague sense they had not been there. I found myself wildly trying to determine which answer, yes or no, was the accurate one. The prosecutor seemed poised to pounce on whatever I said.

"I don't remember," I managed at last. "There was the upset about Mr. Edwin by then, you see, and the men coming for his body, and—"

"Isn't the kitchen and its stock of supplies one of your main responsibilities?"

"Yes, sir, but—"

"Yet you don't remember whether or not oysters had been laid in? Even if you were temporarily distracted by the sudden death of your master, wouldn't the presence of oysters come to your notice eventually? By smell alone, I should think."

I felt my face flush with embarrassment. Mr. Holland was clearly implying he considered me either a liar or a dolt, and he was inviting all present to join him in that assessment.

"I suppose . . . I suppose there were none there," I said.

"Because Isabelle Martin knew there would be none needed," the prosecutor concluded.

There was some curt interplay then between Mr. Clark and Mr. Holland and the judge, but their words passed over me without registering. I was using the chance to try to soothe myself. I hoped I didn't appear as nervous as I felt.

Looking pleased with himself, the prosecutor went to his chair and sat down, and Mr. Clark got up for his turn at me. I told myself Mr. Clark would be friendlier than his opponent had been, but, instead, he led me to the more tortuous path. He began, benignly enough, with the oysters.

"Just to clarify, Miss Willer, on the afternoon Mrs. Martin told you she'd take care of getting the oysters for Mr. Martin, did she say *when* she'd be sending for them?"

"No, sir."

"If she wanted to send for them in the morning, would there have been someone at the shop downstairs able to accomplish the errand in time for Mr. Martin's breakfast?"

"Yes, sir. The first fellows come in very early to accept deliveries."

"So it's possible that was her intention?"

"Yes, sir, very possible."

Mr. Clark asked next about Mr. Edwin's physical complaints and his gloominess when he was ill. I told about the weeping, which seemed of great interest to him. He asked, too, about the frequency of Reverend Dale's visits and whether he'd always come with books, since he was a tutor. I said he had not, though there were sometimes books strewn about on the tables in the parlor when he visited. Then the questions moved onto boggier ground.

"Miss Willer, would you characterize Mrs. Martin, as an employer, to be cool and standoffish or genial towards you?"

"I'd say genial, sir."

"Friendly, even?"

"She was, often, yes—but I never overstepped."

I glanced at Isabelle to see the effect of my careful answer. She was as inscrutable as ever, but I fancied her level gaze said I had not offended her.

"Did she ever converse with you in a personal way? About matters other than your household duties?"

"Yes, she did. Sometimes."

"What did she discuss with you?"

Afternoons in the sewing room came to mind, and mornings in the kitchen, Isabelle and I closeted away with simple tasks. How could a mere factual recounting of conversations capture the delicate tenor of those times, the way our shared chores put us on the same ground, like castaways on a small island, and the way our circumstances were different enough that a certain wariness still kept hold of each of us, so that we seemed on two neighboring islands instead of the same one? It's how women expect to be with one another, so close at times that we know what it's like to be in the other's skin, and yet fearing betrayal or censure with every imparted confidence. It's what we expect because it's what has been, but, I wondered, is it what must be?

"We discussed books—she let me borrow books from her library. During her confinement, we talked about things to do with that. Sometimes she asked after my friends or my family."

Mr. Clark was nodding, but he didn't look satisfied.

"Did Mrs. Martin ever relate the circumstances surrounding the conception of her child?" he said.

"Sir?"

"Did she tell you that it had been the only time she and her husband had had relations?"

My back and my chest prickled with sweat, and my tongue seemed to thicken. I felt like a hiker faced with either fording a risky stream or crossing a dilapidated bridge.

"Yes, she told me that," I answered.

So far as it went, I had not lied. Not outright. But my anxiety did not decrease. I knew about lies of omission. Sippy had taught me about them as a child. Then such lies had been outside my experience, so their immorality was difficult to understand. They were closer, in my childish mind, to secrets than to sins, and secrets were infused with a thrill of pleasure that lies never possessed. But there was no pleasure in what I was engaged in on the witness stand. A weight was pressing upon me. Guilt? Some. Fear of discovery? Some of that, too. But above all else, it was the weight of responsibility, the weight of a chosen decision. However fully or sparsely I answered, I'd be taking sides. Telling the whole truth, as I'd sworn to do, is not always a neutral thing. It is not always the right thing.

"Can you recall Mrs. Martin's exact words?" Mr. Clark asked.

I thought back to that conversation in the kitchen, Isabelle dreamily winding yarn. It was the day Mr. Edwin had the single bed removed.

"She said, 'We had relations only once in all our years.' That's what she said."

I waited for Mr. Holland to object. I thought my face must give me away. I expected him to jump up and ask what more Isabelle had said. I expected him to demand, "Didn't she say 'only once without protection'? Isn't that what she said, Miss Willer? 'Only once without protection,' indicating clearly that relations between them were common, were as ordinary as those of other married couples?" Of course, there was no reasonable way Mr. Holland could have known how much I knew nor how much I was concealing, but extreme nervousness does not reason. I was actually surprised when the next question came not from the outraged prosecutor but from Mr. Clark.

"When did Mrs. Martin tell you this?" he said.

"In April, near the middle," I replied, glad to be veering away a bit from my transgression.

"How are you able to fix the time?"

"It was after her baby died, which was March. And not long after Mr. Edwin's brother had visited from Australia, which was at the beginning of April."

"And after Mr. Sylvester Martin had signed a notarized apology?"

"Yes. Mrs. Martin showed me the paper just the day before."

"When was it that the Martins made the acquaintance of Reverend George Dale?"

"That was in June."

"So, it was *before* the Martins even met Reverend Dale that Mrs. Martin told you her marriage had been almost exclusively a chaste one?"

"Yes."

"And it was, as well, a good deal before Mr. Edwin Martin contracted his final illness?"

336

"Yes."

"Then it was not a 'marvelous story' concocted after her husband's death to explain why she'd obtained chloroform?"

At this, Mr. Holland did object, and the judge said I didn't have to answer. Mr. Clark thanked me, which I wished he hadn't, and sat down.

"I have a few further questions for the witness, Your Honor," the prosecutor said.

I had no cause to feel Mr. Holland was suspicious of me, but I did nonetheless, and the few seconds before his first question came were an agony of dread. My mouth had mysteriously stopped producing saliva and felt coated in dry talc. I was panicked that I'd be unable to speak, that I'd open my lips and emit only puffs of dusty air. I dearly wished I had a glass of water. I had to pull my gaze away from the pitchers on the lawyers' tables to attend to Mr. Holland.

"Well, Miss Willer," he was saying in a skeptical tone, "relations only once. That's quite a thing to be told by one's mistress, isn't it? Even by a genial, friendly mistress?"

I swallowed several times and managed to bring up a small, saving dose of spit.

"I don't know, sir."

"You don't know?"

"I was never in service before, sir. I suppose mistresses may tell their maids whatever they like."

"I suppose they may. But maids may have opinions and make private judgments about what they're told, mayn't they?"

"Yes, sir."

"Even though servants are expected not to remark on their employers?"

I nodded my head.

"Answer aloud, please."

"Yes."

"To be honest, then, Miss Willer," Mr. Holland said confidentially, as if we were two comrades on a park bench, "didn't you find Mrs. Martin's story of a chaste marriage patently incredible?"

"Your Honor," Mr. Clark said excitedly, "Miss Willer has no basis on which to evaluate the plausibility of arrangements the Martins had fashioned in private."

"How about the basis of common sense?" Mr. Holland retorted.

The judge agreed with Mr. Clark, and I thought for a moment that I had been rescued, but, like a stray dog, the prosecutor was not about to give up his bone so easily.

"Miss Willer," he said with a sidelong look at Mr. Clark, "if a friend or a sister had told you the same thing about her marriage, wouldn't you have been surprised?"

Mr. Clark objected again, rising to his feet this time.

"This witness is an unmarried girl, Your Honor," he said. "She has no experience in what may be considered surprising between a husband and wife."

Mr. Holland held up his hands as if surrendering to a policeman.

"Miss Willer, you lived in the Martin house, did you not?"

"Yes, sir."

"And you had occasion to observe the Martins together in various circumstances—at meals, at leisure in the parlor, and so forth?"

"I wasn't *observing* them."

"But you were present at various times as they went about their daily activities?"

"Yes, sometimes."

"Did you ever see or hear anything that would indicate they were on normal terms as husband and wife?"

If I had been on treacherous ground before, I felt surrounded by quicksand now. Whichever way I stepped, I was sure to sink into a position from which there was no exit. In answering Mr. Clark, I had simply left information out, and that had been knotty enough. Now, if I was to carry through on my resolve, I must parade forth in the full mantle of deception.

"Take time to think, Miss Willer," the prosecutor said kindly.

It behooved him to be patient, for the proper recall—of a kiss or a caress or a teasing word—would dissolve Isabelle's story like rain on lump sugar. My disquiet may have exaggerated my senses, but it seemed the whole assembly was leaning forward with listening faces, waiting to know what I would say, waiting to conform it to their own understandings.

"No," I said at last. "I saw nothing like that."

Regarding me pensively, the prosecutor rubbed his chin. Though I wanted to look away, I thought it vital to return his stare with as much composure as I could muster.

"Miss Willer," he said slowly, "did the Martins occupy the same bed?"

"I never saw them in bed."

"Certainly not!" Mr. Holland seemed genuinely horrified. "Let me put it this way: was there only one bed in their room?"

"Yes," I said slowly, wondering if I were trapping myself. "Except when either of them was ill—then they brought in another bed. Sick people sleep better alone."

"But when they were both well, the Martins customarily kept one bed?"

"Yes."

"And you never saw evidence that either of them had slept elsewhere in the house at these times?"

"No."

Mr. Holland moved nearer to me. He was breathing heavily, and I could see coarse black hairs sticking out of his nostrils. He came close enough to speak softly, but instead he raised his voice, as if he would shout me free of my position.

"And yet, Miss Willer," he intoned, "it is your sworn testimony that to the best of your knowledge and belief, Mrs.

Martin's story of a virtually chaste marriage is plausible and true?"

I felt dizzy in the heat of the crowded courtroom.

"Yes, sir, that is my testimony."

I was allowed then to step down. I didn't look at Isabelle as I passed her, nor at anyone in particular. My part was over. I told myself it had been, after all, a very small part. Neither what I'd said nor what I'd not said could, on its own, condemn or exonerate Isabelle. My knowledge was of what lawyers call a circumstance; and circumstances, being things known fully only to those who live inside them, ought not to be judged by others.

Next, Mr. Holland recalled a few people from earlier days—Mrs. Cox, Dr. Cornelius, Mr. Sylvester Martin—and asked them all if the Martins hadn't appeared to them to be living as conjugal husband and wife. All said yes, though Mrs. Cox reminded the prosecutor that the Martins, well-versed in the rules of decorum, did not engage in vulgar displays of affection in front of others.

"Only immigrants indulge their passions like that," she elaborated with a sniff. "Walk down any sidewalk in the Catholic neighborhoods, and you're bound to see more than one rude, uncontrolled embrace. Commonness will out, you know."

All three witnesses had had occasion to enter the Martins' bedroom, and they noted that Isabelle and Mr. Edwin had shared the same bed most of the time. Mr. Clark, in a few quick counterquestions, rightly pointed out, however, that none of the witnesses could really know what had been the state of affairs in the Martins' marriage behind closed doors.

"I'm his father!" Mr. Sylvester Martin protested when Mr. Clark made this suggestion to him. "I know he was an amorous husband!"

"How, sir, can you know that?"

"Why, there was the child. . . ."

"That incident has been explained."

"He complained to me once . . . shortly after the child . . . that Isabelle was holding him off. I'd noticed the two beds, you see, and asked him about them. My wife never took such notions, I can tell you that, no matter what her health, and I told Edwin he was within his rights to demand that Isabelle—"

"Mr. Martin," Mr. Clark interrupted, "isn't it possible that knowing your strong feelings, your son was not inclined to share his views on marriage with you? That he let you believe what you wished to keep the peace?"

"Impossible!"

"Grant me for a moment, sir, that your son and his wife did have a platonic relationship. What would have been your response to him?"

"I'd have set him straight in no uncertain terms! And boxed her ears if he hadn't the spine to do it himself."

"No further questions," Mr. Clark said, lifting his arms in mock defeat and shrugging at the jury.

Mr. Martin stood up and leaned forward, gripping the rail of the witness box and scowling menacingly at Mr. Clark's back.

"My son was a normal male!" he shouted. "It's her was unnatural! Thinking she could dictate when and how a husband may express his affections—"

The judge hit his gavel sharply three times.

"Step down, Mr. Martin, or I'll have you removed," he said sternly.

The old man, red-faced and breathing hard, returned to his place in the audience, looking back over his shoulder to scowl at Isabelle. She kept her chin lifted and her gaze averted from him, but I noticed that she was leaning forward against the rail and that her fingers grasped it tightly. I guessed her father-in-law's tirade had upset her. Indeed, it had upset me and many others who heard it, too, both men and women. Tyranny was less and less accepted in society as a husband's right. But Mr. Martin had reminded us that it had by no means vanished.

I knew, of course, that Mr. Martin was correct that his son's marriage had been only intermittently platonic and then at the insistence of Isabelle, not Mr. Edwin. The old man must have been very frustrated to see that picture distorted. But his harshness erased my sympathy for him, and I felt in no way prompted to come forward and prove him right.

THIRTY-TWO

⚜ THOUGH I was not experienced in matters of law and courtrooms, I had, over the days of Isabelle's trial, been very impressed with Mr. Clark's performance. In asking questions of witnesses, he could seem like a stern father or a sympathetic friend or a curious student. And his interchanges with the judge and the prosecutor were like quickstep dances. Yet none of it prepared me for the forceful eloquence of his closing address.

He began by standing before the jury in such a way that he could look at them and also keep Isabelle in the corner of his vision. He raised his arm and pointed at her with his fingers curled softly toward his palm, so that there was no accusation or harshness in the gesture.

"Gentlemen," he said, "you are being asked to believe that this woman, who for years lived affectionately and obediently with her husband, and who during the whole time of his illness nursed him with tender devotion, was suddenly, one night, without excuse or object, transformed into a murderess."

He shook his head in disbelief, and letting his arm drop, he turned to face the jury squarely.

"Not only that," he said more loudly, "you are asked to believe she committed a crime absolutely unknown in the history of medical jurisprudence. Liquid chloroform has never

343

been used to perpetrate murder because it cannot be administered secretly due to the pain it causes.

"The prosecution would have you believe Isabelle Martin surmounted this problem by making her husband insensible through the inhalation of chloroform while he slept and then pouring the liquid down his throat. I will consider all the challenges that both these procedures entail shortly. For now, let me give you this to ponder: If Mrs. Martin had succeeded in making her husband insensible, why did she stop there? Why interrupt the process of anesthesia, which, if continued, would lead to certain death? Why attempt another operation which might arouse him and cause him to resist? An operation which would have presented enormous—may I say almost insuperable—difficulty to the highest trained doctor? Is this reasonable?"

Mr. Clark went on to review all the medical facts and opinions in detail. I looked from time to time at the jurors. They were listening closely, none of them shifting about or whispering to their neighbors or glancing around, as people who have lost concentration will do. I couldn't read the judging bent of their minds, but they were clearly with Mr. Clark in attention as he finished his summary of the medical testimony.

"Might we not expect her nervous hand to spill some choloroform on her husband's nightshirt, leaving an odor? Might we not expect her untrained effort to result in too much chloroform being poured too quickly, so that some amount must pool, unswallowed, at the back of his throat, irritating the tissues? Yet there were no such signs in the postmortem condition of the clothing or body. There remained, in fact, no physical evidence that she had done it at all."

Mr. Clark paused, looking a bit spent. He had been speaking for two hours, pounding on the strongest part of his argument. Ahead of him lay the more treacherous ground of Isabelle's securing of the chloroform, her story of a chaste marriage, and her relations with Reverend Dale, all or any of which could color the jurors' thoughts.

The judge gave a recess for lunch, which made a break for us all, not just for Mr. Clark. I hurried home for a sandwich, and while I moved about the kitchen, I thought of Isabelle taking her meal in some locked room of the courthouse, perhaps under the eyes of a guard or matron. Would she be able to get food down? I wouldn't, in her place. Even at my remove, my appetite was dampened, and I ate more to subdue the crawly agitation that was afflicting me than to satisfy hunger.

When court reconvened, Mr. Clark turned to the purchase of the chloroform. He said it appeared Isabelle had lied when she told Reverend Dale her husband had a fatal illness and that she needed the chloroform to help him sleep.

"I do not wish to impeach the innocence of Reverend Dale—indeed, I agree with the State that there is no case to present against him—" Mr. Clark said, "but if Reverend Dale *were* on trial, what would you have before you? A man—*an innocent man*—who lied to three druggists when purchasing poison, who threw away the empty bottles as if they were incriminating evidence, and who maintained relations of an exceptional character with a married couple. Yet none of this is considered by the State—nor should it be—as significant enough to cast serious suspicion against his innocence.

"Does it not seem hard, then, that Mrs. Martin's untruthful story about why she desired chloroform should weigh so heavily against her? Especially when you consider her *real* purpose in acquiring it? Could any woman of delicacy have told Reverend Dale what Mrs. Martin later confided to her physician? Surely it is perfectly understandable that she would want to veil such a private and intimate purpose, even at the expense of a small falsehood."

I marveled at how Mr. Clark had both cast doubt upon Reverend Dale's scruples and turned his testimony about Isabelle's lying to her favor. Of course, Mr. Clark's reasoning followed only if the jury believed Isabelle's description to Dr. Cornelius of the nature of her marriage.

In defending the story of the platonic compact between Isabelle and Mr. Edwin, Mr. Clark reminded the jury that both Reverend Dale and Mr. Edwin's father had heard him mention the notion of two wives, that various people had observed separate beds in the Martin bedroom, that Mr. Edwin had encouraged friendship between the minister and his wife, that Isabelle had incurred only one pregnancy in seven years, and that Mr. Edwin had revised his will to allow Isabelle to remarry. This part of Mr. Clark's speech caused me great discomfort, as it touched directly on my testimony, or, rather, on what I had not testified.

Finally, Mr. Clark said it was not his duty to explain how Edwin Martin had met his death, but he asked the jury to let their imaginations sketch in the scene in the Martin parlor.

"Edwin Martin is ill, confined to his bed. The doctor does not think it serious, but Edwin Martin, a known hypochondriac, does. He is in pain and weakened by sleeplessness. His wife has just confessed her procurement of chloroform, and with that confession, has dashed any hopes he might have formed about exercising his rights as a husband. She puts down the vial of chloroform and leaves the room on an errand. In a fit of despair, Edwin Martin snatches up the vial, bolts down a fatal dose, and thus ends his earthly troubles— drinking the chloroform off so quickly there would not be, *as there were not,* any appearances on the soft surfaces of the mouth and throat. When Isabelle Martin returns to the room to sit with her husband and hold his foot, as she is in the habit of doing, he appears to her to be merely asleep. She mistakes his coma for a sound rest. Later, awakened by her maid, Isabelle Martin is shocked to find her husband cold and dead.

"Isn't such a sequence more credible, gentlemen, than that, alone and unassisted, a grocer's wife worked a scientific miracle?"

Mr. Clark paused to look at Isabelle. There was pity in his face. It was so plain and so sincere, the jurors must have recognized it even though, at that moment, they were seeing him in profile. When he addressed them again, his voice was throaty and urgent.

"This woman has been described to you as friendless. She had a friend in Edwin Martin, who in his strange way was affectionate to her and stood by her. Now the fate of this lonely, unprotected woman is in your hands.

"Her husband is gone, but she still has one friend left, and that is the spirit of justice. That spirit will be present at your deliberations. Let it clear your eyes and guide your judgment. It will speak in a firm, unfaltering voice when your verdict tells the whole world that Isabelle Martin is not guilty."

Mr. Clark sat down. This time he had been speaking nearly three hours. A burst of applause sprang up from the audience like a flock of quail startled out of the brush. I myself didn't clap—not because I wasn't moved by the lawyer's speech, but because I was moved in too many directions at once.

ON THE next day, I entered the courtroom with an eagerness akin to a sick fever. Mr. Holland was to sum up, and the judge to give his instructions to the jury, and the jury, officially, to begin to decide. I was anxious to hear the prosecutor's speech—how he'd shape the story from his point of view, and how small or large a difference the absence of my information would make in the fabric of his telling.

Few other people had the intense personal interest I did in Isabelle's case—probably only Mr. Sylvester Martin and Reverend Dale, and I suppose Mr. Clark—yet everyone in court seemed tense with expectation. The assembly of would-be spectators outside was bigger and more restless than on any other day. People spilled into the street, impeding traffic, and the sidewalk opposite was crowded as well. As on every other day, the majority gathered were women. A few men who had arrived early were selling their places in line, and they didn't lack for bidders. Two chestnut vendors were doing a brisk business, too.

I think people must have bribed the doorkeepers because there was a crush inside as well, with many standing in back and along the side walls. The room became overheated with so many bodies. Windows were opened to let in cool air, which helped, but with it came milling noises and occasional shouts from the hundreds waiting in the street.

Mr. Holland spoke, in all, about half the amount of time Mr. Clark had, and he did not sound as confident as I thought he should have, given that many of his points were sensible enough. He said, first, that just because chloroform had never been used to murder before did not mean it could not be used so, and that just because the administration of it posed difficulties did not mean it was impossible.

"What you must decide," he pronounced to the jury, "is whether chloroform was used with criminal intent and, if so, whether the prisoner was the one who used it. Why did Isabelle Martin want chloroform? Why, the day after her husband's death, did she throw it into the river? In deliberating on these points, you must consider the history of the victim and the prisoner."

Mr. Holland walked a few paces away from the jury and stopped in the middle of the area in front of the judge's high desk. He stood appraising Isabelle, as if he himself were deliberating on her guilt or innocence. Isabelle lowered her head slightly for a few seconds. I didn't wonder that she flinched under such a biting stare. But when she lifted her face to meet that stare again, it was the prosecutor who flinched. Perhaps not everyone noticed. It was the merest twinge of one corner of his upper lip, a momentary widening of his eyes. I was close, having secured a front row seat, and I saw. What look had she thrown him? Was it the eerie acceptance I had perceived in her when I viewed her from the witness chair? Was it that practiced look of soft surprise, hinting at both pleasure and modesty, that I had seen her wear so often when a caller entered her parlor?

I thought Mr. Holland should be glad the jurors could not

see his expression just then, could not see she had moved him in some way. As he turned toward them again, his face assumed a drear, angry set.

"This woman," he said, making "woman" sound like a foreign word he found difficult to pronounce, "alleges that in all her married life she had no sexual relations with her husband, save once. Can any man of common sense believe such a tale? There is not a scrap of evidence to support the idea that the Martins did not live on ordinary terms as husband and wife.

"And what are we to make of Edwin Martin's supposed *giving over* of his living wife to another man? The conversations between Edwin Martin and Reverend Dale on this matter show only that Mr. Martin had confidence in the minister and in his wife—unfortunately for him, a misplaced confidence. Yet even if you are prepared to accept Mrs. Martin's remarkable claim, doesn't it strain belief to imagine that Edwin Martin went even further and obligingly killed himself to speed the union of his wife and his friend?"

Mr. Holland paused. When he spoke again, his voice, which was possessed of a naturally sweet quality, gradually tightened and hardened.

"Yes, Edwin Martin was ill, but it was not a dangerous illness, and his doctor, who was well aware of his patient's tendency to exaggerate his condition, noticed no despondency. Indeed, this supposedly discouraged soul ordered oysters for his next day's breakfast!

"There are but two ways Edwin Martin could have ingested liquid chloroform. Either the prisoner gave it to him while he was lying insensible on his back, or the prisoner handed him a glass containing the fatal liquid, perhaps disguised in one of her famous potions, and convinced him to drink it. There was no one else could have done it."

Mr. Clark leaped to his feet.

"I protest, Your Honor," he shouted. "Counsel cannot at this late stage introduce a new theory of the crime. The defense has been built upon the State's assertion from the beginning that if chloroform was criminally administered to the deceased, he must have been first lulled into a stupor."

"Your Honor," the prosecutor replied, "since my learned friend erected the theory of suicide, I feel bound to pose a more probable one. I don't dispute that the idea that Edwin Martin confidently gulped down chloroform handed to him by his wife is without problems, but it is an infinitely more acceptable theory than suicide!"

"We can leave it to the jury to sort out which theories are acceptable and which not," the judge said. "However, sir, you may not introduce an idea for which the defense has no means to make an answer. The jury is instructed to disregard any theory except the one originally proposed by the prosecution."

Mr. Holland nodded and put two fingers to his chin, as if trying to find his place again in his train of arguments.

"My learned friend has seen fit to try to discredit Mr. Sylvester Martin, the dead man's father, to demonstrate that he felt animosity toward his son's wife. Allowances can be made, I think, for a father's grief; and it must be admitted his suspicions, in this matter at least, proved well founded. Also, my friend pressed the point that like his client, the Reverend Dale told lies and threw away bottles, and yet his innocence was not challenged by these things. I tell you, gentlemen, that it most certainly would have been challenged if, like Mrs. Martin, Reverend Dale alone had possession of the poison which caused the death and if he alone could have used it. But these are small matters."

Mr. Holland took a deep breath and leaned toward the jury. He spoke slowly, enunciating every word carefully.

"Edwin Martin was a man with years and prosperity ahead of him. He did not take his own life. Isabelle Martin was a woman who had met a man she liked and admired better than her husband, and when Edwin Martin fell ill, Isabelle Martin seized the opportunity to rid herself of the husband who had become distasteful to her. Much has been made of Mrs. Martin's *devoted* nursing. What better screen for a murderess than to dote on the health and comfort of her intended victim?"

Mr. Holland stopped and looked briefly at each juror.

"In murders of this kind," he said, "we are always, as it were, groping in the dark for the truth of exactly how the deed was done. You may not be able to state with accuracy to your own satisfaction the exact methods or means by which this crime has been accomplished. Nevertheless, gentlemen, the only logical verdict—the only just verdict—is guilty."

Mr. Holland returned to his table. He wore the same drawn look Mr. Clark had shown the day before. Neither seemed sure of success, or perhaps it was simply that their speeches so absorbed their minds and spirits there was no room left for optimism, or for pessimism either. Their jobs were done. How well done was left to others to determine.

The judge's summing up reiterated the important points made by both sides. At first, his recital was favorable to Isabelle. He touched on her devotion as a nurse, and he conceded that chloroforming a person against his will, whether awake or asleep, and then administering liquid chloroform to an insensible person were both procedures so fraught with difficulty that an unskilled person would hardly dare attempt it, as only the greatest luck could render this double operation successful.

"However, gentlemen," he added, "I remind you that fools will rush in where angels fear to tread."

With this, the balance of the judge's remarks began to tip against Isabelle. He hit particularly on the missing bottle of chloroform.

"If Edwin Martin, by intent or by accident, drank the chloroform himself, where was the bottle when the doctor arrived later that night? If everything was right, why would the bottle not be there in plain sight, perhaps even within reach of the deceased? This is the most material element in the case, the thing that presses most strongly against the prisoner. I have waited anxiously for the defense counsel to give an explanation, but he has not, informing us only that Mrs. Martin threw it into the river *the next day."*

The judge looked down at something on his desk and frowned. He looked out at the crowded courtroom, and his frown deepened. When he spoke to the jury again, there was no mistake he was speaking to the audience as well.

"Let no one mistake the personages in this case for romantic figures," he said. "The facts, instead, are vulgar. We have an ordained minister who took advantage of a husband's trust to nourish a perilous friendship with his wife and to spend long, unchaperoned hours with her. I put slender faith in the testimony of such a man. We have a wife who shamelessly read garbage like *The Mysteries of Man,* a type of modern book certain to unsex women. And we have a husband who carried French letters in his pockets. Does this point to indecent habits outside the home or to the fact that the Martins did, in fact, have regular physical relations? If the latter, what becomes of Isabelle Martin's story for wanting chloroform to ward off her husband's so-called unprecedented advances?"

The judge sighed. Clearing his throat, he continued.

"Edwin Martin swallowed liquid chloroform. You must choose between two seemingly impossible theories—murder by a difficult double operation or suicide. I leave you to your duty."

THIRTY-THREE

AFTER THE judge exited the courtroom and the jury had filed out, Isabelle was led away to wait in some private room. The lawyers stayed at their tables talking quietly with their assistants. A few people left the courtroom, but most stayed, not wanting to lose their places to others pushing in from outside. Men stood and stretched and walked over to look out the windows. Ladies fanned themselves, for the room was still stuffy, or chattered together, or nibbled daintily at small sandwiches and cakes pulled from their purses.

I sat for a worried hour and a half. For better or worse, my part was done, but I kept turning it over in my mind, as if I still had the decision before me of whether or not to reveal that the marriage of Mr. Edwin and Isabelle had most definitely not been a fraternal one. I told myself my withholding was of little consequence since the jury had gotten the same information from the fact of the safes found in Mr. Edwin's pockets and the opinions of his father and other acquaintances. I blamed the prosecutor, who had not asked me more specific questions—had not inquired about stained bedsheets or late breakfasts, nor about the quick gleams of lewdness in Mr. Edwin's eyes across the dining table and the answering nervous twitch of Isabelle's fingers. I don't think I could have carried the secret so far if such things had been asked. But however much I tried to excuse myself, I didn't deny that my own will was the main piece of what I had done.

Finally I could not bear the hot, noisy room any longer. It seemed a physical representation of my buzzing mind. Trusting the special pass from Mr. Clark to gain me readmission, I left the courthouse and sought relief in the street.

When I came out of the courthouse, several people accosted me to learn whether there'd been a verdict yet or not. I shook my head, but that didn't stop their dogging me.

"Did the jury have the look of a yes or a no?"

"How is she holding up?"

"Did she face the audience today?"

"They say Clark's speech was fine. Do you think it will do?"

"That reverend, is he in there?"

"When will we know?"

I plowed by them with my head down. They didn't follow, for that would have meant leaving their prime places near the door. Once I entered the crowd beyond the courthouse steps, no one else bothered me, since no one there knew I'd been inside.

The street was busier with commotion than the courtroom, but it provided the refreshing compensations of cold air and the freedom to move around. More people had gathered since morning. It was almost like a carnival grounds, but without the gaiety. The business day was drawing to a close, and office workers on their way home now skirted the edges of the crowd, many lingering to see what they might.

I noticed two nannies conferring with their heads together; they were not looking at each other, but had their gazes fixed on the courthouse doors. Seated on the curb at their feet were two little girls. One had a length of string looped across her outspread hands; with quick, deft lifts of her fingers, she was transforming the circle of string into a cat's cradle, a Jacob's ladder, and other crisscrossed forms. The other girl was watching her companion's movements intently and patting her gloved hands together, either in applause or in impatient anticipation of her turn with the string.

I got into a long line to buy roasted chestnuts. The line shuffled slowly forward every minute or so, and I let my mind be lulled into blankness by having to wait, a much simpler kind of waiting than the one for Isabelle's verdict. It's curious how an experience as common and inevitable as waiting can possess variety—dulling waits, tense waits, pleasant waits, waits full of dread. I suppose there is nothing people do that they cannot make more intricate than it has to be.

I felt a firm touch on my elbow and turned to find Lorenzo beside me. I was startled to see him, but only for a moment. In the next moment, it seemed that, of course, he must appear because thoughts of him had so chafed my mind the night before and had continued to lie durably beneath the engrossing business of the trial like a crayon drawing beneath a wash of black paint.

"I'm looking for you, Hanna," he said, so I'd know our meeting was no accident.

"It's not quite over," I replied, though he hadn't asked.

"Do you want the chestnuts?"

When I said no, he drew me out of the line. He walked to the end of the block, where the crowd was sparser, and I followed right behind. It's strange, but sometimes busy public places can provide as concentrated a sense of privacy as a closed room. When Lorenzo stopped and turned to face me, the peopled street became a confidential chamber.

"You have been thinking?" he said.

"Perhaps too much," I nodded.

"Too much is not good."

"You wanted me to be sure, you said."

"Yes, Hanna, but this is such a thing that you know it or you don't."

There was a hubbub in the crowd near the courthouse. We both turned to look. People were moving up to the doorway, though no one was gaining entry. Their dark winter clothes made them look like swarming ants.

"The jury must be returning," I said. "I've got to go back in."

Lorenzo grabbed my arm.

"What's the excitement?" he said. "You can know soon out here."

"I want to be there. I want to see her. I'm a part of it, Lorenzo."

He still held my arm, but not tightly. He looked into my eyes as if he were searching for something he'd dropped into soft sand.

"Did she do it?" he said in a whisper.

There was a strange sinking in my chest that could have been dread or peace, or a freakish hybrid of both.

"Only she knows that," I answered, "but I believe she did."

"And you are a part?"

"No, of course not, not part of that. Part of the trial, and . . . well . . . part of Isabelle in a way . . . at least I understand what she—"

"Hanna, forget all this. Don't go in."

The commotion in the crowd was spreading. People on the sidewalks were jostling; there was a tumult of noisy talk. The air hummed with speculation.

Lorenzo took his hand from my arm.

"I will not wait," he said.

I looked at him, memorizing the expressive dark eyes, the beautiful line of his mouth, now set in grim resolve.

"I have to see it to its end," I said, and hurried away, my heart thumping. I looked back once, from the courthouse stoop, but I couldn't find Lorenzo. He had not waited even that long.

INSIDE THE courtroom, the people who had gotten up were bustling to regain their seats, and those already seated were squirming around to determine the best view. As the ruffle of activity among the spectators was subsiding, Isabelle entered, and a drone of whispered voices rose up to greet her. Unlike every other time, she did not look out over the audience, but kept her gaze straight ahead, and this made the droning grow louder and more urgent.

Next came the military figure of the judge and the slow file of jurors, and then the courtroom was as still as a frozen lake at midnight. A woman next to me thoughtlessly let a half-eaten sandwich rest on her lap; an oily mayonnaise stain marked the silk around it.

It was nearly five o'clock, and the courtroom was shadowy, adding to the solemnity. A clerk at the side of the judge's bench stood up and addressed the foreman of the jury, who was also standing. It was so quiet, I could hear the scratching pens of the newspapermen.

"Gentlemen, have you agreed upon your verdict?"

"We have."

"Do you find the prisoner, Isabelle Martin, guilty or not guilty?"

The clerk waited. We all waited.

"We have considered all the evidence, and although we think grave suspicion is attached to the prisoner—"

Exclamations went up from several quarters of the audience. The judge rapped his gavel.

"—we do not think there is sufficient evidence to show how or by whom the chloroform was administered."

"Then you say that the prisoner is not guilty, gentlemen?"

"Not guilty."

Irrepressible cheering erupted in the courtroom, people on their feet applauding, women crying, men shouting out the windows and the door, whereupon answering roars of cheers came from the crowds in the corridors and in the street. I pushed past the jostling people around me to catch sight of Isabelle. Mr. Clark had crossed over to her; she had both her hands resting on his arm as if she felt faint, and that gentleman's cheeks were streaked with tears.

"This is an outrage!" shouted the judge. "I will not have this court turned into a theater by such indecent and insulting exhibitions!"

Sheriff's deputies scurried about, shoving people toward the door and shushing them. With great effort, the audience suppressed the din, though sniffles could still be heard on all sides.

"Do not forget," the judge told us, "that this occasion is the most solemn public duty men can be called upon to perform."

Satisfied that no further outbursts were likely, the judge turned to the jury.

"I wish to express my gratitude, gentlemen, for the undivided attention you gave this case and for the cheerfulness with which you submitted to the disturbance of your usual habits and family life."

With that, the judge retired. As I shuffled out of the crowded building and into the boisterous throng in the street, where the entire jury was lined up shaking Mr. Clark's hand, it struck me that the judge had never said whether he agreed with the verdict or not.

THIRTY-FOUR

I WENT straight home from the courthouse. I didn't know when Isabelle might come, and I had realized she wouldn't have her keys. I didn't stop to buy supper things, though I knew there was not enough in the larder to assemble a rounded meal. The spontaneous resumption of regular doing for Isabelle, like food shopping and cooking, seemed somehow indecorous, almost a transgression, but against what exactly I could not say.

It was Mr. Clark brought Isabelle home. He'd tried to take her out for supper, but they were both too well known. The interference of loud well-wishers and a few jeerers had driven them from two restaurants.

"My club will be a sanctuary for me tonight," Mr. Clark said to me, "but, of course, there are no ladies allowed there, so I thought it best to restore Mrs. Martin here, to her own best sanctuary."

Isabelle stood beside the lawyer looking pale and indifferent, as if waiting to be told what to do next. Gently removing Isabelle's hand from his coatsleeve, Mr. Clark passed her off to me. At my touch, she seemed to come awake. She gave me a slow smile, disengaged from me, and turned to Mr. Clark.

"I don't have words adequate to your service," she said to him. "It would be a small, small token of my appreciation, but if I could invite you to a meal sometime. . . ."

Mr. Clark shook his head.

"Lawyers are like dentists." He smiled. "The less often met, the better. I fully expect, dear lady, our paths will not need to cross again."

When Mr. Clark had gone, Isabelle went into the parlor and I followed. Walking behind her, I noticed she had lost weight. She was wearing a combination suit of worsted lace and nun's veiling, and the basque, which was styled to fit tightly to the figure, showed loose folds over her waist and shoulders.

"You didn't expect me back?" Isabelle asked, looking around at the furniture draped with dust covers.

"I didn't know what to expect."

"No matter. It was a prudent decision."

She walked around the room touching things, but she didn't remove any of the cloths.

"I'm glad that's covered," she said, pointing to Mr. Sylvester Martin's portrait. "I've had enough eyes on me to last a long while."

"You looked, in court, to be standing up well under all of it."

"I'm glad the pose was effective. It cost me great effort, Nan, great effort."

"Was it so calculated, then?"

She looked at me warily. There was something in her eyes I'd never seen before, a bitterness and an embracing of bitterness.

"When you're on trial for your life, Nan, everything must be calculated. And when you live as I have been living, shuttled between a solitary, featureless cell and a crowded center stage, you cease to think like a modest person. You cease to be a modest person."

I had always found Isabelle to be someone who carefully considered her own position in all situations. Within her limits as a wife and a woman, she maneuvered with general success to extract what she could and to escape what she could.

360

It was easy to understand that thrown so much to herself as she had been recently, those tendencies would be strengthened.

"You felt very alone, I guess," I said.

"I didn't speak to anyone for days at a time," she answered. "Except for a word or two with Mr. Clark or one of his assistants."

She sat down on the sofa without pulling aside its covering and scanned the room yet again.

"Let's leave it like this, shall we?" she said. "Let's turn our backs on all of it. No sense forsaking one confinement for another."

"You must be tired," I said.

"So tired I don't quite know what to do about it. But you needn't wait. I'll turn down my bed. Go on upstairs, Nan."

"No, I don't want to yet," I said, surprising myself with my boldness. "I'm going to fix myself some tea and buttered toast."

Isabelle stared at me, then leaned her head back on the sofa and shut her eyes.

"Suit yourself," she said.

I was so sure Isabelle would join me in the kitchen, I made enough tea and toast for two. But she didn't come. When I caught myself waiting for her after my snack was done, I emptied the remaining tea into the sink and threw away the extra toast, and climbed the stairs to my room.

I lit my fire and my lamp, washed my face, and changed into a nightgown and a Mother Hubbard wrapper. Then I sat on the edge of the bed and watched shadows move on the walls.

Isabelle had spoken of confinement. I could feel it, too. But it wasn't the house, nor the reminders populating the house. It was us, Isabelle and me. I had kept a secret for her, and in so doing, had helped to set her free. We both knew it. What we didn't know yet was where that had led us. Tonight was my first interchange with Isabelle since my visit to the station house jail, and yet she had been present to me during the past three weeks more strongly than ever. I could not imagine that she would ever be totally absent from me again, but now I wondered if I would be able to abide her actual company. Or she mine.

The next morning, Isabelle slept late. I took the opportunity to open up the parlor; I didn't think she really meant to leave it shuttered and draped. When she finally arose, she made no comment on my actions. She seemed pleased, in fact, going straight to the piano and sitting down to play. Later, she took a breakfast tray in there and ate looking out the window at the ordinary activity of the street below as if it were a show of exotic marvels.

When the doorbell rang, Isabelle intercepted me in the hall as I was about to descend to the street door.

"I don't want to see anyone," she said urgently. "Not anyone."

It was not a caller, but a telegram messenger, and the telegram was for me. I hurried back upstairs, where Isabelle met me on the threshold.

"It's my grandmother," I told her. "Apoplexy."

"You wish to go?"

"Immediately."

I pushed past her and headed down the hall to the kitchen. Isabelle followed, her skirts a whispering wake behind me.

"When will you return?" she asked when I had reached the foot of the back stairs.

Irritated, I turned to her for a moment.

"I don't know, Isabelle."

"Of course. Of course you don't."

"I'll write to you as soon as I do know."

She nodded, and I went to my room to toss a few things in a satchel. When I came down again, Isabelle was sitting at the kitchen table. She held out an alligator change purse.

"This should be enough for the train, both ways, and for sending telegrams, if there comes the need."

I took the purse, thanked her, and departed.

SIPPY'S ATTACK had left her crippled in one arm and slurry in her speech, and it seemed, overnight, to have aged her so considerably that it was clear to all of us she was entering her final days. What would be the length of these, the doctor could not tell us.

"She's always been hardy, I understand," he said, "and she may surprise us with a good number of months yet. But if she were to go tomorrow, she'd have defeated fate already. It's an unusual thing for a woman to live to see all her children into adulthood. And grown grandchildren, too!"

He meant to be encouraging, I suppose, but his pronouncements ultimately signified nothing, and I'd have as soon listened to a card reader, who'd at least have had some respect for the unknown.

Sippy's physical condition quickly leveled out, and the tasks relating to her care were simple and few. She was not a self-pitying person, so there was nothing of the invalid about her spirits. It was a situation Elsinore could have managed without me, and, as the doctor had said, one that might continue unchanged for some time. Sippy herself insisted she was holding out for at least one more spring. But I was reluctant to leave, and not just for the sake of my grandmother.

I did not want to return to Isabelle. I didn't regret what I had done at her trial—indeed, I was sure, given a second chance, I would decide the same way. But I could not feel completely easy about it, either. A man had died, after all. Not a symbol, a man. To stay with Isabelle would be to say I *was* easy with the conflicting streams in my soul. I shrank from that. Especially because I'd be saying it to her.

I knew leaving Isabelle would not relieve me. I probably would never know total relief. Once you've been part of something—or someone—it never has an end. There can be a lessening, some forgetting, an evaluation, but never an end.

I wrote Isabelle that I was leaving her employment and

apologized for the short notice, giving as a reason Sippy's failing health and my desire to be with my grandmother during her last days. I was too cowardly to tell my real reason for leaving, and I suppose I was soft on Isabelle still. She accepted my decision without objection. A box came with my things and a brief note wishing me well. Perhaps she was too tired to argue with me. Or too shrewd.

❧ RE-ENTERING MY family home was not as easy as I had expected it to be. Except for Sippy's decline and her consequent absence from the daily running of the house, things looked outwardly much as they had for years. The same chores reappeared each morning and each evening. I could open any cupboard, any chest, and be sure of what I'd find. The place and its people closed around me with a familiarity that was at once comforting and cramped, just as an old mattress molded to the shape of its owner can still make that owner's back stiff. I felt that my year away had changed me, yet my father, my sister, and even my wise grandmother did not seem to notice. Precisely how I had changed I could not clearly say, but I wanted to be asked about it anyway. I wanted to be wondered at a bit, I guess.

Two weeks into my stay, Mattie arrived to take up residence with us. True to her word, Elsinore had accomplished it despite Mattie's qualms. She was helped in her campaign by Lorenzo's departure for New York and my own quitting of Philadelphia. At first, the novelty of Mattie's presence was diverting. The dinner table was livelier. Sippy left her bed more often, and my father lengthened his sittings at the fireside on the evenings when Mattie and I sat mending and talking. But the talk was only of the far gone past or the nearest future. Soon our life came to seem routine again, and once more I experienced a nagging sense of not quite fitting where I had always fit before.

I began waking up nights. I'd hear the mantel clock downstairs chime three and sometimes four. My and Elsinore's bed was next to the window, so I'd turn on my side away from my sister and stare into the tree branches outside. I wouldn't get up or light a lamp, fearing to disturb Mattie, whose bed stood close to ours. My mind never settled anywhere for very long, circling without object like an ice skater round a small pond. But beneath all my ruminations flowed the distinct yearning to be away from my father's house.

After I'd been home just over a month, I received a letter from Isabelle asking me to come see her off when she left Philadelphia.

"You won't go, of course," my father said.

It was not an order. He obviously assumed I'd agree with him. We were in the work shed attached to our stable. He was sanding mold off our old cradle, which Sippy had had him drag up from the cellar the day before. I'd brought him some hot cider. I had a mug, too, and I sipped carefully at it.

"Actually, I thought I would go," I replied, matching his calm tone.

"You're not obligated to do her bidding anymore," he said, a harsh edge in his voice.

"I know. I want to go."

He turned the cradle upside down to get at the rockers. Then he looked at me and frowned.

"I don't like it."

In the past, that would have been enough to change my mind, or, at least, to influence my actions. But now I felt my heart tighten into a hard knob of resistance. I thought suddenly of Mr. Holland and his hectoring, of how frightening it had been to face him down. But I didn't feel frightened standing opposite my father in the cold shed with the old cradle upended on a table between us.

"I want to see her, and I'm going to go," I said, trying not to sound embattled.

My father looked surprised, but he made no reply, only took to vigorously sanding the rear rocker.

ℛ "I WON'T be in this city again," Isabelle said to me on the pier beside the Delaware River.

She looked over her shoulder, away from the water, toward the city behind us. "I won't miss it."

She turned her face to me and smiled.

"I will miss you, though, Nan. Shall I write? Keep in touch?"

"If you like."

Isabelle sighed. "I understand," she said, as if my answer had been different.

She stepped aside to let by a porter with an especially wide trunk.

"You'll get no letters, Nan. It'll spare you having to answer. And me looking for an answer that's not coming."

"You really think you'll never return?"

"I expect not. Why should I? I've sold off all my interests. I arranged with Mr. Cox to sign over one store to my father-in-law—the one below our apartment. If he's a good manager, it'll see him through. You see, Nan, I'm not heartless after all."

"I never called you heartless."

"Never thought it?"

"Not heartless."

"What, then?"

I found it difficult to meet her eyes, so I looked out over the dark river. Fog hid the contours of the Jersey side. We could have been standing at land's end at the edge of the world.

"Desperate, I suppose," I said. "And destitute."

"Destitute? A prosperous shopkeeper's wife?" She was trying to sound light.

I nodded.

"They called me friendless," she said more seriously.

"You used to call yourself that."

"They didn't count you, Nan."

"It wasn't friendship, Isabelle, made me . . . kept me from . . . it wasn't a *particular* friendship."

"Even you . . ."

Isabelle, too, was regarding the invisible Jersey shoreline, squinting her eyes as if to make out some silhouette more black than the black night or to glimpse one solid, immobile shape behind the shifting shreds of fog.

"Even I, what?"

"In all this business, it may have been only the prosecutor to whom I was a particular person, and he was my enemy."

She had not lost her taste for melodrama.

"Let's step aside here, Nan," Isabelle said as more people began moving along the pier toward the ship. Soon she'd have to board.

She walked to a gas lamp and stopped to dig in her carpetbag. She pulled out a thick blue envelope and held it out to me.

"It's the deed to our building. The shop's on special permanent lease to Mr. Martin, but the apartment and offices above are yours. The shop, too, once the old man has passed."

"Isabelle, I can't . . . A building? *That* building? I don't want it."

"Then sell it," she said glibly, as if she were talking about an old coat.

She waved the envelope at me. "It hasn't got teeth, Nan."

I shook my head no. Isabelle withdrew the envelope, but she didn't put it back into her bag.

"What will you do, Nan, after your grandmother dies, before a new Mr. Testa comes along? Go into service again? To a factory?"

"I'm not afraid of honest work."

Isabelle frowned.

"This isn't a payment, Nan, if that's what you're thinking," she said quietly.

"I don't want it."

"If you had stayed with us for years and years, you know,

367

we would have made some gift or arrangement for you at the end of your service. Edwin was frugal, but he was decent. And he was always open to convincing."

I was startled to hear her speak of Mr. Edwin so calmly. Even to hear her mention his name seemed strange, almost dangerous.

"I haven't been with you for years and years."

"Not as time is normally measured. But don't you think, Nan, that some periods of time carry more weight than others? That one moment can seem to contain a lifetime, while a lifetime can seem to be only one long, slow, self-same day?"

"If you want to tell me something, Isabelle, please say it plainly."

She stepped away from me, just out of the circle of lamplight. When she turned her head, only the tip of her nose and her chin were illuminated. The rest of her face was in shadow, except that her eyes, having somehow caught the light, glittered like a cat's.

"There's nothing plainer than silence, is there?" she said.

"You're wrong, Isabelle. Silence is full of noise and confusion."

She gave the slightest nod of her head. Or perhaps it was only a trick of my eyes.

"You really don't want the house? Not even to sell?"

"Really."

"Surely, Nan, there's some private wish it might smooth your way to? It's not often a woman gets means of her own."

She held out the blue envelope again.

"You'll need these papers either way," she said, businesslike. "Mr. Fisk can straighten it all out."

I took the envelope and pushed it deep into my bag.

"I'm not the only silent one, Nan," Isabelle said softly. "You've never told me your opinion. Do you think I poisoned my husband?"

A sudden puff of wind blew some paper scraps against my skirt. I shook my foot to dislodge them.

"Nan? I'd like to know."

"Why?"

"Secret knowledge is a restless thing. It pushes to be told. To at least one other person."

The cold, damp night felt suddenly colder. The shape and texture of things at the edge of my vision seemed sharper, brighter—the black flutes of the lamppost, the wet slime on the cobblestones, a rusting pile of tangled ship chains.

"Yes, Isabelle. Yes, I think you did it."

She let out a long sigh, as if she had just put down a heavy burden, or was preparing to pick one up.

"You were always a perceptive girl, Nan."

Before I realized what she was about, Isabelle leaned forward and pressed a quick kiss on my cheek near the corner of my mouth. The warm breath of roses brushed across my face. Then she turned smartly around and strode away. The fog closed behind her at the foot of the gangplank. If she looked back at me or at the city, I didn't see it.

AFTERWORD

The Shopkeeper's Wife is a work of fiction, but Isabelle Martin's story is based on the real case of Adelaide Bartlett, who was tried for murder in London, England, in 1886.

Two helpful references were *Victorian Murderesses* by Mary S. Hartman (Schocken Books, 1976) and the transcripts from *Trial of Adelaide Bartlett,* edited by Sir John Hall (Day, 1927). Other useful sources of general information were the Historical Society of Pennsylvania, The Victorian Society in America, Atwater Kent Museum, the Library of the Balch Institute for Ethnic Studies, the Historical Society of Ocean Grove, the photograph collections of the Free Library of Philadelphia and the Library Company of Philadelphia, and the Los Angeles Public Library.

The author is also grateful for a residency at Dorland Mountain Arts Colony in Temecula, California, where part of *The Shopkeeper's Wife* was written.

5